A House of Clay

By the same author:

THE STANDING HILLS

A House of Clay

Caroline Stickland

LONDON
VICTOR GOLLANCZ LTD
1988

First published in Great Britain 1988
by Victor Gollancz Ltd
14 Henrietta Street, London WC2E 8QJ

British Library Cataloguing in Publication Data
Stickland, Caroline
  A house of clay.
  I. Title
  823'.914 [F]   PR6069.T48

  ISBN 0–575–04170–6

Typeset at The Spartan Press Ltd
Lymington, Hants
and printed in Great Britain by St Edmundsbury Press Ltd
Bury St Edmunds, Suffolk

To my father
B. G. W. Sadler

Chapter 1

It could reasonably be said that Ashley Claydon was an honourable man. Indeed, the honour of his family was the life and breath and soul of his being. It is therefore the more surprising that the morning of the tenth of June, 1819, should find him pacing the grounds of his Norfolk estate heartily desiring the death of his wife.

He was a man of eight-and-twenty, handsome rather than not, and with the distinction bred by a family that had called itself old generations before its neighbours. He walked with the consciousness that his position was proud and if his rank had been bought from James I it was neither the action of the present holder nor that of his recent ancestry. Memory was short and though the first baronet had been exalted by his title, the second embarrassed by its acquisition, the third forgetful, the fourth and subsequent holders were heir to a noble inheritance — their only fault lying in a certain diffidence of intercourse with commoners. Their wealth had increased; their portraits had been painted; gilt frames enclosed dark, tired men with eyes that hid whether they understood what they saw; they had tried to do their duty. Although Ashley allowed a certain *laissez-faire* amongst the water-fowls at his lakeside, he was observing them with face and cravat under perfect control.

It was a day which could not decide whether to be good or bad. A breeze chopped the waters of the lake, ruffling the soft under-feathers of a mallard hunting in its shallows; sunlight caught and reflected the green and grey of its wings. It was a lively and delightful scene but Ashley watched it without activity. He was impatient but it could not have been guessed from his pose. He stood with his back to his pleasance, gazing across the park to the oaks that lined his walls. Beyond the trees the Norfolk levels lay bleakly golden waiting for the field-gangs.

Seed that had been sown broadcast was ripening to its fruit but even the knowledge that it was his could not save Ashley from the sudden sickness of spirit that often fell upon him from these broad, Eastern skies.

A movement at the corner of his eye attracted his attention. A rider was crossing the grass. It was clear from the cob he rode and the entrance he had taken that though perhaps not a gentleman himself, he was familiar with the class and familiar with the family. He was now making his way through an avenue of beeches and was intermittently hidden by the young, green growth at the base of the trunks. Ashley, with an air of subdued expectation, allowed himself to walk slowly through the reeds until he had regained the lawn. The two men met as if casually.

Mason was wearing a travelling costume of fine broadcloth with a light cape lying across his saddle. He carried his left leg thrust forward and his excellent boots had neither the virgin correctness of the *nouveaux riches* nor the well-worn comfort of the confidantly old. He eased his leg as though he would climb down but Ashley stayed him with a gesture; it was obviously a ritual.

Ashley did not speak and Mason watched him with eyes that were intelligent and capable but lit more often by self-interest than common sense.

After a moment Ashley said, "My wife is —?"

"She is dead."

"Ah!" The bereaved husband gave a drawn-out sigh.

"All that could be done was done but when once the phthisis has hold —"

"Indeed — and the funeral?"

"It has taken place. Quiet but with due observance. I did not attend."

"You visited my property beforehand?"

"I did. The children were as always."

From where he was standing Ashley could see the curve of the lake beyond the boat-house. A family of water-rails had formed themselves into what, at this distance, seemed to be an orderly group; it was unusual for them to be so exposed. They

8

appeared to absorb him. He said, "I have not seen them for eight years."

"They are strong, silent boys."

Ashley withdrew his attention and glanced at his messenger. "They do not resemble me?"

"They favour their mother. The girl will be pretty."

The father resumed his silence. Mason removed his hat and smoothed hair so naturally curly that an old-fashioned Francophobe might have questioned his loyalty. Ashley remarked wearily, "It is better this way."

"It is necessary, sir — a woman of that birth."

"I could wish it undone."

"Dorsetshire is far away."

He had not understood. His master smiled; he became roused. "You have done me another service, Mason," he said. "I'm indebted to you. I will accompany you to the stables."

With some care Mason transferred himself to the ground. The two men strolled across the shadows of the trees.

The morning had cleared. The breeze that had stirred the waters had dropped and the summer warmth was rising towards an afternoon of heat. Had circumstances been different, it would have been an agreeable walk for the garden was of an individual and comfortable beauty. Before them, the track emerged from the trees and led between the yew hedge that flanked the terrace and the wall of the kitchen-garden. In the tunnel made by hedge and wall the temperature had risen to anticipate midday and the heat reflecting from the earth drew out the sour smells of one who has ridden and bleached the colours that wavered on the bricks. A sound of voices — of laundry-maids lingering in a courtyard — came vaguely between slow hoof-beats, and as they passed a garden door the sweet, thick scent of the strawberry-beds lay dully across their path. It was an hour for friendship and, though they did not show it, their situation and intimacy brought to each man a constriction of the heart.

Mason wondered — and what now? Am I home?

Ashley, noticing a hesitation in his step, said gently, "You are tired."

"You know my travelling."

"You have ridden far?"

"Two miles. I left the coach at Marlingham and hired my hack from the livery. By the by, I met Gascoigne outside the town. He asked whether I were going to Althorpe St Giles as if he didn't recognize me and couldn't be sure of my destination. He meant to slight me."

"As my agent and companion you are above slight."

"He asked me to pass this letter to you."

With his free hand he reached into his jacket and brought out a sealed envelope. Ashley took the letter and slid it over the edge of one hand; it would be impossible to say whether his eyes narrowed.

"I hardly need to read it," he said. "Since you've been away there's been new agitation for a workhouse. Gascoigne is behind it. There are more hand-looms lying idle and apparently their operators eat too much bread — it's causing him concern."

Mason was inclined to think it should. "He has some justification," he said. "Distress is increasing. The monies being expended on outdoor relief are already considerable and likely to rise. It would be cheaper to remove the surplus population from their homes."

"I shall speak at the Vestry. There has been weaving on my estate for generations. It is a respectable trade. I do not intend to lock up its participants for the sake of a slump they could not avoid."

"It may not pass — there are power-driven looms in the North. There was reason for the strike last year."

"I cannot see that Norfolk must be ruled by Manchester — nor that any honourable end may be served by depriving families of their liberty, dividing man from wife and mother from children. You know my views."

In cases, thought Mason, such as these.

They were nearing the yard where they were to part and Ashley, to lighten their mood, asked, "You will dine with me at four?"

"Thank you — yes. I couldn't eat this morning."

"Your leg troubles you?"

Mason nodded. "It eases a little as I walk. A coach may cast you up, down and in your neighbour's lap but it is fundamentally sedentary."

"I should not have sent you."

"Who better to go? And a little arthritis — I don't intend to give in."

Ashley bowed slightly. "It is not in your character," he said.

The evening found Ashley alone. He could not settle. The house, deprived of a mistress, seemed to him to be loud in its demand for one. He noticed sounds that were not there and though he knew them to be imaginary the knowledge did not comfort him. He found himself wandering without purpose in the middle rooms where he adjusted ornaments, noting that a marble table borne by a hideous eagle had been chipped but whether the damage had been done in his lifetime he could not say. In the Gallery, a mottling on the pleats of a blind told him that a window was open and he walked carefully across floorboards to close it. A fine rain, hardly more than a drizzle, was being blown repeatedly against the glass.

He latched the window and then the blind. He was aware of suffering but did not know whether it was his own. For these moments he had built retreats within retreats and in a house of servants he walked in isolation through the styles and furnishings of centuries to his private chamber. The heavy room was unsuited to summer and the scent of the cedar-panelling in the heated air was rich and stifling but the night-cap and gown lying gaily and ridiculously empty on the bed, the new rose-leaves floating in his ewer, the madeira on the table beside the wing-chair, were signs of a routine attention that was necessary to him. It felt welcoming.

He removed his jacket and wrapped himself in an incongruously cheerful chintz robe. Adorned with peonies he unlocked his bureau and took from its lower drawer a small portable writing desk. Seated in his armchair with the desk on his knees, he took from his watch-chain a key he had not used for years. His elbow brushed his wine and he reached up to place the glass on the mantelshelf.

He lifted a sketchbook from the desk and laid it on the closed lid. The binding cracked as he opened it and inside the pages were browning and had fallen loose. Mountains, trees and prospects slid down into his lap. They smelt of age and damp and, to him, something more bitter. He gathered the papers and piled them on the floor beside him until he held only one in his hand.

It was a pencil drawing of a girl — a three-quarter face. She was not beautiful but — as had been said this morning of her daughter — pretty, with a charm he had caught in the turn of her head as she smiled. He remembered how easily she had smiled. The lines of the sketch had faded but the effect of the sitter upon the life of the artist had not diminished since its completion.

Ashley was then seventeen and, prevented by Napoleon from taking the Grand Tour, had been sent by his father on an exploration of Scotland and the Lakes. The sudden death of his tutor-chaplain in the week of their departure meant that he was accompanied not by a middle-aged cleric whose actions were governed by experience but by a young man hardly older than himself. Robert Mason, in training to be a land agent on the Claydon estates and showing exceptional promise, had been glad to accept a position which might bind him securely to a future employer.

Together, their neckcloths tied à la Byron, they set off simmering with romance and ambition. They scrutinised the lakes, they rowed industriously on Windermere, and they admired hovels from the outside. When autumn came they pursued Lochinvar and there in Argyll, where they might rest and be thankful, they rented a house which had a maid. She was an affectionate girl who spoke her little English with concentration and when she discovered that Ashley loved her she returned his feelings without reserve. It was a long winter and Ashley, separated from all communication with his home, did not stop to think of the results of his behaviour.

The girl was afraid. She had no family to protect her and it did not occur to her that a sense of honour would persuade a man of Ashley's standing into marriage. When it did she felt that nothing she could ever do would make him reparation and Ashley, though he did not say so, agreed. Had Mason not proved so staunch in friendship and morality, Ashley might have confessed to his father and applied for some means of escape. He did not do so; neither did he send the news to England — instead, when the snows had melted and the roads opened, he wrote to extend his stay.

What was his despair when his wife was safely delivered of male twins? When, six months later, he was summoned to his father's funeral and the yoke of upholding his family's merit was placed on his shoulders, he returned to Norfolk without mention of his wife. Responsibility did not bring maturity and, his attachment lessened by distance, he drifted towards a decision. Learning that he had now left a daughter behind him as well, he felt that this could not go on — for the sake of his name he would enter his majority unencumbered.

He was able to convince Mason of the strength of his argument. He was well satisfied with his agent's support and did not consider that, in putting his serving man in possession of such a secret, he was ridding himself of one partner only to be bound to another.

The laws of England put the disposal of legitimate children entirely in the hands of the husband; he could, at his pleasure, remove his offspring for ever from the mother and Ashley dispatched Mason to tell his wife that this was his pleasure. She was an uneducated girl and had neither the inclination nor the power to make herself difficult. She understood that she was not presentable and believing that her children would be brought up as her husband's in his household she released them, putting their welfare before her own.

Had she known of Ashley's intentions she would have fought to keep her children. He had a small estate on the Dorset coast which had come to him from a cousin and it was to this location, remote and unvisited by its landlord, that he had them delivered by Mason. Saying that he had found them abandoned, he placed them and a sum of money in the care of a shepherd's widow. She, gaining her living from pauper infants, had little curiosity in their origin; what suspicions she had were directed towards Mason but as a result of his lack of interest in the family on subsequent occasions she took their protection upon herself; because they were young she named them Young and while she lived she did her best for them.

Their mother did not prosper. Materially she lived comfortably but her longing for those she had loved ate into her strength and when she contracted phthisis she died — a humble girl, obliging to the end — and, now that she was gone, Ashley found that it was not she but the existence of a wife that he had wanted dead.

Fear of the coming darkness was growing within him. Soon there would be movements in the corners of the room. He heard the faint sound of church bells blowing across his land and resisted the temptation that they offered. He worshipped in public but had long since given up private prayer, feeling he had no right to ask for intervention. He had done wrong in putting away his wife but, though suffering, was not repentant and would not add hypocrisy to his sins. A future marriage would bring the true blood but he would not think of that now. He had preserved his family name from blemish and what was the misery of a generation compared with that? An individual was only part of the whole and must be bent into its proper form. He wished for light. He would have candles.

He had retired early before the maid had brought the lamps and so he must see to his own comforts. He put the desk on the carpet and reached for the tinder-box that was set beside the fender. Even though it was summer he had had a small fire laid to allow him a moment of warmth and vitality in the night. Striking a spark with the steel, he dipped a match into the tinder and touched it to the shavings in the grate. The shavings caught and flared and twisted and the smells of sulphur and juniper and pine sprang out into the already overladen air. He lifted the sketch from the desk and carried it towards the flames. He saw that the girl was still smiling and holding her gently to his cheek he knelt alone on the floor and wept.

Chapter 2

Some eleven years later the weather had not improved. On a Wednesday in the latter part of May two young women were looking down on Chesil Beach. The elder of the two was in some difficulty with her hat. The reputed mildness of the Southern coast was not showing itself to advantage and the erratic wind which was discomfiting Mrs Dene was, as twilight approached, merely the prelude to something worse.

For the moment, however, their view of the sea was unimpaired and as they sat their horses on the brow of the ridge there was an exhilaration in the aspect that explained why they had strayed beyond their usual path and time of riding.

It was a grey dusk and the sandy grass that fell steeply to the long, pebbled shore had been drained of the colour that made it and the stones and the sea separate. The last of the sun, which was descending the sky directly before them, was drawing a muted tawny from the East Cliff but beyond the cove, and obscured by spume and the approaching mist, the headland was bleak and without detail. The wind, which even at this distance, was spattering the watchers with spray was driving a heavy fog unsteadily inland and its appearance of deadening weight combined with the increasing vigour of the waves gave a curious mixture of stillness and movement to the scene.

The girl showed no sign of stirring and Mrs Dene, who was in fear of footpads, said, to attract her attention, "Does it please you, Sophia?"

Hearing her words the girl turned in the saddle to look at the speaker and in doing so presented a face which was equally likely to attract and repel danger. She was closer to the edge than her companion and was already a decorative addition to the landscape. She was a slim, erect figure in an expensively simple habit and sat lightly on a delicately-built mare of the same pale dun as her gloves. Her friend was riding a sturdy Welsh pony and it was noticeable that while Sophia and her mare were one Mrs Dene was merely seated upon hers. Their station was clear from the quality of their clothes; they should not have been alone in such an uninhabited place but when Sophia turned her head to be seen it was plain that a footpad would have to be bold to out-face her. At twenty she was discarding the common bloom of a girl for the calm and unarguable beauty that would be hers as a woman — but more than this; it was obvious that she was good with a goodness that should be cloistered for its own protection.

She was inclined to alarm people by listening with concentration and considering what was said and now, her expression serene but her intense, dark eyes dilated by the unexpected freedom of the afternoon, she gave her thoughts to Mrs Dene.

"When the sea is meek," she said, "I long for the excitement of a storm yet when I find rough waves they are not to my liking — I see the superiority of peace."

"And this?"

She turned her face towards the waters. "A hidden force is most comfortable to the observer; most dangerous to those in its toils. I pity the fishermen tonight."

Mrs Dene smiled and again put her hand to her hat. "I have heard you say you would sail with them," she said.

Sophia laughed. "I was safely on the shore at the time. Perhaps I would."

A sudden chill brought Mrs Dene nearer to the girl's side. She looked about her worriedly. The horizon, which had been perceptibly growing closer, was almost upon them and strips of mist were being blown inland faster than they could ride. The air, which had been clean and fresh, was now salt and dank and as they watched the white swell of the surf was lost beneath the fog and they could no longer see the beach.

"My dear," said Mrs Dene, "we must leave before the wind drops. Your grandfather will worry if we're late." I have left it too long, she thought, and she is my responsibility. What will Francis say if she is hurt? They turned their horses and began following the ridge back towards the east. It was an unsatisfactory direction. Riding as they were across the wind — their veils fluttering damply round their shoulders — the flowing mists gave them a sensation of wandering from their course that the rise of the hill did nothing to alter. Little by little as their right sides became saturated and they lent away from the wind to protect their eyes they bore to the left believing their line to be straight.

This was unfamiliar country. Tired of waiting for the manservant who was to have come from home they had started at noon from Abbotsbury after a stay of two nights with the Wares of Linton. Although burdened by packages that should have been carried by Joshua they had felt themselves to be unusually unrestrained and taking advantage of their opportunity had ignored the track to Bredy and followed the coastal path. It was to have been a short diversion but the novelty of their unescorted state, their interest in the sights they had seen so rarely and the obvious pleasure Sophia had taken from the sea had drawn them beyond their intention. The path to Swyre they knew hazily from summer expeditions but the hills to the west, the wild and lonely heaths that had fed the girl's spirit, were unknown to them and it was these hills they were riding in dusk and mist.

I am foolish, thought Mrs Dene. What harm can we come to? We have never yet needed a defender. Why should we now? At the most we cannot be more than ten miles from home and surely not that. Francis will forgive me for just this once. He is a fair man; I have never led her into danger before. She glanced across at her charge and seeing Sophia sitting so easily in the saddle, soothing her tired mare and adjusting the leather sack that swung at her side, without trace of the anxiety that was afflicting herself, she smiled and tried not to notice the ache that was growing in her back.

Rosa Dene, placidly intelligent, comfortably handsome, was, at thirty-five, not a woman who was suited to the extremities of climate. Physically the years were treating her kindly but her upbringing in a family which had little money to support its gentility, her marriage to an improvident Ilminster lawyer, the death of her husband and the brief insecurity of unemployed widowhood had made her wary of any situation in which protection was not immediately apparent.

She had come to Bredy Hall in a depressed condition. She had been interviewed by Francis Farren as the bailiffs emptied her house. She had not felt this to be auspicious. They had sat in her dim back-parlour while Francis asked her slow, deliberate questions and she had answered between silences which might have been broken by the clock if it had not been packed in straw. She did not expect to be hired as governess to his orphaned grandchild but for fifty-three years Francis had known what he wanted and got it. He saw in Mrs Dene a quiet, clever woman wearied by the chances and choices of the world; he saw that she would give her loyalty to whoever offered her shelter. There would be no pining for her old life, no sighing for romance; where she was taken she would stay and because she had been hurt herself would be careful and loving to a ten-year-old girl.

Francis was not a sentimental man. In his youth he had hunted not from sport but from the desire to kill; children on his estate had been known to favour him; he was a gentleman of the eighteenth century and those of the nineteenth were uneasy in his presence. He was witty, sharp and sarcastic with a mind more agile and learned than his neighbours. He was fond of Sophia and wished her to have all the advantages his fortune could provide. He had never liked his son and was not displeased that measles and ague had relieved him of the intervening generation and left Sophia to carry forward his blood.

He did not neglect her accomplishments. He allowed her his library as if she were a boy; because she was an heiress he taught her accounts; he dressed her according to her rank; she knew the use of globes. Twice monthly a dancing-master came by carrier and solemnly, beautifully, she danced alone in an upper room. She danced for her new governess the day Mrs Dene, in grey mourning, had arrived to be part of the household and Rosa, complimenting the figures, putting aside her gloves to admire the precise, imaginative sketchbooks, had felt that caring for her would be worth any fear she had of Francis.

She had not expected to like her employer but his complete and courteous dominance took away all the responsibility for decision that had plagued her independence and relaxed her. He showed no tenderness either to her or Sophia but when, after a year of watching her attention to her charge, he came to her room at night she accepted him as her lover almost with relief. She had had no children from her marriage and was hardly disturbed by thoughts of scandal. What anxiety she did have was more than balanced by the security Francis' interest gave her and her gratitude towards him. She was too pragmatic a woman to feel that she had lost her virtue and too discreet to offer others the opportunity to tell her that she had. She had a genuine love for Sophia, an affection for Francis, and, apart from a fear that her pupil's kindness would lead her into harm, enjoyed a life of unexpected comfort and domestic harmony.

And I wish, she thought, as her pony lurched across a ditch, that I were at home now. It was not yet nightfall but the disappearance of the wind had settled the mists about them until they stumbled in a haze that was neither night nor day but a condition of suspended time in which it seemed that they would never again be anywhere but where they were. They rode in a silence so absolute that their own hoof-beats came up to them as a vague surprise. Without noticing it they had left the stone walls and gorse of the coast and the tightly-budded branches of the thorns no longer pointed inland. As they moved among the meadows where the season was more forward they passed banks of red campion covered and muted by the mists and once, when Sophia bent to untangle her stirrup, she was startled by the sudden, harsh scent of wild garlic closing about her.

They forded the Bride knowing they were lost. They had missed the track to Swyre and although the direction of the river, as it flowed down from Bredy, could point them towards home there were no landmarks to tell them where they were crossing. They did not recognize the banks but it seemed a simple thing to follow them upstream. They splashed through the shallows with new confidence but the screen of elders dripping slowly into the river separated them from the sight of the water and little by little, the fog and bushes muffling the soft wash of the current, they wandered from the course of the stream.

It was almost dark when a fence forced them steeply uphill. The neutral tones of the mists had lost the delicacy given to them by the dusk and fog hung still and dead between the trees. They rode wearily, shivering in their damp clothes, across ground that was ridged by sheep-walks, under beeches whose octopus roots lay exposed by the slope. Their hands were almost numb with cold and when they rounded a bend and came upon a camp they had to fumble at their reins to stop.

In a hollow at the edge of the trees a young man was kneeling by a fire. To one side a lantern sat on the steps of a wooden van and its dim flame shining dully through the horn joined with the firelight to throw a hollow, amber glow into the mist. A small cauldron hung steaming from a tripod and as it boiled the man broke from examining a bundle he had cradled on his arm to scatter a handful of leaves into the pot. A grey dog, large and lean, lay by his side, its ears pricked, staring towards the intruders.

"Gypsies," whispered Mrs Dene and turned her pony's head to go but Sophia lent and took hold of her bridle.

"A shepherd, ma'am," she said.

Hearing them speak the dog sat upright, baring its teeth, and the shepherd, seeing him alert, stood up. He was a year or more older than Sophia but there was no boyishness in his expression. His feet were bare and he wore brown moleskins and a heavy drill shirt that looked as if it had belonged to someone else. Mrs Dene, reassured by his profession, thought that there was something uncommon about him and decided it was that he was clean.

The bundle he held in his arms shuddered and gave a mournful cough. He uncovered its face and they saw, wrapped in his smock, an eight-week lamb. He turned aside to lay it on a bed of straw and came back to the fire. Sophia thought, I have not met this man. If I had I would have remembered. He can't see us but he is not afraid. I am always afraid. How tenderly he covers the lamb.

"Come forward into the light." His voice was soft and persuasive and Sophia, still leading her companion, began to move towards the fire. Mrs Dene objected. "He will frighten the horses," she said, looking at the dog.

"He is not frightening them," said Sophia. "Hear how gently he speaks."

The shepherd approached Mrs Dene. "Forgive me, mistress," he said. "I thought you were tinkers. I meant no offence."

"We took none," said Sophia.

He stepped closer to her. He was tall but from her seat she looked down on him. She saw a face, thin by nature, made thinner by circumstance, with eyes old enough to see the ridiculous sadness of life. He had fair hair darkened by the reddening firelight but it was not any physical characteristic that was noticeable about him — it was the self-containment of one who has already spent many years alone on the hills. He is not deferential, thought Sophia, and yet not threatening. From the darkness a sheep-bell clanged and quietened and the horses moved a little on the wet grass.

Mrs Dene spoke suddenly into the silence. "As you may know," she said, "we are Miss Farren and Mrs Dene of Bredy Hall. We were returning home and have missed our path."

The shepherd withdrew his gaze from Sophia. "You'll recognize this hill by day, ma'am," he said. "We're above Toller Valence — Winterbourne Bredy is two miles through the lane beyond." The relaxation of Mrs Dene's figure at these familiar names was so obvious that he became concerned. "Have you no escort?" he asked. "There are vagrants about. You should not be alone."

Mrs Dene looked above his head to Sophia. "We should have stayed another day," she said. "Then Frederick Ware could have brought us home."

"And suppose we had met the vagrants?" said Sophia. "He would have done something brave and been shot. How would we have felt then?"

Mrs Dene stared into the blackness. "We would have felt living," she said.

"If you are threatened," said the shepherd, "give them your money at once and they won't harm you. They're on the tramp for work not mischief."

"Then why do they not work?" asked Mrs Dene. "Are the fields any fewer?"

"There was so little threshing this winter." Sophia let her mare drop its head to the ground. "Now that the machines are here hardly a man is needed. We know that from our own farms, ma'am. Three families left Bredy last month because the parish wouldn't keep them."

Mrs Dene smiled tiredly. "It's my unease speaking," she said. "I wish we were home."

The young man was again watching Sophia. "I would go with you, mistress," he said, "but I can't leave my herd for so long. I could run to the village for a man."

"Thank you but we'll do well enough now that we know where we are. You mustn't leave your sheep."

"No, indeed," agreed Mrs Dene. "Your first responsibility is to your master," and impressed by the darkness, the solitude, the fear of vagrants, she added, "You would not injure him?"

"I would not do what was wrong," said the shepherd.

A faint dissatisfaction made her look more closely at him. "Do we know you?" she said, shivering. "Something about you seems familiar."

"I am Calder Young," he said. "I have a brother and sister at Hammond's farm over to Cheney. Hannah takes cheeses to your kitchens." The water in his cauldron was boiling and he hooked it from the tripod to the grass. The steam, now distinguishable from the smoke, made the women feel how cold they were. Mrs Dene rubbed a stiffened arm and stretched and unstretched her fingers. The weakening fire deepened its light as Calder broke a twig into its ashes and they saw something blue swirling among the grain in the pot.

"You are making fumitory?" asked Mrs Dene.

"No, ma'am," he straightened with a stick in his hand. "Water with a little sorrel and barley for flavour. I would offer you some to warm you but I have nothing to use as a cup."

Mrs Dene shivered again and Sophia, seeing her discomfort, said, "There is the sugar jar I bought yesterday. I can drink from the lid — it will be enough for me." She slid from the saddle and unfastened a satchel that hung behind. From the miscellany of its contents she took a package wrapped in linen and, removing the cloth, revealed a green and white stoke porcelain jar with a romantic and exaggerated view of Weymouth. This she carried to the fire and gave to Calder. While she tied the satchel into her belt he crouched by the cauldron and poured out enough water to fill the jar. Despite its heat he took it carefully between his palms and passed it up to Mrs Dene.

Against the pale gleam of the china his hands were brown and scarred. Seeing him watching her, Sophia looked abruptly back into the pot. The object she had noticed before was now bobbing on the surface of the water. It was a thrush's egg and appeared to be the only sustenance the shepherd had. She held out the lid and Calder, with a slight smile, lifted the cauldron and tipped it so that the egg slipped over into her cup. Her hands shook and a few drops of water slopped on to her glove. I am behaving like a schoolgirl, she thought. Have I had no training?

"Shepherd," she said. "I have never been inside a lambing hut. I would like to see yours."

She felt at once that she had done something wrong. It was natural to her rank to have free entry to the homes of the poor but tonight it did not restore her position; she felt herself impertinent. She looked to Mrs Dene for guidance but her companion was engaged in blowing on her water and did not notice her. To hide her confusion she bent and caressed the head of the dog and, at a signal from its master, the dog gave way to its own inclination and leant heavily against her legs.

She laughed and returned Calder's gaze without embarrassment. "He is playful," she said. "And he a sheep-dog." She stroked the dog under the chin. "Have you no duties, sir?" she asked.

"His name is Watch," said Calder, "but all of us need rest."

He walked towards the van and Sophia followed with the dog at her side, rubbing itself against her damp skirts. Calder held up the flickering lantern and Sophia, with no charity basket on her arm and believing herself intrusive, gathered her habit into her free hand and mounted the steps behind him. There will be nothing to see, she thought. I'm making myself foolish for nothing, but, having entered she looked about her.

As a temporary lodging it would have been agreeable. The floor was swept and the pile of bracken at the far end had its rough-woven blanket folded neatly upon it. A sheep-crook leant against the wall beside a collection of medicine bottles and drenches and a small sack of barley — some of whose grains were now floating fatly jellied in her cooling water. A fustian jacket and low-crowned hat hung from a nail above a pair of wooden-soled shoes. In everything there was the scrupulous neatness of poverty which will not have its dignity defeated — and there was poverty in all except one thing. On a shelf above the bed was a row of books. She went across to the shelf and Calder opened the front of the lantern to give her light enough to read. They were old editions and some were unbound but she could see a *Pilgrim's Progress*, a Bible, a home herbal, something — she could not tell what — by Mary Wollstonecraft, the second volume of *Tristram Shandy*, and on this collection were newspapers which had been read and reread and passed from hand to hand — newspapers she had seen thrown down in magistrates' meetings in her grandfather's house — the *Dispatch*, the *Political Register*. He is a radical, she thought. That is why he speaks to us so freely — as if he were our equal. Perhaps he is.

"The tailor at Cheney taught us our letters. Caleb and Hannah didn't take to it but I read." There was a new tone in his voice that was not shyness or pride but had an element of both. She turned away from his books and faced him. He has been civil, she thought. He offered us water because we were cold.

She said gently, "You have a fine library."

"I buy from the higgler when I can," he said, "but I've had nothing new this winter. Caleb was turned off from the threshing and Hannah and I have kept him."

And I stand here, she thought, and drink from a sugar jar. I know of the hunger but what can I do? I am not yet of age; I have no money and no power. She lifted the flap of her satchel and drew out her Prayer Book. "It is all I have with me to read," she said. "If you would take it you would please me."

He set the lantern on the shelf and took the book in both hands. They were standing close together and it seemed to Mrs Dene, looking at them through her tiredness, the mists and firelight, that there was an intensity about their figures that was misplaced.

"Come away, Sophia," she called. "We have our home to return to."

They left the shepherd at the foot of the hill where the lane to Bredy began. The sea-fog had not reached the valley and they left behind the last shreds of the mist and rode under a sky that was hard and bright with stars. The lantern Sophia now carried glimmered weakly in her hand and she felt a restlessness that she did not wish to be soothed.

"He had a hospitable manner for a shepherd," remarked Mrs Dene.

"Yes," said Sophia. "Yes, he had."

Her companion guided her pony around a rut and came back to her side.

"I thought that dog was going to bite," she said.

Sophia looked at her in surprise. "I was holding its head," she told her. "I wouldn't have let him hurt you."

Mrs Dene laughed. "I know, my dear, but I'm your governess and if there are any bites to be suffered they should be by me."

"But if you are my governess," said Sophia, "I am the more fortunate — surely, then, it is for me to protect you."

Mrs Dene reached across and patted her hand. "How can I send you out into the world with ideas such as those?" she asked. "You'll have no defences."

"I can defend myself."

"No, I think you can only defend others." She sighed and looked sadly at her charge. "You should be more conscious of your position," she said. "I may have done wrongly in bringing you up as I did. I wonder your grandfather allowed it."

"Grandfather," said Sophia bitterly, "thinks to have me

marry and obey my husband and so escape any consequence of my own thoughts."

They rode in silence for a moment. Then Mrs Dene said, "We must do something to make you less serious. The new linen maid can sew; when she comes we'll set her to work. You need a season with Harriet in Town."

Francis was affable at supper. There had been an uncomfortable meeting. Whatever relief the women had felt from riding under their own gateway into the safety of their own courtyard had been dissipated by the sight of Francis, his pistol in his belt, mounting his horse to look for them. "Well, madam," he had asked, "must I search the countryside for you? Is this your care of my charge?" and Mrs Dene, in genuine shame, had turned her face away and received his anger patiently, thankful that she had returned to the custody of one who would never tremble at the fears of the night. Sophia, balancing the lantern on the rim of the unused fountain, stepping down among the bushes of lavender and thyme that grew in the cracks in the flags, had been stifled by the high stone walls and, though held to less blame than her companion had felt it more, and suffered for Mrs Dene's sake.

His mood did not last. Being used to extracting obedience Francis did not allow his displeasure to seep out into sulks or grudges. He had delivered his opinion, given his orders and considered the matter closed. The women were not to ride alone again; neither was Joshua, when bidden to fetch them, to use his discretion and visit the farrier first. Forgiven, they had supped in their habits on a gudgeon and a dish of hashed fowl and retired privately to rest.

Sophia could not settle. The tranquillity that was usual to her light and peaceful room, the composure she gained from its white hangings and freedom from unnecessary ornament, was not to be had tonight. Instead, when she drew the thrush egg from her pocket and placed it on her cabinet, she felt impatient of the chinese wallpaper she had always loved — as if the parading birds and flowers were no longer a wilderness but were suddenly a formal and artificial thing. She opened a pane to let in the night air and, looking down, the sight of the house, so strongly Tudor, so haphazard and beautiful in its familiarity, filled her with an unexpected disquiet. Putting down her brush, she wrapped her dressing-robe over her nightgown and went out in search of company.

At the foot of the stairs she stopped to sprinkle cake crumbs in the goldfish globe. The door of the small drawing room where her grandfather sat in the evening had been left ajar. Standing unobserved in the hall, Sophia could see a softly domestic scene. Francis, his gauntly Roman face contented, was sitting by the fire attending to movements beyond the door. An open book was on his knee and an unplayed flute lay on the music stand by his side. A chinking and rustling subsided and Mrs Dene, now bathed and silked, came towards him carrying a basin. She sat on a footstool in front of the hearth, her back resting against his legs, and, using a long fork, began toasting muffins in a way that spoke more of indolence than hunger. He stroked her hair gently, rearranging the lace streamers of her cap. She turned to smile at him and Sophia, seeing that at this moment she was not Mrs Dene but Rosa, returned to her room, comforted.

Chapter 3

Hester Allen, eighteen-years-old and tired by the heat, had been told to walk with the sun behind her. It was now noon and her shadow was hardly more than a suggestion beneath her feet. She put down her bundle and considered her position.

She had come from Moreton the day before, travelling to Weymouth by waggon to sleep the night with a friend she had met in service, and that morning had made her way across country to take up her appointment as linen maid to the Farrens. She could not read the milestones but her conscientious following of directions had brought her within an hour of Bredy Hall.

It was hot. Around her a blue sky lay motionless on the fields of growing corn. Nothing stirred. No birds flew, no breeze swayed the heavy chestnut flowers on the tree beyond the hedge. The tall grass in the verges, the cattle, the distant hills, all stood suspended in the torpid heat of early afternoon and Hester, small, slim and upright, fragile and vulnerable, in her old green gown and faded yellow sun-bonnet, waited alone in the landscape, like a cowslip preserved in a bell jar.

She undid the strings of the bonnet and took it from her head, feeling at once an increased burning on the back of her neck. She turned the hat from side to side. She had starched it before she left and its tucks were still presentable but it was the only thing about her that had not suffered from her journey and she wanted to make a good impression. She was so young and yet so weary of change. She had an uncommon sweetness of character that had not been broken by a common and bitter story. She was sensitive and loving and in need of a protector; although she did not know it she was afraid of a world which had not yet shown her a reason for its being and, like Mrs Dene before her, she was travelling to Bredy in search of peace.

As a child she had lived with her parents in the north of Salisbury Plain. Her father had poached to help sustain his family and when he was caught had been transported. It was nothing extraordinary — there had been no report in a paper — but the war was over and with it the prosperity of the farms and those who paid rising rates from lessening profits decided to make an example of the Allens. What was to deter men from crime if their families could escape the consequences? To prevent anarchy Mrs Allen and her daughter were refused relief and escorted across the parish boundary. Having no right to support anywhere but the place of their birth they had wandered aimlessly south and west, going hungry and stealing turnips, until the mother died of no particular disease beneath a hedge near the village of Bournemouth.

Then had begun for Hester a life of constant and unconsulted change — of workhouse, of stone-picking, of farm maid — and in this low condition she had seen at close hand the helplessness and humiliation of the very poor. She had seen cart-loads of children sold to the manufacturers in the North; she had seen men willing and desperate for work set up for auction in the marketplace; she had seen them forced to walk thirty miles a day for eighteenpence to feed lives no longer worth the living; she had heard the clang of the bells about the paupers' necks — and from it she had drawn a great longing for security and permanence.

She was naturally quiet, neat and quick to learn and had managed not only to raise herself from field to scullery to laundry but had also been taught, by a kindly and now dead mistress who had noticed her diligence, plain sewing, feather-stitch and drawn-thread work. She hoped to persuade someone to teach her lace-making and the keeping of a still-room. She was a good and faithful servant and wished to increase her talents.

Standing at rest made her feel the heat more. She replaced the bonnet without tying it and the movement tightened the damp cloth of her sleeves against her skin and lifted a breath of sweat and dust from her open neck. She felt unclean. Neither ambition nor fastidiousness would allow her to enter her new employment in this way. She shaded her eyes. There was no cottage near but to her left, beyond the field of budding wheat, there was a wood and from the luxuriance of the hedge that met it there appeared to be a stream. She would take the risk of trespass and use the shelter of the trees to wash and change.

Her bundle seemed heavier as she walked down the lane to the gate. She paused once again at the entrance but could see no one and, feeling conspicuous, she slipped inside. Her heart was beating so hard she could feel its pulsing in her throat but she considered her action important and having made a decision was not one to change her mind. To be exposed for the least time she took the shortest route, crossing the field with the pale, green corn closing behind her like the sea. The dry earth in the furrows crumbled beneath her feet as she stumbled across the ruts left by the oxen but as she reached the wood she heard the soft flow of water and the thick, sour heat of travel was lost in the cool, dark shadow of the trees.

She pushed her way into the bushes, her skirts catching on the brambles, and the hawthorn she passed under shed its last, loose petals on her shoulders, filling the air with a ghost of its sweet and sinister scent. There was movement in the spinney. Outside the field was still and silent but here where the day was less wearing there was the drowsy call of doves and the sudden spring of branch and wing as they flew. The flat sunlight dropping through the trees fell on a pool that was fed and emptied by the gentle stream she had guessed would be there. It was a secret, tangled place of young leaves, of bluebells turning dry and white in the face of June, of yellow flags gaudy at the water's edge.

She approached the pool. The slow current of the stream had kept the water clear and she could see beyond a sloping shelf that the floor was level and deep as if something had been dug from it and the long stems of the unopened lilies twisted down into mud and silt. She could not swim and was afraid of water. She looked at the light dappling the stream and thought of lick-and-promise in its shallows but it would be more effective to bathe and she preferred to be effective.

Putting her bundle down in the grass she untied its knot and revealed it to be a set of new clothing wrapped in her shawl. When word had come that she had been hired for Bredy the Farren's housekeeper had sent her two guineas to buy an outfit suited to the Hall and the result of their gift and her needle lay folded but jumbled before her. There were two new cotton gowns, a large white neckerchief, a cap, stockings, apron and, wound in her underlinen, a pair of flat, leather shoes that were almost new. Inside the shoes she had stored a comb, a green ribbon, a lithograph of a cottage cut from a ballad-sheet and a cheap string of beads a pedlar had given her for mending his coat. These and the clothes she wore were all that she possessed and more than she had ever owned before. She felt the burden they put on her. They represented a rise in status, a step towards the comfort and security she wished to have but they also meant new effort and she was tired.

She knelt in the grass beside them and took out what she would wear. Touching the shoes with a finger she admired them and dreamed a little until she remembered that if she were caught in the wood there would be no position for her. She was an unlikely poacher but gamekeepers were no friends to the unlikely.

Loosening her ties and laces she pulled off her gown and boots and stood at the edge of the pool in her shift. She had grown used to the sound of the birds in the trees and there seemed a great quietness in the wood. A dragonfly was taking its stilted, darting flight among the lilies and she watched it for a moment afraid to go forward. She took a strand of a willow in her hand to steady her. The water was deep but looked restful; she stepped in.

At the time that Hester had been breaking her fast that morning the farm on which Caleb and Hannah Young were employed had been waking to its labours. Five Warrens Farm, across whose meadows Sophia and Mrs Dene had ridden in search of the road to Bredy, lay by the side of Nether Cheney but the village, with its high-walled manor and secretive church, was as hidden from the farmstead as if it had not been there at all. An early Hammond, enriched by the wool trade, had built a house of substance and gables in the hollow of a valley to the east of the settlement. Mullions and ham-stone, dairy and malthouse, orchard and kitchen-garden, huddled beneath the steep slope that led to the village yet it was not a sheltered situation. To the north its fields ran in a long wind-harrowed wedge towards the hills where Calder led his sheep and to the south the combe rose to the desolation of the coastal ridge so that in winter the sound of the sea flowed over the hilltop and swirled down into the valley like the fear of plague.

It was a mixed farm. During the French Wars when grain had been like gold even the blown and salted ridges had been put to the plough and stunted, broken wheat had straggled to the shore but peace and recession had brought the grasslands back and though the level fields on the floor of the valley were still in cultivation there was no longer enough arable land to justify a team of ploughmen. It was for this reason that the brothers and sister Young had hunger in their eyes.

It was a look of withdrawal familiar to all the Southern labourers and interpreted variously by their employers as sullenness, stupidity or insolence. An annoyance to gentlemen whose position had been dignified by Enclosure, an anxiety to farmers pursued by ruin, rates and greed it would not be cowed by imprisonment nor eased by religion but asked for bread. Thirty-four years before the magistrates of Speenhamland had pitied its thin face and agreed that if a man's wages fall below what would feed him the difference would be paid from local rates — and so the wages fell and rates rose and because the rates rose each farmer turned off his men to be paid by his neighbour. And the numbers of paupers grew and the parish overseers adjusted their accounts and year by year lowered the level they called subsistence until the labourers, deprived of the common lands that had aided their parents, bound to their parishes by the laws of settlement, chained in the convict ships for netting a rabbit, watched their families starve in the fields and began to say they would have bread or blood.

John Hammond of Five Warrens was not a harsh man for his time and if his maids did have their whey and his men did dip their hands into the horses' feed he did not comment. He was pressed by tithes and taxes and the desire to live as comfortably as if there were a war and though it would have been a pride to him to work his ploughmen all the year he was compelled by circumstance to let them go — for on the heels of depression had come the machines.

When Caleb was a boy and learning his trade he had accepted that until he was a master horseman his winters would be spent with a flail in his hand threshing the corn he had planted. It was monotonous, aching labour but each of three barns had resounded with seven men and women beating to the rhythm of old ring-changes and holding their poverty at arm's length by the echo of the elm-board floor. Then the machines had spread down from the north and those farmers who bought one could thresh their crops and send them to market in the first, most profitable, weeks after harvest. Thus at farm after farm the flails were replaced by a woman to load and a horse to power a machine and the families who had used them were turned off for the winter to live on the rates — and because the rates rose the farmers, for economy, sacked their men.

Hannah, hired as much for her laughter and good spirits as her work, was an indoor servant and unaffected by the change, Calder — on Marshall's farm — was his master's only shepherd, but Caleb, a junior member of an overmanned craft, was expendable. Hammond turned him off. He went on the parish and the overseer put him on the rounds. Day by day he walked from door to door asking for employ and if there was odd work he had fourpence from the householder and tuppence from the rates and if there was none he had sixpence from the rates. Bread was then one shilling and threepence the gallon loaf and sixpence would not keep him — Calder and Hannah did.

They had little to share. Hannah slept above the dairy with the other maids but had no board and five shillings a week; Calder had a crown weekly from his master, sixpence from the parish and the use of the lambing hut; from this they provided for three. Having lost his place in the ploughman's attic Caleb, with a wary eye for Marshall, joined his brother in the hut and together through the cold winter they set blackthorn traps for hares and slept back to back for warmth as they had done as boys. In February they killed a fox and baked it in a pot beneath the ground. Their crimes were unobtrusive; they poached on sheep-runs too open for the keepers to suspect and when Hannah met them on her free afternoons she did not walk as if she carried corn meal in her skirts. They were young and strong and vigorous and so, though they weakened in the frosts and rains, though they starved until what food they had made them bloated and sickened, they did not lose their health. Caleb endured and Calder thought and when spring came and Caleb returned to Five Warrens Calder put aside his discretion and took his old papers to read aloud in the beer-houses and listen to the talk of those who had suffered as he had done. He looked at women whose children had not survived the winter, at men made bitter and vindictive by the misery of their families, at rich, green fields of wheat and he saw, as Robert Owen had seen among the factories and riots of the north, that in the midst of the most ample means to create wealth, all were in poverty, or in imminent danger from the effects of poverty on others.

While spring revived Calder and calves were brought to the kitchen door for Hannah to cosset Caleb fell back into routine. He was a mild, friendly young man without ambition except, as he said, to "get by". He was patient, slow in his movements, steadfast and loyal; when once he loved he would do so all his life. He played the fiddle doggedly for dances. The pleasures of his world were the soft, warm strength of his horses, the sight of a straight furrow behind his plough and the company of his family who, on the morning of Hester's journey, were once again united. A ram new-bought by Freeman of Swyre had unexpectedly lamed and Marshall, who had been promised its services for his young ewes, sent Calder, as a tried sheep-doctor, to prescribe a cure. There being nothing wrong but a sprain Calder had poulticed the swelling and instead of lodging in Swyre as he had been instructed walked over to Five Warrens to join Caleb. He had left his herd in the care of Watch and the carter's boy and, trusting the dog to ignore the boy's commands, felt no compunction to return before he was expected.

Nor, as dawn seeped into the room and his brother rose to attend the horses, was he in any position to return. Hannah having removed his only suit of clothes to wash over night he was obliged to await her appearance with sheep-crook and shoes his only possessions. He lay in the straw in Caleb's bed and wrapped the blanket closer about him. The light that filtered through the thin thatch and sank in through the floor-level window was of a pale pearl-grey that promised heat, but the sun would not shine fully through the south-facing casement until noon and the long attic room was filled with shadows.

The room was above the stables and looked out across the yard to the dairy but the maids' loft was entered through the farmhouse and so Calder did not rouse himself to watch for his sister. The other men had left for their work and the first stirrings of the day were drifting up in sounds of heavy footsteps, clanking pails and murmurs of stolid, unawakened conversation.

It was a voice that drew him out of bed. He had been aware that something was missing and when he heard the arrival of the cows he realized what it was. The herd was late. The commotion of cattle and milkers that should have set in half an hour before had just begun and he heard a girl say that the gate from the meadow had not been opened.

He had stayed at Five Warrens often enough to know whose task this was. He stood up and walked across the room. Beside the cold grate where the men did their cooking there was a pile of bracken, straw and sacks. Softly he pulled back the coverings and revealed a boy burrowed down into his bedding like a dormouse. He was eight years old, thin, dark and as much asleep as a boy can be. Calder squatted beside him and touched his shoulder.

"Jem," he said. "Jemmy. Didn't anyone wake you, lad?"

The boy stirred and opened his eyes and Calder, seeing that their look was blank, lifted him as gently as if he were a lamb and carried him to the tub that served for bathing. He dipped a cloth into the water and stroked the child's face. The boy was warm with the sweet, sharp scents of hay and sweat. He tried to curl into the arm that held him but Calder, finding him conscious, set him on his feet and put the cloth in his hand.

"Make haste," he said "and you'll be down before master. No one will tell him you were late."

The boy tried to oblige but he had been bird-scaring all the day before and was too tired for independence — and so when Hannah entered, with Calder's clothes upon her shoulder, she found him, serious and tender, easing the small sleeves of a shirt and fastening buttons. She had been brought up in over-crowded poverty and never learned to be prudish and she stood and watched them as the early sun drew the signs of a hungry winter from bodies that were all muscle and bone and sinew and the protectiveness in her mourned that they had never wanted her care enough.

Her brother noticed her and smiled and, passing him the clothes she had laundered, she replaced him as nursemaid and helped the boy with his trousers.

"Jem, my honey," she said, kneeling to lace his boots, "master's looking for you."

The boy steadied himself against her. "He'll whip me, Hannah."

"Not if he can't find you. Hurry down to the byres and be busy."

She listened to him run down the stairs, then got up and uncreased Calder's collar at the back of his neck.

"You're as bad as him," she said.

"You smell good." He looked at her with interest and she took out an oatcake, still hot from the griddle, from the pocket of her apron and gave it to him.

"Caleb's driving the cart to Chilcombe — he'll take you part of your way."

Together they descended to the stables and went out into the yard. It was a scene that was at once quiet and active. The steading was crowded with cattle and their milkers; the cows stood patiently, flicking their tails, nodding their heads so that the sun glinted on the brass binding of their sawn-off horns, and, as the rising day lifted a richly flavoured steam from their backs, their girls leant their faces against the warm hides and let the milk thrum down into the pails. At the edges of the yard and threading through the cattle the men moved in and out of the sheds and grain stores, collecting their tools and loading a brilliantly blue and crimson cart with sacks of barley.

Seeing them watching, Caleb left his mare standing peacefully in the shafts and joined Calder and Hannah at the stable door. When the children had been found abandoned it had been assumed from their sizes that the boys were twins but as they grew older, although the family resemblance was strong, the difference in their build and temperament made people unsure and it was illustrative of the personality of the speaker as to which he considered the elder. Caleb stood with his brother and sister, more placid and thickly-set than either, and their fair hair and alert manner said clearly they belonged together.

"I'm taking the corn to old Briggs," he said, "and picking up wood from Bredy — it's a day's work. I'll —"

"God damn you, boy! You good-for-nothing wretch!"

All movement in the yard stopped. In the centre of the steading, his gaiters white and dripping, Hammond stood with Jem lying on the ground before him. The boy was holding his head and an empty bucket rocked slightly on its side.

"Do you think," Hammond shouted, "I've got money to throw about? Do you think I can run a dairy with the likes of you? Get up before I box the other ear."

The boy lay still and Hammond raised his fist. Hannah took a hand of each of her brothers; Caleb gripped her, restrained by his realism, but Calder's hand was hard and cold and she held him tightly to prevent him going forward. He disentangled himself and walked out into the yard. The cattle were stirring uneasily and he had to push one aside to find the boy. For the second time he reached down and lifted him to his feet.

The farmer glared around him. "Get about your business," he snapped. "I'll turn off the lot of you."

There was an immediate resumption of work and Calder, wondering what to do now, turned to go. Hammond prodded him with the butt of his whip.

"You know damn well I don't beat children," he said angrily.

Calder said nothing but glanced towards Jem who was

cooling his face at the pump. It was true that Hammond was not known as a violent man — but on a farm a blow from a master was not called violence. Hammond prodded him again.

"I wanted you," he said. "I might have known I'd find you meddling."

He reached into the skirts of his coat and brought out a pamphlet. "I suppose you'd have nothing to do with this?"

"It was given to me by a traveller," said Calder. "I passed it on."

"You passed it on. And what is it about and who did you pass it to? I'll tell you. It's about an Act of Parliament — the law, by God, you'd use the law against us — that says parishes should let land to the poor — and who do you give it to? John Hudson with five children already eating their bread at our expense. And yesterday, mark you, what does he do but ask for an allotment on that wasteland over to the Claydon estate. Land that's mine in all but name." He rolled the pamphlet and thrust it back into his pocket. "Now you listen, boy, we know about your habits, the magistrates and I. You keep talking dissent, you keep saying Jack's-as-good-as-his-master and raising sedition and you won't find it to your advantage. It'll be Van Dieman's Land for you and Hudson and all your like. We'll see how saucy you are walking to the hulks." There was a silence broken by the renewed sounds of work. Hammond took off his hat and ran his hand over unfashionably short and thinning hair.

"If you, must preach, boy," he said, "why don't you turn Methodist? T'would take off your fire and reading the scriptures wouldn't do you no harm. Do you have a Bible?"

Calder smiled slightly. "And a Prayer Book," he said.

"Then attend to them. You're young yet and maybe life seems hard to you but God put us each into our own station and it isn't for us to want change. It'll all be rectified in Heaven; the church teaches us that."

Thou feedest them, thought Calder, with the bread of tears.

Hammond patted him roughly on the shoulder. "You're a good workman," he said. "Go back to your sheep. Go back to the hills and try not to be noticed."

*

38

"This near enough for you?"

"It'll do me."

Caleb pulled gently on the reins and the cart drew to a halt. It rocked back an inch and because the slope was deceptive he slid on the brake. He had folded his smock up to his waist and he rested his whip on his corduroyed knees and gazed ahead. Calder, who had taken the journey in unembarrassed silence, showed no sign of moving and they sat together on the high seat looking absently at the view.

It was still early morning but already the heat was growing. Behind them a thin veil of cloud strayed in from the sea but above and before the sky was deepening to the complete and undiluted blue of summer. The dew had risen and the water meadows they had passed had brimmed hedge-high with a pale and gauzy mist but here on the upland they were beyond the cool hollows and, in the face of the sun, the shade from the beechwood that was between them and Calder's sheep lay like a slab on the grass.

A ramshackle growth of honeysuckle, dog rose and guelder stood beside the cart and Caleb hooked it towards him with his whip and picked a handful of flowers. He arranged a nosegay and its succulent, fleeting scent underlined the dry, harsh smell of the barley-sacks and welcome but pungent awareness of horse.

"I'm going to Bredy," he said. "Shall I give this to Miss Farren?"

Calder looked at his brother from the corner of his eye and smiled.

"Miss Farren," he said. "Miss Sophia Farren."

They laughed a little ruefully and Calder jumped down over the wheel to the ground. Taking his crook from Caleb he said, "Come over on Sunday if you get the chance — I won't be grazing the far walks till next week."

"I will," said Caleb — and then, as an afterthought, while he undid the brake, "You read that Prayer Book now."

Calder touched his forelock and waited for the cart to pass. There was a stile into the field that led to the beechwood and he climbed it and began making his way uphill. After a few yards

39

he had to pause to get his breath. He had almost recovered from the winter's deprivations but, like the others, suffered from moments of weakness and the sudden exertion after being carried in a cart was enough to tax him. The morning, indeed, had not been without its emotional trials and there are few things so exhausting as receiving injustice with patience.

He dug his crook into the hard ground and pulled himself on. The faintness passed and he walked more strongly, following the narrow cattle path to the woods. He skirted the edge of the beeches, last year's husks crunching under his heavy shoes. The woods on the other side of the hill were open to his sheep but this piece had been fenced in for game birds. One evening in autumn, while gathering nuts, he had been ordered out of sight by the keepers and returning surreptitiously from another direction had watched them set the man-traps. Knowledge of their position had provided him with good poaching but he would not draw attention to his deeds by trespassing in daylight.

Not, he thought, that his care would make any difference in the long term. He had had warning that his ways were marked and was aware that nothing could come of his present life but transportation. The painful struggle to educate himself, to think beyond the work of his hands, could lead him nowhere but the hold of a convict ship, nowhere but the road-gangs of the penal colonies, locked into irons for insolence of expression. However he wrestled to improve himself there was no possibility of that improvement resulting in benefit to him or his relations. No labourer, let him be as talented, as diligent as he may, could rise out of the morass of Speenhamland to earn more than a starvation wage. He could put nothing by for betterment or protection; he must bend to the winds of greed and prejudice; accept meekly that good craftsmanship would have no reward; rely on crime to feed his family; allow himself to be called the surplus population.

He had begun to turn over in his mind the thought of America. In England what could his ambition do but sit in illegal beer-houses reading the radicals to those too demoralized, too inarticulate and defenceless to ask for change. His

choice was only between opening the eyes of the unenfranch-
ised to laws they could not alter or doing as so many did and, a
little ale going far on an empty stomach, choose to drink instead
of eat — but in America he would not be bound. There, in its
democracy, he would be free to think and speak as he saw fit
and his labour would be his own to sell and not the farmer's to
take for dole.

Reaching the brow of the hill he stopped and looked out over
the distant fields. Before him the long sweep of the high downs
curved across the landscape towards the valley where the
winter-bourne sprang. He was gazing south-east almost into
the sun but it was not yet so fierce that he could not see, among
its trees, the mellow, lichened roof of Bredy Hall.

He had particular reason both for dreaming of advancement
and for considering emigration. On a May night, three weeks
before, a young woman, beautiful, graceful and awkward, had
come to him out of the mists. She had accepted all that he had to
give, answered his eyes and offered him her book. He must not,
on any account, think she could be his — and that was his
tragedy for he had learnt, as he lay alone in the hills, that he
loved her.

He did not think he came of a family which took its love
lightly. Though they did not speak of their affection he and
Caleb and Hannah would always stand by each other and if
they were able to gather enough to pay his passage there would
be no question that his first act would be to save and send for
them. But why should any one of them go? From this hill-top he
could see the whole of his world; from Lyme to Beaminster to
Portland Bill, a half-moon of green and fertile meadows
bordered by a sea now rolling under a thick and lazy swell. This
was his country — as much his as those who said they owned
the land. By what right did they claim his labour in so unequal
an exchange and threaten him with exile for seeing clearly?
What progression of history had meant that he could not ask
honourably for a girl who spoke freely to a shepherd and whose
cup shook when she took water from his hands?

There was a cobweb in the stone wall by his side; its strands
so intricate, so strong for entrapment, so dependent on each

other. He put his finger gently on its centre and, the dew reforming and running together, the whole quivered but did not break. He must deal with life as it was not as it ought to be; he would go back to the hills and try not to be noticed.

The road from Chilcombe to Winterbourne Bredy ran in a long and solitary meander beneath the ridge of the downs. As Caleb drove slowly along it in the early afternoon the air was so heavy with heat that even the pale dust that crumbled from the dried cart-ruts did not rise beyond the hub of the wheels. He gave the mare her head and sat loosely on the jolting seat swaying easily in time with the rough track. Now and again a faint suggestion of the sea filled the narrow lane but so briefly that a walker might wonder whether it was there and Caleb, carrying the intruding smells of farm and cart with him, was conscious only of the close and stifling tunnel of the hedgerows.

He was mildly worried about Calder. Since they were boys they had poached and risked transportation but that had been for a tangible result and in secrecy; to abandon a defensive silence to protest about what would not be changed seemed to him pointless. For Caleb the world was as it was and ever would be. He had suffered that winter with Calder but had seen only that Hammond was more fortunate and harsher than he — not that his misfortune had a wider cause or probable violent result. Everything that was his he considered to belong as much to his brother and sister as to himself and if Calder, who he knew to be an honest shepherd, were hounded out of England he would follow from a stubborn sense of honour but he would go to defy a condition that threatened his family — not because America was a promised land. He would fight an enemy at his gate but would never join a crusade; it was not in him to understand ideals.

It was becoming more urgent to send Calder away but the passage fee presented an impossible problem. To save three pounds from their wages was unthinkable and yet he could see a recklessness growing in his brother that he seemed unable to check; if Calder were to forget himself enough to show blatant defiance of the masters or reveal his feelings to a lady who could not think of him as a man their family would be rent apart without hope of reunion.

The road was lonely and encouraged introspection. As he left Chilcombe, Caleb passed a field of women slowly hoeing swedes and later two boys pushing a hand-cart of seaweed for manure dragged their barrow on to the verge to let him by, but apart from these few signs of existence the landscape was empty and silent. To each side the hay fields stood ready for the reapers and high on the downs small sheep grazed at the beeches' edge, but to the traveller's eye cultivation and human life had come to an end and left the world to a single cart and one young man.

The withdrawn, drowsy and brooding frame of mind induced by the heat, the solitude and thought meant that Caleb did not, at first, recognize that there was another figure in the lane. He was approaching the joining of two tracks when he noticed, vaguely and without interest, a girl stooping to part the grasses that hid the milestone. She looked at it blankly for a moment as if it were in another language and then let the grasses fall swaying back into place. Hearing the sound of the cart she turned towards Caleb but she was too far away and her face too shaded by her bonnet for him to see her expression and when he did not acknowledge her she hesitated and, lifting a bundle from the ground, began to follow the lane away from him.

She held the bundle lightly on her head with one hand and something in her hesitation and the firm, weary patience of her walk began to wake Caleb from his dream. She was taking the road to Bredy and he watched her as the cart began to gain on her path. From behind he saw a slight, straight-backed girl in a lilac gown. The shawl that wrapped her bundle was old and balanced by a hand used to labour but the gown and the white neckerchief he glimpsed beneath the flaps of her bonnet were of a starched neatness not normally seen on a working-girl. She did not look as if she were used to new clothes and yet they suited her.

She glanced to her right as the cart came up beside her, then turned her head away. Caleb began to slow the mare to a stop.

"Are you lost, maidy?" he asked gently.

His voice was soothing and she lowered her bundle to her hip and looked up at him. He saw that there was a tiredness behind her eyes that was more than hunger. Her face was oval and delicate with grey-green eyes and a rim of hair, pale-blonde and neatly parted, yet it was not her charm that hurt him but the air of quiet and defenceless valiance that shrouded her — and Hester, looking up into the sun, saw beneath a broad-brimmed hat, a square and strongly friendly face and within her the desire for rest stirred and reached out towards him.

"I don't know," she said. "I'm for Winterbourne Bredy — for Bredy Hall."

She was standing close into the verge, a haze of Queen Anne's Lace pressing about her, commonplace and beautiful, and Caleb, who loved the fitness of things felt without thinking that this meeting was a settled, looked-for act and was content.

"I'm going to the village," he said. "Will you ride with me?"

For her answer she held out her bundle and he leant over and took it from her. There was a damp patch on one side as if it contained something wet and he laid it in the empty body of the cart where it could dry. Having begun so boldly she now waited, a little uncertain, and he, taking off his hat, held out his large, hard hands to help her; she put her own small, cool fingers into his and he did not notice their roughness.

"Take care," he said. "I don't want you to fall."

A shyness came upon them as they began their journey. She sat beside him on the narrow seat, her skirts smoothed over her knees, her hands clasped in her lap, her eyes downcast. She smelt of clean linen and still waters.

"When I saw you standing there I didn't know if you were a maid or a flower." He looked at her openly, admiring the spruceness of her fern-patterned gown and thinking he was staring at her torn, cloth boots she drew her feet back under the seat.

"I have shoes in my pack," she said.

He smiled. "You going working for the Farrens?" he asked. "They given you new clothes?"

Out of nervousness she told him of herself. "I needn't have

44

left Moreton when my mistress died," she said, "the House would have hired me but Mr Frampton is a hard master and I wanted rid — so when his housekeeper heard the Farrens needed a girl she wrote for me and they gave me a start. I don't want to do field-work again."

The wooded slopes of Bredy's valley were rising into view. Already they were within sight of the Hall. It was right that she should be going there; she was too fine for the fields.

"I'm second ploughman," he told her, "with horses — not oxen. And I play the fiddle; I borrow it."

There was a bend in the lane as it entered the village and he looked straight ahead to drive round it. The sun was very warm.

"I'm not married," he said.

In the small library the Farrens were at whist. Their game was as it always was in a private party. To make a four they were joined by Cates, Francis' personal servant, a man of round shoulders and guarded eyes, who could be relied upon to put the correct number of ivory counters in the hollows of the table before an engagement and promote correct translation into coin at its end.

They showed an assortment of technique. Francis played with malice but did not bear grudges afterward. Mrs Dene was methodical and competent. There had been argument years before when it was discovered that Sophia was playing to lose because it gave others pleasure to win — she now played a cool, determined game marred by the occasional throwing away of chances through a sudden uprising of indifference. Cates' play was calculation disguised by deference to his partner.

Between rubbers they sipped sweet cider cooled in the ice-cellar and picked at a dish of macaroons. Francis had chosen their location as the coolest of the minor public rooms but even with the shade from the elms beginning to creep across the windows it was too hot to take much satisfaction from routing his valet. An urge for improvement having overtaken him half a lifetime before, he had redecorated the chamber in a Strawberry Hill gothic which bore not the slightest resemblance to the relevant centuries and which, having been brought to a simmer by the morning sun, was now depriving its occupants of their aggressive spirit by the heat released from its mahogany walls.

Tiring of the game Francis pushed back his chair and went to lean on the window. It was a house with that exuberance of glass that only an Elizabethan could commission and as he rested his knee on the low sill with the bright light obscuring his age there was an air about him of the buck he had been. He had thrown his coat over the folding steps and, with his cravat tied freely primo tempo and his thumbs in the pockets of his white marcella waistcoat, was a model of summer wealth.

Mrs Dene yawned behind her fan and Sophia, who had recently been surprising her bookseller with requests for unsettling literature, retreated into a private world of last night's reading. Cates counted the money.

"There's to-do in the servants' hall," said Francis. "I can see one of Hammond's carts leaving. There's no reason for it to be here — the new maid must be arrived. Yes, I see her."

The women got up and, with a slow shush of silk, joined him at the window. From this vantage they could look down on the rear courtyard, larger and more serviceable than the one to the front, and see Caleb manoeuvring the cart into the lane. At the door of the offices beside their housekeeper, a clever woman who did not admit to fifty, a young girl was standing with a posy of faded flowers raised to her face.

Francis laughed. "Will Mrs Harding be pleased with her bargain," he said, "or will she not?"

Mrs Dene shook her head mildly in reproof. "She is a pleasant, willing-looking girl," she said. "Do you not think so, Sophia?"

"She's delightful." Sophia moved a little to avoid the sun. "I hope she will be happy here — it would be a poor thing to travel from home and be sad."

Chapter 4

For the third year the harvest failed. The crops, which had been alternately forced and retarded by the wayward weather, were thin and the seed-heads rolled to nothing in the hand. Four reapers died of starvation in the fields and Lord Winchilsea, speaking in the Lords, said that this was not exceptional. The labourers did not need to be told; as the threshing machines began to seek grain amongst the empty husks and children searched the hedgerows for roots and weeds those who had already suffered saw another winter of cold and hunger before them and felt they could bear no more.

The farmers, having brought the disappointing yield safely into their barns, turned off the harvest workers and lowered the wages of those who were left — and this, throwing more on to the parish, raised the rates and the overseers cut the dole and said a man may live on less bread than had been thought. Still the numbers coming for their pittance did not lessen and to discourage their persistence the authorities increased the humiliations attendant to relief. Young men with field-craft in their hands were set to break stones for the roads and over these roads women harnessed into shafts were forced, like animals, to pull carts.

Yet even these measures did not prevent men from asking for their one and a half gallon loaves a week nor women for their one and one sixth — and when they received it they did not show gratitude. Over their day's diet of water and a pound of bread they began to see visions.

There was movement through the summer. In June, before the hay was gathered in, ricks were set alight in Kent. This was a traditional way of proclaiming distress but break with tradition was to follow. In France, in July, a revolution threw down a king and in England a general election with its tiny

47

electorate routed the Tories after years of rule and Radicals waved the tricolours while the Whigs cried for reform and declared that Old Corruption was dead.

In late August in Lower Hardres four hundred labourers destroyed a threshing machine and were met by special constables and the army. As news trickled westward murmurs of men in green gigs spreading word of a Captain Swing, who would lead the labourers back to their rights, were heard at every turn. Letters signed by Swing were delivered at night to farmers, threatening their ricks and machines. The demand "Bread or Blood" took new meaning, magistrates summoned troops to their aid and found them already engaged elsewhere, fires burned and country gentlemen prepared to evacuate their families. JPs used, in their delicacy for the rights of property, to send children to gaol for breaking trees while berrying — so that prison governors complained that their convicts were not old enough to dress themselves — found they were confronted by adults asking that their wages be raised to be sufficient to feed a family.

In backwaters of the counties rumour lapped at the shores of complacency and washed away resignation. John Hudson, who had been refused an allotment and whose wife had died of debilitation, Abel Marler whose daughters had been transported for stealing eggs, and others, began to talk of taking what they needed by force.

And amidst this tumult ordinary lives were led. Caleb learned to walk the path to Bredy in the dark and before July was over he and Hester were handfast. Hester, who had understood his character from the first, willingly put aside her worldly ambitions for the greater comfort of a strong, enduring love. There was no prospect of marriage as things were but another wage was added to the pool which would send Calder to America and another name added to those for whom he would send.

Caleb, cherishing her for her brave fragility, courted her with a gentleness that her employer found laughable. He carried her flowers bound about with ivy; on their free Sundays they walked solemnly down the lanes, his hat in his hand; he bribed a boatman with stolen oats and took her mackerel fishing from Chesil Bank. She never lost her fear of water but fear was her way of life and she put it aside. In September, when the apples were ripening and the leaves were still green, they lay together in the long grass and thought no harm would come of it.

They did not flaunt their love before Calder nor did he resent their happiness but it was a matter of occasional, bitter reflection that both he and Caleb should have found their lot at the same time in the same place. Sudden, inconvenient love seemed to be a family trait and he wondered, as he had often done, about the parents he had never known. He was in a restive, discontented mood. As the troubles had spread across the country and magistrates had issued notices warning against riot Caleb and Hannah had bound him hand and foot with promises of quiet, putting their safety into his keeping. He was not one to gossip of his private feelings but in a family as close and loyal as theirs it was not possible to keep so great a matter secret. His brother and sister knew him too well to underestimate the strength of his affections and it made them afraid; the Prayer Book he kept beneath his blanket was now never mentioned nor was there any teasing about the night in May. It was always in their minds that if he did not endanger them by approaching a woman who he should hardly dare to look upon then he would surely break out into active support of Swing. They did not want him transported for love of a girl and pressed him into his promise by making him think of them. He had no desire for violence nor confidence in the result of changes gained by threats but felt restrained. He had taken to grazing his sheep on the south side of the downs so that he could watch Sophia ride out for exercise. Once he had left his flock to his dog's devices and walked to Bredy church for morning service. He had stood at the back with the poor, holding her Prayer Book, and been rewarded with a short sight of Sophia entering a private box-pew from a side door.

This was foolish and tantalizing behaviour but he was not in a condition to help himself and Sophia, who thought she had seen him as she crossed the nave, had less understanding of her own feelings but was equally unsettled and without concentration.

Sophia, of a naturally fervent and affectionate disposition, was being awakened. Intense, restless and idealistic, she had been reared in isolation with books and solitude as her companions. Her mind formed by her elders for duty, given religion as her diversion, with no contemporaries to laugh her into convention and with a successful, unorthodox relationship continually before her eyes, she had learnt the manners of her age without growing into the beliefs that gave them life. She carried the forms and habits of society like a shell to be discarded when outgrown.

Clever, inexperienced and lonely, generous and loving, she looked piercingly before her and did not realize she wore blinkers. She had met a man who affected her and from curiosity — to discover how he thought — she read what he read and plunged, ripe by nature and circumstance for persuasion, into the undercurrent of her times.

It was not difficult for a young woman with ready money and a determined mind to look on heresy. A note and a purse of guineas altered the wares her bookseller sent her and Francis, discovering her occupation, put confiscated periodicals at her disposal. It amused him that she was reading radical literature. He put small value on female intellect and considered that if she did form unusual convictions it would be immaterial to the course he had planned for her. A woman's opinions were private and irrelevant; her duty was to obey — and, not believing that she needed anything more, he gave her free rein and laughed to hear the names Owen and Cobbett on her lips.

Sophia did not laugh — but she thought she began to see a lighter, less oppressive world where there would be more laughter for her. There was a want in her that had not been quenched by her way of life and now she sat alone by candlelight reading of education, equality and choice and saw that they were good.

The red moreen curtains swaying slightly in the wind were the only signs of autumn in the room. Outside in the gusty twilight the first weakening leaves were being driven from the elms and the racked clouds fled inland from the sea but inside all was warmth and comfort and the occasional mizzle of rain could not be heard above the crackling of the fire.

Seven men sat about the dining table at Bredy Hall. Sophia and Mrs Dene had lately left them and the cloth had been removed. A scatter of unconsidered raisins lay on the polished wood. Now and again one of the men would trifle with them, running them through his fingers, as he stared at the silver-gilt fruit basket in the centre of them all. In their turn the visitors were watched by the crowded Farren portraits, showpieces and miniatures of past generations with here and there, disturbingly, the eyes of Sophia. A slow and heavy turning towards business was in the air.

Francis dipped the long stem of a toddy-lifter into the large rummer before him and filled the tumblers of those who had not chosen port. A scent of hot brandy rose from the moving spirit.

"And for that reason," he said, touching the pipette to the edge of its vase so that the last, clinging drop should transfer to its rim, "I thought it wise to confine this meeting to the principal landowners. With the tenant farmers urging the rabble to riot we cannot extend our trust."

"There is collusion between them," said Dasent. He was a dark, thickset man in his early forties, given to a stolid and sometimes bitter melancholy. As he passed them down the table the squat, flint-glass tumblers looked suited to his hands. "No sooner do the peasantry ask for higher wages than their masters tell them they might have 'em if the tithes were lowered — and the riot appears on the parsonage doorstep. You must look to yourself, Mingay."

He nodded at an older man seated opposite him but Philip Mingay was not one to be intimidated by the idea of a mob. Blonde and blinking, too cold in his feelings to have married, he was vicar of Nether Cheney and squire of a large estate towards Bridport; he intended to leave both position and estate intact to a nephew.

"The church demands of the farmers no more than it is agreed they should pay," he said.

"But agreed by whom," asked Sir John, "when it is you who are their landlord? The labourers are distressed."

51

It was some months since Lady Abigail Ware, Sir John's wife, had entertained Sophia and Mrs Dene at their home near Abbotsbury but had Sophia known it she had been frequently in the thoughts of the family at Linton. Their eldest son, Frederick, who Sophia had correctly assumed would have put himself in danger to protect them from vagrants, was now twenty-six and beginning to feel the want of a wife. He was, like his father, pleasant, easy-going, attractive and rich and the number of girls available to him was large; the number, however, who were eligible, was small and Sophia, with her proximity, inheritance and youth, was prominent in the Wares' consideration. Throughout the summer while Sophia had slept badly, ridden the hills and wondered where her salvation lay she had been watched and discussed and rejected for being too serious; but this afternoon, as they had dined, Frederick, smiling and unembarrassed, had been impressed by her beauty and had suspected that her gravity was not an expression of her character but a vacuum waiting to be filled.

His neighbour at table was not an advertisement for matrimony. Edmund Kitson of Askerwell had married his second cousin, Maria, five years previously at the age of thirty and his devotion to his wife and growing family was causing him to replace an open disposition with an anxiety to give away nothing which could be of advantage to them. Where before he would have flicked a coin to a child who held his horse he now looked on that child as a potential drain on his income through the poor rates. Neither did a hidden physical timidity make insurrection attractive to him.

These were the men who would be harmed most by rebellion; they were the magistrates in whose hands lay the preservation of law and order; six of them owned most of the south-west of the county — the seventh, Robert Mason, representative of the Claydon estates, acted in all things for his master and had his interests at heart.

"Distressed, by God," said Dasent, fingering his glass. "I should be well pleased if a plague were to break out among them; I should have their carcasses as manure, and right good stuff it would make."

"One matter is certain," said Kitson, as Sir John turned slightly away. "You couldn't use a contrivance to dig it in. There is nothing spoken of by the men but the destroying of threshing machines."

Sir John removed a lace handkerchief from his waistcoat and dabbed a spot of port from his hand; a stain more crimson than the liquid spread across the thin lawn. "It would be as well if they were broken," he said, "there is no advantage to the farmers now that they are common and they can no longer race each other's corn to market."

"You would pander to the crowd?" asked Mingay.

"I have a disaffection for men's deaths," said Sir John coldly, "whether from hunger or revolt."

A gust of wind flickered the candles and the dullening fire briefly expanded its glow. Francis leant from his chair and pulled the bell-rope for a maid.

"You appear to have a sympathy, Ware," he said. "I take it Swing has not yet called for your assistance."

"As you know," said Sir John, "that is not the case." He took a letter from an inside pocket and unfolded it. "I have myself received this letter in the course of attending to my sister-in-law's Sussex estate and do not consider it without favour. If I may read it?" He looked about him for a variety of assent. "'We,'" he began, "'the labourers of Ringmer and surrounding villages, have for a long period suffered the greatest privations and endured the most debasing treatment with the greatest resignation and forbearance, in the hope that time and circumstances would bring about an amelioration of our condition, till, worn out by hope deferred and disappointed in our fond expectations, we have taken this method of assembling ourselves in one general body, for the purpose of making known our grievances, and in a peaceable, quiet and orderly manner, to ask redress; and we would rather appeal to the good sense of the magistracy, instead of inflaming the passions of our fellow labourers, and ask those gentlemen who have done us the favour of meeting us this day whether sevenpence a day is sufficient for a working man, hale and hearty, to keep up the strength necessary to the execution of the labour he has to do?

We ask also, is nine shillings a week sufficient for a married man with a family to provide the common necessaries of life?'" He lowered the paper. "This was delivered to the magistrates and myself on the village green. There were more than a hundred people assembled and no violence was offered us. It continues — 'Have we no reason to complain that we have been obliged for so long a period to go to our daily toil with only potatoes in our satchels, and the only beverage to assuage our thirst the cold spring; and on retiring to our cottages to be welcomed by the meagre and half-famished offspring of our toil-worn bodies? All we ask, then, is that our wages may be advanced to such a degree as will enable us to provide for ourselves and families without being driven to the overseer to experience his petty tyranny and dictation. We therefore ask for married men two shillings and threepence per day to the first of March and from that period to the first of October two shillings and sixpence a day; for single men one shilling and ninepence a day to the first of March and two shillings from that time to the first of October. This is what we ask at your hands — this is what we expect, and we sincerely trust this is what we shall not be under the painful necessity of demanding.'"

He put the letter flat upon the table and waited for comment.

"Affecting to the sentimental," said Mingay, drily, "but gets us no further. You will notice the threat at the close."

"Indeed," Dasent drummed his fingers, "we would have to be babes to think it representative." He pushed his glass towards Francis and picked a grape from the fruit basket.

"I also," went on Mingay, "have had communication from our friend the Captain but not couched in such amiable terms." He took what appeared to be a torn flyleaf from his coat and passed it to his neighbour. "I am without my reading-lens, Kitson. If you would be so kind —"

Kitson drew a candle nearer and tilted the paper into the light. "'Sir,'" he read, "'Your name is' — I can't make this — ah! — 'your name is down among the Blackhearts in the Black Book and this is to' — confound this writing, I — 'this is to

54

advise you and the like of you, who are Parson Justices, to make your wills. Ye have been the Blackguard Enemies of the People on all occasions. Ye have not yet done as ye ought. Swing.'"

There was a stirring among the listeners as if the wind had again found its way into the room. Francis adjusted his cuffs.

"None of us," he said, "need be reminded of our French neighbours these past forty years. Let us remember the tender necks of our families."

Kitson shivered and poured himself another measure of port.

"My aunt," remarked Mingay, staring at the portraits, "who was a girl at the time of the Terror, had her hair cropped and wore a scarlet ribbon about her throat out of sympathy for the well born. It was not a fashion I cared for myself."

"And yet," said Dasent, "knowing the results of revolution, we can neither reband the yeomanry nor raise special constables. The intransigence of the middling class is hardly credible."

"There is much sympathy among them for the destitute," Sir John folded his letter and returned it to his pocket. "I have heard a magistrate in our own county say that those who did not destroy their threshing machines should receive — if their ricks were fired — only half the insured value of their grain. This would surely encourage masters to re-employ their threshers and remove families from full support by the rates."

"By God," Dasent spat his grape pips into his palm. "We could do with fewer on the rates. And you're no help, Farren. Why the devil did you bring in a girl from another parish to be your linen maid? She'll be chargeable to us soon if you turn her off."

Francis regarded him coldly. "Are you suggesting I don't have linen enough to give work to a maid?"

Dasent shifted uncomfortably in his chair. "No, naturally not. I —"

"Then let us attend to our business," said Francis, "and leave my laundry to me."

But Dasent's glass was again empty and he gave a brandied laugh.

"I'd pull down my cottages about their ears before I'd let

55

new workers stay to gain rights. Take a leaf from your book, eh, Mason? I hear Norfolk's depopulating." He laughed again.

Mason did not join him. "We find it expedient," he said, "to destroy unnecessary cottages and let our labourers live elsewhere. We do not find the distances they are obliged to walk from home to work dissuades them from employment. I am Overseer and it is my responsibility to prevent undue expense to the ratepayer."

It was the first time he had spoken since the women had left and having expressed himself with concision he returned to silence. Francis watched him with interest. He saw a man, heavy but well kept, with a stiffness in one leg which forced him to lean back in his chair, giving his demeanour an arrogance which was veiled in his speech. It was plain from his appearance that his eyes gave the same critical observance to his mirror as they did to those around him. He was known for his precise and detailed management of the Claydon lands and, though he had made no friends in his visits to Dorset, was admired for his dedication. To Francis, who chose his servants with deliberation, he was a commendation of the judgement of his employer and it was Ashley's judgement on which he let his mind play.

It had not only been the Wares who had been considering Sophia's future. As she neared her majority and ripened into a woman Francis had meditated on her prospects and, though the project was not yet fully formed, was deciding to promote an alliance between the Claydon and Farren estates. Though, to his knowledge Ashley had never ventured into Dorset, they had met occasionally in Town where Francis' son-in-law was banker to the Claydon purse. As a man Francis found Ashley upright, gentlemanly and cold. That he was now thirty-nine and neither married nor sullied by scandal was to the good — displaying to Francis' satisfaction a character strong enough not to have been entrapped into marriage by a flattering mamma and discreet enough to conduct his private liaisons with as much reticence in the face of the world as Francis had done himself.

In rank the match would be admirable. Although Ashley was noble Sophia was of more ancient lineage and her present and potential inheritance both substantial and adjacent to Ashley's

Dorset land. Ashley would benefit and though Francis himself had no admiration for a title which had been acquired over the counter, he did not underestimate the ignorance and gullibility of others who would esteem Sophia more for being a Lady and he wished her to have all the advantages he could acquire.

It was true that Sophia had shown a reluctance to marry and a distaste for being in the power of a husband but modesty was no bad thing in a girl who would therefore preserve her reputation. And her protestations against being owned? To Francis these were less than the buzzing of a bee. Women were not formed of independence and the strong sense of duty he had taught her to hold coupled with a child or two to take her time and love would force her into the ways of a wife.

He did not think sentimentally of the loss of her company; he had brought her up for the continuation and furtherance of the family and it would be weakness to alter his intention now. He would visit her when he pleased and if he found his domestic circle too greatly diminished by her going would look about him for recompense and take it.

"And it is our responsibility as magistrates," he said "to prevent revolt in our district. I have here —" the door opened and a young maid diffidently entered their view. Francis made an encircling gesture which indicated a general adjustment of the room and she began quietly to snuff candles and tend the fire as he continued, "I have here a list of names we have all put forward as potential troublemakers. I will read them aloud and we may consider how to remove them — John Hudson, labourer, Five Warrens Farm; Isaac Briggs, labourer, Rowden Knapp Farm; Calder Young, shepherd, Marshall's Farm; Jack Marlow, carter, Labour-in-Vain; Abraham —"

"Strike Marlow from the list," said Mingay, "he's been dealt with. I suspected him of stealing swedes and swore an oath against him. He has six weeks in the House of Correction — it will be enough to temper him."

"This may be a ploy we can use for them all," said Francis, running a finger down the list. "It will save us the trouble of trials. As gentlemen we are all entitled to make such oaths."

"There is one," Dasent took a small leather purse from the

57

floor by his feet, "who we could dispose of more permanently. I was riding over the downs yesterday and met one of your keepers, Mingay. He was on his way to you but when I found why I took it in my charge. He gave me this," he reached into the bag and brought out a small Prayer Book bound in kid. "Shepherd Young living so near the preserves they suspected him of taking birds and searched his hut while he was elsewhere. There was no game and nothing of value except this —" he pushed it across the table towards Francis and it swivelled a little on the polished wood. "It has your grand-daughter's name in it, Farren. In her hand. The keeper can spell and thought it of interest."

Francis lifted the book and opened the cover. He raised his eyebrows fractionally at the inscription. "It's unlike Sophia to mislay her possessions," he said, "but like her not to mention a theft. I think we have this one for transportation, gentlemen — or," he turned the book and considered its cost, "for hanging if we chose."

Sophia was in an unusually frivolous and contented mood. Her conversation at dinner with Frederick Ware had been amusing, and, the gentlemen having turned to business, she was not obliged to attend them in the drawing room, and was now in her bedchamber occupying her thoughts with future entertain-ments.

The visit to her London relations was to take place in a fortnight and now that it was almost upon her she was looking forward to it with cheerful expectation. She had very few family ties — her only relatives apart from her grandfather being her Uncle and Aunt Garnam and their nineteen-year-old daughter, Harriet.

When Francis' own daughter, Arabella, had married into banking the match had been looked upon by her contempor-aries with some disfavour but, the dowry demanded having been only ten thousand pounds and Rowe Garnam having risen to the heights of mercantile splendour and the tables of earls, it was now agreed to have been astute.

It was certainly convenient for those who wished for

diversion and Sophia, in her present condition of half-under-stood restlessness, was — with the date of her return firmly in her mind — glad of the promise of company and dance.

They had missed the Season. If Francis had ordered haste there would have been haste but as he preferred to dispose of her hand privately and did not consider her to be lacking in social grace he was willing to let his women enjoy a leisurely approach to their holiday. Nevertheless he wished them to cut passable figures in the monde and materials and pattern books had been sent for from Bath and Bristol in order to do credit to their station. Some of this preparation was now spread upon Sophia's white counterpane where she had laid several new gowns to plan their packing.

In dress she knew her own mind. Despite the fashion she had not raised her skirts to her ankles, nor had she allowed elaborate ornament, whalebone, padding or undue puffing of sleeves. The result was a simple, sometimes slightly severe, elegance which allowed her to move more freely than her over-dressed sisters.

She was trying on an afternoon gown of russet levantine — pacing the room to feel the flow of the soft, twilled silk — when she heard footsteps running to her door. Agitated movement was unknown in this house and she reached for the handle to discover its cause but before she could turn it there was a single, furious knock, the door was flung open and Hester — gentle, restrained Hester — pale hair falling down about her neck rushed from the passage and almost into Sophia's arms.

"Hester!" said her mistress. "What do you —" but the sight of the wild face drove all accusation from her speech.

"Hester," she repeated more gently, "my dear. What is this?"

Hester twisted her hands together. A summer of food and devotion had rounded her and her arms, where her cuffs were folded back, were shapely.

"Ma'am, ma'am!" she cried. "Shepherd Young is called for a thief. He'll be transported. The master wished for hanging!"

A cold rush of fear fled through Sophia's body. "Be calm," she said. "Explain slowly or I cannot understand you."

Hester struggled to contain herself. "Miss Farren, please. The gentlemen are counting the men they think will be Swing. Letty was snuffing the candles and heard them. They have searched Calder's hut and found your book and say it is stolen. I walk out with his brother, ma'am, and know it was given. He would never steal from you, miss."

Sophia let out a breath. "Then we are safe, surely? He has only to tell them I gave it."

"Oh, Miss Farren," Hester touched her sleeve. "You don't know how it is with us. He could swear on his knees and they would not believe him but a word from you and no one could speak you nay."

Sophia looked across the room. On the cabinet a blue thrush egg was lying. "They will transport him?" she asked.

"Yes, yes," Hester was in tears, "or hang him."

"I will speak to them." She took the girl's hands from her arm and walked out of the room. Apart from a single lamp the gallery was in darkness. Through the mullioned windows she could see grey clouds moving against a greyer sky and, in the coach-house, the glow of firelight through an open door. She heard Hester lift a candle and follow her but she did not wait to have her way lit.

She thought, She believes it will be easy for me. That because I am Miss Farren I may talk to these men as their equal. That it is a simple thing for me to go down among them and tell them that their action is unjust because I willingly gave to a shepherd something of value to me. I am a lady and supposed to be charitable but they, and I, know that I have been given my tenets as an adornment — not to be put into use — and I also know, as they will guess, that there was something in my gift that was beyond ordinary charity — something not appropriate to my position, something not innocent. And yet — a book to a poor man. What harm is there in that?

She descended the stairs and walked strongly towards the meeting. Her hands were clasped and it was not until she looked down that she saw that they were white.

The double-door of the dining room was before her; she grasped the handles and entered.

60

Chapter 5

"Less pace, Joshua. I'm in no hurry to be home."

The driver drew gently on the reins and the two carriage horses slowed from a trot to a walk. Joshua turned his head to look over his shoulder. "You'll be cold, ma'am," he said.

Sophia smiled. "Nonsense. The afternoon is beautiful and I have been doing my duty all day. Let me enjoy myself a little."

She was sitting at ease in the rear of the landau with both sides of the hood folded down for her to watch the passing scene. It was the first day of October and, despite a white sun which shone low in the sky, the air had begun to feel crisp against her face. Over her afternoon gown she was wearing a redingote with a shawled fur collar and this combined with the lace veil thrown back over her bonnet and the silver hand-warmer in her beaver muff gave her the feeling of being simultaneously cocooned in warmth and comfort and free to experience the outside world.

The journey to London was to be begun the following day and for the past week she had been engaged in paying farewell calls on the county. Today she had attended the Wares in the morning and was now returning across the downs from the manor house to the west of Martinstown where George Dasent's crushed wife had plaintively insisted the handwarmer be filled with fresh embers. It had been her final call and the afternoon was hers to use as she would.

Autumn was flaring about her. The leaves in the hedgerows had turned without dropping and the brilliant crimsons, yellows and scarlets which are so unexpected and so easily forgotten coloured the verges beside her. The glowing, translucent fruits of nightshade hung their poisoned heads amongst the branches and the seeds of black bryony, ripe and danger-ous, clustered about their twisting stems in plump temptation but all edible berries, all hazel nuts, sloes, rosehips and crab apples had long since been gathered by the hungry and it was only in the most well-protected woods that beechmast and acorns lay littered on the ground.

In the stubble the gulls were stalking grain but the gleaners had left nothing and the cries of the birds, harsh and melancholy, were one with the scent of the sea and the pale, flat sunlight that spread across the abandoned fields.

To Sophia they brought no lonely thoughts. The restlessness that had occupied her since May had taken a new turn. She had crossed a chasm, she had walked out of her restricting female life into a room of powerful men and prevented them from exerting that power over another more defenceless than they by her quiet insistence that their accusation was false and that she would witness against it at any level.

She remembered with satisfaction how confounded they had been, how hampered by courtesy to their host's granddaughter, and with what concealed outrage they received her interference. She had been afraid of the damage she would do to her reputation but found to her surprise that though she was now looked at with enquiry she did not care. Indeed, the incident had given her the taste of a new and intoxicating strength. What she was to do with it she did not know. Like Gulliver she found herself able to loosen her bonds but not to leave a country too small for her.

Her only active measure had been to send Calder, through Hester, the three guineas he needed for his passage.

"By God, miss," Francis had said when his guests had left, "you set them askance." He had settled on the arm of a chair smoothing his coat-tails and watched her sardonically. "It seems I've bred a fighting-cock," he had said. "We must get you a husband — he'll stop you giving books to shepherds."

"It was a Prayer Book," she protested, "because he helped us find our way."

"Yes," he had said, smiling, "yes," and because she did not trust him she had gone immediately to her cash box and given Hester the fare she knew Calder needed for America — with advice to go at once. Being raised with such wealth herself she did not know the value of money and, even in such a situation, did not think to offer enough for a whole family to leave, nor did Hester, holding such riches and promise in her hand, dream of asking for more but both women, in their different worlds, took consolation from the Pennsylvania shore.

She was envying emigrants and looking out over the downlands towards the sea when she noticed a figure waiting at the edge of the road. They were driving across the long hill-top that led to the valley into Bredy and she saw, sitting on the milestone at the joining of two tracks, a man with a dog at his feet. He stood up as the carriage approached and she was certain, before she could see him clearly, that it was Calder. With a curious wrenching of her heart she saw that a traveller's bundle lay in the rusted bracken at his side.

Sitting up a little on the leather seat she spoke to Joshua. "Draw in when you reach the shepherd," she said. "I wish to take my leave."

Calder stepped forward as the landau slowed. The wheels were almost upon the verge and standing as he was on the grass, raised above the surface of the road, their faces were level.

He looked directly into her eyes and she felt that he could see more than she knew of herself. Autumn hunger had begun to tell and he was thinner than he had been when she had seen him last, tending his sheep beneath the Toller woods. He was wearing the moleskins and drill shirt she had known him in and with them the shoes and fustian jacket that had been in his hut. His hat and sheep-crook lay on his blanket-wrapped pack. He was carrying away all his possessions to a foreign, and perhaps unwelcoming, land and to her the sight of such poverty, injustice and courage was almost unbearably poignant and she did not dare to question further her pang at their parting.

Yet even with this restraint upon herself she noticed he wore a blue neckerchief she knew him not to have owned before and, to her discomfort, found herself calculating that as it was a male garment and not new it must have been the gift of a man. She did not want him fêted by women and this thought, unseasoned as she was in her ideas of equality, shocked her.

"Joshua," she said. "I believe I dropped my scarf upon the road. Please go back on foot and retrieve it."

They did not speak as the driver climbed down from his box and, with the appearance of one engaged unwillingly in subterfuge, trudged back along their route.

Calder thought, I love this woman I have hardly met. I walk and she rides and looks at me with such open, uncertain eyes. This silk and velvet girl — I cannot believe as I stand here that I could presume to think of her. What does she smell of? Nothing I have smelt before. She has risked herself for me, has given me my freedom yet if I told her of my heart, if I put out a hand to touch her I would disgust her. How could she help it? She sits there in her furs, so pale in her face. This is the last time I shall see her — and I love her.

"I have not thanked you, Miss Farren," he said. "I leave today and Hester told me where you would be driving."

Sophia stirred slightly and abruptly and the body of the carriage rocked a little on its springs.

"It was no hurt for me to help you," she said. "I was glad to do it." A faint flush rose in her cheeks and she dropped her eyes. Then, because he did not speak and she was afraid of silence, she looked up again. "Hester told me you would sail for Philadelphia from London," she said. "Surely you will not walk there? You will be taken up for a rioter. I go by sea myself to avoid the troubles."

"I have some experience of fishing. I'll go to Weymouth and try to work my way along the coast. Once in the sight of the Justices is enough."

In the small wedge-shaped spinney behind the milestone a rook cawed and was joined momentarily by its neighbours. What birds will he hear next autumn, Sophia wondered. Will they sound as desolate?

She took her hands from her muff and laid it on the seat beside her. Reaching into the folds of the redingote she pulled out a mesh purse. She slid aside the gold fastening and shook two sovereigns into her soft, kid palm. What she had about her hands — the gloves, the purse, the coins, the muff and silver warmer — were of more value than what Calder could earn in a

64

year and, watching her, he felt a conflict of sensation — an anger that he who had worked harder than she should be so obliged to her charity, a pride that it was his independence that had led him to this situation and that would sustain him in his new endeavour, a pity for this cosseted girl who was so different from her peers and thus condemned to bewilderment and loneliness, and a searing hurt that he could not take her into his arms and tell her that this was not what he wished for from her.

She lent forward tentatively holding her cupped hand over the side of the carriage. Her eyes were shy and pleading.

"This is all I have with me," she said. "Would you take it to please me? You have so far to go and so little to help you."

He did not move, conscious of his need and roughness, her wealth and kindness, their parting — and she, thinking she offended, said again, "To please me."

He stepped closer to her and looked at the coins. A breeze stirred the lace of her veil pressing it briefly against her lips and again the scent unrecognizable to Calder — the soft astringency of bohemia-water — drifted to him, beckoning while underlining their separation and difference. Her eyes were so naked he could not refuse her. He smiled.

"I would not take all you have," he said, "but I will gladly take half." He lifted one coin from her palm — his hard, scarred hand as gentle in its touch as if she had been a lamb — and once more the flush showed delicately on her face.

"I shall always remember you, Miss Farren," he said.

"And I will think of you, Mr Young."

She took her hand back into her lap and clasped it with the other. "You understand that I can do nothing large," she said, "I cannot buy land and put men to work. My private money is in trust until I marry and I don't inherit until Mr Farren dies. I have only what he allows me for my pocket and I must account for that."

"We must all account to the Mr Farrens of the world," Calder replied and there was a hardness in his voice she had not heard before.

"You are sorry to leave your country?" she asked.

"This is someone's country," he said bitterly, "I don't think it can be mine. I've laboured all my life and for what? Our masters treat their animals with more favour than us. I would rather stay and help to make my land a fit place for Englishmen to live but it's pointless for someone of my position to think such things. I would not last a twelve-month."

"And you will be wary in America?" she asked, tightening her hands. "It isn't only here there is scandal. I've known men — not of your class — who have crossed the Atlantic and say the behaviour to emigrants on ship and in port is shameful. You will not let yourself be tricked?" Again the breeze which was rising from the sea fluttered the edge of her veil and she smoothed it absently as if she would be relieved to be interested in her minor actions.

He smiled. "I had no easy upbringing," he said. "The working people here are not gentle. I can look after myself amongst my kind."

But not mine, she thought, not mine and I will not know where you are.

"What will you do?" she asked.

The horses were restless in the wind, lifting their heads to the flavour of the cold waves and the call of the gulls riding the high air. Calder motioned to his dog to remain and walked to their side to soothe them before returning.

"If I try to succeed alone," he said, stroking Watch, "I doubt if my life will be very different and I feel — I feel I must do something with it. There are many Ideal Communities in America where men and women of all stations combine together for each other's good. I've cut names and towns from journals and shall try to join one and hope to be improved." He smiled again. "I've heard that in those with many gentlefolk there's a free choice of tasks and so much writing of poetry and little digging. Perhaps a pair of strong arms will be welcome."

Sophia laughed. "I've met no one like you," she said. "I hope with all my heart you succeed — but, I think something troubles you. Is it the distance you must go?"

Something hurts me, he thought, and it is not the distance.

"No," he said, "these fields have been my world and so London or America it's all the same to me but," he looked down at Watch, at the thick fur ruffled by the wind, "it's my dog. I don't know whether I may take him aboard. My family will follow me later and would bring him if I sent word they could but they have no money to feed him. I couldn't leave him with strangers; he's worked by my side and is more than a beast to me."

He laid his hand on Watch's ear and the dog, unconcerned, leant its large head upon his thigh.

"I will take him," said Sophia, softly.

Calder looked at her with surprise. For all his irrational love of her he had thought her protection of him a patrician dislike of injustice, a rejection of the degrading selfishness of her class — he had not thought her able to be touched by the sentiments of the poor and it was both a new revelation and a new torment to him.

"If you would allow me," she repeated, "until your family leave I will care for him."

"Thank you," he said, "thank you, ma'am, — and, Miss Farren, if you would be so good would you keep your eye upon my sister? Caleb can see nothing but his girl and Hannah is pretty. She will have no one to guard her."

"I will," she said. There was a trust in his gratitude, an implied value of her that brought her close to tears. I must not show my emotion, she told herself, with every word and look I become deeper enmeshed.

"It's late, ma'am."

Sophia turned sharply on the seat and dropped her purse. Joshua had considered his employer and come back without being heard.

"Yes," she said, startled. "Yes, we must return."

And so, she thought as the driver climbed bulkily on to the box, we part and I have grown older. She opened the carriage door and Calder lifted the dog on to the floor at her feet. The dog whined and its master took its face between his hands and laid his cheek against its head. The rank smell of sheep mingled with Sophia's delicate scent. When he stood up and closed the

67

door upon the oddly assorted pair his eyes were bright and liquid.

"Would you shake hands with me, Miss Farren?" he asked.

"Gladly," she said, "gladly" and, as Joshua gathered the reins and encouraged the horses, she took off her glove and put out her uncovered hand. For a moment her small, white fingers were within his and then the carriage moved away — and it was not until she could no longer hear him that he said "Sophia".

Chapter 6

The soft autumn weather of breeze and sun and suggested frost continued through the first week of October and into the next. On the second Monday of the month, when the wind in Norfolk came flowing in its long, slow, unhindered course across the open country, washing was being hung out on a rope strung across the shared garden of a row of workman's cottages.

The buildings were a terrace of small houses which, though constructed plainly, had walls of that marled flint and brick which can appear over-ornamented and darkly garish when the light catches the glassy surface of the stones. The large windows on the upper storey would have told the occupation of the inhabitants even if the heavy, wooden rhythm of the looms had not carried to the lane outside. Weavers must have clear vision and the finer the work they do the clearer it must be — the windows had been enlarged in happier days.

But the depression in trade did not seem to be lowering spirits on this cool and gusty morning and as Nathan Hearne approached the gardens from the rear he could see — according to the full, wet flapping of the laundry — the lower half or quarter of two women and a girl and hear their voices, with accents as broad and level as the fields around them, breaking into laughter.

The laugh of a good-natured woman was a luxury to Nathan and part of the weariness that was a consequence of his journey fell away as he opened the gate. Hearing the latch and the scrape of the lower bar where it always caught the path, the girl — who could not have been more than seven — peered out from beneath a sheet and, with a cry of "Nathan!" ran bounding along the cinder trail and jumped into his arms. With the ease of long practice he lifted her in a bundle of home-woven skirts and apron on to the wall and, leaning back himself so that his pack was resting beside her, allowed his pockets to be rifled.

He was heavily laden. It was not yet eight weeks since Asa Burton, the last manufacturer stubborn and old-fashioned enough to employ hand-loom weavers on the Claydon estate, had put up the shutters on his Marlingham warehouse and withdrawn to private life and despair, and the remnants of his workers, left without master to pay them or putter-out to provide their materials, were not yet organized sufficiently for independence.

There were few of them to supply. The power-driven looms of the northern towns, thriving and multiplying in raucous industry, had drained the life from the older ways and one by one, unable to compete in speed or price, the agents of the hand-looms had lowered their wages and lost the fight for trade.

Colonies of talent where weavers were skilled in fancy goods and figured clothes survived but this year the excise duty on printed cottons had been repealed and who would pay dearly for a hand-woven pattern on their gown when they could buy cheaply from the prosperous mills? As craftsmen the weavers had died in their sleep and now, like Lazarus rising from the grave, they looked about them at a world they were not prepared to meet. They had been born to weaving and knew no other work. In a country of starving labourers and burning ricks they had nothing to offer and nowhere to go.

In the parishes about Marlingham where Ashley's farmers were shaking their heads over their harvest and complaining of their tithes the weavers had not work enough to pay their rents. Robert Mason riding out on his great brown cob, reading in the estate-room of Claydon Hall, considered their problem in the business of the day. The finances and administration of the estate were in his hands and he liked his province to be well run. As the weavers fell upon the rates he served eviction among them and when they left their homes he pulled down the houses at their backs. Without work or shelter they crowded into independent villages or wandered to the cities on the tramp —

and so their distress was not witnessed by Ashley or registered in his accounts.

Nathan Hearne and his bulky pack were, on that fresh and breezy morning, an obstacle to Mason's smooth operation of affairs.

The terrace of cottages lay on the Marlingham side of the village of Althorpe St Giles. Half a mile to the east, beyond stubble and willows straggling the borders of drainage canals, were the walls of Ashley's park. St Giles was Ashley's home village; he appointed the vicar, he visited the school, he owned the land and it was remarkable among the arrangements of tenure that the rent of the weavers' terrace was paid not to him but to a lady of advanced years who held a lease from his father and who resided complainingly in the market town.

The payers of this rent had always been weavers. As the recession bit into their trade and they found their vegetable gardens and their fieldwork at harvest too little to support them, the occupants of three of the five houses sold their looms to their neighbours, loaded their possessions on to a hand-cart and set out for the north — but the Greaves, the Yates and Nathan stayed. They had between them the equipment, the experience and the determination needed to work without the supervision of an employer and they put their resources into a common pool and agreed to cooperate with one another. They were eight adults and two children and they worked early and late, covering each others' weaknesses, sharing their orders, their profits and loss, and Mason, watching their endeavours in a village that was otherwise entirely in his grasp, knew they could not hope to succeed in these modern times and was irritated by the unrealistic struggle which was bound to descend into an application to himself, as overseer of the parish, for poor relief.

If he had noticed Nathan earlier that day as they passed in the street he would have felt that application to have grown nearer.

The weavers could no longer afford either to buy their raw materials in bulk or to hire a waggon to take large consignments of finished cloth to the wholesaler and were obliged to carry their goods themselves. It was a burdensome task undertaken reluctantly by all except Nathan. For him the ten miles into Norwich along the straight grass tracks lined by the dogwood and withy bushes, whose height was irrelevant compared with the depth of the sky, gave him a freedom and ease of mind he could not achieve at his loom.

He was a tall, slight young man with a mild and far-away look in his eyes. Although in this industrial age he appeared as if he should have been a monk — in a less secular era he would have seemed unsuited to the habit. He was, like his work-fellows, a Dissenter by birth but had been visited by no enthusiasm for religion. He was afflicted by a vague and transient pantheism, a sense of the transcendental that was fed by his solitary journeys. His presence was soothing to the old, the young and sick but those of his friends who were hale and hearty were inclined to wonder whether they did right in sending him out alone.

He had not yet proved unequal to his duties but rather had returned from his forays more richly laden than necessary. It was his custom when walking to take a clod of the heavy red clay from the fields and fashion it into an animal or an inhabitant of the village. The extra leisure he had gained by carrying counterpanes to Norwich on Saturday evening and remaining in town until collecting a pack-load of yarn on Monday had given him the opportunity to make several delicate and interesting figures and it was for these that Abbie Greaves was searching his pockets as he leant against the garden wall.

The younger of the two women — mother of the children and wife of Luke Greaves — set down her half-emptied basket at her mother-in-law's feet and, raising her hand in greeting to Nathan, kicked off her pattens at the back door. She entered the house, followed at speed by her daughter — now holding an ass, a cockerel and an all-too-recognizable baker's boy — and the sound of Nathan's return being called up the stairs was heard.

Nathan hunched his shoulders and levered his pack off the wall. The momentary rest had increased its weight and he was a little off-balance as he made his way past the turned potato plot towards the door.

Margaret Greaves fastened the last shirt to the line and stood with the basket at her waist. She looked at the young man sadly. She was a dark, strong-boned woman in her middle fifties and though there was a shadow of the Romany in her appearance there was none in her actions and John, her husband, had learnt early in their marriage that to tease her of it caused her pain. She wished for no change or loss of respectability and the sight of the yarn piled on Nathan's back reminded her of the insecurity of their position.

"The carrier's come, I see," she said, and Nathan told her kindly, "I've brought new orders with me."

He made an ungainly ducking motion to lower his pack under the lintel and went into the kitchen. Mary was standing on the bottom step of the narrow stairs talking to the men above and she hurried down with the same quick movements as her daughter to clear his way through the apparatus of laundry.

Manoeuvring himself up the inconvenient staircase he emerged into the workroom. The noise of the looms had ceased as his arrival was announced and five men of various ages were clustered about the opening. Through their legs as he gained their level Nathan could see a thin, nervous boy take the ass from his sister and walk it along the frame of a loom.

"Give us your hands, lad," said John.

Nathan was pulled up the last, most tiring, step and the straps that bound the pack to his chest were unfastened by more helpers than were adequate for simplicity of action. They were standing in the room where he slept and when his bag had been removed it was placed against the wall where the four pallets for himself and the Yates' father and sons were stacked to clear the floor. It was a long, sagging chamber, propped from beneath by rafters bought from a demolished cottage, and crowded at awkward angles, by four looms. A doorway had been knocked through to the neighbouring house and beyond its hooked-back curtain the other four looms could be seen.

There was not a face watching him that did not have strain

and hope apparent on its features and Nathan did not dally with his news.

"Jackson's has closed," he said. "There are bankruptcy dealings on hand and they say that he'll run from his debts."

The men stood heavily and Jed Yates sighed and looked out of the window, past his sons, as if there was some comfort to be found there.

"I had trouble getting rid of our work," Nathan went on, "but Eliot's of Mercer Street took it. They'll buy any figured counterpanes still on the loom but after that only calico at $1/1\frac{1}{4}$d the piece."

"When I was a boy it was 6/6d the piece," said John quietly.

Jed turned back from the view. "We must do what we can," he said, "until we reach better days."

Nathan glanced at him and continued. "Robert Mason is back," he said. "I saw him go into the druggist's as I came through the town." He paused. "I've told the women none of this. I wanted to protect them."

John gave a short, soft laugh and rested his hand lightly on Nathan's shoulder. "Protect them?" he said. "God help us. Do you think we can?"

In an upper room of The Bull in Marlingham a serving girl was fumbling with a tray. She had never attended Ashley Claydon before and her recently acquired manners were not equal to his presence.

He did not appear to be aware of her. He was standing at the sash window above the entrance porch absorbed in the activity of the market square but his personality was such as to fill the room and as she set the table for two she could not help but make small clatterings of cutlery and disarrangements of the cloth.

The places laid she attempted to retreat. Ashley turned towards her; his eyes moved coolly over the silver and glass.

"I have not seen you before," he said.

"No, sir." She made an awkward curtsey.

"You have managed very well. You may tell your master I said so." He took a florin from his waistcoat and held it out. She did not move. Seeing that she had been struck by the imbecility of one unused to gentry he walked across to her, put the coin on her tray and held open the door.

When alone Ashley went back to his vantage point and returned to his unseeing observation. He was tired but did not feel ready to sit and take his ease. The congestion of the streets that always accompanied County Court day was still in evidence and, having been upon the Bench since nine that morning, looking out on the crush of market stalls, waggons, loiterers and bullocks being driven erratically home was a relaxation and distraction to him.

He disliked his duty as a magistrate; he did not care to be in judgement on any man — but his position called upon him to judge and he was obedient to the voice of conscience.

The years since his wife's death had not left him untouched. In outward appearance he was immaculate. His face, always handsome, wore habitually an expression of severe calm as if the surface of a swiftly running stream had iced over so completely that only those familiar with deep waters could tell that the current still moved in its depths. His aspect was gentlemanly; his character rigid. He had, in his youth, committed a sin for the sake of family honour and in his anguish, his weakness and guilt, had determined that his action should have been worthwhile. With the obduracy of one of uncertain mind he had dug his fingers deeply into a frame of rules and drawn it to him. He had become obsessed with what he considered to be the code of gentlemanly behaviour — with honour, dignity, integrity and courtesy, with the maintaining of tradition. He believed it was upon his shoulders to preserve society in the rural paternalism to which he had been born and did not spare himself in the stemming of progress. Reserved and confident in public, his private self was a limestone cliff — of massive solidity to the onlooker but worn and riddled by hidden tunnels where secret things flowed in darkness. Fears and hauntings eddied in his mind and turn where he would he could see no light.

A knock and shuffle at the door brought company. At his invitation two manservants entered with the makings of a meal and were followed by Mason. It was only the second day since

Mason's return from Dorset and a look of subtly-ordered intimacy passed between Ashley and himself. Neither was demonstrative in his affections or given to conventional ties but the bonds that had grown between them were strong.

A waiter was at odds with the erection of the gate-legged table. Mason watched with growing disdain but feeling Ashley's eyes upon him contented himself with throwing down his gloves on a chair and folding his cloak over them. He stood tapping his fingers on his leg until the men had gone.

Ashley smiled. "My dear Mason," he said. "You should consider the frailty of mankind."

Mason shook his head and approached the tables. "If something is to be done," he said, "then let it be done. Slackness is beyond my understanding."

"He was merely over-eager."

"The result was the same." He lifted the bull-emblazoned cover of a serving-dish; a hot and savoury smell of mutton-chops spread into the room and settled into dew on the china lid. There was also on the side-table a cold fowl, a tureen of potatoes which had been subjected to some indefinable kitchen process, and an almond tart.

"I thought I ordered bread," said Mason.

"At your elbow. The maid brought it previously." Ashley took a seat with his back to the window.

"Is everything as you wish?" Mason enquired. "You asked to dine lightly."

"Yes, yes. I have no stomach for my meat after sitting with Gascoigne."

Mason speared a chop with a long, two-pronged fork and raised his eyebrows. Ashley made a languid gesture over his plate and Mason helped him to mutton; onions were discovered to be lining the dish.

"Yet you always carry your point," he remarked.

Ashley took up his knife. "But at what expense of my energies?" he said. "Today we had Reuben Briggs before us. The son of an old family. They have laboured in these fields as many hundred years as you may count. Now there is no threshing for him and, fearing the winter, he puts his name to a

76

round-robin asking for the machines to be broken. A civil request with no harm offered. Nothing would suit Gascoigne but we commit him for riot."

"And did you?"

"No, he has six weeks in the House of Correction and is then to present himself at your office. You will, if you please, find work for him. But, to come to this decision, we had to retire to prevent the populace seeing that we were not in accord, and I was obliged to agree attendance to another vestry meeting."

"About a poorhouse?"

"What else? There are occasions when I feel that I have shot an albatross and must wear it about my neck for the rest of my days. Will there never be an end to this workhouse question?"

There will be an end, thought Mason, but it will not be to your liking. And on this subject — He put down the spoon with which he was portioning potatoes and took a document in a sealed envelope from his outer waistcoat. "I have completed the buying of the weavers' row as you requested," he said, passing it to Ashley. "I could have persuaded Mrs Tannahill to accept a smaller annuity but I knew you did not want her pressed." Ashley held the envelope in both hands and Mason watched him with a hidden, cold amusement. He had been surprised by the strength of his employer's enmity for the weavers' combination. What was to Mason a venture doomed to limp to overdue destruction — a matter that, at its outset, had been worth mentioning only as general gossip — was to Ashley dangerous and revolutionary. If workmen could prosper without the natural order of master and man would they not look further at the hierarchy and think its gradations unnecessary? Proper station must be upheld; like James I, Ashley thought, "No bishops — no king", and Mason, for his own power, liked to encourage his master's obsessions if they were convenient to his own purposes. Ashley, he thought tightening his grip on the horn handle of a knife, my Ashley — if I had been born in your place what could I not have done?

Ashley noticed the whitening of his agent's knuckles. "Have I overtaxed you?" he asked in concern. "I know you came home

77

only yesterday and your travels tire you but — you seem unusually agitated."

"When I return from a journey," said Mason, "I feel — I like to have things under my hand. Though, naturally, I'm willing to go to Dorsetshire; it's part of my duty."

"Yet there is something different this time," Ashley said gently. "My dear friend, you have not been over-indulging in laudanum? I know your pain is great."

A fierce and consuming anger burned momentarily in Mason's heart. What do you know of it? he thought bitterly. You who have no stomach for your food because you are tired. My whole life is deception, every day I see, every step I take is a disguise of my pain until you have come to think I should be always calm. And if I am not? Shall I tell you that my mind is disordered by the remembrance of a son, a complication, that I carried to Dorset under my cape years ago? That I have watched your children grow as you have not and have witnessed the removal of one prevented by an arrogant girl who did not acknowledge me? No, because I divine you begin to see the futility of a childless man preserving the honour of an inheritance and I do not trust you. My hands tremble. I will be composed.

"I take only what the apothecary recommends," he said. He turned the remaining meat dish and began dividing the fowl between them. Ashley had often remarked that watching Mason carve a bird was like observing an anatomical operation and now he smiled again. "Have pity on the cook," he said. "Leave her a little on the carcass."

"I like to be thorough," said Mason drily. "The bird was for our eating," but at Ashley's request he did not cut quite down to the bone and left part of a wing for broth.

"And of the apothecary," said Ashley, laying the envelope in his lap and holding out his plate. "I have it on drawing room authority that he means to marry his daughter to you. He believes it will raise him." Mason deftly gathered the soft, white flesh between the point of the knife and the fork and passed them to Ashley. "Let him look to himself," he said. "When I marry it will be to no one's benefit but my own," and this putting another matter into his mind, he asked, "What of the weavers? Do I evict them?"

Ashley looked down at the dismembered fowl and sighed.

"Yes," he said. "Yes. I go to London tomorrow — but you will know what to do."

Chapter 7

In a white-panelled bedchamber in Brunswick Square, where Sophia had gone at Harriet's invitation to talk while finishing their dress, all was quiet concentration. It was late evening in mid-October and the jagged, smoke-stained sunset that had streaked the London sky had been forced out by wooden shutters, lace blinds and heavily festooned curtains of rich blue velvet. A fire of Sunderland coal burned slumberously in the basket-grate and its warm light mingled with the flames of beeswax candles to mute and soften the thick Turkey carpet and bright oak floor. It was a room of more conspicuous wealth than anything Sophia had been used to and she felt the life in it to be muffled by its density — and yet it was pleasant and well fitted to her cousin.

Sophia sat upright on a Chinese stool before a rosewood dressing table and fastened a necklace of gold filigree about her neck. She had been fully dressed for some time but had brought her jewellery in her hand in order to have some display of trivial occupation to ward off any further interference from Harriet and her maid. Having resisted their attempts to add ornament and curl her hair she had sat before the oval looking glass with its two brass candle-holders and attached her long earrings with slow attention. An austere tiara of matt Etruscan gold, that was out of time but suited her as well as it had suited her mother, lay in the litter of silver and porcelain toilet articles before her.

The candle flames swayed slightly in the warm current of air from the fire and she watched herself in their soft reflection. Her skin was very pale but looked delicately flushed against the white satin and gauze of her gown. It was a costume completely without decoration and so was similar only in its colour to that which would be worn by her cousin.

In the glass, beyond her own plain figure, she could see Harriet standing to be dressed by her maid. Harriet was a fair, blue-eyed girl, neither tall nor short, and of a mild and happy prettiness that accorded well with the ruffles and flounces of the latest fashions. In middle-age she would be plump but now her rounded body gave the impression of a lively agility on the dance floor that promised well for the evening's ball. She stood now with her arms outstretched as the maid adjusted the cushions of down padding that would hold the puffed sleeves away from her shoulders and tied the small rolled bustle about her waist. Absorbed as they were in their tasks neither young woman noticed Sophia's eyes upon them — nor would they have thought her interest misplaced if they had for they considered the correct display of female attractions a serious affair. Harriet, good-natured and expensively domestic, was content to be brought up for a wealthy marriage and was preparing accordingly. With some care the maid transferred a gown of a floating white net over a pink satin slip from the bed to her mistress. Together they laced and hooked, teased and smoothed until the full skirt was an unblemished bell, the embroidered hem just so — and Sophia thought her delightful cousin wanted only a sprig of angelica to look like the perfect iced dessert.

The gown perfected to her satisfaction Harriet rustled over to the dressing table. Sophia sat to one side of the stool that her cousin might have her share of the glass. In place of angelica the maid clipped on a necklace of diamonds and pearls, adorned Harriet's ears, hung a dainty *ferronière* in the centre of her forehead, and, patting her sugarplum mistress cheerfully on the back, retired to the linen press for their carriage clothes.

Harriet looked into the glass and regarded both their reflections with complacency. At nineteen years old she was fortunate in being entirely sure of her world. She did not understand Sophia's dissatisfactions and felt that her own intelligence was greater than her cousin's. She was fond of Sophia when they were together and rarely thought of her when they were apart. Tonight she felt their appearances complemented each other — Sophia severely classical, herself softly romantic — and would be to their advantage. She picked up Sophia's tiara and eased it on to her cousin's head; the gold gleamed dully against the dark hair and Harriet felt strangely as if the moment were solemn.

"Now," she said, discarding the mood, "we are ready for the game."

"My dear," said Sophia, "you know I do not play."

Harriet was unconvinced.

"But Sophie," she unstoppered a scent bottle and dabbled attar of roses on to her neck, "we must have husbands." She replaced the stopper. "And that — that is not so bad, is it?"

A diffidence in her tone made Sophia suspect. "Harriet," she asked, "are you thinking of one husband in special?"

There was a silence and in the shadowed depths of the mirror she saw the blush rise from her cousin's low dress and colour her face. Sophia turned on the stool and laughed gently.

"Harriet," she said. "Oh, Harriet, I believe there is."

Harriet, suddenly shy, laughed also and Sophia took the shaking bottle from her hands and put it down.

"Who do I look for?" she said. "Who do I particularly admire?"

Harriet examined her nails. "Mr Henry Thompson," she said demurely. "He has a Kentish estate and is — oh! so handsome."

"And does his suit prosper? What of my uncle and aunt?"

"They find him most agreeable. He frequently visits the house."

Sophia stroked her cousin's arm. Though she herself had no desire to marry the idea of love had recently become compelling to her.

"And you?" Harriet asked. "To be almost of age and no public engagements must seem very dreary — but, then, stuck away in the country where nothing happens I suppose you know nothing else."

Sophia smiled. "Sometimes we do lack for company," she said.

The return of the maid interrupted them. They moved towards the door and allowed themselves to be helped on with their gloves, given their fans and have their cloaks fastened about them before descending to the hall where the party would gather to leave.

Rowe Garnam was already standing by the fire taking a cup of negus against the cold. He was a broad, capable, intelligent man and the obvious strength of his legs in their tight breeches and silk stockings looked more apt for a hunting squire than a banker. Though he rarely saw her Sophia was a favourite with him and as he watched the young women walking down the curving stairs he did not let his fondness for his daughter keep him from privately acknowledging that his niece, wrapped as she was in white velvet, was the more elegant and had the greater presence of the two.

A sweep of padded silk across the floor brought his wife to his side — and with her Mrs Dene who was not dressed to go out. Mrs Dene's position — now that she appeared to have been promoted from governess to companion — was ambiguous and Mrs Garnam had not yet fixed on a serviceable pattern for when she should accompany the family and when remain at home. Mrs Garnam was her father's daughter and, understanding his mind, had a suspicion that Rosa Dene was more to him than a member of his staff. Having Francis' astuteness without his ruthlessness she held her peace and did not speak of a situation which seemed to suit everyone concerned but felt herself in a position in which it was difficult to show neither too much familiarity nor too much reserve. If Francis had joined them, as he had intended, for a fortnight of their month's stay she could have judged better but the troubles among the field labourers which were drawing so many useful men back to their provincial seats had detained him in the country. Tonight, having been assured by Mrs Dene that an evening of solitude was quite acceptable, her slightly Roman face under its feathered turban was relaxed and she took her husband's arm out to the carriage in firm expectation of pleasure.

The carriage, which was more like a closed brougham than anything else, held four with ease. Sophia and Harriet sat with their backs to the horses. The noise and rush of the city at night had taken Sophia by surprise and as they rolled uneasily south and west, now stopping, now starting, pushing through the throng, their wheels grazing the hubs of other wheels, she sank into the silence of a traveller.

The hustle of street trade, the dazzle of houses of entertainment, the rapping of begging and selling hands against their windows, were foreign and sinister to her. The chaos, crowds and squalor of London had made her feel both her position as an heiress — a young woman cocooned not merely by a competence but by great wealth — and her powerlessness to use it to advantage. In Dorset, although a death by starvation was no less a death, the scale of poverty was so much smaller she felt that if she were in possession of her money she could do a nameless something to protect the poor around her; here in the city, where the numbers of the destitute were so vast, she was conscious that she was a voice crying in the wilderness.

Her thoughts were vague and without direction and she wished for guidance. She had been in a languid and trancelike state since she had arrived in town. She was mechanically and sensuously savouring London life with an emotion that was not enjoyment but had much in common with it. Sleepless and suffering from nightmares of confinement and the sea she did not connect either this or her physical and passive acceptance of sensation with the departure of Calder Young. Still, with all her theory, it did not occur to her that she could love outside her station and her insistence on being driven to the docks to see the emigrant ships had been, she thought, from interest only.

Her grandfather remaining in Bredy had given her a freedom from constraint she could not have had if he had been by her side but she smiled to think that their separation might instigate both a greater freedom and greater constraint. Unwilling to risk losing Watch in the city she had left the dog in Hester's care in the kitchens of the Hall and, having little trust in Francis, warned him that if Watch were harmed or happened to vanish she would apply for a position of governess. Having given her word she would keep it and considered the dog's safety to lie in Francis' new value of her determination.

Gleaming cliffs of stuccoed houses were about them and they must prepare to descend and wish joy to a daughter of fortune who was to dance into her coming of age that night. The carriage slowed before the portico and the light rain that had been falling bleared the window and obscured their view. Outside Sophia could hear the murmur and stirring of the poor who had gathered to see the rich arrive. A manservant opened their door and waited to hand them down. Beyond him footmen in powder and livery lined the wide, stone steps to the Greek columns of the entrance where two or three gentlemen stood taking the cool night air.

"If we dally for each other our appearance will be ruined," said Mrs Garnam. "We must forget our manners until we reach the hall. Do you agree, my dear?"

Her husband was straightening the brim of his hat. "You, Harriet and I will dash in a body to the door," he said, "and then I will return for Sophia." He looked across at his niece and she nodded. With a drawing-up and smiling the Garnams gathered themselves and stepped down into the street. Arranging his family on each arm her uncle led them sedately towards the house and Sophia watched them through the thin mist of rain that glinted and sparkled in the light that glowed from the door.

For a moment, as she rested alone in the carriage, part of but separated from the activity of the night, time seemed pregnant and encapsulated as if it marked a change in her life — as if the dark interior were the still centre of the turning of the earth. Sounds were distant; she noticed that small pieces of swansdown from her cousin's cape were clinging to the plush seat; she smelt the bright scent of water falling on brushed stone and because the growing intensity of awareness perturbed her she did not wait for her uncle to return but rose and stepped out alone.

And so Ashley, standing a little apart from the other men but exchanging words with them, saw her revealed, serious and pale, and pause for an instant on the footrest before she moved towards him. Her air was grave; her manner detached and formal and in her face and youth she had a fresh and living beauty he had not seen equalled. In the simplicity of her dress and the dignity of her bearing he saw the image of the woman of birth whose pride in herself was unaffected by vanity and was captivated by its glamour.

But as they stood, each in their own abstraction, the world went on about them. The chaise behind her, jostling for position in the swarming street, thrust itself through the inadequate gap between Sophia's carriage and the landau passing the other way. The resultant clash of entangled wheels, the raised voices of the coachmen and jeers of the spectators alarmed the horses and as Sophia stepped down on to the ground the carriage twisted and rolled and the wheel caught the hem of her gown, ripping the gauze and holding her fast by the stronger satin. To take the safest way she tried to go back into the body of the carriage but her shoe ribbon was also trapped and no movement was possible. My foot will be crushed, she thought, another inch and I will not dance again. Well, then, what use will there be in panic?

"Madam."

She looked up calmly and Ashley, standing before her with his pocket-knife, thought that he had never yet gazed in such eyes.

"You are in danger," he said. "May I help you?"

"Pray do, sir," she replied. "With haste."

He knelt at her feet to see what was to be done. The driver was at the horses' heads but in the commotion the wheel scraped minutely back and fourth on the cobbles, alternately pressing the soft flesh of her foot and releasing it enough for the passage of a knife.

With three firm strokes Ashley cut away both the ribbon and the hem of her gown. She stood still and unembarrassed by the servants and onlookers milling foolishly about her but when an acquaintance called from the crowd "What Ashley? On your knees to a woman?" she turned her face away and flushed with an anger that was not for herself.

Ashley, as if he had not heard, straightened and led her forward from the carriage. Taking the side where her gown was torn he offered her his arm.

"May I take you to the maids?" he asked.

"Thank you," she said simply and putting her hand within his arm she walked beside him into a strange and fashionable house with her dress in ruin and her thin shoe ripped from its

86

bands and it was as if she returned in comfort to her own home. Her mind was occupied. She was puzzled by her rescuer. Something about him reminded her of someone she could not place. For a moment his eyes had seemed familiar. He had a peculiarly drawing voice, compelling and persuasive, and almost against her inclination she was attracted by him.

As they entered the door and he prepared to pass her to the family that claimed her Ashley said, "I will reprimand the driver for the inconvenience he has caused you."

"Oh, no!" She looked again into his face and met his eyes frankly.

"Sir," she said gently, "the accident was caused by the chaise at our back. It would not be honourable of me to blame him," and once more as she spoke she felt that there was something recognizable within her grasp and became conscious that her arm touched his.

When she had been taken by her aunt and cousin and he had related the event to her uncle Ashley did not return upstairs to the ball. With that reserve that made even his most aimless actions seem deliberate he wandered into a lower room that had been arranged for guests to do nothing in particular. Above him was the stamp, shuffle, stamp of those engaged in a hearty country-dance and the pressure on the ceiling caused the chandelier to swing backwards and forwards sending shadows swaying into the darkness in the corners of the room. Candle grease spattered the floor beneath and in the marble fireplace a pyramid of dampened culm balls burned with a brilliance that hurt his eyes. There was a table of refreshments but he did not approach it; neither rout-cakes nor syllabub could interest him.

He was unsettled. An emotion he thought belonged to the young had risen up within him and was beating on the walls of his mind like an animal that has just realized it is caged. An admiration for grace and beauty had slipped beneath his guard and fired the rash and urgent longing that had led him to squander his life so many years before. He would restrain his response until his impulse to know more of her was subdued. His past behaviour did not qualify him to show interest in a woman — yet had he not suffered for his misdeeds? Did his constant struggle towards right not count to his merit? And were not her first words to him a soft and kindly reminder of honour?

A school-fellow of his, Sir John Jeffrey — a landowner detained in town by the marriage of his son — entered the room and, seeing Ashley standing unoccupied and absorbed, hesitated before taking anchovy toast from the table. Ashley withdrew himself from his thoughts and greeted him. "The lady I brought in," he said, "do you know who she was? She had come with Rowe Garnam, my banker."

"Aye," Sir John lifted the lid of a cheese-dish and decided against it. "She's his niece. A Miss Farren of Dorsetshire. I heard her mentioned. Her grandfather's got a pretty estate. You look damnable odd, Claydon. Did the wheel nip you?"

"Thank you," said Ashley. "I am quite well."

Sir John poured two glasses of madeira and offered one to Ashley. "A fine-looking girl," he said, "if my boy weren't wedding —"

"You will oblige me," said Ashley and stopped.

Ah, thought Sir John, ah — and attended to his wine. "It was a mercy she was not crushed," he added.

"Yes," said Ashley. "The danger was real." He raised his glass to the light. "I will wait on her tomorrow. It was the custom of our youth, Jeffrey, and I do not like to break tradition."

Chapter 8

It was a matter of some concern to the more prurient clergy of the country that it was rare for a working-girl of the lowest class to reach the altar without having proved her fertility. Hester Allen was no exception.

It was of equal moment to those sensitive gentlemen that the rural magdalens were not inclined to exhibit shame or repentance for their fall from virtue, as decent girls would do, but rather accepted their condition as the course of nature. Here again Hester did not show herself extraordinary.

She did not come from a family which had ambitions or religious scruples; she did not, in practice, come from any family at all and the affection and attachment of the brothers and sister Young were to her like the warmth of a sheltered room to one who has walked alone in the rain. She trusted Caleb absolutely and when he wished to lie with her she, who had borne the weight of so much cruelty, did not think to tell him that love was wrong but entered gladly into an expression of her trust.

She was not without her cares; she had no illusions that actions have no consequences and knew that she set herself upon a course that would have a more speedy and fruitful harvest than the one taking place around them — but the juice of the apple is sweet, a kind man's loving answers other hungers than those satisfied by bread and the soft September evenings were warm and long.

It did not surprise her that she became pregnant at once. There was a popular saying amongst those likely to find themselves in straits that it was the good girls who were caught and, a good man being in the case and the world being as it was, it seemed inevitable to her that a heavy and life-long responsibility should be the outcome of so brief a time of pleasure.

Caleb's joy, his gentle devotion and solicitude for her well-being were balm to a spirit which had been menaced by indifference and uncertainty for eighteen years but could not reconcile her to their predicament. She did not resent the child but feared for its welfare on this harsh earth and did not know how it would forgive her for bringing it so unnecessarily into existence.

To Caleb her condition was not a subject for philosophical query. He had chosen his life's partner and it was as natural as the seasons that their commitment and union should be followed by children. Because their parents were poor their lives would be harder than those more comfortably born but he had hope that Calder's emigration would bring them all to a prosperity beyond imagining in Dorset. The insult paid to his family, to craftmanship and honesty, by the hounding of his brother had adjusted his mind to thoughts of departure and the slow settling of his loyalties had pointed him to the American shore. Though he had never had Calder's restlessness and urge for change he could now sail with less turbulence of feeling than had been suffered by his brother as he had stood on deck amongst the steerage passengers and watched the last of England.

Meanwhile as he waited for Calder to provide the means for their journey he must attend to the problem of caring for his family now. Since the harvest he had been at work spreading dung on the stubble, this week he would help to pull the one field of beet Hammond had planted and the next he would take out his team for the winter ploughing. He could probably count on being in work until the middle of December but then — thanks to the machine — there would be no threshing for him; he would be turned off and fall back upon the parish.

Without a wage to keep them or a home to take them to a wife and baby were a deep, though willingly-accepted, anxiety. On being told Hester's news he had gone at once to his master and, explaining his situation, had begged to be kept on until spring and allowed to clear an old shed or erect a hut from hurdles in which to begin his married life. His requests had been refused.

Hammond — who in these times of trouble preferred to have his workmen under his eye — offered to let him remain in the bachelors' attic but he felt his financial position would let him carry no superfluous labour and it was not incumbent on him to provide accommodation for those who were not in his employ. He was aware that Caleb was a hearty worker and would gladly hire him again when the need arose but he was not a charity. He was sorry that Hester's condition would cause distress but Caleb should have thought of that before he tampered with the girl.

For the first time, as he stood with his hat in his hand pleading for so little, Caleb began to understand his brother's way of thinking. Who was Hammond to have the yea or nay over his life? What had led to the one being man — the other master? He, who would have laboured conscientiously all his days on this one farm — as he had done since a child — was to have less recognition of his worth than would have been given to a beast. If they had been cattle, if Hester had been in calf she would not have been refused the shelter of a byre. A stubborn determination to do right by her grew in him. He would house his family and while he lived in England he would not beg again.

On the third Sunday in October, when Ashley Claydon was again being announced in Brunswick Square, two figures were making their way wearily up the last steep incline before the hill ran down to Chesil Beach. It was late afternoon on a grey and blustery day that was lit suddenly and occasionally by bursts of racing sunlight. Whenever the wind flared out the girl's skirts the young man clutched her as if she would be blown down and whenever the ground and weather were smooth enough for them to walk side by side they held hands.

The land here was wild and heathlike with thickets of gorse fluttering their brilliant, yellow flowers and patches of exposed earth where gales had ripped the rough grass out of the sandy soil. It was open moor, a strip of scrub running along the coastal ridge, neither fenced nor cultivated, and coveted by the adjoining Mingay, Farren and Claydon estates all of which were considered by their agents to have first claim of ownership.

"We'll rest at the top," said Caleb, "before we choose a place to build."

Hester held more tightly to his hand. "You're sure, you're quite sure we're not trespassing?"

She was wearing a large, woollen shawl that had once been Sophia's and the soft, dark material passed over her head and pinned beneath her chin made her face a perfect oval. In the breeze her colour was as fresh and glowing as a Tudor miniature.

"All the masters think they own it and say they own it and want to enclose it but now it's still common land." He guided her carefully around a rabbit hole.

"Then, why," she asked, "when John Hudson wanted an allotment here, did he ask Mr Hammond first and be told no?"

"Because he's too weak-headed to take his rights. Even for his family. It's 'Yes, sir. No sir,' with him and then a bad deed on the sly. I've had my fill of it. Mind your feet on that stone."

"You sound like Calder these days," she said.

"I should have sounded like him long ago." He lengthened his stride to reach the summit and pulled her gently after him. A buffet of wind at their backs rocked them a little and he stood behind her to protect her from the cold. His arm encircled her beneath breasts that were ripe and full and tender with their coming child.

From this vantage point they could see the long, pebbled beach laid out before them, tawny and fretted by the thick, white foam of a slate sea. The sky was low and heavy with cloud but, as they watched, it parted and for an instant in the distance Portland Bill gleamed like a new-caught mackerel. The air was keen and exhilarating and though the wind blew from the land up here there was the chill scent of the waves and the thought of the voyage being taken came to them both.

"Will he have reached port yet?" Hester leant back a little and, under the loose edges of her shawl, rested her hands on Caleb's arm.

"Not yet. We don't know what day he sailed but he'll be at least a month at sea. Aaron Kaye's daughter over to Vinney was seven weeks."

She was silent, looking out over the distance that was a seven-week journey, and then she asked, "He will send for us, won't he?"

Caleb held her closer and bent to rest his cheek against hers.

"He'll send," he said softly. "You need have no fears of that. Come, sit with me out of the wind."

He loosed his hold on her and again taking her hand led her a little downhill. Pulling out the piece of sacking he had been wearing beneath his shabby jacket he spread it on the grass for her and she, sitting to one side, left room enough for him. Arranging her skirts she remembered they were not alone.

"Where's Watch?" she asked.

Caleb raised himself to his knees and whistled. Immediately the great, untidy dog bounded over the ridge and began roving back and forth before them, scouring the earth with an unlovely, snuffling grunt.

"That dog is getting fat," said Caleb, settling at Hester's side and putting his arm about her. "He misses his work."

Hester laughed. "Miss Farren found him to be moping for Calder," she said, "and ordered him to have chocolate, warmed, every morning. He has a china basin and she gives it to him with her own hand when she is home."

Caleb regarded the animal with friendly envy. "Perhaps he'll bring his basin when we move into our hut," he said wryly, "we'll have need of it."

Hester shivered and he drew her closer so that she could rest her head on his shoulder. With the hill at their backs and a thorn tree, still clinging to its battered, rusty leaves, at their side they were sheltered from the wind but the thought of their near future was enough to chill her. Let Caleb tell her as he may that this was common land and their squatting only a makeshift for a few short months she could not rid herself of fear. She admired his initiative and determination to care for her and the child but she knew enough of the gentry to suspect they would not let legality interfere with destroying an irritation.

Down on the shore pale rushes, hollow and brittle, were rustling together and now and again the wind caught the white spray and drew it up into the air where it hung for a moment like lace over the waves. She closed her eyes and nuzzled her face into his shoulder. He smelt of worn corduroy and clean horses and safety.

"Tell me of America," she said. "Tell me again."

And so he told her all that he knew and all that she had heard before — of the forests wider than from here to Bristol, of the mountains higher than the West Cliffs piled one upon the other, of rivers and lakes where the fish were free to all, of bears and settlers and the communities where work and results were shared and every new child of equal value — and she listened gently to his romancing and neither believed nor disbelieved him but let herself be soothed.

She did not allow herself to dwell on emigration nor to think forward more than a day at a time. Apart from a little tiredness and nausea and a need to be told things twice her health was staying good but to keep it so they were delaying their wedding day as long as possible to let her continue working at Bredy Hall.

There she would have the benefit of proper food and warmth and would miss spending the worst of the winter in a turf hut. She was not afraid of her master discovering her condition. Francis was not harsh on pregnant maids — regarding their fall merely as a humorous illustration of the carnal frailty of mankind. She was not afraid of Pennsylvania. What she feared were the months between her dismissal and their leaving. They had no choice but to live as squatters but she was sure it would be seen by the magistrates as defiance. If they could keep themselves clearly separate from the troubles that were approaching from the east perhaps all would be well. She wanted no part in retribution, no Captain Swing, no tricolours or black flags flying. She was so young and so damaged; if they could leave in peace she would never cease to be thankful; her ways were domestic and loving and Caleb was her promised land.

Chapter 9

"You are an excellent subject, Sir Ashley. I wish all my sitters were so still." Harriet Garnam raised her small silver scissors from the silhouette she was cutting and considered the effect so far. Satisfied with her talents she looked narrowly at Ashley and began to cut again. Snippets of white card fell down into her lap.

"Would you prefer to be pasted on to black or green?" she asked.

"Oh, green," he said. "Nowadays I prefer not to see things black and white."

They were seated in the front drawing room in Brunswick Square on a damp afternoon in late October. It had rained heavily an hour before and the sound of carriage wheels spraying water from the puddles still reached them on the first floor but the sun had just come out and Ashley's profile, as he sat on a Sheraton chair placed sideways to the window, was sharply defined.

He was relaxed. He had paid several calls on the household since the night of the ball and the naturalness and ease of a family circle in which he was not the object of active husband-hunting was more than agreeable. At this moment the tea-board had just been brought in and Mrs Dene, who had been upstairs supervising the packing for the return of Sophia and herself to Dorset, was seeing to its arrangements on the table at Mrs Garnam's side. Sophia was sitting on the striped satin sofa next to her cousin, her own white silk skirts overlapped by Harriet's muslin.

"Of course, as you were saying, Sir Ashley," said Mrs Garnam, lifting the lid of the teapot and considering the colour of the water, "times have changed. I can remember my grandmother — your great-grandmother, Sophia — draining all her used tea-leaves on a holed saucer and eating them with sugar and butter. She would give me a spoonful as a dainty but I never cared for it."

Ashley moved slightly to reply but was held by an imperious wave of the scissors. He glanced at Sophia from the corner of his eye and she, smiling, rose to take him his cup.

"Sir Ashley," said Harriet. "You must positively not move until I'm finished. You'll overthrow all your good behaviour."

Sophia approached him, carefully holding a full cup in both hands.

"I hate to disoblige a lady," he said, "but I'm prepared to do so under certain circumstances."

He leant forward and took the saucer from Sophia. For an instant their fingers met but she neither drew away nor looked conscious. I like his touch, she thought, in surprise. How strange the world is. She turned away to bring him sugar and as she did so she remembered suddenly another sugar jar and a night in May beside a shepherd's fire — and blamed herself for her constant dwelling on the insignificant past. She held out the porcelain dish and, watching him take his measure, was again struck by the disorientating sense of recognition that was so frequent and so puzzling.

Ashley, sprinkling the coarse grains into his cup in performance of the small details of the social round, noticed her expression as she moved back to her seat. He believed that she was attracted to him — not as coquettes were attracted by the wealth and status he could give them but genuinely for himself — and her interest was like rain on seed lying in earth that was parched but fertile. His heart seemed to twist within him like a suffering animal and his need to love and be loved lay defenceless at her feet. Feelings he had tried to deaden had grown new life and yearned towards her. She appeared to him an honourable young woman, serious, sympathetic and without affectation, and yet the strength of her character was softened by a delightful and feminine warmth. He had unbent enough in her company to assay the occasional humorous remark and these comments, dry and creaking, were met by her with a look of understanding and a low and delicious laugh. He had not yet told himself that he would definitely court her but, in truth, he was a lost man.

The surrender of his well-known preference for the single state had not gone unnoticed by other occupants of that drawing room and though there was no interference with his advance his progress towards an intimacy with Sophia was being over-looked with keen attention. Harriet, who was herself smarting under the enforced departure of the handsome Henry Thompson for his unruly country estate, felt that she was particularly perceptive and practical in affairs of the heart and had guessed Ashley's intentions from the beginning, approving them for one of Sophia's sober disposition. She would not have cared to marry him herself for she found that although he was always scrupulously pleasant to her he often made her feel like a schoolgirl but she noticed that her cousin never suffered any awkwardness with him and she told her mother she considered it a suitable match. Mrs Garnam, having already made observations of her own, asked Mrs Dene whether she thought Francis would give his consent and received the answer "I do not doubt it". Mrs Dene was herself in favour of the connection believing that an older man of proven sense and integrity was what Sophia needed to steady her and protect her from her increasingly unorthodox views.

The object of everyone's surveillance was being deliberately obtuse. Despite her distraction, her habit of starting awake in the night, her inclination to fall into aimless reverie when she should have been conversing, she had enjoyed her stay in town and did not want to open her eyes and see that it had brought new complications into her life. She had sat idly by in many shops as her aunt and cousin ordered assistants up and down ladders; she had trounced the family at Pope Joan and been trounced by them at Commerce in her turn; she had discovered that "taking exercise" meant a half-hour drive in the carriage; she had bought Watch a collar of soft, green leather and she wished these trifles to be the sum of her experience. Glad as she was that Harriet was on the verge of a proposal she did not want to receive one herself. Tomorrow she and Mrs Dene would take ship for home and she was eager for that to rule a line beneath this interlude and allow her to take up her real life where it had been left.

And yet — to what did she return? To a pastoral existence in which all her sympathies lay outside her own class. Because she was a woman and, though rich, without control of her money it was possible for her to say that the troubles were no concern of hers and to sit and sew a fine seam while the countryside burned around her — but this did not satisfy her. The Sunday before last the rector of the fashionable church the Garnams chose to patronize had preached on the text "I was an hungered and ye gave me no meat", and Sophia had meditated on its instruction.

She believed that if her Creator had given her intelligence, a feeling heart and a privileged position it was for a purpose. She must look about her and consider why the labourers were rising against their masters, whether their cause was just and what practical measure could be taken to prevent the likes of Shepherd and Ploughman Young floundering in the slough of despond. Arson, riot and violence were abhorrent to her yet if her kind did not allow the peasantry to provide for their needs from heavy labour did they not themselves sow the seed of this foul harvest? "Let the rich be taught," *The Times* said, "that Providence will not suffer them to oppress their fellow creatures with impunity. Here are tens of thousands of Englishmen, industrious, kind-hearted, but broken-hearted beings, exasperated into madness by insufficient food and clothing, by utter want of necessaries for themselves and their unfortunate families" and she —

"Miss Farren, I have —"

Sophia wrenched herself from her musings and stared about her, wide-eyed and mentally dishevelled.

Ashley had moved his chair to face inwards and was holding a piece of closely written paper in his hand.

"I have interrupted your thoughts," he said.

"They were leading me nowhere." Sophia waved her cup vaguely and Harriet, seeing disaster imminent, reached over and took it from her, placing it on their side table beside the silhouette materials. Sophia folded her hands in her lap and composed herself.

"You were saying, Sir Ashley?" prompted Mrs Garnam.

"I have here," he said, addressing himself to Sophia, "a letter from Collingwood, a magistrate of my acquaintance in Battle. He knows of my opinion of the sad condition of our labourers and the present unfortunate consequences and has written to me of his own experiences. As you return to the country tomorrow and were expressing sympathy with the requests of the rioters I thought it might interest you to read it."

"Thank you, I —"

"Oh, read it aloud, Sir Ashley," Harriet took a tart from a plate that Mrs Dene was handing round. "It would interest us all. There's hardly a man capable of dancing left in town and Henry — Mr Thompson — has been drawn back to his estate by the scoundrelly behaviour of his men. He says, mamma," nodding her head at Mrs Garnam, "that more than a hundred threshing machines have been broke in Kent by the rascals. His neighbour, Mr Becker, a Justice and overseer, had his property completely gutted by fire and at another place — I forget where — when a barn was burning the labourers cut the leather hose of the water-engine and stood calling for potatoes to roast in the flames!"

"We live in dangerous times," agreed her mother, stirring her tea. "If you would read us your friend's comments, Sir Ashley, we would be grateful."

Ashley, whose face had again lost expression as he listened to Harriet, held up the letter and, in a cold voice, began. "'I have seen three or four of our parochial insurrections,'" he read, "'and been with the People for hours alone and discussing their matters with them which they do with a temper and respectful behaviour and an intelligence which must interest everyone in their favour. The poor in the Parishes in the South of England, and in Sussex and Kent greatly, have been ground to the dust in many instances by the Poor Laws. Instead of happy peasants they are made miserable and sour tempered paupers. Every Parish has its own peculiar system, directed more strictly, and executed with more or less severity or harshness. A principal tradesman in Salehurst (Sussex) in one part of which, Robertsbridge, we had our row the other night, said to me these words "You attended our meeting the other day and voted with me against the two principal Ratepayers in this parish, two Millers, paying the people in two gallons of bad flour instead of money."'" His voice had grown warmer and Sophia, her eyes fixed upon him, drank in an attitude she had never heard from her own kind before and resigned part of her denial of his interest.

"'"You heard how saucy,"'" he went on, "'"they were to their betters, can you wonder if they are more violent to their inferiors? They never call a man Tom, Dick, etc but you d——d rascal etc, at every word, and force them to take their flour. Should you wonder that they are dissatisfied?"'" These words he used to me a week before our Robertsbridge Row. Each of these Parochial Rows differs in character as the man whom they select as leader differs in impudence or courage or audacity or whatever you may call it. If they are opposed at the moment, their resistance shows itself in more or less violent outrages; personally I witnessed but one, that of Robertsbridge putting Mr Johnson into the cart, and that was half an accident. I was a stranger to them, went among them and was told by hundreds after that most unjustifiable assault that I was safe among them as in my bed, and I never thought otherwise. One or two desperate characters, and such there are, may at any moment make the contest of Parish A differ from that of Parish B, but their spirit, as far as regards loyalty and love for the King and laws, is, I believe, on my conscience, sound. I feel convinced that all the cavalry in the world, if sent into Sussex, and all the spirited acts of Sir Godfrey Webster, who, however, is invaluable here —'"

"Mr Thompson will not let them riot," said Harriet firmly, "Mr Thompson will ride with the cavalry —" Catching Ashley's glance she subsided. From the landing a clock, which informed its viewers of the movements of the moon, was heard to chime the quarter.

"'Stop this spirit,'" read Ashley, "'from running through Hampshire, Wiltshire, Somersetshire, where Mr Hobhouse told me the other day that they have got the wages of single men down to six shillings per week (on which they *cannot live*), through many other counties. In a week you will have demands for cavalry from Hampshire under the same feeling of alarm as I and all here entertained: the next week from Wiltshire, Dorsetshire, and all the counties in which the Poor Rates have been raised for the payment of the poor up to Essex and the very neighbourhood of London, where Mr Geo Palmer, a magistrate, told me lately that the poor single man is got down to six shillings. I shall be over tomorrow probably at Benenden where they are resolved not to let Mr Hodge's taxes, the tithes or the King's taxes be paid. So I hear, and so I dare say two or three carter boys may have said. I shall go tomorrow and if I see occasion will arrest some man, and break his head with my staff. But do you suppose that that (though a show of vigour is not without avail) will prevent Somersetshire men from crying out, when the train has got to them, we will not *live* on six shillings per week, for living it is not, but a long starving, and we will have tithes and taxes, and I know not what else done away with. The only way to stop them is to run before the evil. Let the Hampshire Magistrates and Vestries raise the wages before the Row gets to their County, and you will stop the thing from spreading, otherwise you will not, I am satisfied. In saying all this, I know that I differ with many able and excellent Magistrates, and my opinion may be wrong but I state it to you.'"

There was a brief silence as he concluded the letter and then Harriet, who was pleased neither by her lover's return to the country nor Ashley's reception of her hopes of Henry's valour, said irritably, "And so they are all to have more wages for no more work, the idle creatures." She brushed a fragment of card from her skirts to the carpet.

"They must feed and house themselves, Harriet," said Sophia, ashamed that a member of her family should meet Ashley's news with such misunderstanding. "Now they do not make a living from their labour."

Harriet pouted in a way that charmed her Henry. "But there are so many of them," she said, "surely so many are not necessary to us."

"They're here now, my dear, and must be dealt with. Everything must always be dealt with as it is. A problem does not go away for the wishing."

"They could go into workhouses and be out of the way. Mamma, is there tea? — Not that they have anything to complain of. If the farmers don't pay them enough to buy food the overseers make their wages up to survival — but if they were in workhouses they would have to be grateful."

On the mantelshelf, flanked by two pot-pourri vases, a Staffordshire shepherdess was strumming a lute while, at her feet, a lamb was smiling blandly at a duck. Ashley stared at it and tried to contain himself.

"Miss Garnam," he said frigidly as the cups were passed to and fro, "do you consider it part of our country's tradition that a man may labour honestly and yet be unable to support his family? And should he then be taken from his home and locked into a Bastille as if he were a vagabond? There have been workhouses in the past but the majority of men have been free and who is any one of us to decide to take away that freedom?" Harriet did not reply and Sophia, who was watching Ashley with alert and earnest eyes, said, "You make me think of a shepherd of our district — Calder Young — who was grossly ill-treated for no fault of his own and forced out of his birth-right — to live and work in his home place — by the dishonourable and underhand actions of men who considered themselves his betters."

Ashley had achieved a slight protection from his sins by being unable to think of his children as adults. The Youngs with their trades seemed to have no connection with himself or the infants they had been and while his guilt had grown his offspring had remained in the cradle — but with this sudden intrusion of the past into the present he paled and became aware of the beating of his heart. Sophia, noticing the small signs that he had been affected, admired his sense and sensitivity. He is a reformer, she thought. He dislikes the status quo as I do; he wishes for progress and is not afraid to speak his mind. She gazed at him intently and her aunt, catching Mrs Dene's eye, wondered at the forms that courtship takes and decided they would have a match at last.

"And if," Sophia went on, "faced by hunger and injustice, these men break out into disgraceful behaviour then, as you said, Sir Ashley, who are we to stand in judgement? How many of us can look into our hearts and pasts and say that we are without sin?" And what of my heart, she thought, what of my feeling for, my obsession with, a young man not of my class? Is it only obsession? And if it were not would it be sin? I speak of the levelling of mankind but do I mean it? "And when we transgress," she continued, "instead of harsh treatment is it not better that a kindly hand sets us back upon the path we should walk? I read in *The Times* that a magistrate in Canterbury has sentenced machine-breakers to only three days imprisonment to encourage moderation on each side. There is a man who understands the labourers' plight."

"But it hasn't worked, Sophie," said Harriet, standing up and shaking out her skirts. "The fires are still burning. Now, if you will allow me, Sir Ashley, I'll make a copy of that letter to send to Mr Thompson's sister. Sir Ashley? —"

If you knew what I had done, thought Ashley gazing at Sophia, would you forgive me? Would you look softly at me then? He noticed Harriet beside him and passed her the letter.

"Would you prefer me to copy it?" asked Mrs Dene, half-rising from her seat.

"No, no," Harriet said, grasping the connecting doors to the back drawing room and throwing them open. "She likes to see my own hand."

"His sister," said Sophia. "Do we believe her, Sir Ashley?"

"I think," he said, smiling, "we do not."

With an unembarrassed laugh Harriet ran to the far side of the room and began rummaging in a secretaire. After a moment of consulting together on writing materials her mother and Mrs Dene followed.

For the first time Sophia felt uncomfortable in Ashley's presence. She felt herself to be sitting awkwardly and did not know how to place her hands and feet. What is the matter with me? she thought. I do not know what to say or what is the meaning behind his words. I cannot tell whether I wish to encourage him. And yet — encourage what? Perhaps I begin to see phantoms and will end as miss-ish as any other girl.

She said, "Your business with my uncle is finished?"

"Yes," Ashley uncrossed his legs and moved his chair an inch towards her. "It was a trivial matter. A transfer of funds after the purchase of some cottages. I wished for an excuse to make holiday and chose that. I would have come for other reasons if the sale had not been completed." He listened to the laughter in the next room. "I stay for others," he said.

Two days later there was, among the correspondence that arrived by post-horse at Claydon Hall, a letter from Ashley to Mason. It informed his agent that he was travelling to his estate in Dorsetshire for an indefinite stay. He intended to journey by land to observe the unrest in the country and must instruct Mason to deal gently with any signs of uprising that should occur before he had returned. He wished his friend to have no fears for him.

Robert Mason sat at his desk in the estate-room of the Hall, in the last of the autumn sunlight, looking long at the letter and neither supplicant nor servant ventured near him.

Chapter 10

Rosa Dene, lying drowsily against her lace pillow, looked younger than her age and was glad to be home. She lay watching Francis build up her fire before he left and, absently, she raised her hand and brushed it over the hollow beside her where his head had been.

The comforts of her own territory were more to her than the blatant luxuries of town. The heavy, oak furniture, the dark, mythological tapestries, the unsteady heat of the flames and the sound, on wild nights, of the lost sea-wind were the outward marks of the security provided by the man kneeling at the other side of the room. She admired him and trusted his judgement.

Putting the last of the coal in place Francis stood and brushed his hands. He adjusted the fastening of his chintz dressing-gown and returned to the bed, looking down on her through the velvet curtains. In his gown, his loose trousers and Turkish slippers his years did not tell on him. "So," he said, "Claydon arrives within the week and Sophia is already soft towards him. We should have the match quick arranged. He's not a man to chase about the country after a Miss if his mind were not made up — especially in these times. And at — what? Thirty-eight? Forty? He'll be wanting an heir as soon as he may."

"It was a friendlike notion asking me to carry his message for opening his house."

"Yes. I think we need have no anxieties about his meaning."

She shifted a little on the pillow. "There'll be scurrying amongst his servants tonight."

Francis put his arm against the bedpost and leant on it. "I doubt it," he said. "I'll wager Robert Mason will have had the whole house in master's condition all these years. Nothing to do but remove the dust-sheets." He considered. "This will put his nose out of joint. That house has been his own domain these twenty-two years and putting one account with another he's been more an intimate than an agent to Claydon in Norfolk as well. He won't take kindly to a mistress and I doubt Sophia will sit on a cushion eating strawberries when she's wed. He won't be cock of the walk anymore."

"Oh, Sophia is gentle with everyone."

Francis raised his eyebrows. "Is she though? Our little Sophie is not the girl she was. I remember her at the magistrates' meeting sweeping down among us to clear Young's name. For two pins she would have sent for pistols and called us out."

Mrs Dene smoothed the counterpane. "She suffered for it afterwards," she said, "with the headache."

Francis shrugged. "Why wasn't she born a boy? Then we should have seen some doings. However, as she was not we must have a husband to curb her. Prayer Books to shepherds!"

"She doesn't need curbing. The book was a —" She sensed his opinion and stopped.

"Rosa," he said, stroking the wood with a finger, "don't be innocent. When did she show love for work-dogs before? Why this one? I should have hanged it while she was away."

The fire hissed and flared as gas escaped from a coal. Mrs Dene sat slightly at the sudden noise. "She appeared to be taken with Sir Ashley," she said. "I didn't guard her too closely because I knew you would approve but neither did I push her towards him. She must feel the decision is hers."

She lay back, her face open to him, and he looked down on her with his hard, unreadable eyes. He touched her lightly on the cheek.

"Sweet Rosa," he said. "My sweet, sensible Rosa. I'm pleased to have you home."

The desolation of the western heaths, the violent skies hanging above bare woods and dark tumuli did not prepare Ashley's spirit for his entry to his Dorset house.

He had left London in defiance of his past and, seated in the cold interior of his carriage, with the collar of his travelling cloak turned up about his ears, had considered the arms carried by himself, his coachman and valet, and thought that if preparation to repel memory were as easily made he would now have been a different man. As they rolled through the wet, brown landscape — hearing the news of mayhem in the inns at night, being stopped at crossroads to account for their presence, witnessing the dank smoulderings of yesterday's arson — a flat, sweating anticipation overtook him. It was therefore strange to him to walk into the square, hamstone manor to be greeted by servants who had worked a lifetime for him and find an absence of any attack on his sensibilities.

In this unvisited place he had no reference points for his guilt. A sin committed long ago and far away and brooded upon in secrecy in eastern lands did not receive new life from a situation that was fresh and new in his experience. The sweetness of his burgeoning feelings for Sophia, the pleasure of seeing her in her home speaking so tenderly to a pale and clumsy maid, the yearnings roused by watching her from a distance galloping the gorse-covered cliff-tops with her dog at her side, all served to divert his mind into thoughts that were affectionate, spiritual and carnal and encouraged other obsessions.

Nor was he allowed time for dismal introspection. Francis was not a man to kill one bird where he could kill two and, as the disturbances gathered pace towards the west and magistrates rode about the county bullying or cajoling labourers according to their whim, he kept Ashley at his side, and in frequent contact with Sophia, by offering to exhibit his neighbours and the country by their riding together on Swing business. Ashley was not reluctant to take this opportunity and it was on one such journey to Hammond's farm to view a fire-threat found nailed to a shed that he broached the subject of offering for Sophia and was accepted by Francis readily.

That he should make this proposal while riding to the farm that housed his son and daughter did not strike him as incongruous. He had never asked Mason for details of his children's lives and the little he knew did not include their places of work. His ignorance, his habit of drawing shutters down in his mind, his preoccupation with Sophia and a new line of heredity did not lead him to speculate on the condition of his previous children or wonder whether their safety was endangered by disorder.

Sympathy aroused in him by the plight of the labourers had not abated but he was a man of his class and where poverty and hunger erupted and over-stepped the law he sided with the judiciary in desiring to block what they saw as anarchy. That Ashley wished to suppress unrest by light sentences and higher wages and Francis by harsh sentences and constant fear seemed a mere subtlety to the latter who was impressed by Ashley's informed interest in public affairs. Every man of authority was now needed and Francis, who found his present life much to his taste, was glad to offer his future son-in-law a share in thwarting revolution.

Swing filtered towards them like the spread of typhus — now running along lines of obvious contagion, now advancing by underground streams — and like an epidemic that is rising to its peak it flourished and strengthened and there seemed no means to end it. Ricks burned and Fire Offices refused insurance, masters smashed their own machines and workmen gathered to demand food and pence — but this was no longer the extent of the troubles.

Factories and foundries were now being destroyed; poorhouses were torn down; in the Southampton sawmills £7,000 worth of property was reduced to ash. Rioting began to last for days; in Salisbury the shops were closed and their windows barred; at Pyt House, west of the city, in a parish where Lord Arundell said that the poor had been more oppressed and were in greater misery than anywhere in the kingdom, four hundred labourers with hatchets and crow-bars were surprised by the cavalry who shot one man dead and wounded six; in the Vale of Wylye the road to Warminster was barricaded by rioters and a battle fought with the yeomanry for possession of their prisoners — and, in the last days of November, as the Whig Ministry took office, the troubles reached Dorset.

In the small drawing room where the family sat in the evening Sophia was at her needle. She held a piece of white-work in her hand. As yet it had no particular design or purpose but the soothing monotony of the stitches relaxed her. She had recently come from the kitchen and a small, brown stain on the hem of her gown was still damp.

Giving Watch his accustomed dish of chocolate had become an anticipated event for her. She had only had the opportunity to try it once before she went to London but now it was for her alone to do and she enjoyed it. Liking the dog's abandonment to pleasure she would sit on a stool beside his basin, her fingers lightly resting in his coat, and ignoring the splashes he threw off until the servants whispered that such attachment was unnatural.

Since her return to Dorset she had been freer in the taking of amusements as she was freer in many things. The lassitude and passivity that had afflicted her in town had fallen away with the resumption of her more active life and, as she rode or walked or played for Ashley, she felt a new and curious physical strength. Though she still did not wish to give herself in marriage she was aware that Ashley's interest represented a possible change in her condition and so gave her a confidence to defy the restrictions of the old. Despite the troubles she wished to ride abroad and Francis, no longer trusting her quietness and eager to hide her unexpected corners from Ashley, allowed her to do so in the company of a groom. If he had forbidden her she would have disobeyed him. Her challenge of the magistrates and journey to London had broken her routine of submission and much of her fear of everyday existence was gone. What remained was her dread of an aimless drifting that would carry her to old age without having made use of her fortune or position.

This evening she sat and sewed alone. Her ribbons were crossed neatly at her throat; her thread was drawn with regularity; there was no sound but the ticking of the eight-day clock; no light but the fire and two wax candles; she and the room and the night were the image of tranquillity and Francis, entering the scene in restrained elation, thought that she was his Sophia and the moment auspicious for his news.

He went to the cabinet and poured himself a glass of brandy, then crossed to the fireplace and leant with his elbow on the mantel, the tails of his riding jacket hanging near to the flames. He looked at her closely.

"Does Sir Ashley come with you tonight?" Sophia asked.

"No, he's gone home. Where is Mrs Dene?"

"At the lodge-house. The youngest girl is sick."

Francis tapped his glass on his bottom lip but did not speak. For an instant the firelight caught the moving liquid and cast a swaying amber glow at the ceiling.

"Have you returned for the evening?" said Sophia. "Shall I fetch someone to take off your boots?"

"Shortly, shortly." Francis was watching her with fervid eyes. He was always a man to have some strong intention lying concealed within him but tonight Sophia thought the excitement of the times was unusually revealed in his manner.

"Would you have wished Claydon to have supped here?" he went on. "Again?"

Sophia let her work rest on her knee. "I'm always ready to welcome guests," she said.

Francis laughed. "Your father never had half your spirit. I'll be sorry to lose you."

"Lose me?"

He sat on the edge of the wing-chair opposite hers. "Come, Sophie, use your wits. You can see I'm pleased by something. I rode over to Five Warrens with Claydon this afternoon. He offered for you and I accepted."

Sophia folded her white-work and set it aside. She stared into the fire. After a moment's silence Francis put his glass on the floor. He leant forward and said more gently, "His circumstances could hardly be bettered and I've witnessed for myself how well you suit each other. You know I wouldn't give you to a man you disliked."

She got up slowly and stood a little vacantly by her chair.

"You didn't ask me," she said.

"He'll ask you himself in time. I congratulate you."

Sophia was clasping and unclasping her hands. "I'm not yours to give," she said.

"What? Ah," Francis made a dismissive gesture, "a figure of speech. I would not have accepted the offer of a man you found distasteful."

She turned her head to look at his face and it seemed to him that something in her eyes was slipping.

"You did not ask me," she said again. She moved as if she were going to step forward but had changed her mind. Looking about her as though there were others in the room she raised her arm. For a moment she held it in the air — then lashing suddenly down she struck her work-box from the table. The wood splintered as it hit the fender and pins, silks and thimbles scattered across the floor. She watched them rolling.

"You did not ask me," she said.

Mrs Dene, returning from her nursing, found her services again required. Francis, who she found pacing the hall, waiting for her whilst gnawing a chicken-wing, beckoned her into the small drawing room and, before she had had time to take off her cloak, showed her the debris of the work-box whose contents had been crushed underfoot by their owner. That owner, instead of rejoicing in an excellent match, was now residing silently behind the closed door of her chamber.

He admitted freely that the general turbulence of the day and his triumph at Ashley's proposal to unite their estates had led him to an unwise choice of words in conveying the news to Sophia and cursed himself roundly for losing hold of a lifetime of calculation. He added a few phrases concerning the foibles and inconsistencies of the female sex and apologized for not being completely master of himself — a thing Mrs Dene had never seen necessary before. He then instructed her that she was to approach her charge and bring about a more amenable frame of mind.

There was no sound within Sophia's chamber as her governess listened outside the door yet Mrs Dene knew her well enough to be certain she was not sleeping. She took its handle and pushing it open an inch said her name softly and entered.

The candle she carried was the only light apart from the fire and a pale moon-glow from the uncovered windows. There was a great stillness in the room as if a moment before the birds now frozen on the Chinese wallpaper had been battering at the glass for escape. Sophia had half-drawn one of her bed-hangings and was lying motionless on the rumpled counterpane with her back to the door.

The silence, the bleached whiteness of the bedstuffs, the moonlight, the ceiling and the background of the walls, the corpse-like pose of the girl sent an eerie tremor over Mrs Dene's skin and she was glad of the movement and slight companionship of the flames.

Sophia, lying on a sodden pillow and clutching the sheet in her hand, was torn between willing Mrs Dene to leave her to her suffering and longing to reach out to be held and comforted and set back on the path of duty as if she were a child. What had begun, as she strode away from her grandfather, as a few hot and relieving tears of temper had unexpectedly and agonizingly become the bitter heart-grieving of those who are mourning for the unending cruelties, pettiness and entrapment of mankind. Her life and body were not another's to give — yet how much true choice was there for her between now and death? Calder Young and his family were born free Englishmen — yet how far was their position from slavery?

Feeling a useless and painful weeping welling within her she moaned faintly and Mrs Dene, taking it as invitation, came forward and sat on the edge of the bed. She rolled Sophia gently on to her back and saw the glittering eyes in the blanched face. For perhaps five minutes she did not try to bring the girl to speak but wiped away the sparse tears that escaped despite the fight against them and stroked her forehead as she had done for childhood fever and nightmare; occasionally she murmured something meaningless and soothing.

At last Sophia showed signs of discomfort and they propped the pillows higher in the bed so that they could sit upright against them with their arms about each other and the counterpane covering the skirts of their creased gowns. Sophia leant her aching head against Mrs Dene's shoulder.

"He shouldn't have told me as he did," she said. "It's for me to choose. I could never be a society wife — a name, a figurehead. When I — if I take my vows I will do it sincerely — so I must be the one to choose. I can't take half-measures."

Mrs Dene stroked the dishevelled hair that was brushing her cheek.

"Don't let a few hasty words prevent you doing what would be for your benefit. Your grandfather is proud of the proposal made for you — that was why he was too quick in his answer. If you turn away a good man because of that it will be nothing but a different kind of pride and foolishness."

Sophia stirred in a way that showed she was listening but did not reply. Mrs Dene went on, "I want you to be happy and cared for. So does Sir Ashley. The world is being turned upside down. What if you lost Mr Farren and your wealth? Independence can be a cold, barren thing for a woman, Sophie. Take your opportunity while you may."

"You have not remarried and are content."

"Is that what I am?" Mrs Dene stopped her stroking. "Well, I was never a romantic. But it's been pure chance, my dear, this content of mine, and Fate is offering you a better."

In the dusky room the various dim lights were throwing an unusual reflection on the window-panes. Sophia regarded it with half-conscious puzzlement. Finally she said, "I'll bathe my face."

They put back the coverlet and climbed off the bed. As Sophia went stiffly to the washstand Mrs Dene shook out her skirts and walked to the window. With her hand on the curtain she looked out on the night and the coloured clouds.

"Sophia!" she said suddenly. "There are horsemen outside."

The alarm in her voice caused Sophia to put down her jug and cross quickly to her, leaving a trail of water on the floor. The two women craned together at the figures in the courtyard. Sophia blew out Mrs Dene's candle and the loss of its shine on the glass enabled them to make out three riders and an unmounted horse. As they watched Francis moved out into view and settled firmly into the empty saddle.

"There are men on foot beyond the gate," said Sophia. She opened a pane to call down, her wet hands glinting, but as she did so the men clattered out towards the coast and she, looking past them at the reddening sky, recognized the light of fire and did not need to ask their destination.

Chapter 11

Caleb was tired. He rested the stone he was carrying on the low turf wall and wiped his forehead with the back of his hand. It was a cold night but weariness and exertion had made him feel clammy. His trousers were tied beneath the knee yet a cool layer of air between the worn corduroy and his legs made him conscious of his body and its conflicting sensations.

He went inside the hut and sat heavily on a pile of cut bracken in a corner. The heat he had thought he felt left him and he leant back in the shelter of the two walls and pulled his neckerchief more securely to his ears. Taking a turnip from his pocket he bit through the tough, gritty skin and chewed as he looked at the sky.

There was a long, dragging rhythm to the sea tonight. The sound came over the ridge of the heath with a peculiarly detached melancholy and this, with the moon that gave the atmosphere a milkiness that was not quite mist, made the small combe where he was building seem intent and isolated. Over the walls he could see the rusty skeletons of dock shivering their seeds in the night-wind and for a moment a bat swooped like a pendulum between a pair of thorns.

Lack of time and of materials he could use without being accused of theft were making the progress of his shanty a slow business. He had no pride in his work. He was ashamed that he was bringing down the delicate girl he considered to be his wife to this level of poverty. Longing to give her pretty gifts, a house to live in, a bed to sleep on, he was angered that his craft should not reward him with the means to provide such simple needs.

Though he did not approve of Swing and would not have rallied to a mythical Captain had he appeared on his white horse he was unable to suppress a truculence in the face of orders that was noticed by his master. He wanted to be unseen until their emigration yet thoughts of his Hester made him surly. He began to sympathize with the frustrations that led to wage demands and the sending of incendiary threats. A fear that it was in him to burn down the sheds that had been refused as shelter to his love sometimes troubled him at night and it occurred to him that if Calder had taken an active part in rebellion it would have been deliberate and well-calculated but that he himself would be prompted by the more dangerous moment of passion. He was a patient man being goaded beyond his strength to endure.

Tonight his exhaustion was not merely emotional. He had risen at five that morning to prepare his team for the plough. That, he thought, was the time he loved most of all — going into the warmth of the stable, a lantern in hand, with the dawn almost breaking and the gentle snufflings of the heavy mares and the rustlings of their hooves in the straw to welcome him. The quietness of small sounds was all about him as he poured out the chaff and beans for the feed and when he took the brushes and groomed her with long, gentle strokes his leader would pause in her chewing and turn her head to rub her muzzle against his shoulder, her hay-sweet breath hot upon his neck. It calmed him to remember it but that morning, as with all others, the soft hour of animal companionship had soon been over and he had brought out his team for the last week of winter ploughing. Sitting sideways on the land-horse, rocked by a gait that was both lumbering and graceful, he had gazed at the turned fields where a hare lay flat-eared in the frost and yearned sickly for his brother to recover him from a life where his craftsmanship was unvalued.

To set up the plough and stand behind it in his own breath, empty-bellied and anxious for the future, knowing there were ten miles to walk before the acre was finished was a hard labour and as the sun sank behind the elm copse he was glad to give his horses to a fellow ploughman who passed the gate and come to the heath to work on his hut. For three hours he had cut turves with his hay-knife, tearing the grass-roots from the thin, chalky soil, and had stacked them along the top of the low walls, reinforcing them with stones. Next week he would be out of work and back on the rounds and did not know how often he would be free to build.

Finishing the turnip he rubbed his hands on his thighs. His palms and finger-ends were smoothened and powdered by earth. He drew them over the ground where a dew was forming and the wetness untightened the skin. He could do no more tonight. By the time he had walked back to Five Warrens in the dark it would be half past nine or later and he must check whether someone had settled his horses to their feed. He hoped Hammond had not noticed he was not there; trouble would make a dismal ending to the day.

Standing up he took the knife from the wall where he had left it and thrust it into the leather sling at his belt. At the entrance to the hut he stopped to shut an imaginary door and smiled at himself. Putting his hands in his trouser pockets he walked tiredly back towards the farm, his shoulders slightly hunched against the cold. The wasteland with its hollows and ridges, rabbit-holes and tussocks, offered rough going and Caleb, wrapped in his thoughts, was forced to keep his eyes low and concentrate on the dim presence of obstacles in his way.

Occasionally he lifted his head and stared through the grey moonlight unable, at a distance, to distinguish sky, hill and shadow. The wind slid gently over his body, drawing a shiver slowly down his spine, and always as he walked there was the faint surge of the waves washing the beach.

As he climbed the slope that led to the valley of Five Warrens he became uneasy. The fields were cultivated here and as he strode sturdily up the incline he grasped the edging of the dry-stone wall and pulled himself on. There was a strangeness in the sky; a glow that should not have outstayed sunset. A suspicion, that part of him laughed at, blossomed in his mind and he almost ran to the summit of the hill.

Across the floor of the valley, beyond the farmstead, a fire was burning. There was a shallow terrace between the orchard and the steep rise that led to the village which was used as the second rick-yard and there, as he stood looking down on it and trying to catch his breath, he saw the fluctuating orange and scarlet of a stack in blaze. From this distance, with the wind blowing from the sea, he could hear nothing and though he could see dark figures moving in front of the fire and the flames, now contracting, now gusting out like a woman's hair, the absence of all sound of agitation made the scene unreal and separate from him.

For several minutes he watched without feeling. He had helped to beat out rick-fires before. A badly-built stack will over-heat and kindle of its own accord and the black silhouettes of the men with hooks and women with buckets were part of a routine that would end in the cursing and sacking of the builders — but none of the stacks had been slackly tended this year. Knowing nothing of that morning's fire-threat he thought quite coolly that Swing had reached them and an incendiary was at work on the farm. He wondered who it had been — John Hudson? Abel Marler? a stranger? — and then its reality began to sink into his mind and old loyalties to master and place took hold and he scrambled over the wall and ran, stumbling in the darkness, down the slope towards the farm. He took long, jumping strides with his arms out as if he expected to fall and as he cleared the first meadow and was far enough down into the hollow to be out of most of the wind he caught the first bitter tang of smoke and glanced up to see the progress of the fire.

At first he thought it had lessened. The bold block of flame upon the hillside had gone and left a thin, vertical streak of fire that a hearty thrust of water could extinguish. A thick, dark-grey felt of smoke hung heavily above it and a sudden golden spray of sparks rose from its centre and danced like bees about its crimson head. It had a harsher, fiercer colour than it had done and, as the breeze found its way into the yard and shook the smoke, small, brightly red flames ran like the springing of poppies along the ground, consuming in a moment's brilliant heat odd twists of straw, and jumped on to a ladder that leant against the wall.

The wall? His mind was slow with tiredness but the thought came into it as he ran towards the farm lane that you could not see the ricks from here. He was so low in the valley that the terrace was hidden by the farmhouse and if he could see fire it was in the buildings and more dangerous and destructive.

117

He scrambled over the wall that ran beside the track. The gate into the yard had been left swinging and this — being unheard of — made him look back down the lane expecting to see the incendiary in retreat, but all was dark and empty except for the loose, gauzy streamers of smoke that trailed indecisively over the far hedge.

There were signs of a hurried desertion in the yard as if its occupants had been called for urgently and had thrown down what they were carrying and fled elsewhere. A wheelbarrow stood abandoned in the centre, a short shovel lay broken on the ground and at the entrance to the grain-store a sack of oats sagged untidily and spilt its dust-white seed on to the stone. A flickering pattern of light and shadow like a late sun glancing through swaying branches dappled the yard and through it Caleb ran in anger.

From the youth of the yard-fire it must have been started later than the rick's. It would have been simple for the arsonist to hide in the yew walk at the edge of the orchard until the barton had emptied of people rushing to save the hay and then return to the yard and the country beyond, beginning another fire as he went. And the damage he had chosen — the revenge on the farmer for the pauper existence the labourers were forced to endure — was to light the door of the stables.

To Caleb — gentle, steadfast and tender-hearted — it was an act of inexcusable callousness. That the horses — the faithful creatures who so willingly pulled the plough — should be left to have their living flesh burnt from them was an outrage to him. Already, as he neared the stable door and felt the brilliant heat that made his eyes stare and his head draw back, he could hear the stricken stirrings of chained beasts and the irregular booming crash of a powerful hoof smashed in fear against a stall partition.

His own team were housed alone to the rear of the yard but in the main stable, with the men's attic above it, there were three pairs of mares and geldings and two of the mares were in foal.

Pulling off his neckerchief he wrapped it about his hand and, snatching at the metal latch, wrenched open the door. The whole of the wooden surround was alight and thick layers of dirty, yellow smoke fell slowly out into the yard. He could not see into the stable but putting his arm over his face he dashed himself inside. A single spark glowed abruptly on his sleeve and he pinched it out as he looked around.

Tendrils of flame were reaching into the room and he kicked the straw away from the doorway to delay their spread but he could not protect the stairs by stamping and the open attic above, acting as a chimney, drew the fire upward so that it appeared like ivy entwined with the rungs. Soon the attic floor would kindle and then the thatch.

The horses were pulling at their tethers and the rattle of the chains, the snortings, the crackle and hiss of the flames whipped on their terror so that they rolled wide-eyed and kicking in their stalls. A smell of singeing — an acrid, smithy scent — was present beneath the smoke, as if their feet and hides were being caught by sparks, and sweat gleamed hot and pungent on their flanks.

Caleb edged into the stall of the nearest mare. He knew her for her good nature and spoke soothingly as he unfastened the chain from her halter, but the natural horror of an animal for fire prevented her from recognizing that he meant her no harm. He pushed her gently towards the door but she would not move any nearer the flames. He put his shoulder against her chest but she squatted like a jack-rabbit with her teeth showing. He found himself saying, "Come on, girl, come on, come on. There's my beauty", as if he were in the fields. His face was wet with heat and dripped a salt grime on to his lips as he spoke. He was still holding his neckerchief and he tied it around her eyes but he had nothing to disguise the smell of burning and again she would not move.

With a sudden rushing sound the flames reached the ceiling and ran along a rafter. A hay-net that had been hanging from a hook blazed brightly and, its rope breaking, fell scattering fire into the stalls. At the far end of the stable a horse screamed.

Caleb snatched up a long handful of straw and twisted it into a torch. Reaching to the ceiling that was dropping charred wood amongst them he lit its end and pulling his neckerchief from the mare's eyes showed her its streaming, ragged flames.

She backed awkwardly and he followed her, holding the torch in her face. Again she backed and again he followed, stooping for another twist of straw to light from the first. With fire in both hands, that were slimed and slippery and tense, he manoeuvred her towards the door.

"We have him!"

The unexpected voice startled him. The mare, thinking she was menaced from all sides, panicked and Caleb, trying to prevent her leaning against the crumbling stairs, let the straw burn down to his fingers and burst the skin on his palms. He dropped the fragments of the torches and looked for his accoster. The smoke was now like a winter fog lividly coloured by the northern lights. He shielded his eyes with his blistering hands but could see only that three gentlemen stood in the doorway — and had no knowledge to tell him that he had met his father.

Chapter 12

The kitchen of Five Warrens Farm at two o'clock the following morning did not present an image of order and masculine beauty. It was a long room and so dimly lit as to be a relief after the unusual and vicious illumination which had afflicted various parts of the valley that night. The inconveniently small windows looked out on the leafless currant bushes and espaliered pears of the kitchen-garden but their moonlit shapes were hidden by the layer of clinging smoke that now lay on the glass like the dust on ancient wine-bottles.

A stench of watered ashes and burning horse-flesh still hung heavily about the yard, eddying in the wind like a body trying to be washed upon the shore, but even had the room overlooked the farm-buildings its windows would not have let in the light of fire. Nor would they have framed their expected view. The stables and men's attic which had been discovered in flames with their destroyer red-handed in their midst were now fallen pitifully into rubble. The efforts of the special constables and loyal labourers who had run to the farm at the heels of the magistrates determined or reluctant to quell a riot had prevented the spread of the conflagration to the other buildings but the rapid consuming of the old thatch had brought the roof into the stable and cast all combustibles into its fiery furnace. Two horses had been burnt alive in their stalls and a third, which had lain twitching and stinking in the yard, had been shot. The much-anticipated arrival of Nether Cheney's antique fire engine had caused the entire contents of the stew-pond to be pumped into the yard and its glistening storm-wrecked appearance now belied the mildness of the night.

The descent of the rescue party upon the fire had been opportune. The Reverend Mingay, before riding to Weymouth for a clerical meeting, had left word with his housekeeper that he would call on Sir Ashley on his return journey. When, therefore, Hammond's rick was attacked and Mingay, as the nearest Justice, was required a messenger was dispatched to Pierston House and Ashley, still booted and in possession of his horse after leaving Francis, had agreed to accompany Mingay back to Five Warrens — mustering all available anti-revolutionaries on their way. Ashley's devotion to the pattern of life which was threatened by rebellion and his passionate and romantic spirit, now re-emerging after so long a repression, combined to make him ride with a vigour which gave Francis no fear of his success with Sophia and it was with satisfaction that his future father-in-law saw him take the initiative in entering the stable and apprehending an arsonist so much younger than himself.

It was true that the rioter — a known discontent — had shown little inclination to struggle beyond an attempt to thrust a hysterical plough-horse between himself and his arresters but courage had still been required to go into a burning building and confront a desperate and muscular labourer who had a knife in his belt and the prospect of a noose before him. Francis, as he sat in the kitchen from which all large water-carrying containers had been hurriedly looted, was congratulating himself upon the annexation of Ashley and considering the prospect of a grandson in his own image.

There was a small, tame fire smouldering in the wide hearth and Francis, who had pulled up a Windsor chair so that he could lounge with his feet on the settle, was heating a poker in its midst. He had undone his stock and his normally gaunt face was drawn and shadowed. Much as he relished such activities the events of the night, coming after an already full day, were telling his years and he was more aware than he wished to be of several of his joints. He had a pewter plate on his lap and was eating mutton pie and cold potatoes with a flat spoon. A tankard of Hammond's best ale was standing on the scrubbed stone floor.

As the door opened, a waft of charred timber came in, and with it the Reverend Mingay. Mingay shut out the night and stamped his boots on the flags, leaving a deposit of cinders and ash behind. Though always of a cold and bloodless demeanour, tiredness made him appear incapable of any emotion beyond a certain effortless cruelty. He was drying his hands on a white lawn handkerchief after washing them under the pump. Seeing Francis he nodded and Francis pointed with his spoon at the dishes of food on the table.

Mingay reinserted his handkerchief into his pocket and, taking a plate from the dresser, went to the long oak table and began cutting pie.

"Where's Claydon?" he asked.

Francis removed the poker from the fire and inspected its tip.

"Spewing in the privy," he said. "He swallowed smoke." He eased the glowing end of the poker into his tankard where a fizzling and a surge of froth agreed that he had heated it enough.

Mingay, whose willow-pattern plate was now hidden by barley bread, crumbling cheese and the section of pie which contained the most mutton, sat in the corner of the settle and, leaning his head against its high back, closed his eyes. Francis returned his feet to the floor.

"A good night's work," he said.

Mingay smiled coldly, showing his teeth. He opened his eyes. "Very satisfactory to catch one in the act," he said. "There'll be a few potential incendiaries round here who'll think twice now."

There was an empty dog-spit amongst the cooking apparatus in the fireplace. Francis pushed it with the poker and the cage moved slowly round.

"It was fortunate for us there wasn't a full-scale riot to put down," he said. "With a few minor tradesmen who rely on our households as constables and the tenant farmers with bird-guns we would've been hard pressed. I wouldn't trust the labourers as far as I could throw them."

"My keepers and their prisoner should reach Dorchester within the hour. I sent a message to the barracks with them." Mingay divided the bread with his hands. "This Young," he asked, "he's the brother of the shepherd who emigrated, is he not?"

"Nicely put," said Francis. "Yes, a troublesome family altogether. Ideas above themselves."

"But now you have Claydon and all he entails. We may wish you joy."

Raising his eyebrows Francis said, "You're becoming an old woman, Mingay."

"I like to know what my neighbours are about."

Francis laughed. "If you're thinking of the wasteland on the cliffs," he said, "we may come to an arrangement between us. An Enclosure Act should be easily managed to our good. Hammond's claim is as small as his farm and can be discounted."

"And," said Mingay, brushing a crumb of cheese to the floor, "we shall have no unpleasantness with squatters now."

"No." Francis lifted his tankard from the hearth. "No. There are some things best got rid of."

In the double privy behind the house Ashley was spitting down one of the holes. He was shaking and though he had unburdened his stomach, bile was rising to his throat and burning through the after-taste of smoke. A sudden shuddering overtook him and he was forced to lean against the damp wall with sweat seeping to his skin. He took off his cravat and wiped his face and mouth.

He had learnt Caleb's name. He had exerted himself that night in his guise as a magistrate; he had conducted his actions with resolution and strength and experienced the continuing intoxicating renewal of youth that was expanding his vision and filling his mind and limbs with a sweet increase and savour of energy — and in a moment, standing in a dark farm kitchen waiting for a rush-lamp to be lit, he had learnt a young man's name and been transformed.

His reaction had been physical. An immediate retching had brought him out into the air and an urge for privacy into the confines of the closet. Holding his cravat over his nose he shovelled earth into the box but the acid reek of vomit hung about the hovel and he threw his neck cloth after the earth and went unsteadily outside.

The privy was at the end of a gravel path that edged the garden and instead of returning to the house he followed a grassy track that led uphill towards the orchard. He held himself upright by clutching at the wall and when it ended and he entered the trees he leant with his back against a trunk. He had a heavy giddiness as if he had taken too much port and as he rested against the lichened bark, looking up through the gnarled branches, the stars swung slowly in a sinking sky.

The night was full of distant sound yet seemed so quiet. There had been a frost last morning but at this early hour the cold was mild for November and there was no crispness underfoot. The grass was longer here and brushed him to the knee with dew. When he moved his foot he felt the soft slide of a forgotten apple.

So, he thought, Fate has punished me. Flesh of my flesh. My son is violent and criminal; a felon. Is his nature a result of my desertion or does he merely take after his father? It seems that neither of us has loyalty or honour. But I have tried — I have tried since my failure and am served thus. Where is the honourable course now? I could protect this thug from his well-justified deserts by letting it be known I sired him. I need not even reveal his legitimacy; I'm of a rank to have such errors winked at. Or I could keep silence — sin by omission — to preserve my family name and the feelings of my bride and let this arsonist be punished for what I saw him do. Did he hear those horses scream? Smell them in their agony? I hear him now — his foreign, western voice. I feel his rough sleeve in my hand. Lord, is this deliberate? Are you testing me? Have I not tried enough?

His mouth was sour and scummed with sickness and the long draughts of air he drew in to calm his uneven heart had a rancid, bitter taste. The news makes me vomit, he thought, and so I must have accepted it yet my mind does not acknowledge a connection. Reason puts together the evidence and gives me a son but whatever is myself says that he is not of me. What do we have to bind us? If I had not married his mother I would think nothing of this. If I had not loved and had taken her lightly. But if is so large a word.

There was a rustling in the grass. He turned his head and saw a farm-girl walking tentatively towards him. She carried an earthenware jug of milk and when she was close to him she stopped, holding it before her like an offering. In the dusk and the shadow of the trees he could not see her clearly but was aware of an apprehension that made him conscious of his exposed throat and unshaven face.

"Sir," she said and, in the litter of leaves, made an awkward curtsey. "Sir, I heard you were unwell."

She was unused to gentlemen and, made nervous by his pale scrutiny, almost pushed the jug to him. He took it from her but did not drink.

"You are the prisoner's sister?" he said.

A shiver went over her as he spoke and she nodded.

"Turn your face to the moonlight."

Obediently she lifted her head towards the moon. She was an ordinary work-girl with a cheap shawl crossed over her chest and pinned behind. Her clothes were creased and smoke-stained and there were the marks of tears on her cheeks. He untangled a piece of blackened straw from her hair and she flinched in silence. How can I tell if she resembles her mother, he thought. My memory is not so long.

"Have you come to plead for your brother?" he asked.

"Yes, sir." She turned towards him so that the shade of a branch darkened her brows. Again he felt no recognition, no summons to kin and when she met his eyes there was no answer in his blood. His paternity seemed academic and theoretical.

"If we do wrong," he said, "we must suffer."

"Oh, sir," Hannah put out a hand as if she would touch him and quickly drew it back. "There was a mistake. Caleb is so gentle. He'd never harm a living thing. Please, sir, be merciful."

"Family feeling is deceptive," he said. Once more, he thought, my character is revealed in my children.

She did not understand him; she was tired and did not know what to say.

"He loved his horses, sir," she said.

126

On a dark afternoon in mid-December Sophia was promenading the Long Gallery at Bredy Hall. She carried a copy of the Dorchester *County Chronicle* which she occasionally brandished beneath the walnut swags. Ashley, pacing by her side, listened to her with a concentration underlined by his appearance of pending illness. Sophia walked firmly, looking now straight ahead, now directly into her companion's eyes, and Ashley, accommodating his stride to hers, took fewer steps to keep her by him. Outside the rain fell at an acute angle and at intervals was blown in violent gusts against the glass.

"You see me to disadvantage," she said. "I can't control my feelings. The world used to seem so safe."

"It does you credit. If more people had felt deeply for the poor this horror would not be upon us."

And how, he thought, can I bring you into my world where there is no safety at all? Do you know what you walk by? The long, sleepless nights since the fire blurred his reason. He felt himself to be the embodiment of evil, the repository of all sin and weakness. Lying in the empty, early hours in an unfamiliar house, with the childish comfort of a lamp denied him by his own restriction, he struggled with temptation until the words he used to argue came from without and whispered softly in his ear. An easy martyrdom was offered him. The self-indulgence of *mea culpa* beckoned with enticing arms. A confidential conversation here, a smoothing over of evidence and offer of recompense there would free his son from the consequence of his savagery and himself from the inevitable sequel of guilt. The delicious satisfaction of baring part of his secret could be his without complete disgrace — but he had taken the easy path years before. Was all that he had striven to become since then to be abandoned for the convenience of his conscience?

He looked at Sophia as she stared at the rain and thought that if hag-ridden eyes were a concomitant to marriage they would make a perfect match. Nothing had been said between them on the subject of their union. He had never considered himself to deserve her love and now, for her sake, wished his proposal unspoken. Francis, hoping to delay until he could be sure of landing his fish, had made much of Sophia's womanly concern for the impoverished and advised Ashley not to approach her on any tender subject at this time. Sophia, herself, could see that his involvement with Caleb was causing Ashley to suffer and respected him for his sensibility in both this and in not courting her while he was so circumstanced. Yet, though she talked freely to him on public affairs, she had become shy in other ways. She could not tell him of the white and tragic Hester. He knew that she had discovered Hannah and a maid from the Hall walking to Dorchester with food for the gaol and had ordered a cart to convey them but she had not been able to reveal to him the full reason for her action. She had been offered an extraordinary intimacy with this man who trod at her side so gravely and if she accepted it she could next year be carrying his child as Hester carried Caleb's. The enormity of this silenced her. Is my reticence modesty, she wondered, or a sign that I could not completely share myself with him?

"Oh!" she said, "but to have Swing so near us — among a family I know so well. And such cruel, cruel violence. I still can't believe it."

Ashley frowned into a pier-glass. "I saw it with my own eyes," he told her.

She laid her hand on his arm as they walked. "I don't doubt you," she said.

It was the first time she had touched him in this way and, for a moment, he covered her fingers with his own.

"What can I do," he asked, "but tell what I saw?" There was an appeal in his words which begged her to release him from his duty but the history that had put the pain in his voice was unknown to her and she was too young to be practical.

"Naturally," she said, "you must say what is true however hard it may be — but I wish you didn't have to stay here as a witness. It's bitter for you to be away from your own people when you could be protecting them from harsh sentences on the Bench. All tolerant magistrates are needed now."

They had reached the end of the Gallery where Watch was stretched upon a needlework rug in the bay of a window. As they turned to repeat their walk, with Sophia's skirts sweeping roundly across the polished floor, the dog rose and padded companionably at Ashley's side. Absently, Ashley let his hand trail and caressed the thick fur on its head.

"I think the Justices' tolerance will soon be immaterial," he said. "I hear through my agent that many magistrates in Norfolk have been raising wages instead of using force and have written to the Home Secretary to recommend it — but all he's done is send out that appalling circular abusing their efforts and demanding resistance to menace of property. Mr Farren had a copy."

"He approved of it."

"I do not. And then, of course, the Special Commission which is being sent to try the prisoners specifically because the Government fears the leniency of the local magistrates. I'm the first to want to avoid riot and anarchy but is Australia the answer? There are more than fifty men awaiting trial at Dorchester and most of them, I'd swear, driven into being creatures of the mob by hunger."

Sophia watched him running his fingers over the dog's rough ears. He is morally and physically brave, she thought. He is tender and strong and unafraid to oppose the views of grandfather and the others. Everything he says is compassionate. Whenever I meet him I feel an indefinable quality which sends an excitement through me. I breathe with claustrophobia and he offers me space. Why then do I hesitate to accept him? Perhaps Mrs Dene is right and it is only a foolish pride that prevents me.

"There's a letter in the paper," she replied, "from a man of the county who, ten years ago, parcelled out eight acres of his land to the poor for allotments. He says that when he first resided in the village he found the people neglected and uncivil — thieves, poachers and mischief-makers. They are now attended to, contented, laborious and honest. He says," she stopped and rustled in the paper to find her place. Ashley looked out of the window at the rain beating steadily at the outbuildings and sodden woods. Watch flopped heavily to the floor at his feet. "He says," Sophia repeated, "'Years ago I suffered the country's revenge for encouraging the good and punishing the dissolute — I had my plantations twice broken down and destroyed. During the late tumults they have come forward as a man to protect my property; no disturbances whatever have occurred.'" She closed the paper. "A little fairness and kindness and after false starts he has had his reward. If Caleb Young had been treated justly how different things might have been. God help us — why do we not learn?"

"God help us," said Ashley, "indeed."

Chapter 13

On the thirteenth of January in the new year their Lordships of the Special Commission arrived in Dorchester at five o'clock in the afternoon. They were preceded, in that grey and wintery twilight, by mounted yeomanry and were escorted by the local constables without their staves in order to show that this addition to the procession was a compliment and not necessary for their protection. As they crossed the low stone bridge into the town they were greeted by dignitaries headed by James Frampton of Moreton House near Tolpuddle, who had been so active against Swing and so outraged when Portman, a fellow magistrate, had offered to raise his labourers' wages.

The following morning they attended divine service at St Peter's Church where the Reverend Pickard delivered a valiant sermon — speaking against the infidel and revolutionary spirit which was abroad, lighting on the qualities and duties of a true patriot and, after alluding to the recent events in the county, urging the enforcement of more punctual and correct discharge of religious obligations as the best mode of preventing disturbance.

Thus invigorated their Lordships entered court. Mr Baron Vaughan sat in the central chair with Mr Justice Alderson on his right. Also on the bench were three lay commissioners — the Earl of Shaftesbury, Earl Digby and Mr Wollaston, Esquire. Upwards of fifty JPs answered their names and a Grand Jury of twenty-two was sworn. It was a disappointment to Francis Farren that he was not among the jurors.

The talk the evening before, amongst the party gathered at George Dasent's decaying manor with its descending, box-edged carp-pools and its view across Martinstown and the open hills, had bandied the likelihood of who would or would not be on the jury with all the mixed hopes and expectations of a group whose opinions were similar only in their ignorance of a conclusion none of them could possibly know.

The inevitable overcrowding of Dorchester at the coming trials and the inconvenience of either putting up at a noisy inn or driving to the town in the dark of the morning had been the subject of much conversation amongst the gentry of the county and, as a neighbourly act, Dasent had invited Francis, Ashley, Mingay and Sir John and Frederick Ware to stay at his home for the duration of the sitting. The Wares were previously promised to friends in the town but their place had been filled by Sophia who had insisted on accompanying her grandfather although, by Ashley's request, she was not to attend Caleb's trial.

For her the hours after dinner had been spent in a subdued and sober mood seated in a recess in the drawing room helping Mrs Dasent sort her silks and appearing to consider — not the words of the men about the fire — but the particularly unfortunate floral carpet. Neither Ashley nor Francis believed her absorption and, in different ways, were unsettled by her presence but to Mingay and Dasent she was merely Miss Farren and to her hostess she was a quiet and soothing guest.

Ashley preferred to take as little part in the conversation as possible. He felt unwell. A nervous constriction in his chest and back which had begun to trouble him in the past two years had returned accompanied by a curious numbness in his left hand. It had always been his habit to draw whatever small article he was holding along the edge of his other hand and now he passed his glass of hot brandy gently along the offending fingers in the hope that the warmth would free them. He was sickened by the advent of the trial. He determined not to dwell on it and yet could think of nothing else.

"We can only trust," said Dasent, arranging his feet among the setters lounging before the hearth, "that a severe example will be made of the guilty."

"Considering that alarm and excitement have prevailed throughout the kingdom," replied Francis, leaning back in his green leather chair, "I think we need have no fear of that. Now that the burnings have reached Carlisle there's barely a part of the country untouched. I'm not a Whig myself, as you know, but I trust them to deal out justice firmly in this matter."

"If the law is not properly administered," Dasent agreed, prodding his dogs absently with his toe, "I couldn't say to what extent these disturbances mightn't reach nor whether we could long continue to enjoy those blessings which we now possess under the constitution of the country — steering, as it does, a middle course between the tyranny of the higher classes on the one hand, and the despotism of the multitude on the other."

Under cover of reaching for a skein of rose Sophia glanced at Mrs Dasent but years of married life had left her face a saddened mask.

"If we turned to the cause of the troubles —" said Ashley.

Francis uncrossed his legs and recrossed them at the ankle. "I think we all appreciate that they're much in error who would attribute the whole to one cause," he said.

The Reverend Mingay, who had been sitting on an upright tapestried chair stroking his black silk stock, leant forward slightly. "Distress is said to have produced it," he informed them, "but, upon investigation, I cannot find that the distress of this year has been greater than that of the last, nor that the prices of those articles necessary to the subsistence of the labourer have lately increased."

Ashley put down his glass and flexed his fingers. "We cannot doubt," he said, "that distress is one of the causes."

"But much has been done," Mingay replied, "by the influence of wicked men and it has been greatly increased by the mal-administration of those laws which were originally intended for the relief of the aged, the sick and the infirm. One of these abuses has been an encouragement to early marriages and in consequence an increase of population; and —"

"Well, Claydon," Dasent broke in, "what do you think of early marriages?"

Ashley hesitated. "They produce untold misery for all concerned," he said.

"But not late ones, eh?" Dasent laughed and looked at Sophia but to all appearances both Sophia and Ashley were deaf.

"And the system," went on Mingay as if his host had not spoken, "of paying the labourer a part of his wages out of the poor's rate has done much to degrade him in his own estimation; and the extension of education — of which I have never approved — whilst it has tended to make him feel more acutely the privations of his state of life has not gone far enough to teach him the duties of society." One of the dogs asleep before the fire woke enough to roll lazily on to its back and look with drowsy hope at Mingay. He ignored it. "It is thus that wicked men," he said, "have proved too successful in practising their evil arts upon them. They have given them to understand that they are labouring under grievances of a most disastrous character and that there exists a determination amongst the higher classes to oppress them and they thus endeavour to sever those bonds of society the maintenance of which is necessary for the welfare of the community."

"And also," said Dasent, reaching to the mantelshelf for the tobacco jar, "they cause the labourers to assemble together for the purpose of discussing the best mode of redressing their grievances and teach them that they owe all their evils to the mismanagement of the farmer and to his employment of machinery." He took a rack of new churchwardens and began to pass them round.

"Fortunately," Francis said, selecting a pipe, "the law has provided a remedy for these things and as magistrates we're empowered to move on all subjects connected with danger to the state."

This, thought Sophia, is Caleb Young they are speaking of — this danger to the state. Everyone in the court will think this way. He will be transported for sure. Oh, God, why did he give way to his worst self? What broke his last loyalty and self-control?

"Amelia!" said Dasent sharply. "The tobacco jar is empty."

His wife started and got suddenly to her feet. The silks she had been winding slid in confusion down the smooth surface of her shiny black skirts.

"I'm sorry, my dear," she said. "I'll fetch Martha at once."

She walked hurriedly to the door and Ashley — who was the

nearest man to her and had bent to gather up the tangled threads — was left with his hands full of blue, purple, green and crimson silks. The numbness was fading and there was almost no clumsiness in his fingers as he dropped the skeins into Sophia's cupped palms but she noticed his paleness in the face of the solemn and revolting duty that awaited him in court and such a passion of tenderness overtook her that if he had offered himself to her then, at that moment, she would have accepted him. The incident had diverted the company's attention and Francis, seeing Ashley entangled with yarn, was reminded of a new aspect of affairs which touched home ground.

"You'll be glad when this trial's over," he said, nodding at Ashley as he rearranged himself on his seat and Sophia turned back to her task. "The trouble amongst the weavers is unhealthy close to your estate. How far is Norwich from your place? Fifteen, twenty miles?"

"Ten." Ashley took up his glass which had grown cool. "Yes, the riot by the bombazine weavers has ruined their manufactory but, fortunately, doesn't seem to have spread to the outworkers or we would've had General Ludd machine-wrecking as well as Captain Swing. I have weavers on my estate who are being dealt with by my agent but he's sent me no news of needing force yet."

"Well," said Francis, "a show of judicial force this week should make any other unnecessary."

"Let us hope so," Ashley replied. "The thought of further violence — it chills my blood."

The morning of the opening of the trial found Sophia in the Farren's landau before the dawn had broken. She was accompanied by her grandfather and Mingay but Ashley and Dasent had decided to ride and were preceding the carriage with a groom before them. It was piercingly cold and both sides of the landau's hood were firmly shut but even with rugs wrapped about their legs and canisters of hot water in their laps the passengers were wondering whether the exertion of riding might not compensate in warmth for the more exposed position.

The journey from Martinstown was begun slowly with only lanterns and the warnings from the riders to keep them to the road but before they had reached Dorchester a still, grey light had spread over the fields and their pace had quickened. Across the exposed heath Sophia could see the low, barren outline of Maiden Castle whitened and softened with frost that gleamed fitfully as the weak sun rose. Occasionally the wind carried a bitter handful of sleet and the men on horseback sat down into the wide collars of their overcoats as it stang against their cheeks. A few shabby catkins hung in the hedges but there was no green growth and Sophia, rustling her boots in the straw in the carriage, thought — if I am ever tried let it be in high summer when hope seems easier to reach. As they entered the town they were slowed again by the traffic. Carts, carriages, horses and walkers were progressing towards the prison and the court and, though the numbers were not enough to halt them, they were obliged to return to a more moderate speed. On the verges the remnants of camp fires could be seen where families of accused men had slept out over night; a ballad-seller with his tray looped round his neck was making his way, half-asleep, through the obstacles; working women in pattens with their skirts tucked up through their pocket-holes to reveal red petticoats and with shawls wrapped over their heads were carrying milk-cans and wheeling goods on barrows to their market-stalls. The scene might have been medieval.

The crowd became thicker as they neared the High Street where Sophia was to be left in a private room in the King's Arms and Francis and Mingay, as local magistrates, attend court for the swearing of a jury. Ashley, whose duties as a witness were unlikely to be needed that day, was to see to the stabling and then join Sophia at the inn. Although she could not see him, Sophia's mind was on Ashley now as they drew towards the prison and the day.

The street was congested outside the prison gate and the long shadow from the buildings beyond fell on the women waiting, like penned cattle, to greet their men. They were silent as they stood and the children they had with them drooped tiredly at their skirts and cried quietly with fear and cold. White faces, white breath and the white walls of the gaol hung in Sophia's memory. A dark girl nursing her baby inside her jacket stared passively through the carriage window as it went by but gave no sign of what she saw. Sophia leant forward to look for Hester but could not make her out among so many.

They had passed the women and were approaching the crossroads when the unnatural silence, that made the creaking of the carriage and the fall of the hooves seem so loud, was broken. A moaning that was like nothing she had ever heard rose in the road behind them. Francis let down his window to lean out and on her side Sophia opened the door and looked back.

Above the heads of the crowd she could see that the gates of the gaol had been swung round and the women and children had surged towards them for a sight of their men. She thought she saw Hannah but could not be sure and before she could ascertain it the dragoons rode out of the yard, pressing the women back to clear a path for the prisoners to walk to court. Husbands, sons and fathers — ignorant of the laws that bound them, weakened by threats of transportation and the noose — came out into the light and the lamentations of their families. They cried out to the women as they recognized them and the shouts of the haggard men as they urged their wives to keep their courage and the weeping of mothers and children in anguish for future partings was a frenzy of suffering and grief that was new in Sophia's experience. Sick at heart, she turned her head to glance at Ashley and saw something glint on his face as he raised his gloved hand to his eyes.

They did not know Caleb — with his head shaven to show he was a felon — was already at the court. His crime was so desperate in the eyes of the law that he had been held alone in a cell beneath the County Hall and was, as the Farrens rolled by, being led through the gaolers' room and up the stairs to the prisoner's box. He had not seen a window for more than a week.

Neither could they tell that the judges considered one act to be without equal in the ill-doings of the times — nor, because he was a witness and did not hear Mr Justice Alderson deliver his charge to the jury, was Ashley present to listen to his lordship say: "The last offence which it will be necessary for me to mention is that of arson, and it is the worst offence which the late events have brought before our notice. It is one of the deepest moral die, easy of perpetration and difficult of discovery and is very properly punishable with death."

Ashley was no stranger to a courtroom and, beyond his reluctance to take part in the judgement of his fellow-man, there was nothing intimidating to him in the apparatus of the law. Similarly, their robed and wigged lordships were not the figures of mighty and unavoidable terror to him that they were to those of lower rank. Nevertheless, Francis — watching from among the spectators and seeing Ashley's rigid face and frozen composure as he answered the prosecutor's questions with a clear and precise account of apprehending Caleb Young — thought that he was either a colder fish even than the Reverend Mingay or that there was something seriously amiss which he could not place. He noticed that after a first glance as he entered the witness-box, Ashley did not once look at the prisoner — and that he did not release the bible after his oath but retained it and kept his hand upon it throughout his evidence. He seemed disorientated as he stood down — which was odd after so straightforward a case — and Francis, a little disturbed, left his seat and went out into the entrance hall to meet him.

He discovered Ashley in the corridor, walking with his shoulder so close to the wall that his coat rubbed the panels and brought away the dust and flakes of old paint.

"Good God," said Francis. "You look as if someone's stepped over your grave."

With difficulty Ashley focused on his friend. "Sophia will help me," he said.

Francis, startled by both the comment and the familiarity, did not reply and Ashley went on, "But it isn't my grave. Or only in a way."

There was a press of people in the passageway and a messenger, hurrying towards an inner room, knocked against Francis and pushed him almost into Ashley's arms. Taking

Ashley by the sleeve he drew him the last yards into the hall where they stood in a corner behind the backs of a group of argumentative solicitors' clerks.

"Come," he said, "we know that death sentences are being handed about like sweetmeats but how many are being carried out? Your conscience may be tender because you don't agree with most of us how Swing should be treated and yet you have to witness against this rough — but he'll only be transported. And that's not so hard, eh?"

Ashley, whose mind was shifting like cargo in a heavy sea, gathered himself enough to nod. Beneath his feet the floor rose and fell. Father, he thought, I have left undone those things I ought to have done. I have not done as I ought. But Providence has sent me another — a woman who will save and punish me.

"You're shaking," said Francis. "Have you an ague, d'you think?"

Ashley laughed shortly. "Yes — I have a sickness," he said.

Chapter 14

It was difficult for anyone acting on behalf of Captain Swing not to incur the death penalty, for though — to the disgust of Mr Justice Alderson — breaking a threshing machine was not a capital crime, there was little else for which the same could be said. Under the Acts so thoughtfully provided for the safety of the kingdom any person destroying — or beginning to destroy — any building used in carrying on a business was guilty as a felon and should suffer death; any person who robbed another or was part of a mob who demanded and received money of a householder should suffer death and any person forming a member of a crowd in which one person did a violence to another was also guilty and should suffer death. There did not appear to be sufficient awareness of the penalties for protest on the part of the labourers for as Baron Vaughan complained, "There seems to be some impression that unless the attack on an individual is made with some deadly weapons, those concerned are not liable to capital punishment; but it should be made known to all persons that if the same injury were inflicted by a blow of a stone, all and every person forming part of a riotous assembly is equally guilty as whose hand may have thrown it, and all alike are liable to death." The punishment for firing a rick was, of course, death.

However, with the coming of the Special Commission the sword of Justice was, as Brougham told the House of Lords, unsheathed to smite, with a firm and vigorous hand, the rebel against the law — and the unhappy men thrust so precipitously into the county gaols were soon to learn that they had been in error to think that the hunger and despair which had driven them into protest would make the judges look with lenience on their crimes. On the contrary, the fact that after so few months of riot there were almost two thousand men and women waiting trial proved the seriousness of the affair to the judiciary and the need for a repression so thorough that there would be peace for years to come.

The first Special Commission opened in Winchester in December and the sentencing began. Two hundred and eighty-five people were charged and of these, one hundred and one were ordered to hang. Having put terror into the hearts of the guilty the judges relented and left only six to die. The rest of the condemned they sent to join their companions on the transport ships sailing to separation for ever from their families and homes. The Governor of Van Diemen's Land, waiting to welcome them, thought it a favourable comment on the system that many of the rioters died at once from diseases induced by despair and that of those who survived the journey a great many lived their wretched lives dejected and stupefied with grief and care.

In the overcrowded cells the prisoners heard of the punishments given out. They heard of three brothers sentenced to die for knocking at a kitchen door at midnight and receiving half-a-crown from a servant; they heard of William Sutton, a carter-boy of eighteen with one shilling and sixpence a week and his food and a good character from his master, sentenced to death for taking four pence; they heard of two youths of eighteen and twenty sentenced to hang for accepting three pence and a promise of beer at the Greyhound. They expected no mercy for themselves and got none. When a man whose wife had died giving birth, pleaded to be allowed to take his eight month old child to Australia with him for he had no family to care for it the judge responded that he should have remembered that before.

And so when Caleb was led out of the small, damp cell that confined him and up into the body of the court, he knew with part of his mind that his life was over but the strangeness of it — the disorientating nature of so sudden and drastic a change — made the situation seem unreal and drugged him with its phantasmagoria. The noise and light confused him. His hands which had been burnt on the night of the fire were suppurating; the low fever brought on by the infection in the wounds made him giddy and the people ranged about the room altered their colour and closeness as he looked at them. He could not see Hester and Hannah and was glad they were not there to see him fail. So many gentry and such terrible authority embodied in the judges gave him no confidence in the effectiveness of his innocence. He felt guilty; he had resented his master, he had planned to emigrate, he was leaving an undefended girl and child behind him — all this, surely, must add into a guilt.

The question of his guilt on the matter which concerned the court was soon decided. He had had no money to hire a counsel to speak for him and because he was charged with a felony he could not give sworn evidence in his own defence. No one had told him that he was allowed to cross-examine the witnesses and if they had the knowledge would not have turned him — after a lifetime of deference and manual labour — into a wit who could persuade an assembly of gentlemen to disbelieve the testimony of one of their own kind. The prosecution had intended to call both Ashley and Mingay to describe catching him in the act of arson but in the event it was felt that Ashley's account was clear enough and when Caleb was asked if he had anything to say to the jury he felt that his stumbling account of the true facts was spoken in another tongue.

The donning of the black cap began to bring him to a realization that there was a meaning to the day. Wild with all regret, he stood crippled and bound by his upbringing listening to Baron Vaughan enumerate his crimes and his only outward sign of emotion was the placing of his hands on the rim of the box so that the glistening marks of sweat and pus remained on the well-worn wood.

"We have come," said the judge, "to the painful conclusion that it is not consistent with public safety to spare your life." He nodded his head as he spoke and the front point of the cap shook like a bell-flower; Caleb watched it as he used to watch the oats trembling in the fields. "As a proper example and sacrifice to be made on the altar of the offended justice of your country," the judge went on, "you must prepare forthwith for that great change which now so suddenly awaits you." The cap nodded and shook. "All hope of mercy is excluded from you — and in a life so properly forfeited to the state as yours the heavy penalty of the law will be rigidly exacted."

There was a larch-chip fire burning in the gaolers' room and as Caleb sat on a bench in the antechamber the smoke which evaded the chimney wafted out and enveloped him in its sharp-sapped scent. From the floor above he could hear the scuffle and tramp of a group of prisoners being herded into the court for a combined trial. In the room beside him two gaolers were untangling chains and the rasp and clank of the iron filled the narrow space. He thought of Ashley and his acceptance of the sincerity of his witness did nothing to weaken the bitterness he felt. You gave me no chance, he thought, you believe your eyes in the dark before my word. If you were here, Sir Ashley, I could tell you that if you had been there in my place and worn a smock instead of a coat and a straw hat instead of a beaver you'd have been standing in the dock not sitting where you were. If you were here I'd put my hands round your sleek throat and choke you.

"I hear you're for the drop."

Caleb looked at the head gaoler — a heavy, middle-aged man with flakes of rust from the chains on his worsted jacket.

"Yes," he said.

"Never mind, lad, they'll bring it down and you'll see Van Dieman's Land. Give the judges a few days to keep you afeard."

The second man — shorter and thinner in a red wool waistcoat — came over carrying a pair of manacles and fetters he had taken from the wall.

"You won't cheer him that way," he said. "He'll be leaving a sweetheart behind. They all do."

Caleb stared down at the floor and tried not to think of Hester.

"Are you going to give us any trouble?" asked the first man.

Caleb shook his head.

"Then we'll lock your hands in front — it doesn't look as if you can hurt anyone with them."

He lifted the manacles out of his assistant's arms and fitted them round Caleb's wrists. The cold metal was smooth on the inside as if they had been worn many times before.

"Put out your feet."

Above them, as the assistant crouched down to fasten an iron about Caleb's leg, a sudden, muffled wailing broke out in the court. The gaolers paused and listened. There was a commotion, as though the spectators were rushing forward to reach the prisoners, and a turmoil of men shouting and the vivid, heartrending shrieking of women. The headman squatted beside his companion and began hurriedly forcing Caleb's ankle into the other iron. The thick links of the chain between them scraped across the floor.

"They'll all be down in a moment," he said.

The sound of the door at the entrance to the courtroom being opened warned them of the arrivals and the rush of air billowed the smoke back into the inner room. They could still hear the cries of the families above but their sorrow became a background for the uproar of departure from the dock. Eight prisoners and their warders came down the stairs and into the room. A youth was weeping and howling, lying back in his companions' arms and trailing his feet so that he was manhandled and dragged into the corner of the room. He lay on the floorboards, distraught and abandoned to his misery, rocking himself and kicking out at anyone who stood within reach. The men were still calling farewells to their wives and the warders were yelling for quiet, exchanging news of the sentences with the gaolers and milling among the new convicts with the fetters that would deliver them safely to the transport ships. The clamour of despair rebounded in the crowded room and filled Caleb's head until he thought his skull would break apart. He fell into line to be driven away, willing to suffer anything for solitude and peace.

Dusk was falling as the condemned men came out into the street but to Caleb the grey light and the cold of the January evening were fresh and startling after the twice-breathed air of the cells and the smoke-ridden confinement of the room where they had been chained. The cart that was to take them to sleep at the gaol was waiting just beyond the door and as they walked towards it, with the awkward gait of men in irons, it came to him and clutched at his heart that he would never again be free to walk unguarded nor sit, as the driver sat, on the box of a cart with the reins held in unbound hands. His eyes filled. There were lamps burning in the shopwindows and for an instant the unfamiliar business of a town and the turmoil of the women and children, struggling to touch their husbands, sons and fathers once more before they parted, merged in his mind and sight — but, as the warder pushed him up into the body of the cart, they separated and he turned round in the straw and searched for his sister and Hester.

The cart was shaking as the last of the convicts climbed in and the women mobbing about it clutched at the clothing of the men inside and held up children to be bidden farewell. He could see no one who was not weeping and the cries of "Don't go on so, old mother, 'tis only for life I'm sent", and "Don't you fret, girl, 'tis only fourteen years and maybe I'll live to see you all again" tore at him as the horses moved off and his chance to see Hester fled away.

"Caleb! Caleb!"

Her voice attracted him and he knelt up and leant out over the edge of the cart. The families were running now as the horses gained speed and amongst the desperate faces he saw both Hannah and Hester reaching out to take his hands. Hester was wearing Sophia's old shawl and it fell from her hair as she ran, exposing the suffering that wasted her. Side by side the two girls could not force their way to him through the crush but Hannah, falling behind, pushed Hester forward with all her strength and Hester's small, rough hands were in his. He strained over the frame of the cart, not thinking of the pain his wounds caused him, and the warder who rode with them looked at Hester's red eyes and turned away.

"Caleb," she said, the tears shining on her thin face, "Caleb, I shall never see you more."

The noise of the partings, the children screaming and the rattling of the cart overwhelmed them and even though they were so close he could hardly catch her words.

"My love," he said, "don't you be frightened. Wait for Calder. He'll send for you. A new life for you and the child in —" His throat contracted and he pressed her cold hands. She was stumbling now as she tried to keep up with the cart and her skirts were tangling with her legs and the people about her.

"I want you," she said. "I can't bear it without you."

The cart jolted over a cobble and her hands slipped out of his. She fought among the women to regain him but she had lost her place in the crowd.

"Wait for Calder," he said again. "Go to America", but there were too many people calling around her.

"I can't hear you," she cried — and as the cart drew away and its escort of constables rode to each side of her, she stood, alone and helpless, in the road and said again, "I can't hear you."

At six o'clock on a bleak evening in the following week the governor's carriage drove out of the prison gates. As it emerged from the entrance a young woman on horseback left her two companions and rode towards it. Mr Godfrey Weyden, wrapped in his overcoat and anticipating a goose for dinner, did not at first realize that she was approaching him but when he did he took an interest.

She was — so far as he could see in the dark — riding a pretty dun mare and had an elegant figure dressed in an expensive habit. On coming up to the carriage window she raised the veil she had worn as some slight protection against cold and gossip and he saw that she was extraordinarily lovely but with overly intelligent eyes which marred, in his opinion, the true beauty of the female face. He himself had a plain and practical wife and he loved her. He rapped on the glass behind the driver for the horses to stop and lowered the window.

"Mr Weyden?" asked the rider.

He bowed.

"You are the governor of the gaol?"

"I am, ma'am."

The girl gathered up her reins in her soft leather gloves.

"I am Miss Farren of Bredy Hall," she said. "I'd be most grateful if you would spare me a moment to talk of a prisoner you hold."

Mr Weyden inclined his head.

"I'm at your service," he told her.

"The prisoner's name is Caleb Young."

"Ah," the governor rested both hands on his silver-mounted stick. "Miss Farren," he said gravely, "if you're hoping for a reprieve it isn't me you should apply to. I have no power in the matter — and if you'd take my advice you'd go home and not waste your efforts on something which will not be granted."

Sophia did not reply and in the silence one of the carriage-horses snorted restlessly and scraped its hoof against the road. From the gaol there came a faint reverberation as if a heavy door had been slammed.

"The other two death sentences have been commuted," Mr Weyden went on, "but the judges are determined to have one hanging to deter other malcontents. Young is unmarried and that — with the serious nature of his crime — should help to discourage sentimentality at the execution. We want as little public disturbance as possible."

"It's on the subject of his marriage that I wish to speak to you," Sophia said. She hesitated. "It's a delicate matter. He —" She removed a hand from the reins and straightened a strand of her pony's mane. "My maid is with child by him," she said. "She's always been a respectable girl — as, indeed, we all thought Young a worthy man until he proved otherwise — and fell into this common situation under the promise of being wed. I believe that she and Young truly love one another. I also believe that recent events and the threat of staining her child with illegitimacy are unbalancing her mind. If you would allow a marriage ceremony to take place before the hanging it would be a generous act."

The governor looked down at his boots. His dislike of the conversation lay — not in the lady and her request — but in the answer he was forced to give.

"My dear madam," he said gently. "Your concern does you credit and I would oblige you if I could. The prisoner has already asked me this and I petitioned the magistrates on his behalf but they have refused him. They are my masters and I can do nothing against them."

Sophia stared into the darkened, cloud-swept sky. "May those responsible for this horror answer for it on the Day of Judgement," she said bitterly.

"Amen."

She turned back to the carriage window and Weyden saw that her eyes were wet with tears.

"I must beg one other thing of you," she said. "After the death would you release the body to me? I would pay the burial expenses. It distresses my maid to think of what might become of the remains."

"She need have no fear," Weyden said, "nor you compromise yourself in such a manner. Sir Ashley Claydon has already arranged that Young be delivered to him and laid in consecrated ground. He has an estate on the coast which includes a disused chapel and the body will be put to rest there."

Sophia lowered her veil to hide her feelings. "Thank you," she said and her voice was unsteady. She gathered her pony to leave but as she did so the governor called her back.

"Miss Farren," he told her. "My sympathy is entirely with you. I would let them marry if I were free."

"Oh," Sophia gave a short, broken laugh. "Oh, no doubt we would all act differently if we were free."

The night before the execution Caleb was taken — by his special request — to the governor and there, before a great oaken desk, he heard the final assertion that he would not be allowed to marry Hester. Mr Weyden had not been unkind but the news he had had to give was too cruel to allow even the greatest kindness to penetrate it.

As he was led back along the dim corridors Caleb walked heavily and painfully. He could not get used to his irons. The flesh of his hands was raw and shreds of skin hung from his palms. At intervals he shook convulsively with fever but mastered himself sufficiently to return with an apparent and false fearlessness. Even now he could not persuade himself that his experience was real.

All day he had heard the gallows being erected — the scrape of saws, the hammering of nails, the whistling of workmen, the thunk as they practised the fall of the trapdoor. He had been worried by what would become of his body after the hangman's work but the governor had assured him that a benefactor, who wished to remain unknown, had arranged to give him a decent — if not Christian — burial. He suspected Miss Farren and was relieved that no surgeon would have the use of him. Miss Farren would care for Hester until Calder sent for her — surely, surely, she would.

His cell was almost completely dark. Only a pin-point of light through the badly-closed Judas hole in the door added to the starlight from the small barred window. Because he had been away when the prisoners threw out their slops for the night he had not been able to empty his chamber pot and he stumbled against it in the gloom. His bowels had been loose and his bladder weak and the liquid diluted the excrement and ran out into pools on the ground. The stench was so great he could feel it in his mouth.

He thought how angry his brother would have been over the indignities man thrust on man and the knowledge that he would never again see Calder nor build the home in the New World wracked his suffering mind. Crouched like a beast in its dirt, he wept — not for anguish for himself — but for Hester and the injustice of the world, for his girl and the baby he would never hold. He beat his burnt hands against the flagstones and raged against leaving Hester but there was no one to hear him who cared and he became tired and could protest no more.

The night was long and the silence made more terrible by its breaking. In the cell next to his a prisoner intermittently droned a psalm. There was the inevitable, melancholy rattle of chains as men on bare boards changed their position. Around midnight there was a frenzied burst of screaming that died as abruptly as it had been born and, most horribly, there was a soft laugh that faded so gently into a sigh that listeners could not be sure that they had heard it at all.

The hanging was to be at eight and even if he had slept Caleb would have been woken early by the bizarre, excited sound of the crowd that gathered outside the gaol to see him die. When the governor, warders and chaplain came to bind his hands behind his back and walk him to the gallows Weyden took pity on his fouled clothes and they brought him a suit of pale fustian to go to his death respectably.

By order of the judges the convicts who had not yet gone to the hulks were to watch their fellow hang and, as he mounted to the scaffold on the upper part of the gaol, Caleb looked down into the yard. He saw many weeping and others burying their faces in their smocks unable to cast their eyes upwards. He slipped on a step and a warder gripped him by the arm to steady him.

As he appeared on the wall the noise of the crowd died away and, for a moment, as he looked out over the heads of the quiet people beneath, to the hills beyond the town and the painfully, piercingly dawning sky, he felt absorbed by the space and emptiness and was at peace. Then the hood was drawn down over his face and the grief of his innocence and the parting from those who needed him returned and wrenched his heart so that he breathed in sharply and lifted his head to stand firm.

Hester, watching from below with the child inside her, saw the white linen of the hood take the fine rain and cling to the gentle features so that the face she loved was a mask, blank and eyeless, before life had left it.

The chaplain concluded his prayers. The hangman slid the noose about the waiting head and adjusted the knot below the left ear. He took the lever and the trap-door fell and the people below saw the fettered body plunge and jerk and swing to the side. The gaoler beneath the scaffold stood ready to catch the legs and pull to break the neck but the work was done and the burden swung more slowly, twisting a little in the wind.

Nothing more was needed but the burial and for people to say in later years that the snow would never lie on the grave nor flowers bloom.

Chapter 15

The pale light of the setting moon entered the mullioned windows of Bredy Hall and threw a latticed pattern of shade on the uncovered floorboards. Where the shadows were interrupted by beds the grey bars were disjointed and angular and as the moon followed its course they glided from one position to another. Hester sat upright against the wall watching their progress.

She liked it here in the attic. There were sheets on the seven beds, chests for the maids' belongings and an old satin screen about the washstand in the corner. It seemed luxurious and safe. The girls did not even have to sleep in couples — although they often did for warmth in winter. Listening to their regular breathing she thought tenderly of their companionship. In the months she had been there she had grown to know their nocturnal habits — who snored and denied it, who woke in starts from nightmares, who had to be forcibly roused in the morning, who retold their dreams at breakfast — and the intimacy pleased her. She would miss their presence. They were her friends and a fortnight before two of them had proved their regard by accompanying her to Caleb's burial.

She understood the value of that gesture. The words for what she was had changed and with the loss of her respectability she would inevitably lose her place among people like these. She was no longer the cherished, handfast girl whose pregnancy promised well for a fecund marriage with a hard-working man — she was contemptible, a woman shamed by a hanged felon, and the child Caleb had planned for was a convict's bastard. The hut on the downs would now never be finished and soon she would have neither work, home nor means of supporting herself. She could see no way of improving her situation. Her grief was so great she had no wish to live but it was the thought of the malice which would be shown her child that was determining her to protect it from certain suffering.

Caleb had told her to wait for Calder but she had no confidence in his ability to help her or in a Fate which would allow her to be saved. For nineteen years she had lost everyone she loved. She thought of her own mother's death so long ago — a hard and hungry passing beneath a hedge and no one but a small girl to comfort her — and sometimes the figure in the ditch had Caleb's face and sometimes the body on the rope turned round to be her mother.

Something would prevent aid from Calder — that was the natural course amongst the poor. He would want to help her but find himself without the means to do so — just as these sleeping girls sympathized with her plight but could do no more than stand by a graveside with her.

There had been few mourners there. He had been brought to the overgrown ground of the disused chapel on a Wednesday and the local masters, fearing further unruly demonstrations, had not given leave to their servants to attend. Only Francis, who had stood in the graveyard himself with Sophia and the white-faced baronet who owned the land, had granted permission for two girls to support Hester and, at Five Warrens, Hammond did not have the heart to deny Hannah the right to follow her brother's body to its rest. There was no religious service but the girls had gathered bunches of catkins, gorse and dog mercury and Sophia left Ashley and walked through the long grass to lay the first snowdrops on the new earth. Under the heavy sky the white flowers and the brilliant yellow gorse were fluttered and valiant in the wind.

With this ending she had become completely alone in the world; she had nothing and no one but the responsibility that moved in her belly. All her life she had behaved with a quiet and sustained courage; she would not change that now.

Taking care to make no sound she put back her covers and slid down on to the floor. Standing in her shift in the moonlight she looked for the last time at her companions. She felt no anger at her situation — merely a lethargic acceptance of her decision and the circumstance that had led her to it. Picking up the bundle of clothes from the foot of the bed she walked softly to the door and passed out of the room, moving like a phantom — a white figure against white walls.

The door opened on to the landing at the head of the back stairs. She stole half-way down the first flight — keeping to the edge where the old wood did not creak — and stopped at the turn. In the shadows she dressed herself and wrapped her shawl around her. The house was silent. It was the time to sleep and its inhabitants were sleeping; Hester, isolated by her experience, was filled by the emptiness and sense of exclusion common to those not included in routine. She felt threatened; she had not yet left but already her intention had put her outside the proper numbers for the house.

Holding fast to the corners of her shawl she followed the stairs down into the darkness of the hall. Two dogs guarding the door started up but they knew her and slumped back into quietness on the flags. She let herself into the kitchen. No one was yet down but the fire in the range was never put out and a warm, red glow lit the portion of the room nearest to it and shone on the copper pans hung on the first rafter for this aesthetic purpose.

In a basket beside the fire Watch lifted his head and prepared to join her. She ran across the floor and, kneeling down, pressed him back into lying. Burying her face in his rough fur she thought of his master and Caleb.

She needed both hands to draw back the bolts on the door to the yard and, in the deserted room, the noise seemed fit to rouse the dead. The night-air, rushing in upon the fire-warmth, was like a draught of mountain water. Stepping out into it she closed the door behind her. There was a thin frost and on the stones where water had been spilled last evening there was a delicate sheen of ice like the coating on the fruit they had candied for Christmas. It cracked in a hundred filigree lines as she trod on it.

The path past the stables would lead her through the kitchen-garden to a gate in the wall. She took it with caution. The direction was wrong but it was safer than risking the raising of an alarm by passing the lodge-house. Once in the village street she walked back beyond the Hall and left the road for a footpath pointing to the sea.

There was so little light. The moon did not show the way clearly and as she entered the wood and began to struggle uphill, slithering on the fallen beech-leaves, the branches twining overhead enclosed her in darkness. Here the silence was interrupted by small patterings and rustlings and a sudden flapping of unseen wings but her own breathing and the stumblings of her feet absorbed her. Although the fear of being watched touched her she was not deflected by it but, like the Romans who had walked these hills before her, kept straight towards her destination.

She intended to reach the shore before dawn had broken and brought the fishermen from their beds. The air was still and the sound of the sea prowling the beach met her while she had miles still to walk. Over the fields and hedges, so beautifully burdened by frost, the waves shifted and swelled and brought before her thoughts of Caleb and the day she had gone with him to the wasteland to choose where he would build. Life was so terrible, so harsh and desolate; the only gift she had to offer her child was oblivion. Covering her face with her hands she halted and stood alone in the darkness waiting for the convulsion of grief to leave her.

A day of work and a night without sleep were telling on her. She was more tired than she could say. She sank down where she stood in the meadow, crushing the hard, white grass beneath her. Her skirts draggled in the earth and frost but she did not stir to move them. Her feet were hurting and she took off her shoes; shoes she had been so proud of last summer. A wind rose and came soughing through the hedge nearby, rattling and swaying the bare twigs.

A time she could not define passed and she raised herself to continue her journey. She did not put back her shoes but did not notice it. She cut her foot on a stone but did not feel it. She saw a lantern shining in a barn but did not know whether it was the sun nor recognize that she did not know.

Dawn was breaking as she reached the coast at Swyre and the first intimations of day were glimmering through a mackerel sky and gleaming on a leaden sea. A rolling swell was grating the pebbles to and fro but the breeze, which had blown up off the land, was stiffening and would drive any small vessel away from the shore. The threat water had always offered her now seemed welcoming and opened beckoning arms. It was here that Caleb had brought her fishing; she knew where the boats were kept.

Her feet, bare and bleeding, crunched the broken shells and slid on the tangled seaweed as she walked along the beach. The rank smell of brine was stong and cold. She came to a cluster of rowing boats upturned beyond high-water. At this month of her pregnancy it was hard to roll a boat over and drag it down to the foam but she felt the need to be great and succeeded. There were no oars or rowlocks but she took up a piece of driftwood to use as a paddle and when she had crossed the first waves the wind would be enough.

Before she set the craft in the sea she waited a moment watching the sky. The light was broadening and shone down in a silver path to the surf; all was movement and glitter and to each side streaks of a deep, heavy blue were intruding on the grey. With all her strength she pushed the boat into the waves and held it as it took the water and twisted back towards the beach. Gathering her skirts with one hand she held them against the old planking of the boat and waded out from the shore.

Twice as she tried to climb in the dinghy it turned about and took her to the beach but the third time the wind helped her and, as she sat shuddering on the seat, a gust lifted her and the boat and took it gently on to a current running to the west.

She drifted slowly in the growing dawn. Far to the east Portland became a shadow and then a rock. The small boat pitched and shook on the waves and the cold, salt water slapped full-face on its side, sending showers of spray on to her sodden skirts. The cliffs were without their true colour and rose like slate from the shore. In the early morning light the gulls began to cry. The water here was deep and restful; she lowered herself over the side.

Chapter 16 ·

Towards the beginning of March a letter arrived at Five
Warrens Farm. It was post-paid and was addressed in an
untutored hand to Caleb and Hannah Young. In it Calder told
his family to be of good heart for the future. He had arrived
safely in Philadelphia after a rough passage in time to see in the
new year in a New World. He had been supporting himself by
casual work and was about to go up-country in search of a
community but was first sending this letter by a returning
seaman to tell them all was well. When he was settled he would
write again but for the present they were not to be discouraged
— this was truly the land of promise; their faithful and
affectionate brother, Calder.

Hannah — rightly — did not believe that things had been as
easy for him as he described them in his letter but his confident
attitude and effortless concealment of difficulties gave her hope
and courage. Good humour and cheerfulness were as natural to
her as the colour of her eyes; they had survived the adversities of
her childhood and the prospect of poverty until death but they
were not derived from a state of mind too self-centred to be cast
down by the misery around her. Her feelings were soft and
tender and it was only her exquisite appreciation of the small
joys of life that perpetuated her gaiety. The absence of Caleb
and Hester had left her empty and dejected and the waste and
pointlessness of their going grieved her deep in her spirit. Their
loss had condensed her urge to care and cosset and the
reappearance of her brother — even in so distant a form — gave
solace to her loneliness and combined an object for her love and
the prospect of joining one strong enough to outface the world.

She had been frightened by the injustice that had left her
alone. However damning the circumstances of Caleb's arrest
she did not believe that it had been in him to harm his horses

and the comment made at his trial — that the men's attic was above the stables and therefore attempted murder could not be left out of consideration — was ludicrous to her. She did not know who the incendiary had been but was sure it was not Caleb. Their powerlessness terrified her; men like her brothers were so small when they stood alone against the prejudice and self-preservation of the gentry. Where would Calder have been if Miss Farren had not been prepared to risk her character for him? And where were her family now? Calder in exile, Caleb hanged, Hester and the unborn child lost without a grave to hide them. Hannah had been sewing baby-linen from an old tablecloth begged from her master; she had given it away unfinished.

Hammond was being kind to her. He had derived no satisfaction from Caleb's death and wished the deed undone. Although he approved the strict rule of law and did not hold with men of ideas a man's life in exchange for an animal's seemed too harsh a retribution and when that man was one he had seen mature, had had taught a craft, had watched at work and play, he could not find it in himself to persecute the sister left behind. For that reason when he heard that she had had a letter he went to her and advised her not to seek for new employ — as rumour had suggested she would — but to bide where she could be sure her brother could find her.

Ashley returned to his duties as a magistrate the day after he arrived back at Claydon Hall. He had no rest. There had been less arson in Norfolk than in the south but, nevertheless, the machine-breaking and rioting for wages had filled the gaols and every Justice was needed to work in court. Ashley, entering his home at midnight, had found a note awaiting him begging for his presence on the Bench at his first convenience, and it seemed to him that a charitable and lenient interpretation of the law would be the beginning of reparation to the son who, no doubt, now watched him in judgement.

He had been away from his estate since the middle of October and, though he had been in constant communication with his agent, was bound to be, to some extent, out of touch with local affairs. To rectify this and to have an old friend about him he had summoned Mason to take breakfast before he left for court.

It was only a few hundred yards from the Queen Anne house with the smooth lawn, that Mason inhabited at a nominal rent, to Claydon Hall and he arrived — in a double-breasted coat against the cold — in good time. Even on a damp and threatening February morning the breakfast room was a cheerful place. The large bay-window that looked out on the now barren pleasure-grounds caught all the light there was to catch and the white panelled walls, the white cloth on the circular table and the white background on the *toile de jouy* chintz curtains seemed to reflect that light and dash it on to the silver on the sideboard. The darting fire, the glistening china, the aroma of coffee and warm bread all added to a light-hearted and jaunty aspect which was in direct contrast to the master of it all.

Mason had been expecting signs of strain on Ashley's face but the extent of the ravages of guilt shocked him and a genuine affection and concern moved in his breast. If a cadaver had been wrapped in a morning-gown and invested with the ability to breakfast it would have appeared as Ashley did that morning. His skin was a dull yellowish-white and seemed to cling to the bone beneath, his eyes were larger in some way and more noticeable and Mason observed that, on this usually immaculate man, two of his nails had been bitten. There was a series of straight lines indented on the cloth beside his plate where he had been drawing with a fork. He did not look like a man who had had the sharp edge of an anxiety blunted by the acceptance of a proposal but, for the first time in their relationship, he had not confided his private affairs to his agent and because of this Mason did not feel free to ask what the outcome had been. He could not imagine an ordinary young woman turning down the opportunity to be Lady Claydon but Sophia had not seemed to be an ordinary woman. He disliked her. He detected in her an arrogance disguised as humble uncertainty which he would not be able to bend or cajole to his will. That she had a tender conscience and a self-dramatizing urge to put an idea of justice before a proper respect for her own station had, he felt, been demonstrated to him by her defence of Calder Young and this inconvenience would mean he could no longer adequately manipulate Ashley if she became mistress of the estate. She would have Ashley's ear in an intimacy he himself could not rival and Ashley's actions would progress in what husband and wife thought to be a straight and logical line but which to the more materialistic Mason would be a sequence of unpredictable tangents. He would lose his importance to Ashley and possibly — if his dislike was returned — his situation as agent.

To add a particular cruelty to this hypothetical loss it would occur just as his regard for his friend and master had grown to a new intensity. He admired beyond measure Ashley's ruthlessness in the matter of Caleb's trial. The cold-blooded witnessing against a son whilst knowing that the rope hung over him was something he doubted that he could have done himself. It was one thing to abandon children or aid a transportation but another to bring about a death. Had he been in Ashley's position he would have dealt beneath the counter to arrange passage to Australia; he envied Ashley his ability to take the more vicious and decisive answer. He knew of Ashley's obsession with honour but could see no connection between cause and effect in this case. The subtleties of concepts were not within his understanding; he could observe their results on others and manoeuvre the holders of beliefs into paths of his devising but could not enter into an empathy with any ideal except the idolization of power.

They greeted one another without any display of emotion at their reunion or comment on the past event which was in their minds and on their faces. Taking breakfast together was an old-established habit and this and their normal reserve enabled them to act as if they had nothing to disturb them. The exchange of everyday remarks, the unfolding of napkins and buttering of toast warmed Ashley. He was glad to see Mason again; there was relief in being with the one person who understood the reason for his malaise and yet, because of Sophia, there was now also something unsatisfactory about

Mason's connivance at the years of pretence and his lack of condemnation of the witness against Caleb. He began to wonder if he would not have been a better man if he had not had Mason's loyalty.

He thought, as he sat stirring a swirl of cream round and around in his coffee, of other loyalties. Remembering a morning that he had ridden to the sea with Francis and Sophia he shut his eyes momentarily against its fierceness and made his agent pause in his eating fearing an attack of illness in his friend. He had known nothing of Hester and her condition until that day. To him she had been only a thin-faced maid he had once seen walking to the gaol with Hannah. Sophia had not come to him to ask for help in bringing forward a marriage because he was not a magistrate with power over the prisoners — and those who had the power had not thought to mention such a trivial matter to a stranger. What interest could he have? And so he had learnt of the circumstances when he had gone to Bredy Hall on the morning before he was to leave for Norfolk and found the house in turmoil because she was not there.

A messenger had come from Swyre to say that a boat small enough to be handled by a girl had been found drifting by the mackerel-fishers towards Burton Beach. Draped over the seat had been a fine-quality shawl which one of the fishermen thought he recognized as having been worn at the hanging of Ploughman Young by the woman he should have wed. She had been an object of interest and he had looked at her for some time. He remembered seeing her when Young had taken her out with a line last summer and she had been a frail thing then.

The conclusion to be drawn was obvious. They had tied the boat to their own and put about to search for her body but had found nothing. On reaching home to report their suspicion they had met the hue and cry and returned their news. There could be little doubt of the truth of what they feared; a cowman who had sat up overnight with a sick heifer reported having seen a girl walking down in the direction of the shore and a pair of shoes thought to be hers had been found lying forgotten in a field. In the confusion the clothes had not been sent with the message and the Farrens were to ride out to identify them.

Ashley had gone with them. While the horses were being prepared and Sophia went to put on her habit Francis had told him the details of the case. Francis, himself, was saddened that a pretty, willing young thing like Hester, who should have served usefully in a household until she bred the next generation of labourers, should have been wasted in this way. He thought it fitting that if her body was found it should be laid beside Young's in Ashley's churchyard and to this Ashley agreed.

There was a poignancy in this quiet and unobtrusive loss of an unborn grandchild that was more piercing than the heavy drama of its father's going. The mother was spoken of as a gentle and delicate creature and the knowledge that she was not a farm-slattern but a girl — like his own wife — who had trusted a man so much worse than herself, cut him like a blade of grass across the skin. He had stood alone on the grey beach, listening to the retreating roar of the tide as it withdrew from this desolate coast, waiting for the Farrens to finish their sombre business, and wondered in what cold deep the deserted girl rolled now.

The child she had taken with her into that unhallowed death was more than lost family to him. It was the absence of the old ways in which he believed. Hester had found herself without her natural protector and had not faith enough in the masters of her world to choose to live. Here was a representative of the sick, the weak and the helpless, who had given an undeniable retort to the question of whether paternalism survived. He knew that Sophia planned to approach Hannah and offer her help if ever it were needed but would that guardianship be met with the same lack of comprehension? Or did these girls understand modern ways better than he? And was all that he strove to preserve dust in his hands?

"At least," said Mason, helping himself to half a kipper which had been making its presence known "the trials are almost over and you can soon have some peace. It's a pity the Special Commission didn't sit in Norwich — then you needn't have had any part of it."

"Oh," Ashley replied, leaning back in his chair. "I'd rather be on the Bench. I know the sentencing hasn't been harsh here but it's safer to do something yourself than leave it to others."

To Mason this seemed to have an uncomfortable relevance to his fear of losing his position but he mentally reprimanded himself for being over-sensitive.

"It's true," he said, "that the rioting amongst the labourers and weavers is dying out but they may be just biding their time and need a severe example. It hasn't only been ricks that have been damaged — there were threats made to pull down the workhouse at Smallburgh and the one at Forncett was partly demolished. Barely a step from revolution."

The kitchen cat, which was not allowed in Ashley's rooms, pushed open the door and stalked towards the fire. It curled on the rug and was instantly asleep. Mason began to push his chair back but Ashley gestured for him to leave it.

"Perhaps we need a revolution to take us back to where we were," he said. "There was once a time when those of us who were able took care of the poor."

A flicker of old feelings rose in Mason. Fairy-tales, he thought, he believes in fairy-tales — perhaps he's preparing for a full nursery. He followed Ashley's gaze out of the window.

"There are buds on the willows in the park," he said.

Ashley turned back and smiled. "I can always rely on you to notice the small things of the estate," he said.

Chapter 17

"Sophia, take care. Don't — oh, let me send for the steps to be brought."

"No, there's no need. I can just — ah! Yes, I have them. I thought they were here."

Sophia turned carefully on the stool, holding out a flat wooden box. Standing as she was on the round seat with her starched underskirts pressing her gown into a diameter wider than the whole stool she appeared to be hovering in mid-air. The three pine legs wobbled on the uneven flags and she steadied herself on the shelves as she climbed down. She eased the lid off the box and Mrs Dene, who had been waiting to catch her if she fell while reaching to the back of the top shelf, looked with interest at the treasure.

Inside the box on a lining of pleated silk that had once been yellow was a row of five spoons with broad bowls and handles of white enamel dotted with small green stars.

"My mother brought them with her when she married," said Sophia. "They'd been her mother's — given to her at her wedding."

"How pretty they are," Mrs Dene took one from its nest and weighed it in her hand. "You can't imagine anyone making such things now."

"I thought I'd have one brought to me in the evenings with my sleeping-draught," said Sophia. A tendril of hair fell down over her eyes and, being occupied in holding the box and lid, she shook her head to dislodge it.

"Yes, indeed." Mrs Dene put the spoon back into its place and sank down on to the chair behind her. "Oh," she said, "I'm tired — a few minutes rest."

They were engaged in checking the household inventory before the spring-clean and were in one of the smaller pantries which opened from the still-room. Both wore linen-wrappers and Mrs Dene carried the red leather inventory book and pencil which she now pushed into her large front pocket. "Read me Harriet's letter again," she said.

Sophia placed the spoons beside a bowl of brown eggs and sat down on the stool. She searched inside her wrapper for the small silk bag tied to her waist and drew out a paper thickly covered by erratic blue writing. "'My dearest Sophie,'" she began "'What do you think? I have such news! Dear Henry — I may call him that now — has proposed. We are to be married in the autumn. Papa and mamma are delighted. He will be your cousin and I hope you will love him as much as I — or not so much but enough as anyone would and must. Only think he followed us to Bath to make his declaration and has spoken and is gone back in three days! His estate is quiet now that the rogues have been tried. You —'" Sophia paused and held the letter closer to decipher a word.

"Her writing is atrocious," said Mrs Dene, looking over to it, "and the lines so crossed one above another that they can hardly be read. She doesn't change."

"Oh," said Sophia, letting her hands drop to her lap, "but isn't it good for someone near us to be happy for once. This winter has been so long." She turned a little on the stool to gaze at the window. The old damask rose whose dry stems scraped at the glass was not yet in leaf and the only sign of life was from the ivy. "I'd like to see things green again," she said with a sigh.

That she was distressed was plain in the dark grooves beneath her eyes. She did not know what to do with herself and it was to curb her restlessness and drain herself of a strange, aching energy that she had undertaken to ascertain the contents of the house. There was also in her a compulsion to be sure that all was where it should be that had arisen since the discovery of Hester's disappearance. She was bitterly grieved by the girl's suicide and that no body had been found and thus no burial could be held and no line drawn conclusively beneath a life made the sorrow worse. She had laid flowers on Caleb's grave for both him and Hester but such ritual gestures could not comfort her. The horror of the past months confused and distracted her as if she were trapped amidst the beating of great wings and the joyful news of her cousin was light and shelter to her darkened mind.

Of her own marriage plans she was not clear. She still did not know what her position was with Ashley nor what she wanted it to be. She did not love him but her admiration of him — and of the principles of honour and justice which he had upheld despite the suffering they cost him — had grown substantially during the course of his stay in Dorset. That she had always been strongly drawn towards him by some unfathomable familiarity to something that always escaped her memory was plain in her remembrance of their meetings. He was so sure of what was right and yet so sensitive; she was so lost and ineffectual. She had been quite unable to strengthen Hannah whose care had been entrusted to her by Calder Young; she was deeply troubled by the despair in the countryside that had followed the crushing of Swing, by the callousness of the landowners and by her own isolation and powerlessness — if she was united to Ashley she would have a rock on which to lean and an ally in her struggle to make some small change for the better in the world. Yet she did not love him and through all her inward debates there ran the strange, subterranean feeling that she loved someone else but could not say who. It was a thought of the same elusive quality as the uncanny recognition of something in Ashley and she dismissed both as romantic delusion.

At dinner that afternoon Sophia put a suggestion to Francis. It was five o'clock and, because there had been a sudden gleam of sunlight after a heavy shower, the curtains had not been drawn. Dusk was now almost complete but during the soup there had still been reason enough to look out at the water-drops shining on the branches of the elms. It was the first time in the year that they had sat down to dine by daylight and as she had gazed absently through the runnels on the rain-washed glass Sophia had noticed the first sturdy nettle pushing up through the gravel on the path. Things were again growing and putting out shoots. The eternal resurrection of the natural world which can seem so heartless to the bereaved was beginning the burgeoning that would smother the decay of the year before. Sophia, who had gained no consolation for the recent deaths from received religion, was pleased by the mindless repetition of the seasons and thought of Harriet.

"Grandfather," she said as the bowls were cleared away and a maid, shielding a burning taper in her hands, began to light the candles, "has Mrs Dene told you of Harriet's news?"

Francis dabbed at his chin with a napkin. "Yes," he said, "and a good thing it is for her father. From what I hear of the young man he's no scholar but his land is very respectable and, of course, can be increased to a considerable degree when he inherits the Garnam money. Or if Rowe prefers to keep trade in the family no doubt Mr Thompson will be willing to have one of the younger sons brought up to banking. Times change and there isn't the stigma there was. Rowe's no great age and can afford to wait. It's a pity he had no son of his own."

The curtains rattled as the maid drew the old but rich red moreen across the darkening windows. The two silver, three-armed candelabra on the table and the four single candles in brackets on the panelled walls had all been lit and their pale flames shook in the air currents from the fire and the movement of the curtains. Once again they were enclosed by the intimacy of night and winter.

"I was thinking," said Sophia, leaning back slightly to allow shoulder of mutton to be put on her plate, "that perhaps I might go to Bath and travel back to London with the family. We'd be bound to be invited to the wedding and I could just as well take the opportunity to go early. I'm sure Harriet would like my help and I know I'm in need of a different scene."

She looked down at a tureen of boiled potatoes and Mrs Dene, who had been adjusting a dish of macaroni placed too near the edge of the table, glanced at Francis. An almost imperceptible gesture of interrogation and assent passed between them. Sophia's interest in the details of a wedding and the request to visit a place she would normally avoid but which would give her an increased likelihood of encountering Ashley seemed to them both an excellent portent for the future.

"Yes," Francis said, "since they're so near and you've never travelled overland before I don't see why you shouldn't join them. Two birds with one stone."

Such a ready agreement surprised Sophia. She was aware that her grandfather had little sympathy for the anguish the past months had caused her; he would be unlikely to feel that her vagaries deserved to be pandered to and though he had never been niggardly the expense incurred on such a journey was not to be thought of lightly. She had expected to have to persuade him into permission and this abrupt surrender cut the ground from her feet. Perhaps he mistook her need for change for a robust indifference to the suffering around her.

"If you would write to Uncle Rowe," she said, "I could ride over with Joshua. We could arrive in two or three days."

Francis put down his knife and reached for his claret. "You'll do no such thing," he said. "You'll remember who you are and what's fitting for your station — a thing you've been far too inclined to forget recently. You and Mrs Dene will take the landau with Cates to escort you and two men on the box. The country may appear to have quietened but you can never be sure. In fact," he took a mouthful of wine and replaced the glass, "I can spare a week to go as far as Bath. I haven't seen them for two years. We'll take post-horses from Dorchester on and sleep one night on the road."

The letter was dispatched that evening and Rowe Garnam, who was sparing a month from business to take the waters, learning that his family was about to descend upon him immediately wrote a cordial invitation that justified his niece's sanguine hopes of his hospitality. It was the first holiday he had allowed himself for more than five years and he thought ruefully as he strolled to the Pump Rooms with his wife on his arm, that what with daughters, suitors, rumours of renewed riot and country cousins it was proving far from quiet.

None of his wry amusement at the turbulent nature of his days of rest was evident in his reply and no sooner was it received than orders to pack for an indefinite visit were given at Bredy Hall. Mrs Dene was to accompany Sophia to London and had private instructions from Francis to consult with his daughter and between them do all that they could to encourage Sophia to think of herself as Lady Claydon. If it could become a settled thing in her mind that she was bound to Ashley she would feel that she had given her word and the match would be complete.

They left for Bath early one morning at the beginning of March. It was a wild, grey, blustery day that set the horses fidgeting and shaking their heads in their traces. The high elms behind the house thrashed branches on which the first leaves were in bud. To Sophia, seated alone with her back to the way they would take, there seemed a faint disloyalty in relinquishing her home not for the adventure of Pennsylvania but for a search for succour amongst the fripperies of town. She felt that somehow she was capitulating to the way of life that was expected of her.

She rearranged her rug to cover her fur-lined boots and tried to shake off her foolish notions. She was wearied by sadness and confusion; Harriet's frivolity would make her see things in perspective once more — she was convinced of that. Yet, as the carriage pulled out of the courtyard and she leant to look out on the familiar façade of the house, she felt that it was for the last time and that she would not return.

Chapter 18

Through the half-open connecting door between his bedroom and dressing room Mason could hear the sound of water being poured into his bath. It was seven o'clock on a breezy morning in late March and, now that the maid had drawn back the curtains, he could lie against the many pillows at his back and around his leg and watch the branches of the ash in his garden being flung repeatedly towards the church. There had been a great twittering amongst the birds at dawn but the wind had risen in the past twenty minutes and nothing could be heard of them except the occasional squawk of a rook as it was swept up by an unexpected gust.

He had been awake for some hours but, being in need of warm water to help ease his tormented body back into the semblance of health, had lain where he was, thinking. For the first time he was afraid that his influence with his employer was weakening. There was a difference in Ashley since his return from Dorset. Whether love was strengthening him or the horror of the trial had made him reckless of the character he had built so carefully over the years and given him the desire to bring retribution down upon his head Mason could not decide but there had been a change which was noticeable in a hundred small ways. He no longer seemed to have the need of a rigid outer skeleton of convention; he was less detached in his manner; instead of responding coolly to the blood-thirst of the more savage of his peers on questions of riot and disorder he invited argument; as Mason had seen he allowed the kitchen cat the freedom of the house and yet he was more violently against the weavers' cooperative and all combinations of labourers than he had been before and he looked as though death were waiting for him. It appeared to be a subtle alteration of personality rather than opinion; as if he were keeping the same course but ran under a different sail.

For the first time Mason found it politic to be quiet about the divergence in their views on the world. Previously he had felt able to talk openly of his approval of a harsher regime than Ashley thought necessary — trusting in his friend's courteous reserve and need of his particular qualities of loyalty and acumen to prevent a rift — but now he began to feel insecure. He was being supplanted; Ashley no longer leant on his worldly wisdom to the same degree and there was a loneliness in it for him which fostered a spite against Ashley and all that was Ashley's that made him take pleasure in petty tyrannies in his dealings with the tenants and workers of the estate — and the knowledge that those he hurt believed him to act entirely on the orders of his master made such cruelties sweeter.

He was not, however, a free agent. Ashley's new tortured independence was leading him to give direct instructions on the management of his lands as he had rarely done before. He had informed Mason that all threshing machines on the Claydon farms were to be destroyed and had taken an interest in seeing that it was done — and here was another example of the change in him. Did this interest mean that he no longer trusted his agent to carry out an order that clashed with Mason's own favoured remedies for unrest?

I'm not happy, thought Mason as he listened to the preparations in the dressing room, about the effectiveness of the punishment of Swing. We will have revolution yet. For all the severity of the Special Commission the spirit of rebellion was not quelled. Though the majority of the labourers — men and women who were aware every day of the absence of those with whom they had grown up, who had seen their neighbours marched away in chains — were exhausted and demoralized there was a minority who had not been quashed. Isolated fires still burned in the night and only this month in Wiltshire, where the law had done its worst, a mob of labourers who had struck work had had to be dispersed by the yeomanry. Nor was this the only outrage; there was a desire for revenge abroad that had not been present in the riots — a bitter, black desperation that manifested itself in the secretive maiming of cattle and in violent acts directed at members of the gentry believed to have been responsible for the defeat of Swing.

If this mood had been general perhaps it would have been easier to crush. Widespread hanging and transportation had broken the will to resist their earthly fate in most of the labouring population — surely perseverance in such sentencing would complete the restoration of peace? But there had been another reaction amongst the poor. A brand was burning in the religion of dissent. The emotional, uneducated rabble, thwarted, threatened and downtrodden in matters of the world, were casting themselves without inhibition into the waters fished by the travelling preachers. Reports came that "the glory" became visible to a convert's eyes. "By some" claimed a follower, "it was seen as a light, by others as fire falling among the people." It was a rejection of tradition and the example of the gentry but religious mania is not a crime and, however undermining to the status quo ranting may be, a man who obeys his master meekly cannot be hanged for privately clamouring to be washed in the Blood of the Lamb.

To Mason the startling imagery of these sects was a simple transference of the threats of the Swing letters to a temporarily more mystical setting, but to his master it was an expression of the cowed nature of labouring men who had been hurt too deeply.

In Ashley's view the unnatural fervour of the conversions was a sign of the longing of the chastised to return to the duties and loyalties they felt were closed to them by the malice of their betters. Petitions for mercy to be shown the convicted were being drawn up by those of the gentry who believed, like Ashley, that the poor were contrite and would return to their old obedience if the old love were offered them. Mason, himself, despised such weakness and romancing but could not reveal the extent of his scorn to Ashley.

A double knock on the connecting-door and the sound of the maid removing the last water-can from the room heralded the most agonizing moment of Mason's day. The usual urge to stay where he was came into his mind and was, as usual, rejected. Carefully putting back the covers, he eased the pillow from

171

beneath his left leg and dropped it to the floor. With slow determination and closed eyes he turned in the bed and sat upright as he lowered both feet to the carpet. His night-shirt had ridden up and the bulbous, misshapen ravages of arthritis were revealed. A laudanum-sweet sickliness swam round him and he glanced with a mixture of hatred and desire at the bottle waiting on his cabinet.

In a movement of ferocious self-discipline he stood up and began to walk. The pain was so great this morning that he let out a soft, suppressed hiss with every step. Ten paces to the chest of drawers — turn — six paces to the wall — turn — eight paces to the window seat. He paused at the window, holding on to the shutter with white knuckles. Beneath the boisterous ash a drift of daffodils was streaming in the wind. There were violets, too delicate to be visible from this room clustered under the budding beech-hedge. Yesterday he had had a clump of celandine dug from the edge of the lawn and placed in a pot on his library desk. All was rebirth and regeneration and he walked in pain in another man's house.

Moving was breaking down the stiffness in his joints and he left the window and gained the dressing room without having to rest. Bath-sheets were spread over the floor and as he sat on a cushioned stool at the side of the tub he noticed that they were already damp with steam. Another knock stopped him as he was lifting his foot to the water. A servant came in holding a small tray.

"Sir," he said, "a letter came from the big house very late last night and the messenger said it would wait till day." Mason took the note and nodded at a large jug of cold water as he undid the seal. The paper was dated half past ten of the evening before. He watched the servant pour half the contents of the jug into the bath and then read the lines.

"My dear Mason," it said, "Would you be in the estate-room at nine this coming morning? I am hardly returned but I must leave again. The petition for mercy to be shown the Norfolk convicts has been completed and it is agreed that Paterson and I wait on Lord Melbourne with it at the earliest opportunity as representatives for the county. We depart for London tomorrow noon and, naturally, I must speak with you first. AC" He acts independently, thought Mason, but naturally he must speak with me. Naturally. He noticed the servant still standing attentively in the room and put the note back on the tray. "No answer," he said, "except my compliments."

"Mamma," said Harriet, "I'm worried about Sophie."

They were in Harriet's opulent bedroom folding yard upon yard of shimmering, filmy blue silk that was to form part of her trousseau.

"Oh," said Mrs Garnam. "Why?" She stopped the hand to hand passage of the cloth and let her arms drop slightly, pulling the material a fraction so that it slid from the bed and lay in soft, tumbled layers on the floor. Mrs Garnam looked at the silken pile philosophically and returned her attention to her daughter. They were free to discuss Sophia without an ear to the door as the subject of Harriet's worries had chosen to enjoy the sudden, delightful spring sunshine by driving out on errands for her cousin.

Harriet sat on the bed where the material had been and stirred the tangled silk with the point of a satin slipper.

"It was last night," she said. "We were in her room together for a long time after we were undressed. We were talking about Henry. Then I came back here but I'd left my brush behind and I went back. It was only a few minutes later but I thought she might be asleep and I just opened the door without knocking — I was very quiet. And Sophie wasn't in bed, Mamma, she was sitting by the fire — and she was crying."

Mrs Garnam looked interested. "Crying," she said thoughtfully.

"Yes, I went in and asked her what the matter was. All she said was that the smoke was in her eyes. But she was crying — and we'd been so happy all evening and busy the whole day with my preparations. There's no sense to it. Is she jealous, do you think?"

Mrs Garnam stared sightlessly out of the window where the long-missed scene of white clouds and blue sky was plain above the roof-tops.

"Your grandfather told me that she'd been upset by the riots," she remarked.

"Oh," Harriet said, dismissively, "even Sophie wouldn't let a few paupers make her ill."

"No," Mrs Garnam gathered a few folds of the silk in her fingers, "I don't think it's that — or not entirely. And she does look ill. I —" Harriet's maid coming into the room interrupted them.

"Oh, Susan," they both said.

"Ma'am," said the girl, "this card was just left."

"I didn't hear the bell," said Mrs Garnam.

"No, ma'am. Jane was in the hall and opened the door before the gentleman could ring. You said you were out to callers this morning."

Mrs Garnam took the card. "I did, didn't I? I wonder who — oh!" She glanced at Harriet and smiled. "Sir Ashley is in town. Did he know Sophia was here, d'you suppose?"

Harriet slipped off the bed and looked at his name engraved on the card. "I don't know," she said, "but, for sure, we'll see a change in Sophie now."

"For better," said her mother, "or worse."

Chapter 19

Even in the residential streets the noise — at this time of late morning — of hawkers, errand-boys, passers-by, carriages and delivery carts was such that the sound of Sophia's own horses was lost in the general clatter. She had been out for almost two hours collecting packages for Harriet and placing orders for the various fripperies that her cousin felt essential for a prosperous marriage. Two dozen double-hemmed cambric handkerchiefs lay in their box on the seat opposite her accompanied by a dozen evening gloves, three velvet reticules with tortoiseshell clasps, two dozen openwork stockings and a mother-of-pearl fan — none of which seemed to Sophia to have the slightest importance on the matter of a wedding.

She was herself in band-box condition. Harriet, aghast that she could intend to carry her autumn clothes over into spring, had taken her by the arm and marched her into the Garnams' dressmakers directly they had arrived in London and though Sophia had preserved a plain and simple style she had not been able to prevent Harriet putting her in possession of another new wardrobe. Nor at that time had she wished to do so. She had wanted to be submerged in trivial pleasures and to fill her mind with the nonsense of a fashionable young woman; concerning herself with the real griefs and injustices of the world was painful and fruitless and she longed to learn to giggle behind her fan but the hope of driving the past from her thoughts by the adoption of a way of life that was alien to her nature had faded like a trodden flower and she rode in her open landau in quiet, contained desperation.

I will endure, she thought. I must endure. There will be a call for me at some time for something — I cannot have been put on earth without purpose. They also serve who only stand and wait. God, is my whole life to be only waiting? These silly, foolish toys I've bought for Harriet; this unnecessary new gown — how much bread would they have bought? I wear lavender — a mourning colour. Can I do no more? I dream at night of a girl washed in the turn of the sea; I hear the gulls and a child crying. Do the dead dream if they lie unburied? I cannot stay here and I cannot go home. I should take this silk in both my hands and rip it from me as if it were unclean.

They were in the square next to her own now and the horses had slowed to a walk behind a tangle of tradesmen's vans. There was a railed garden in the centre of the road and in this morning of warm April sunlight the bright, young leaves on the trees and the soft grass between the paths looked tranquil and beckoning. A birdseller was pushing his barrow of caged finches behind her and a barefoot girl with a tray of violets was singing her wares at the garden-gate. For a moment the sweet scent of the flowers and the song of the birds conquered the noise and smell of the city and she was calmed by their illusion of peace.

"Miss Farren," said a voice by her side.

She was startled by the greeting and the sudden movement she made in looking for its giver sent her veil swaying so that she had to smooth it to clear her view.

I meet her again, thought Ashley, in London in a carriage, still and serene. How beautiful she is and how much more so because there is pain in her eyes. She has felt for me and for the family I killed. Can she love me? I need her.

"Sir Ashley," said Sophia. "How strange! What do you here? Oh, I'm glad to see you." Impulsively she put out her hand and he took it and held it in both of his. Like two exhausted swimmers flung upon a rock in the midst of a torrent they clung to the familiarity which events had made grow between them. The driver glanced suspiciously behind him but the footman recognized Ashley as a gentleman used to calling on the house and nodded for the horses to be stopped.

Ashley still held her hand and an anticipation began to move in her body so that she was conscious of all that touched her and the texture of her clothing was rough against her skin. She could feel the blood coming to her face and her heart

176

quickening. This is how it is, she thought, the moment which decides a life — a woman's life. This man with the white, ravaged face who makes my hand tremble will ask me a question which will name my future. I see it in him. He has a voice which draws me. I want to be near him. If I say yes I go to a world from which I cannot return. All will change. What more perfect emigration? Let go — let go of my hand.

"This garden," said Ashley, "does it belong to your Square?"

"No," her voice caught and she paused to control it, "but my aunt is friendly with its owners. We walk there."

Ashley released her hand and unfastened the door of the carriage. "Go back to the house," he told the driver, "and tell Mrs Garnam that Sir Ashley Claydon will bring her niece home."

I am agreeing, thought Sophia as she stepped down in a rustle of silk, by this action I agree before I am asked. What seemed so foreign and unthinkable in October is achieved now without discussion or reason. Is this how all unions are decided? Do I do right?

Ashley offered her his arm and she took it, her glove sliding over the fine cloth of his coat. The long, loose folds of her French shawl brushed his leg as they walked and dipped to the ground behind. At the gate he paused and bought violets which she held in her free hand like a tender, palpitating bird.

Inside the garden the air was warm and sultry. The gravel, newly-raked from its winter disuse, shifted beneath their feet. Upright, understated and elegant, lithe and wealthy, they walked together under the limes. At the raised pool in the centre a nurse-maid helped her charges sail a wooden boat; on a bench near them a governess sat reading to three girls who were watching the yacht. Ashley guided Sophia past this crowded place and on to a path sheltered by laurels.

Her presence was like balm to him. He had not known she was here until the Garnams' servant had told him at their door and the gift of her was, to his tired and haunted mind, a token of divine mercy and approval. Her acquiescence was surety for his second chance to be an honourable man and the intoxicating promise of this grace gave his manner a bold assurance that was more positive than his normal stance. He knew her to be direct and unflirtatious; she would not have come with him alone to this place to play with his feelings. Here in this city which was natural to neither of them she would agree to be his wife and possessing her would be a reclamation of his youth. The children of her body would be untainted by their father's guilt and the family name he had sinned to preserve would go untarnished through the generations. Above the laurels the trees hung leaves already smeared with soot and above them the blue sky shone like Lakeland waters. They were almost at the railings that enclosed the garden and would have to turn back.

He wheeled slowly about, still holding her arm. After a few steps she broke their silence.

"Why are you here?" she asked. "We thought you were at your home."

My home, he thought, is nowhere without you; you are my fulfilment and my love.

"I came with a fellow magistrate," he said, "to petition for mercy for those condemned in Norfolk. We twice waited on Melbourne and persuaded him — much against his will — to reduce one death penalty to transportation for life. It was as much as we could expect from such as he," he paused and looked again at the sky, "but it was something — there's been enough hanging."

How ineffectual I am alone, she thought, I could not even beg a marriage for Caleb Young. I can do nothing as Miss Farren. Surely it is meant that I should be the wife of such a man whatever my inclination?

"I think there's a different feeling in the air," Ashley went on, "a weariness of violence and this modern cruelty. It's held by a minority but at least it's felt by some. There's a rumour that Cobbett will be tried for encouraging sedition as he was back in 'ten. The government expects to set an example to discontents by crushing him as they did before but I think his accusers will find their noses bloodied. And what then? Perhaps a return to the allowing of independence to the countryman." He stopped suddenly and faced her. She was still carrying the violets in her free hand and as he dropped her arm she stroked them convulsively, crushing the outer petals and wetting her gloves with their dew. In the sunlight her veil threw a delicate tracery of net and flowers on to her pale skin. Now, she thought, it is now.

"Your grandfather will have spoken to you on a matter of the gravest importance to me," he said. His face was serious and almost hungry.

"Yes," she said, so quietly that it was hardly more than the expiry of a breath.

He reached forward and took her hand. Again she felt the distracting sense of recognition that afflicted her in his company but this time — strangely — it was almost a physical sensation and the memory of another hand and the bidding farewell of Calder Young came, uncalled and unconnected, into her mind. Ashley covered her fingers with his and, taking it to his face, kissed the glove that was damp with the trace of violets and held the unresisting hand to his cheek. He gazed at her with a look of such intensity and suffering that he was forced to close his eyes to protect her from his need.

"I'm not worthy of you," he told her. "If you knew what I am — but, God help me, I can't bear to be without you."

Sophia, bound with the tension of the moment she knew to be already decided, shook in his grasp. If I pledge myself to him and the generations that will come through us, she thought, I become a female name on the roll of his family's history. I give myself up to him completely and for ever. If it is a mistake it is for always. Yet if I am unhappy — what of it? Life cannot harm me in the ways it can harm the Hester Allens of the world. My misery would be sugared and trivial. The thought relaxed her and Ashley, feeling the stiffness leave her, knew that he had won and opened his eyes.

"Will you?" he asked.

"Yes," she said again — and again it was as soft as a sigh.

He put her hand gently back on to the violets and, raising both of his, he lifted the veil from her face so that she was revealed and naked before him. His face and the inch of throat above his cravat were very close now. What was it that made a man's smell so different from a woman's? One man's from another's? There was the scent of warm woollen cloth and starched linen, the aroma of eau de bergamot and something sharper and more intimate. It was arousing; she liked it.

It was only as he retook her arm and began to walk her out of the garden that she realized that there had been no talk of love — but she thought as she matched her pace to his that she had preferred it that way.

Francis, who was never one to let his fields lie fallow, received the news of the intended marriage before his own letter to Claydon Hall informing Ashley of Sophia's whereabouts could be passed on to its recipient. In his own manner he was jubilant and instantly organized his affairs by presenting Mrs Dene with the title of Upper Housekeeper — a sinecure which would keep her with him without giving the evil-minded sufficient hold to insult her to her face — and preparing to leave for London.

His approval of his future grandson was increased by the decision with which Ashley was acting now that Sophia had brought herself to the point. The ceremony was to take place in town as the most convenient station between their two estates, on the earliest day which would allow Francis and his party to arrive and the marriage settlement to be agreed. Sophia would carry with her £30,000 and the promise of the inheritance of Francis' land and wealth. In return her grandfather and uncle would extract for her a jointure of 10% of her fortune, provision for any child who would not be Ashley's principal heir and sufficient pin money to cover her private expenses without allowing her enough to finance any radical scheme which might appeal to her.

There was one fancy in which Francis was prepared to indulge her. Sophia had written to him mentioning that Ashley had instructed her to hire a personal maid and she wished her grandfather to approach Hannah Young of Five Warrens with the offer of the post. She was aware that the girl had no experience but was prepared to train her and was particularly eager to have her maid from her home county; if Hannah was reluctant because of the part Ashley had played in one brother's trial or for fear of losing touch with the other brother she was to be pressed until she agreed. She did not mention the promise she had given to Calder to care for his sister and Francis, seeing in this ready acceptance of a lady's maid and imperiousness of tone a new value of her own station, dispatched himself and Mrs Dene to Five Warrens and combined his authority and her persuasions to achieve Sophia's wish. The three travellers sailed for London before the fortnight was out.

In town the preparations were going forward. Harriet was, initially, inclined to be put out that her glory was to be stolen but when she discovered that Sophia intended to continue her eccentricities by marrying within the month and with little pomp, refused a trousseau, did not laud Ashley in time which could more profitably be spent praising Henry, neither filled the house with her exuberance nor languished on a sofa demanding attention for maidenly fears and regrets, she was able to take an animated interest in the proceedings.

She persuaded this curious creature of a cousin to abandon the old custom of marrying in a richly-bedizened day-dress of whatever colour the bride favoured and to adopt the fashion which had begun to grow in the higher ranks of being wed in white. To Sophia this detail was neither here nor there but, as Ashley had expressed an admiration for the white evening gown she had worn at their first meeting and she had devoted herself to pleasing him, she agreed without argument.

Ashley, himself, had returned to his duties in Norfolk and the two letters Sophia received from him on the subject of magisterial business were puzzles to Harriet which could be accepted as billet doux only on account of the mention of the overhauling of the Claydon houses and jewels and the gifts of pearls and Limerick lace which accompanied them. She did not wonder at Sophia's lack of distress at the absence of her lover for she herself was again experiencing the discomfort and anxiety in Ashley's company which always made her feel like an awkward schoolgirl.

And so the participants in the feast gathered in the city and the day approached. Mrs Dene, who — out of Francis' sight — had shed tears for the loss of her charge, found Sophia in a collected frame of mind. Although she was naturally fearful of the alteration in her state and conscious of her new responsibilities she was not overwhelmed and the out-grown governess reported to Francis that she congratulated Sophia on being diffident but generous in her attitude to Ashley; she did not mention the reminiscences and endearments which passed between Sophia and herself because they would not have interested him.

On the morning of the wedding Sophia climbed the attic stairs to show Hannah her gown. The farm-girl, who had once ridden a carrier's cart as far as Weymouth to see what a town was like, had been prostrated by the sea-voyage and the noise of the journey from the ship and was confined to bed. The terror of Calder being unable to reach her, of being wrecked and of passing the dead Hester floating below the surface of the waves had acted on her bereaved mind and sea-rocked body to produce a physical malady that Mrs Garnam had announced would be the better for complete rest until the Claydons were to leave for Norfolk. Out of sight and unimportant as she was no one thought to mention her name to Ashley and Sophia, preoccupied as she was by the change in her own life, trusted in the nobility of Ashley's mind to reconcile him to Caleb's sister.

Only the immediate family and Mrs Dene were to attend the ceremony and the wedding breakfast in Brunswick Square and, Ashley having no male relations whatever, Rowe Garnam was to act as groomsman. The party, in fine array, departed for St Peter's in good time and ribboned carriages. Rich as honey, gorgeous as peacocks, they entered the nave like the progress of the Queen of Sheba. The church was so cold that their breath misted in the still air and when the bride moved slowly to her lover the soft draught of her skirts swayed the candle-flames that burned against the dark morning. Draped in white satin with a wreath of beaten silver leaves holding her veil and orange-blossom shaking slightly in her arms she stood on the marble memorial stones as pale as a wraith and Ashley, with his heart beating unsteadily and his left hand almost numb, thought — she is my sanctuary — and yearned for the comfort she would bring.

Later, when the healths had been drunk and wishes made, Hannah stood on a chair in the attic to watch the Claydons drive away to spend two days at Ashley's London house with its view of disappearing orchards. The servants gathered on the steps to cheer them away wore the gloves and caps they had been given as favours but all about the crowded room lay the lengths of muslin to be made up into reminders of the morning. Surrounded by such affluence Hannah could hardly credit the ease of life they seemed to represent. She had been cosseted in this rich, well-ordered house as she had never been before and this, the glimpse of the city streets she had had on her way from the wharfs and the tales of the town-bred maids gave her an impression of wealth and prosperity that sank deeply into her mind as she recovered her strength. That she would be the personal servant of a lady and follow a man already so vitally entwined with her life seemed unreal and uncanny. She watched Ashley help Sophia into his carriage as if he were a creature from her dreams and wondered what her place would be in his house.

Chapter 20

In the dark interior of the carriage Sophia leant back into a corner with her eyes shut. In the other corner — far enough along the seat to avoid touching her — Ashley sat in silence watching her face. It was an old coach and more substantial than the modern conveyances but had been resprung and refurbished to carry that unusual thing — a Claydon bride — and on this stretch of good road which was taking them the last miles to the Hall the effect was a solid and lumbering comfort.

Behind them the all-purpose vehicle, which carried the larger luggage and the maid, lost and gained ground so that Ashley could sometimes hear the rattle of its harness and sometimes not. He preferred to hear nothing. It was only after the wedding that he had discovered who Sophia had chosen as her servant and it was not conducive to the peace of mind he had hoped she would restore in him. That it was his instruction to her to hire a maid which had led to the situation did not soothe him — nor, indeed, did Sophia's explanation that she was fulfilling an obligation to Calder in caring for the girl. She seemed to have been on more intimate terms with his children than made him happy and an account of Prayer Books and poaching given during a private moment at the wedding-breakfast did not make the relationship entirely clear. He did not wish to begin their marriage by criticizing her personal arrangements and, naturally, could not tell her that his objection to having Hannah in his home was that she was his daughter — but the sound of the wheels that followed him was like the remembrance of sin and stirred the mud of his guilt.

He lifted a corner of the blind to see where they were and a shaft of warm May sunlight divided the coach and fell across Sophia's face. As soon as he noticed this he laid the blind quietly back against the glass but it had disturbed her and she stirred from her sleep. She opened her eyes and as wakefulness came back to her she turned towards him and smiled. All youth and freshness were in her smile and he put out his hand to her as if he would grasp her to be sure that she was real. She took it in her own and slid across the seat to him so that her skirts, which dragged on the new plush, were tight on the side closest to him and lay bunched and abandoned on the other. She pressed her face against his cheek and rested her head on his shoulder.

"I meant to let you sleep," he said. "You looked so tired when we stopped at the inn."

She made no answer except to squeeze his hand. Her bonnet was lying on the unused seat, with its ribbons thrown across her book and parcels, and her hair brushed his face. The scent of some herb or flower he could not name came from it. It was so long since he had been familiar with a woman that although her openness was a joy to him he was frightened by it and had to fight his inclination to withdraw into his old detachment. Like a snow-field that is beginning to break his tenderness came in rushes like the sudden small slides of ice which warn of avalanche. Now, with an awkward movement, he raised his arm and put it round her. In a moment the tension of her skirts and the awareness of elbows made themselves plain; she braced herself against the floor and tried to pull her gown from under her; he inched about on the plush wondering how you did this; the swaying of the coach shook them into an easier position and on the box the driver and footman were witness to a remarkable action — they heard their master laugh.

This is my Sophia, thought Ashley wrapping his arms tightly about her as she leant back against him, my Sophie. Not Miss Farren, not my rock and saviour, my Sophia. A living woman, warm and perfumed. Beneath her dress he could feel the laces he had tied for her that morning; he had tied them precisely and caught her watching him in the mirror with an odd amusement in her eyes that had made him smile in return and stroke her as if she were a cat. He tightened his arms further and felt her breathing quicken and grow shallow.

Strange, he thought, strange to have found that this creature was flesh.

"Ashley," she said, with a laugh like a gasp, "give me some air."

"I beg your pardon," he released her but as she was raising herself to smooth her skirts he took her gently by the shoulders. In the five days of their marriage she had already learned that he was a man of pauses and she waited motionless until he bent his head to her and kissed the white skin on her neck. Touching him softly on the leg she leant forward and took her bonnet from the seat.

"Where are we?" she asked.

"Almost home. We passed through Marlingham while you slept. In a moment we'll be at the village and then home. Shall I put up the blinds?"

"Yes, do." She tied the broad ribbons beneath her chin and raised the blind on her own side. The light swept into the carriage and suddenly the brass fittings, her rings and the silver top to Ashley's stick were dazzling. She shaded her eyes with her hand and looked out.

The journey from London had brought her through country entirely foreign to her. The flatness of it, she had thought as she stared interested and aghast from the dusty window, the flatness. How can land be this flat? It was as if the Creator, having made the East, had found it untidy and had reached down and sliced off the hills and valleys leaving a cleared surface behind. Yet there was a curiously ragged and unfinished look to the countryside and the straggling brick villages. She had felt such a desperate need to break away from her old surroundings that she had not fully considered the effects of being taken to those which were new. And this will be my home, she thought, for the rest of my life. I am a stranger here.

Many times in the past days panic had begun to swell inside her and had been firmly suppressed. She had known that the first months of marriage would bring the loneliness of change and refused to be cast down by it — putting her trust in the feelings she would have a year from now. She was determined to ignore her frightened reactions to the necessary adjustment of her way of living and to accept that there would be times when she would stand in tears amidst the alien corn — but already she found that the things which disturbed her were different from those she had expected.

Mrs Dene was not one to let her charge marry in ignorance of carnal knowledge and Sophia, who had considered the intimacy of such behaviour astonishing, had been ready to disguise a distaste or even repugnance for her duty. She had found this to be unnecessary. Ashley was a gentle, tentative lover. He had a look of pleading which brought out in her a protective wish to please — yet always for her it was as if she made love to an echo of something she wanted more and for both of them there was tenderness without fever. She had not thought that physical passion would be important to her; she thought of it now.

No, she had told herself earlier that morning, my difficulty is all around me and will remain — the land. I am of the West and this is the East. It is a country of straight lines — what is not low ground is sky. Where is the sound of the sea? Already I yearn to be riding the cliffs instead of this endless, endless travelling in a coach along level roads. These drainage canals; those annoying little willows. And, oh, Mrs Dene — where are you? I want to be young enough to be in your care again.

"Ah," said Ashley, "we're entering the village now."

"Althorpe St Giles?" Sophia sat further back on the seat and tried to remember that she was the lady of this manor.

"Yes." There was a peculiar tone in Ashley's voice and she glanced at him unable to decide whether it was triumph or anger. He was staring at a terrace of workmen's cottages with long weavers' windows and the expression on his face did not explain his thoughts. The word "hatred" jumped into her mind but she dismissed it, knowing him to be a loving man.

A movement at her own side of the coach distracted her and she turned away.

"Oh, Ashley," she said, "look, people are coming to their gates."

The news of their arrival was being cried through the village and, as the carriage passed, the women, children and old men who were not in the fields were hurrying out of their houses and making their homage to their landlord and his wife. Sophia felt herself under scrutiny and, despite her wish to shrink back, bowed and kissed her hand as they were drawn past the inquisitive eyes.

"Everyone likes to see a bride," said Ashley, "I do myself — this one."

Sophia smiled but she noticed that the people here were barely less destitute than the poor of her own county and that they did not cheer or call good wishes — nor did Ashley stop the coach to speak to anyone. I'm tired, she told herself, and beginning to imagine things.

They turned the long corner out of Althorpe and she saw for a brief moment, through a gap in a row of elms, the turrets and chimneys of what must be her home. A cold alarm spread through her. This was so absolute, so final. She felt herself to be Miss Farren of Bredy Hall but the world said she was Lady Claydon of this parish. What if she could not act as this person that she was should act? I have no business here, she thought, none, none — let me go home.

"We're slowing," said Ashley. "Why? We're not yet arrived."

The coach stopped completely and, as the footman jumped down, a leg rode into view on Ashley's side. It was a leg that, though stout, was lying easily in its stirrup and was clad in Wellington breeches strapped under the foot of a well-made, round-toed boot. Sophia, who was avoiding the humiliation of tears by strong self-discipline, drove herself to notice that the clothing and the horse they accompanied were those of a gentleman and prepared to meet a neighbour. Behind them the luggage-trap jingled and creaked to a standstill and the servants' conversation died away.

The footman opened Ashley's door and the rider moved his mount up to a suitable position to speak. Ashley sat forward in a manner that had all the inherent courtesy of leaving the carriage without the inconvenience of doing so.

"Afternoon, Claydon," said the voice that was flatly nasal. "I mistook the day you returned. Been at your place paying a wedding call."

"How kind," Ashley inclined his head. "Perhaps I could introduce you to my wife now."

The rider stepped down from his horse and Sophia saw a man in late middle-age with a browned complexion that said he took an active interest in supervising his farms. He held his hat in his hand and approached the door. Unable to think what correct deportment for a bride should be Sophia looked at him in a way that was gravely friendly.

"My dear," said Ashley — and Sophia, giving him a surprised glance at this public endearment, was touched to see that he, in his own way, wanted to shout his possession in the marketplace — "this is our neighbour, Mr Edward Marsh of Ketting House on the other side of Marlingham. Marsh — Lady Claydon."

Sophia and Marsh bowed and Marsh, storing the details to tell his wife, looked across the carriage at the blue silk figure who sat so silent and tranquil against the padded seat and thought that the rumours of Ashley's prize had been true.

"Honoured, ma'am," he said. "I hope we'll see you at the County Ball next month."

"Thank you," said Sophia — and her throat, contracting with the embarrassment of introductions, made her voice softly husky. "Whatever my husband wishes."

"I think you'll meet us there," said Ashley, smiling. "My wife has shown me that I'm not too old to dance and you know I like to play my part in gatherings."

"Yes," Marsh tapped the brim of his hat with his fingers. "That reminds me — it wasn't like you to miss the meeting. I know it was the day before you left for town but you're so hot against the workhouse I was sure we'd have you there."

"What meeting?" Ashley ran the edge of his hand against his leg and his haggard face which had begun to be genial sank back into bleakness.

"The combined vestry meeting — all of us in the district. The poors' rate is becoming ludicrous. I know your opinion, Claydon, but really — something must be done."

"Why was I told nothing of this?" Ashley laid his hand on the seat beside him as if it were something dead; the familiar pressure was building in his chest.

Marsh looked startled. "But you were," he said. "I was with Gascoigne myself when he gave your invitation to your agent." He laughed shortly. "Well, has the perfect Mason slipped at last, eh? Not quite faultless after all. I'll wager the note's in his waistcoat pocket at this moment. What of his £800 a year now? — But you've had your money's worth out of him, eh? Nothing so neat as Mason's estate — unless it's his accounts." Traces of envy and dislike were apparent in his voice and he remembered himself. "This is no talk for the occasion, ma'am," he said. "If you'll excuse —"

"A moment," said Ashley. "What decision was come to?"

Marsh replaced his hat. "The old weaving-sheds at Pointer's Piece go to auction on Wednesday. We'll join what rates we have on hand from all the parishes and bid for the land. It's a good situation for a workhouse to cover the area."

The severity of the silence that wrapped Ashley as they drove on did not disconcert his new wife. On the contrary, the obvious ferocity of his abhorrence of the scheme gave her confidence and security. This was the man she had aimed to marry — the man who was angered by what his neighbours saw as merely economically expedient. She relaxed into a desire to enter her new home.

Ashley suddenly reached out and grasped her hand. He held it firmly, shaking it abruptly to emphasize his words. "This project must be stopped," he said. "I will never be party to the breaking up of families. Never. Never again. I will never see a family split."

The high-pitched chime of a clock striking midnight reached Sophia as she lay alone in the bed. By an accident of judgement in maids who could not have known their lady's preference the mattress had been plumped exactly as she liked it. She was tired from the journey but not so exhausted that she could not enjoy the luxuries that surrounded her. Stretching her arms back over her head and her pointed toes down among the sheets she arched her bathed body in a languorous physical content-ment. An oversight by the servants had left dried lavender where it had caught in a fold of the linen and she brushed it over the edge of the fat, duck-down billows with one foot. As she moved, her knuckles brushed the hangings behind her head where the Claydon arms were embroidered in old silks and silver thread. It amused her to have the device so prominent as if serious hereditary business was expected of her in this place.

She was already familiar with the bull and eagle which now represented her. From the pair of portly gryphons, which brandished the heraldic shield at the entrance to the hall, to the flat of the fork she had used at supper the beasts stared at her, reminding her that she had become a point in their history and must live up to them.

With every passing hour that task seemed harder. Her whole setting was so different from what she was used to and what she had imagined. There was the delightfulness of the house. Ashley had shown her an engraving of the front face and she had known that — allowing for the artist's flattery — it was attractive but the charm of it, the welcoming prettiness had escaped both the engraver and herself. She had been taken completely by surprise at her first sight of it. The façade with its cupolas and clock-tower, its symmetry and balconies, its warm, soft brick and pale stone decoration was like a motif stitched into a sampler by a clever child; a child who, given the faded work-things of her mother, had chosen colours that were obvious and muted — red brick, yellow gravel, green grass, blue sky — all brought down to a faintness that was beautiful.

As they turned in at the elegant wrought-iron gates and drove the last yards between the smooth lawns, with the yew hedges and the Flemish gables of the servants' offices to each side, she had thought in wonder — how did this delicate toy come about? How does it fit with the character of this man — my husband? And what of a girl raised amidst dark panelling and hills where the thorn-trees lean to the wind?

For a moment as she was led over the pierced stone bridge that crossed the turfed moat where the wisteria had its roots, through the deep courtyard and into the crowd of serving men and girls gathered in the hall she had felt too disorientated and foreign to grow into part of the estate. The lightness of the rooms, the elaborate ceilings with plaster like whipped cream drooping from the spoon, were not her background. But, she had told herself as she ran her glove over a soldier carved upon the banister, she had uprooted Hannah with the arrogance of a gentlewoman who knows what is best for the poor and this arrival must be ten times worse for her. Then there was Mason — a strange souvenir of her girlhood to find, courteous and brooding, at the threshold of her future home. He was a link with her past and if he could live — however coldly — in two worlds so could she.

It had reassured her when Ashley had asked permission to leave her in order to attend to the matter of the workhouse. Just as in the coach it had strengthened her to see him angry this manifestation of his concern gave her confidence in her decision to be his wife. Warm water, loose clothes and spiced wine had restored her spirits and, pushing the fancies of tiredness from her mind, she abandoned herself to the enjoyment of an end to travelling.

It was a pleasure to be alone in this comfortable room and no longer to be waited upon by unfamiliar figures. Sophia, with her round West Country vowels, and the maids, with their sudden rises and inflections, were slow to understand each other and she was glad to have bidden them goodnight. They had told her that this was not the master's usual room but had been prepared particularly for the bride — and the bride, who did not know where her husband was, was happy in the choice. There was no fire but a smoky tang of applewood used to drive out any damp still lingered in the air. The carved mahogany posts and tester of the bed, with its salmon-pink counterpane and hangings, shone with beeswax. The two candles still burning illuminated a spread of white-painted panels beneath the Mortlake tapestry that covered the four walls and cast shadows on the ceiling that merged with the darkness in the corners. The chair was satinwood; the carpets were Moorfields; all was of the finest and for her. This was the room where she would bear her children and grow old.

Stealthy movements in the dressing room disturbed her. A chink of jug and basin and murmur of voices roused her from the drowsiness that was overtaking her despite the wish to stay alert. She pulled herself further up the pillows. Across the dusky room she saw the connecting-door open and Ashley come in with the slow, over-emphasized movements of one trying not to wake a sleeper. In his long, white robe he looked Roman and stately.

Sophia turned back the covers and ran across the carpets to him. He gathered her up and pressed her against him so that she stood on tiptoe to keep her balance. He rocked her a little from side to side as if she were a child. How scented she is, he thought, always so clean and warm. I'm not so tired now and need never be again. Perhaps I should lock her in this room and keep her for moments like these. This room — women like so many little things about them; they have silver jars and combs; they drape their shawls. This is a woman I have with me.

He pushed his fingers up into her hair and she let her head fall back supported by his hands.

"I wanted you to come home," she said.

He did not answer but, instead, lowered his face to her neck and kissed it with abrupt, hungry kisses. His mouth was dry and hard and for no reason she could name she was afraid.

"Were you — were you successful?" she asked.

He raised his head. He had a blank pallor on his skin and an empty expression in his eyes that could, she told herself, have been the candlelight.

"Yes," he said. "I bought the land that was to be auctioned. My price was so good. I'm safe this time." He paused and seemed to be thinking of something else. "Mason was too ill to go to the meeting and put my point. The doctor was called. He was ill."

He bent and lifted her from the floor. Carrying her to the bed he set her down lightly where the sheet was thrown back. She began to lie down but as she drew up her legs he knelt and caught her foot.

"Look," he said, caressing it, "the reason why we're here. You can still see the mark where the carriage hurt you."

Sophia watched him stroking the unblemished flesh. "There's no scar, Ashley," she said gently but he did not seem to hear.

"Everything evil leaves a mark," he said, "but if I love you enough it will go, won't it?"

Chapter 21

Under the trees, where the grass was longer, Sophia and Hannah picked up their skirts and scrambled down the short slope to the lake, with their hands full of gown, shawl, books and fan, and last year's fallen twigs and ash-wings crackling beneath their feet. Seen from this distant part of the water, the house shimmered in the haze of July.

"Oh," said Sophia, "it's so hot. I wish I could take down my hair."

"'Twouldn't be any cooler, ma'am" said Hannah, opening her mistress' fan and passing it to her, "not with it hanging down your back."

"I suppose not." Sophia undid the broad ribbons of her wide straw hat and waved the fan slowly over her face and neck. Hannah, standing slightly behind her, remembered her duties and rearranged Sophia's muslin skirts before smoothing her own. The work of a lady's maid was less laborious than that which she was used to but was full of small fussings that she found hard to keep in mind. Not, she thought, that her mistress was demanding in trivialities — she seemed rather to accept them as part of her own responsibility as Lady Claydon and often gave the impression of being about to shake off the attentions shown her as she would shake off tiresome pups. Her new life seemed to irk her and, though Hannah had rarely met her when they lived in the west, she thought that Sophia had had something about her then which she did not have now. It was only an intuition that the missing zest had been replaced by a concealed hurt and puzzlement that appealed to Hannah's ready sympathies and prevented her from delivering only what her wages demanded. Instead, eager as she always was to mother lost lambs, she considered that Sophia had done herself an injury in marrying a man as cold and cruel as the master and stood in need of faithful service. She did not understand why Sophia had made this marriage but thought, obscurely, that she had been coerced — women of Sophia's rank being bred to be sold to rich men just as women like herself were born to labour — and though she considered wealthy servitude to be better than hunger and dirt she did not think it paradise.

"Will you sit down, ma'am?"

Sophia turned at the sound of the rolling Dorset voice and smiled at her maid's earnest face. She was becoming used to the odd outbursts of concern from what should have been a rough country girl — and liked them. It alarmed her that she should be in need of affection so soon after her wedding but she could not deny that she found a responsive softness in Hannah that she did not find in her husband. Nor, she was forced to admit, was that all. Several times she had caught herself studying the girl's face in the hope of discovering the resemblance to Calder. She walked with the shepherd when she walked with the maid; over and over again she saw his eyes as he thanked her on the Bredy road, heard his voice as he called to her to come into the light of his fire; she felt a strange longing to receive his dog which Francis had not thought to bring to London and which she had summoned directly a servant could be spared to fetch him. She even used his Christian name in her imaginings and it disgusted her that her mind should be absorbed by any man other than Ashley. The fault, she told herself looking back over the shining waters, is mine. I'm too childish to appreciate Ashley as I ought. At the present I'm too concerned with myself to see the good effect he has on the county; when I'm more used to this place it will become clear. But she could not hide from herself that whatever she had expected to result from Ashley's radical example had not materialized and there seemed a curious emptiness about him in his everyday life. Nonsense, she said to herself sharply, I must think not of how bad things are here but how much worse they'd be without him.

"No," she said aloud. "Thank you — I'm not tired."

She had come to this bank by the water intending to read in the shade but now that they had arrived she felt an impatience of the whole scene and a rush of home-sickness that was like a physical pain. I'm here, she thought looking at the wavering park, I'm here for ever.

"I'd rather walk," she said, "out of the grounds and by the river."

Hannah placed the shawl more securely over her arm. "Shall I fetch a footman, ma'am?" she asked.

"No," Sophia waved away a wasp that was hovering around her. "We'll go alone. The country seems quiet just now."

The soles of her thin sandals slithered on the grass as they climbed back up the slope and Hannah put out her free arm to grasp her firmly by the elbow. It was a farm girl's familiar gesture and welcomed by Sophia who was learning to dislike a distant manner.

Together they walked out of the copse and across the open turf into the avenue of beeches that lined a green drive to the wall of the park. Once outside the gate they found themselves on a path that ran among the fields of corn leading down to the river. It was a path Sophia had taken only twice before but it led into places that had a hidden, secret quality — a feeling of separateness from the world — that soothed her. Sometimes they followed the path beside hedges where the dog rose dropped late petals and the haws were forming; sometimes they walked waist-deep amongst the rustling barley where the poppies coloured the corn like a conjuror's red smoke. The sun burning in the fullness of a Norfolk summer drenched them in heat and when they stopped beneath a lime and looked up into the brilliant, translucent leaves they were overpowered by the rich, honied scent of the hanging flowers and the buzzing of the bees that worked them.

In the lane that curved past the fields and spinneys the verges were yellow with toadflax and drifts of meadowsweet that frothed against the hazels. It was so quiet here that the sound of stones dislodged by their feet or the crumbling of the dust-dry ruts seemed to break a rule of silence. They passed a pair of cottages where the linen spread upon the bushes did not disturb the appearance of desertion and both women thought how strange it was to see houses built of brick.

They stopped again beside the slow river and this time Sophia knelt among the grasses on the bank and put her hand down between the reeds into the water. In parts weed almost closed the channel and in an inlet opposite her seat water-lilies with shining white cups choked the current. Upstream the river widened and a moorhen darted out from the pillars beneath a mill.

Sophia clasped her hands behind her neck and stretched herself up into the sun. The water from her fingers was cold on her skin. She closed her eyes.

"How lovely," she said, "how lovely it is."

"A bad day to be tramping," said Hannah.

Sophia reopened her eyes and as if she had asked a question Hannah pointed. "There, ma'am," she said, "along the track and beyond the mill."

Standing up Sophia gazed across the dazzling river and saw a group of people struggling towards a decaying barn. They were of all ages and shabbily dressed — the women's clothes draggling slackly around them telling of underskirts now long sold for more necessary things. They carried an assortment of oddly-shaped pieces of wood and at the rear of the procession three men wrestled with a hand-cart loaded with larger boards and poles. Two children ran ahead and wrenched open the doors of the barn.

"Pour souls," said Hannah. "Pour souls."

"Who are they?" Sophia raised herself on tiptoe. "What are they moving?"

"They must be weavers. Those are dismantled looms. I went to a weaving-shed in Bridport once and there used to be that journeyman weaver in Cheney until he died. Do you remember, Miss F — ma'am?"

"Yes, but I never saw his loom."

They watched as the first figures to reach the barn put down their burdens and went back to help with the cart. The children were swinging on the door but at a cry from one of the women they jumped down and ran to take the pack from her shoulders.

"Isn't that path they're using private?" said Sophia. "I thought it was Sir Ashley's."

"Do you want me to question them, ma'am?"

"No, no. Let them be. I was just thinking aloud. The Norwich weavers are such radicals and we've seen enough trouble."

"They look too starved to give trouble, ma'am."

"I wasn't thinking of it being made by them." Sophia picked up the fan she had laid on the grass. "Come, we'd better go back."

They returned to the parched lane and began to make their way slowly home. Now and then Sophia trailed her fan along the hedgerow and struck at a nettle, sending a patter of small seeds down among its leaves. Always true to old customs, Ashley had not put his female servants into uniform and Hannah, upright and sturdily graceful in her new sprigged cotton gown, looked more like a poor relation than a retainer as she followed her mistress towards the fields.

"Are you happy here?" Sophia asked suddenly.

Hannah, who had been watching a butterfly as her thoughts wandered from the kitchens to Philadelphia to the sea, was startled by the personal nature of the question. "Yes, thank you, ma'am," she said. Sophia smiled sadly. "You couldn't say anything else, could you?" she asked.

Feeling that she was being criticized Hannah searched for something else to say without telling any of the truth that would be unacceptable to an employer. "The other servants are friendly," she said, "I don't know how things are done in a big house but they think it's just because I'm a foreigner. They laugh at my voice but there's no harm meant."

"I worry that I shouldn't have brought you away from your home. It's hard to be so far from everyone you know."

"I've no family here, ma'am," said Hannah simply, "but now I've no family there either."

The meaning of this made Sophia wince inwardly. Guilt by marriage, she thought. She looked at the ground in front of her and said, "Is that why you came? I ask because I realize now how terrible it must be to live dependent on the man who witnessed against your brother. I've noticed that you avoid my husband as much as you're able."

What can she know, thought Hannah, of how much necessity

drives people in my condition to do what we wouldn't do if we had the choice? Does she think those weavers are choosing to enter that barn? There was anger and bitterness in her thoughts but her affection for this unhappy, pampered woman and her gratitude for all she had done for Calder made her look charitably on her mistress as she would on an imbecile child.

"I came because I wanted to be away from Five Warrens, ma'am," she said. "I didn't think I'd see much of Sir Ashley — and your governess was so kind and persuading and Mr Farren wouldn't take no for an answer."

Sophia smiled again. "My grandfather can be bettered if you stand against him."

"No, ma'am," said Hannah. "That's for the gentry. I have one brother hanged and another running from transportation. And Hester —" Sophia stopped and turned round violently to face the girl. Hannah stared back at her as she would if she had unwittingly disturbed an adder. Fear of authority came swilling icily into her veins. She had forgotten her place.

"Forgive me," said Sophia, shaking her head once sharply. "Wicked, wicked thoughtlessness. What use am I?"

Hannah did not reply. Nervously she rubbed the edge of her hand back and forth across the shawl she carried. Noticing this mannerism — so prominent in Ashley — Sophia scrutinized her maid for signs of mockery but could see nothing except distress — and something in her face which again reminded her of her husband. Does he suffer, she thought, as much as this girl? And if so — why? He has so much power; he could give her prosperity for life with one stroke of his pen while she may not provide for herself by working all her days. She fears me now because she has reminded me that my kind have caused her family's destruction. I am doing my best for her and it is not enough.

She put out her hand and patted the girl's fidgeting fingers. They looked at each other across the divide of what they had been taught they were born to be and as they walked on they also took a step towards friendship.

On the lawn outside the house Sophia gave her hat and fan to Hannah, telling her to take them inside while she herself went to the stables to see whether Watch had arrived. With her arms full of paraphernalia Hannah made her way to the flagged path that ran around the building and began to follow it, intending to enter by one of the servants' doors. Her feet hurt and her heels — unaccustomed to new shoes — gave her a sharp, rubbing pain as she put down each foot. She did not want to look at them in case she saw blood — until she knew it was there she could walk normally. She was alone for the first time that day; there were no sounds whatever and feeling free from observation she leant against the wall. Raising her full arms she covered her face with her hands. The brick was smooth and warm and put out its soft, dry smell into the more sharp and delicate scent of Sophia's belongings. Why did I come here? Hannah thought miserably. Oh, Caleb, Caleb — I'm lonely. What if Calder doesn't write?

She had not lied in telling Sophia that she was happy here but it was a meagre happiness that consisted in being neither hungry, thirsty nor cold. A terror of what the gentry could do haunted her actions and she longed to bury herself where none of their rank could touch her. If Calder would only send for her it would take her to that promised land and give her what she needed most — someone to cherish and love. For several minutes she rested against the wall in an almost animal state of yearning and then — from close-by — she heard a sudden stifled oath and the sound of a man falling heavily against a table.

Running a few paces along the flags she passed the two windows of the estate-room and came to the entrance. Both the French door and the heavy shutter, that protected the rent-rolls and payments at night, were propped open. The office was bright with the sun and she could see plainly the predicament of Robert Mason who, having put too much pressure on his weak leg, had collapsed against a small table that had stood at right-angles to his desk. The table and ledgers lay scattered on the rush mat and Mason, with his back to Hannah, was trying to right himself by dragging on the top of the desk. The veins straining on his neck and the short rasps of his breathing made the pain of his unsuccessful struggle apparent.

Although she knew from village history that it was he who had discovered the Young infants abandoned in the hills and had placed them with the widow she had loved she had never spoken to him and understood only that he was a hard man with a hard reputation. Already she had seen the ruins of cottages he had ordered torn down to lower the local population and had witnessed the weariness of the field-gangs who now had to walk miles to their labour. She had not yet gained a settlement by having worked a full year in the parish and was not eligible for poor relief if she were turned off and her sympathy had been all for the wretches driven away from their homes — but seeing the agony of the man distracted her from the cruelty of the agent.

With an instant's hesitation she went into the office and put down Sophia's things on the chair by the door. Mason, with his leg stiff and twisted beneath him, glanced over his shoulder at the intruder and, seeing her, relaxed. There was a second chair, for visitors, placed facing the desk and taking him firmly by the waist she put his arm round her and lifted him awkwardly on to the seat. He was no small weight and as she knelt and gently straightened the offending leg she shook a little from her efforts. More familiar with tending to ploughmen and carters than gentlemen she forgot herself and began adjusting his shirt and stock. The fine cambric reminded her of their positions and she looked up at him. He was smiling and it was not a smile to put her at her ease.

She sank back on her throbbing heels and he took her face in his hands and examined it as if it were a contract. Since she had come to the east she had become used to this inspection — supposing that it was the way of gentry and must be suffered. She disliked his touch but she had no fears for her safety. The weeks she had been at the Hall were enough for her to have been told the gossip of the house and there was no scandal attached to Mason — who had never been known to notice a maid unless she fell short in her duty. His vice lay in apothecaries' bottles and was excused by his condition. Whisperers said he indulged himself too much but his skills were not impaired and nothing definite could be spoken against him. At this moment his eyes were as cold and penetrating as always but the acuteness seemed to swim out from somewhere far away and there was a sickly tang to his breath.

He turned her head slightly to each side. Her features and colour, he thought, are like her mother yet there is something of the Claydon about her. Nothing I would see if I didn't know who she was but something I can't define. He had a spiteful pleasure in her presence at the Hall and the situation of Ashley who had thought to slide so easily from his old friend to a new life. It appealed to him to have Ashley's daughter ministering to him and calling him "sir" and this concern — shown of her own volition — pulled at what there was of tender feeling in him.

He was not a carnal man; some years before he had kept a widow in a quiet street in Norwich — a handsome, barren, agreeable woman — but the complications and risk of it irritated him and after six months he had given her the means to start a dame-school near her home town of Worcester and had washed his hands of clandestine arrangements. He despised men who could not contain themselves and, though this failing in Ashley had been so useful to him, had always looked down on his friend's impulsive sensuality. He had admired Ashley's rigid control of this weakness through twenty years and thought it dead but now his choice of a young and striking bride and his eagerness to found a second family proved it well alive. Mason, softened by Hannah's sympathetic care and jealous of Ashley's receipt of his wife's companionship, thought suddenly that what was sauce for the goose — The heat of her walk and the lifting had covered her skin with a glistening film of moisture; there were dry marks of his fingers where he had touched her as if he had walked on dewy grass. She smelt hot and in health.

"I need the room straightened," he said. "Johnson's coming about his lease. Help me on with my jacket."

She stood up, and he glanced at the clock on the side-wall but the sun was shining on the glass, obsuring the numerals.

"What o'clock, is it?" he asked.

Hannah, relieved to be released, was opening his jacket and did not look up.

"I don't read well, sir," she said.

"Don't you?" he smiled his cold smile again. "Would you say then you were no wife for a professional man?"

Chapter 22

In the dim drawing room Sophia sat with her legs outstretched in a long-chair and one velvet slipper hanging loosely from her crossed feet. Its pair lay upside down on the carpet — as did the embroidery she had been toying with — and her book lay unread on her lap. It was past ten on a September evening and a fire was burning on the hearth where she and Ashley were sitting. Neither of them had wanted much light and the flames and a single candle on the tables beside their chairs were all that they had allowed to be lit. A pastille was smouldering in an incense pot on the far cabinet and the perfumed smoke curled up into the dark corners of the room.

In a warm and trancelike state Sophia saw Ashley playing with Watch. The dog had taken a fancy to him and, in return, Ashley seemed able to give a freer affection to the animal than to any person he knew. He was leaning forward in his chair rubbing the dog's rough chest as it sat upright at his feet. Taking the shaggy ears he held them out like wings, flapping them gravely up and down. The dog lifted its head and pushed its nose into his hand and be began to stroke its head more softly with the shadow of a smile on his thin, tired face. Sophia stood up in a rustle of taffeta and, losing her other slipper on the way, crossed the rug and sat on the arm of Ashley's chair. With his free arm he encircled her.

"Both my pets," he said.

She drew his head against her breast and kissed his hair. The muscles of her face began to constrict but she subdued the impulse and no tears reached her eyes. Taking his hand from the dog he placed it lightly on her stomach and looked up at her inquiringly. She shook her head sharply but then, regretting her impatience, said gently, "No, love — perhaps next month," and he laid his head against her once more.

He had not expected this. He had destroyed his low-bred family for the sake of the name of that family and now was trying to atone but the means of that atonement — a son born of the correct kind of woman who would honourably carry forward his banner of tradition — did not come. It confused him. His wife was young, loving and willing — even, at times, eager for something he could not seem to give — yet there were already nights when he could not bring himself to touch her and others when he could do no more than hold her tightly in the darkness until she asked him to let her go. Once, in the morning, there were the marks of his fingers on her arm.

He could not understand it; there were ghosts about his bed and in his dreams. A mental malaise, as if the numbness in his hand were creeping to his brain, clouded his thoughts until he felt like a stranger to his life. He suffered a growing suspicion of Mason but could not say of what he was suspicious and the matters of the workhouse and the weavers swelled and entwined themselves in his mind like bloated seaweed. He held Sophia closer and she stroked his hair as he gazed into the fire.

The sound of purposeful footsteps disturbed them. The steps approached the door and Ashley remembered his invitation earlier that day.

"That will be Mason," he said.

"At this hour?" Sophia uncurled her stockinged feet from the leg of the chair and folds of her heavy Turkey-red skirts fell slithering to the floor.

"He was playing at whist with the Pearsalls and I asked him to take a glass of wine on his way home."

She got up, trailing her fingers along his arm.

"I didn't hear wheels," she said, pushing on her slippers. "I suppose he did come in his gig?"

"Yes. No, I didn't either. A pity he's had to give up riding but his leg gets no better."

"I think it warps him. The pain —"

The door opened and a footman gave Mason's name. He came in and, seeing Sophia, bowed.

"Do I interrupt you, ma'am?" he said. "Sir Ashley —" He left the sentence unfinished.

"I was going to my room," she said and glanced at the servant. "A glass for Mr Mason, John, or will you take something more? Cold beef? A little fruit?"

"Thank you — I have supped."

"A biscuit?" asked Ashley "And another of madeira, John. This bottle won't last."

"Yes," Mason remained standing. "Perhaps a biscuit." He was in evening-dress with full-cut trousers strapped beneath his Spanish leather pumps to hid his disfigurement. His appearance was easy and immaculate but in front of Sophia he felt loutish. He did not doubt that he was the superior by natural right but his was the superiority of intelligence, work and ability and hers was the assumed superiority of position and wealth. He had managed this man and this estate for twenty years yet this arrogant girl could call it hers and dismiss him if she chose to use a little midnight persuasion. She offered him food as if it were she who had grown old here and knew every turn of its seasons. An urge to do her a violence was becoming more frequent with him. He wished to humiliate her — to push her down into the mud of the lake until she choked. He looked with his cold, unrevealing eyes from her, as she picked up her book, to Ashley, who leant forward to help her, and thought — this place is mine as much as yours; no accident of birth can disguise that it is my talent that maintains its good name and prosperity and one day — one day — I will force you to acknowledge it.

He stood back politely to let Sophia pass and when the door was closed behind her he walked stiffly forward and, at a gesture from Ashley, took the long-chair. They were not as comfortable together as they once had been but still, in their ways, they could not do without each other's company.

"Was your evening enjoyable?" Ashley asked.

"Yes, it was but," Mason adjusted his leg by pulling at the trouser around it, "I heard some news. You remember Burton's Longhorn heifer — the one that took second at the Show? Hamstrung in the field. The cowman found her this morning — not dead but they had to kill her. They say —"

The footman returned with a tray of wine and biscuits and

Ashley pointed for him to light more candles. When they were alone again Mason went on, "So it appears the county is not settling and we may see more trouble yet. This is not the only case we know of — which reminds me I've been giving some thought to the weavers."

Ashley shut his eyes briefly at the mention of the word. That the weavers had not been driven back into proper subservience to a master by their eviction from his cottages seemed a standing accusation of failure on his part and their occupation of the millers' barn on the very threshold of his park poisoned all that he saw. To Mason they remained nothing — the world had changed leaving the handlooms obsolete and the tiny, pathetic cooperative was merely the last twitch in the trade's death throes. If Ashley would leave them be they would disperse of their own accord in a year or two but Ashley was not content to let them alone and it was convenient to Mason to show his friend that his help was indispensable.

"I talked to Marlow as we decided," he said, as Ashley fixed his eyes on him, "but he said the mill was his own and there was no advantage in having a good barn go to waste. The barn, of course, is not good and the root of his obstinacy is a sentimental sympathy with the rascals — but I didn't say that knowing it wouldn't shake him and would bring the scriptures down on my head. He's found the Lord, incidentally, and has become a hedge-preacher on Sundays like too many of the rabble." A candle in a silver stick beside him guttered and he trimmed it with his fingers. "I thought how incommoding it was to have this spur of private land intruding on the estate but that, I hazard, will prove the remedy." He saw that Ashley was interested but not enlightened and continued, "He's a miller and depends upon his waterwheel. The river runs to each side of him through our meadows. We have but to divert the course of the river a small distance to put an end to his business. A simple ploy that's been most effective in other areas and with our experience of drainage channels will be easily effected. Not that we'll have to actually employ it; a threat to do so will be enough to remind Marlow to render unto Caesar."

208

Ashley nodded and leaned back in his chair "Yes," he said, "excellent. You were always one for ideas. Yes, do it."

Mason reached out for a biscuit and Watch rose sleepily and padded across to rest his head on the agent's outstretched leg. He winced and Ashley called the dog away.

"Your knee doesn't improve?" he asked.

"No," Mason sighed and crumbled the biscuit in his hand. "Hannah told my cook a receipt for a poultice but it's had no effect. The thought was kind."

They had become used to referring to her and were careful to avoid words that would betray them but each had feelings they found difficult to conceal.

"And Hannah herself," said Ashley. "These past two days —I've noticed she's looked sickly."

"Oh," Mason threw an edge of the biscuit to Watch. "She's had a letter from her brother in America. The housekeeper read it aloud to her and now there's bad feeling in the kitchens — the staff feel he's rising above his station."

In the barn only one loom was working. An order had been given by the wife of the seed-merchant in Marlingham for three counterpanes of an intricate design — one for herself and two for her daughters' bottom drawers — and Nathan, who was the most skilled in figured weaving, was immersed in the complicated pattern. The swinging of the lathe, the throwing of the shuttle and the pressure of his feet on the treadles made a rhythm that irritated the nerves of his companions. Not all of the weavers were present to hear the poverty knock. Ted Yates and his sons were out delivering finished cloth and Luke Greaves had walked to Norwich to carry home yarn but Luke's wife, Mary, and his parents were sitting on straw-stuffed sacks about an upturned barrel. At the open door of the barn the two children had tied a piece of old rope to the handle and were skipping in time to Nathan and a chant they had picked up in town:

"Bread-tax'd weaver, all can see
What that tax hath done for thee,

And thy children, vilely led,
Singing hymns for shameful bread,
Till the stones of every street
Know their little naked feet."

At the end of the rhyme they changed places — the boy who
had been turning the rope passing it to the girl and jumping
into it himself.

"Bread-tax'd weaver, all can —"

"Be quiet," their mother said softly and then louder — "be
quiet. Be quiet! Be quiet!" She put her hands over her ears.
"Stop them Nathan, make them stop!"

Margaret Greaves leant over and put her arm around her
daughter-in-law's shoulder. Mary burst into violent tears and
Nathan climbed out of his loom and crossed to the startled
children. As Mary's cries subsided they could hear his mild
voice soothing them and sending them down to the river to
play. When they had gone he crossed over to the Greaves and
sat beside John. After the sunlight in the doorway the barn
seemed dark. "I can't bear it," said Mary, hiding her face
against Margaret. "I don't mean to be — oh, God! What shall
we do?"

Margaret patted and rocked her. She used no words of
comfort and knew that Mary expected none. The apathy of
prolonged fear and despair had not yet reached them but was
not far away. A daily diet of two pennyworth of oatmeal and
potatoes preserved them physically but not mentally and
would not do even that in the approaching winter. Three
counterpanes were lifting them from destitution now but the
calico that was their usual work did not fill their mouths and
there was nowhere they could turn to improve their trade.
Fellow weavers they met on the roads brought tales of leaving
homes emptied of every article but the loom, of women forced to
give birth standing with their arms about their helpers' necks
for fear of fouling the only bedding, of the pamphlet advocating
infanticide, of charitable ladies visiting the poor and finding
families dead amongst their rags. And to the starving there was

worse than this — they heard the testimony of those who had left their parishes and the thin drip of poor relief to tramp to the factories they feared and despised only to be turned away as useless for the work required. The last resort had proved an illusion and if Sir Ashley was not merciful there would be no new life amidst the powerlooms — there would be a dispersal to the parishes of their births and the hunger and humiliations of the auctions and stone-breaking and rounds that had fed Swing.

John Greaves smoothed the paper that lay on the barrel. "We know Robert Mason will have been behind this threat with the river," he said. "Maybe Sir Ashley doesn't know — he leaves all to his agent. And his lady looks a gentle-heart."

"Ladies don't read petitions," said Mary, drying her face on her sleeve.

Her father-in-law looked at her with eyes that were almost blank with sadness. "Well, dear, perhaps he's softened by being wed." He held up the paper and began to read, "Most honoured Sir, we the undersigned do humbly beg that a most heavy grievance be —"

"We know the words," his wife stood up. "Come, if you're to visit the house while you're sure Mason's in town you'd best be moving."

With their hands she and Mary brushed away the straw and cotton threads that clung to the men's dilapidated clothes and tied their neckerchiefs and as the two thin, shabby men walked out into the sun the women stood in the doorway and watched and waved.

Nathan and John followed the path that Sophia and Hannah used to reach the river. The corn had been cut and gleaned and the hedges were turning. In the autumn sunlight the colours were sharp and clear and the chatter of the starlings searching unprofitably amongst the stubble was shrill in the still air. They met no one on their journey and when they reached the park and began to see the intimidating Hall between the trees they were conscious of their trespass and did not know where they should apply.

Nathan touched his companion and pointed towards the lake.

"That maid," he said, "I've seen her with the lady."

Through the brambles that were growing at the edge of the copse they could see a girl exercising a dog. Both she and the dog were watching them but did not seem unfriendly. Nathan took off his hat and went a few steps towards her. He stumbled slightly in the long grass and Hannah instinctively reached out to save him even though they were yards apart. When she looked into his dreamy eyes she saw that he was smiling and had not seemed to notice his fall.

"Beg your pardon, miss," he said, "but could you help us?"

A warmth was spreading over Hannah. As she stood in the cool sunlight beneath the reddening leaves she felt all the comfort of summer and when this thin, pale young man asked for her help it increased within her as if she held some young creature in her arms. She shook herself like a dog leaving water and smiled back. I know what this is, she thought. Mercy on me, I have a taking for him. He may be a tinker and I have a fancy for him because he almost fell.

Seeing her hesitation, John said, "We're weavers, mistress, and want to see the master for business. Can we go to the Hall from here?"

Hannah looked at him reluctantly. Her eyes were full of laughter and strayed back to Nathan as she spoke. "Surely," she said, "but I can't give you leave. My lady will see you if Sir Ashley won't. I'll walk with you."

She brushed the dog's head with her fingers and began picking her way over the grass. As she passed Nathan she laughed aloud and he, who had not noticed her confusion, was not offended but drank in the sound he heard so rarely. The three began walking towards the house with Watch behind them. As they came out from the shelter of the trees a soft wind, with a hint of rain, lifted the brim of her hat and Nathan, tall enough to look down on her as she walked beside him, touched it with one long gentle hand and held it down. She drew away but seeing that there was no boldness in his mild eyes began to laugh again. Lost and gone, she thought — oh, my handsome, lost and gone.

John and Nathan exchanged a glance above the head of this curious, obliging girl. Her voice was a stranger's and each charitably excused her behaviour as foreign ways.

"Did you come from the south country with your lady, miss?" John asked.

"I did," said Hannah.

Nathan looked before him at the light reflecting on the many windows of the house. They were crossing the turf that surrounded the Hall and would soon be at a door. The girl would go to her mistress and they to her master and the laughter would be gone.

"And will you be staying?" he asked. "Do you like this place?"

Hannah lifted her face to him. "How can I like it," she said, "when I have no friends nor kin and no one to care for?"

He smiled again slowly. "Well, now," he said, "we've got neither bread nor meat to offer but that's a lack we can remedy." He was not looking at John but could sense the surprise at his familiarity. As he watched Hannah's face colour, without being turned from him, the usual forms of courtship did not seem important. "When you have your free day I'll come for you if you'll walk out with me."

Hannah sighed as if she were tired by happiness. "Yes," she said, "I'll walk out with you."

Chapter 23

"No! Ashley, Ashley! No!" In her resplendent evening-dress Sophia backed away from him as if he were a serpent. Her rich lace wrap slipped from her bare shoulders and as it fell she picked up her wide satin skirts and ran. The door of the drawing room dislodged a sketch as she flung it open against the wall and a maid carrying hot water backed against the banister as first her mistress and then her master ran past with violent faces.

Sophia plunged into their bedroom and crossed to her dressing table. She was panting and the locket about her throat was sticking awkwardly to her skin. Her hands shook as she unlocked the drawer and lifted out her cash box. With trembling fingers she took the small key from her chain and unfastened the box. It was empty. She slumped on to the stool and, resting her elbows amongst the brushes and jars, held her head in her hands. Through the beat of blood in her temples she heard Ashley come into the room. He closed the door and approached her.

"Sophia." He stood behind her and put his hands on her shoulders. She hit them away with her fists.

"You have," she said breathlessly, "you have taken it!"

"Yes," his voice was hard but had a tremor. "I told you I had. I —"

"It was mine. Mine by law. It was in my marriage settlement that it should be paid to me every year. You had no right to it."

Ashley thrust his hands into his pockets to hide their convulsive clasping.

"The money was to be paid to you but becomes mine as soon as you receive it. All that you have belongs to me. Perhaps I should remind you that everything you possess —

your jewellery, clothes — is my property and may not be sold by you. I was entitled to your banknotes."

She looked about her dazedly. "But how did you — my box was locked."

"Naturally I have keys to every lock in this house."

"Oh God," she covered her face. "Then I have no privacy, no freedom at all."

"My love," Ashley took his hands from his coat, "the laws are to make you free — free to be without the responsibilities that weigh on men. I'm your husband and should think of these things for you." Sophie, he thought, Sophie — believe that I'm doing what's right for you; love me for it.

"It isn't fitting," he went on, "that you set yourself against my policy for the estate. Financing those weavers would be pure defiance of my rule." He touched her shoulder again and she shrank away from him. "Sweetheart, I did you a great favour yesterday. You know how strongly I feel that men should not act without masters yet when you pleaded with me — you and your maid — I withdrew the instructions that would have rid me instantly of that Jacobin group. The river will not be diverted. Mason tells me the cooperative will die a natural death but I'm not so certain and I take the risk for love of you."

Sophia stared at him in the mirror. "You humiliated me," she said "by consulting Mason before you'd grant me this — favour. And now you leave me penniless because I was to give them a little food and trade. What price Swing tonight?"

He turned away abruptly and took a few furious paces back and forth.

"The situation is entirely different. The field labourers wished to return to the old ways — these pestilential weavers would have us all upside down and in revolution."

"They're doing no harm, Ashley. Just trying to gain a living."

He grasped the bed-curtains to steady himself.

"If inferiors are to prescribe to their superiors," he said, "if the foot aspires to be the head — to what end are laws enacted? No — it's the indispensable duty of everyone — as a friend to the community — to endeavour to suppress them in their beginnings." He left the bed and came to stand behind her once more. There was only firelight in the room but their faces stood out pale and stricken in the glass.

"Sophie," he said. "You're so young. You must trust me to know what's best. I can't leave you able to provide for undesirables. Concern yourself with what's suitable. Will you come down to the hall?"

"No."

"The carriage will be ready."

"You must make my excuses to Mrs Marsh. If I went with you tonight I'd disgrace your name. Let me have the headache or spleen or any of the things we women have."

"Very well."

There was a moment's silence. The division between them had never before been expressed in anger and it was bitter and painful to them both. Ashley waited as if he expected Sophia to speak and when she did not he turned away and strode out of the room. He closed the door quietly and she thought — he does that for the servants.

It was warm and dark in the room. There was a faint crackle and spit from the fire and the glow of the flames shifted and wavered on the tapestried walls. Sophia sat in pearls at the heart of her husband's ten thousand acres and mourned — I have nothing I can give and so I have nothing. The shock and rage that had risen at her discovery was dying and a numbness was spreading in her but it was a numbness she recognized as the pause before grief. A laugh that sounded small and broken came from her and stopped suddenly as she was surprised by it. After all, she asked herself, what has happened? A husband has exerted his authority over his wife. An ordinary event applauded by almost everyone. She held her head in her hands and closed her eyes. Oh, God, she thought, let there be more than this. After such desperation, such seeking and hope of unity, let our marriage be more than petty, commonplace unhappiness. She remembered her acceptance of him and how she had dismissed her fears by saying that her misery could never be as great as that of Hester and her kind; she had not tasted then the slow poison of gradual disillusionment and the ebbing of faith. There was such loneliness in their marriage; she recognized it in Ashley as well as herself but could not reach him and her efforts to touch his emotion were as if she were coaxing open a container she suspected to be empty. If she could give him the son he craved perhaps it would be different but no child came and she had began to be repulsed by his touch. How much more so now? Before they were wed she had longed to be in the shelter of his strength and certainty. He had shown his strength and she was powerless.

A tear — and then another — welled and spilt out of her eyes. With blurred sight she searched the open drawer for a handkerchief and dried her face. There would be no weeping; tomorrow she would rise as usual and begin a disciplined and adult life.

A soft knock disturbed her and she looked at the door. Hannah entered with a candle in her hand. Even in the dim light she could see the distress on her mistress' face and her maternal nature was roused by the anguish. Nathan Hearne was the yeast that was working her spirit but its rising engulfed all calls on her tenderness. In this dark room the woman who Calder loved sat in pain from the actions of the man who had hanged Caleb. Putting the candlestick on a chair she crossed to Sophia and took her in her arms, dabbing the glistening lashes with the edge of her shawl.

"Oh, my lady," she said. "There now. There's my moppet."

At this unexpected demonstration Sophia laughed and for several minutes tears and laughter mingled, and threatened to become hysteria before she calmed herself and sat holding Hannah's arm and gasping.

"Hannah," she said when she had regained control of her voice, "how much is the passage to Philadelphia?"

"A little over three guineas steerage, ma'am," Hannah replied, puzzled, "and take your own food. I don't know what it is for gentry."

Sophia's face creased again but this time there was anger and disgust in it. "In my purse," she said, "I have a sovereign and a six-penny piece. It's all that I have and my husband would've taken it from me if it hadn't been in my pocket. I am a rich woman, am I not? The fortunate Miss Farren who married a baronet — oh, Hannah, Hannah. I can't even give you your fare to join your brother. I should have sent you all when he left but I didn't think of it. Forgive me — I've been blind and thoughtless in so many ways."

Hannah held her as if she were a child. Thoughts of what might have been — and the question of what she now wanted — kept her silent and the sound of the window rattling was loud in the room.

"The wind is rising, ma'am," she said. "At Five Warrens we would've heard the sea."

Sophia listened to the worsening night that held no roar of waves. "How far away it is for both of us," she said. "And I've brought you here and can't help you or your friends."

Hannah released her and moved behind the stool to undo her headdress. The heavy coils of scented hair with the ropes of pearls twisted between the braids fell down over Sophia's back and shoulders and gleamed against her pale skin. Hannah began to undo the plaits and take out the silver pins. As Sophia gave her the brush Hannah said, "There is something you could do for me, ma'am, if you had a mind."

"Oh?" Sophia shook her head to loosen the untied hair. "Then tell me and I'll do it gladly if I can."

Hannah watched her hands as she passed the brush through her lady's hair.

"Perhaps you heard, ma'am, that I had a letter from my brother, Calder, in America."

Yes, thought Sophia, I did — and you did not mention it and so I did not ask.

"I did hear," she said. Through the mirror she watched the flames play in the grate. There had been another fire in the night — on a hillside in cold May weather; a man had said, "Come forward into the light," and she was here in darkness.

"Ma'am — you're trembling." Hannah stopped brushing.

"No." Sophia said, "No. Is your brother well?"

"He flourishes. He wasn't used to the abundance of food and his stomach was awry but now he prospers." Again she ran the brush through Sophia's hair, dividing the strands with her fingers. Sophia leant back into the action as if she were being stroked.

"Did he find his Ideal Community?" she asked.

"He's lived in five, ma'am, but not for much time in each. At two they would have him on his knees a-praying or calling for repentance until his head was reeling, at another he was hardly better than the slaves and a fourth broke apart with quarrelling — but now he's settled and happy in his ways. He walked more miles than he knows in his search and wrapped his feet in the skin of a cat to stop them bleeding." Her voice was full of pride and excitement at this adventure among places and people so different from what she knew.

"But what does he do?" Sophia glanced over her shoulder. "He told me — I remember him saying it — that a strong arm might be needed. Was it right?"

Hannah pushed Sophia's head gently back to face the mirror. "He's the same as here — a shepherd. The men are all farmers or work in the smithy by day but in the evenings they have schooling — and that's what I was asking, ma'am." She laid down the brush. "I was never quick with my lettering, ma'am. The housekeeper read out the news for me but — Calder loves his lessons and was strong against being kept from books over here. He's bitter-angry about the magistrates that time when you —"

"Yes," said Sophia.

"The other servants don't like it, ma'am — they say he doesn't know his place. No one will write a letter back for me. Mr Mason is always seeking me out but he was there that time with your Prayer Book and I don't trust him. So — would you write for me, ma'am?"

Sophia moved the trinkets on her table. "This letter," she said, "he will not know — you would have to tell him of Caleb and Hester?"

Hannah was quiet and then, in almost a whisper, "Yes, ma'am."

"You understand," Sophia said, "that whatever disagreements we might have Sir Ashley is still my husband and I can say nothing disloyal to him?"

"Yes."

"Then I will write for you if you tell me what you would say."

Hannah let out a sigh. "Thank you," she said, "thank you; and, ma'am — that sovereign and sixpence. We could use it for postage."

Sophia smiled, "Indeed we could. And where would we send it? What is his address?"

"Pleasant Waters, Pennsylvania, ma'am."

Sophia rested her hands on the drawer and laughed outright.

"Pleasant Waters," she said, "Pleasant Waters — how we'd all like to be on those. Oh, Hannah, fetch me the paper and pen and ask your brother to send me a breath of his air."

Chapter 24

In the pastures of Pennsylvania, where the forests hid threats to sheep not dreamed of in England, the shepherd now pursuing his calling with shoes on his feet and a heady freedom from magistrates and keepers, had matters on his mind apart from wolves and bears.

He received letters from two women in the name of one and the news he read in, and between, the lines occupied his thoughts and changed his intentions. The news of Caleb and the gentle girl he had loved had been a profound shock and hurt to him. He did not believe that his brother — so patient and with such need to be unnoticed by the law — had lost his senses and committed arson — but, with his own experience, it did not surprise him that Caleb should be blamed unjustly. The sorrow and futility of the deaths overwhelmed him and as he lay in the dormitory for the unmarried men, and thought of the winter nights he had slept in the straw in the farm-attic sharing his brother's warmth, tears of anger and grief would come to his eyes.

He blamed Ashley Claydon. The life he had led of deprivation in the face of plenty — had not fostered a Christian resignation or inclination to turn the other cheek and he began to think it would be sweet to be revenged upon the baronet by taking from him what they both must want most — his wife. Nothing had taught him to respect the institution of marriage as the only, and the unbreakably sacred, form of bond between a man and woman. He was familiar with the unorthodox relations among the sexes in many of the communes; in the backwoods, through which he had travelled, couples consorted together until a preacher happened by to perform a ceremony; he himself had had no parents and Sophia had been raised by a grandfather who lived openly in sin. He was more aware than she had been of her feelings for him and, though it revolted him to think of her as Claydon's wife, he did not imagine that there had been love on her side. Despite his own independent and venturous spirit his upbringing had left enough fatalism in him for him to believe that people led their lives according to patterns not of their choosing. For all that he knew Sophia had been contracted to Ashley by her grandfather to merge their estates. Though she said nothing against her husband in her letters it was plain from her tone — and the fact that she wrote — that she was not happy with him. If she had had children to damage he would not have considered approaching her but it appeared that, despite her husband's desire for an heir, there were none — nor, as she put it in Hannah's name was there "likelihood of issue". His natural arrogance was blossoming in a country where each white settler was free to rise as high as his neighbour and in a community where a member was judged by his behaviour and talents — and even the women were thought equal — and, though in England he would not have thought it possible to pay court to a woman of Sophia's rank, he now felt that his enduring love for her allowed him to do so. Nor was it only pride and revenge that urged him to take her from her unhappy home. The gentleness that made him a good shepherd also drew him to succour her. From her apologetic explanation of why she could not send Hannah to America he had learned that she was kept penniless and the knowledge that she was a humiliated prisoner of the vicious Claydon determined him to go to her aid. The cruel removal of the family he had been planning to receive, and Hannah's growing affection for a man who seemed unfit for a pioneer's life, meant that he was no longer the vanguard of an emigrant dynasty but was free to decide his own future.

The letters from his settlement to the old country were sent among the loads of iron-goods that were carried from their smithies to New York. From there — at a cost of twenty-five cents — the Black Ball packets sped them at unheard-of speeds to Liverpool. With the various delays involved he could reckon on his letters reaching Hannah within three months of sending and was sure he could rely on a prompt answer. A gap of half a year between replies did not distress him unduly. He was not used to a fast pace of life and needed time to improve his education enough to be a companion for a gentlewoman and to persuade such a woman to break her vows and enter the wilderness for his sake. From his first reading of Sophia's hand he began to court her — gently and obliquely — and as the fierce Pennsylvanian seasons strengthened and hardened him he determined to return and claim what should have been his own.

"And pray tell Miss Farren —"

"He always forgets you're married," interrupted Hannah.

Does he? Sophia thought. I wonder. "Oh," she said, "your brother's so far away and never saw Sir Ashley — why should he have noted my name?" She smoothed the weather-stained letter and went on reading "that I bear always in mind that it was she who set me upon this Free Life and that I keep her Prayer Book by me Always and Always. It is a Keepsake and Rememberance. England is often-times in my thoughts and there are those in it that I long to look upon as a Hart desires the Stream. I close now with right good wishes to you, Hannah and to your lady who holds your pen. Your faithful and affectionate brother, Calder."

They were sitting in a window-seat in the Long Gallery where the sunlit elegance and harmony of the room mocked the stifling lives lived by the inhabitants of the house. More than a year of marriage and service had put its marks upon them in different ways. Hannah was better fed and enlivened by loving Nathan, a man who needed all her care and more, but remained haunted by the loss of Caleb and, although she and Sophia had moved close to friendship, the fear of those in high rank his death had engendered prevented her from putting all her trust in her mistress. She looked on Sophia as a caged leopard who chose to be tame now but could turn and ravage her at any time. Sophia, herself, was aware that, despite her approaches, there was a holding back in Hannah that threw another loneliness into a marriage that was all sour disillusion. The hopes she had had of her union with Ashley had faded almost as quickly as the violets he had given her in London. She had longed to give so much of herself and had found it rejected. He had claimed her as his wife but after an initial, brief interlude of uneven and forced emotion had withdrawn from any attempt at understanding. They no longer lived as husband and wife; hardly had they entered their home when the tender passions of their first nights had been replaced by a strange, dark striving to father an heir and as the months showed it to fail so did Ashley's ability to pay his conscientious, routine attentions fade and die.

Alone in the heraldic bed, listening to the sounds of her husband's tormented sleeplessness beyond the dressing room door, Sophia — mentally and physically hungry for love — searched her mind for what could have divided them. It seemed now that they had never had opinions in common and the captivity in which he kept her tried her patience almost beyond endurance. In order, as he said to protect her from the vexations of the world, he let her accept almost no invitations nor receive company in the house and would not allow her to stray beyond the park unless it was in a closed carriage. He was invariably courteous to her and would occasionally accept endearments and caresses, as he had done in the early months of their marriage, but asked for her views on no matters of importance to him and rather than be with her he would sit alone in rooms with the blinds drawn down.

She knew him to be ill but suspected it was a sicknesss of the soul more than of the body. Bound to him by the law and her promises, she could not leave him even if she were prepared to do so but the empty, destructive years stretched ahead of her like a prison sentence and what harm, she thought, what harm could there be in taking a little comfort from the letters of a man an ocean away?

"Yes," she said, putting down Calder's letter and picking up some newly-written sheets that lay on the table before them. "We've answered his questions and I believe we've given all our news — what little there is of it."

"You didn't say, did you, ma'am, that Mrs Thomson is with child?"

Sophia dipped the pen in the inkwell and made a word clearer. "He never knew my cousin — it would be of no interest." She glanced at Hannah and smiled. "You think of it because of your Nathan," she said. Hannah laughed. "Think is all, ma'am," she said. "Trade is no better and to wed is to bring forth mouths to feed."

"For some," said Sophia. "For some."

They fell silent as she folded the papers into a package and sealed it with wax and ribbon. Her nib scratched loudly on the parcel as she directed it; the address always gave her pleasure to write.

"Does Mason still follow you?" she asked.

Hannah took the pen and dried it on a cloth. "Yes," she said, tiredly. "In his way. Forever wearying me with his 'Hannah, bind my leg.' 'Hannah, you're so gentle,' 'Hannah, shall I teach you to read?' and I must suffer him for Nathan and the rest. I can't abide him."

"Nor I." Sophia leant back into the corner of the window-seat and rested her arm on the sill. She flexed the fingers of her writing hand. "This affliction in his leg," she said, "I think that constant pain exaggerates whatever is already in a character. If Mason had been a kindly man he would have become more kind — but he was not."

"He's an opium-eater," said Hannah. "Sometimes he stinks of it."

"Yes," Sophia tapped the glass sharply, "and what does that do to his judgement? The whole estate is in his hands."

No longer feeling secure that any correspondence she put into the letter-bag would leave the house unread by its master Sophia sent Hannah into the village to see the packet posted. Although she had too much pride to complain to anyone of her husband she sent her letters to Mrs Dene unstamped, trusting her to pay the carriage, and Mrs Dene — drawing her own conclusions — willingly did so and was sick at heart for her beloved girl. The money Ashley gave Sophia for the innocent practice of writing to her old governess was used for passage to America.

The afternoon was fresh but mild and Hannah enjoyed the

freedom of the open air. On her way back, however, an observer would have noticed that, on hearing the wheels of a gig behind her, she looked about for an escape into the fields and, finding none, was obliged to accept a seat beside the agent of her household. If the observer had been travelling in their direction he would also have seen that after an apparently agitated conversation the driver drew to a halt and ejected his passenger before they had reached the Hall. He then drove on striking his horse unnecessarily and did not look round at the maid who seemed to be shaking.

In the estate-room Ashley sat in the chair behind the desk rubbing his eyes with the thumb and forefinger of one hand. The cadaverous aspect, which had overtaken him after the death of Caleb, had returned after its short-lived banishment in the early weeks of marriage, and his thin, white face was spectral in the afternoon sun.

A jug of coffee stood on the edge of the desk and as he poured it into his emptied cup his arm trembled, almost spilling the contents on to the form that lay before him. He was applying himself to the questionnaire on the administration of the poor law that had been sent out by the Royal Commission, and the conviction that history was crushing his beliefs beneath its rolling wheels did nothing to heal a spirit that was wretched and distraught. Only the knowledge that he had no heir prevented him from the final sin of ending a life unbearably painful to him.

As he sat in the quiet room with the shadow of a loose tendril of ivy swaying gently on the wall, he asked whether he could trust himself not to succumb to temptation. He was in terror of his state of mind; he felt his intellect to be crumbling. Madness, which had always waited on the horizon for others, now walked close at his side and there was a sweetness in its breath. He had only to look into its eyes and there would be no more responsibility; if he could not have his wife's respect he would have her pity.

He steadied his cup in both hands and drank in long, deliberate gulps. The physician Sophia had insisted he see had told him that coffee would clear his head and, though it did not, he took it for her sake. He loved Sophia no less than when he had married her. Indeed, much of the rift between them had been caused by the seriousness with which he took his duty to protect her. Whatever magic he had hoped for from her in giving him serenity had not occurred and he did not blame her for it. What had he expected? She was hardly more than a girl and he was a man of twice her age with experience he had begun to long to confess to her.

As he thought of this indulgence he closed his eyes and the uneven pounding of his heart mingled with the muffled voices that he was never sure that he could hear. He dared not laugh or cry and when Mason came into the room it was to find Ashley sitting like one who had died.

Mason threw his cloak and hat on to a stool. The noise withdrew Ashley from his thoughts and he opened his eyes on to his friend. The sight shocked him. He knew his agent to be a man of strong, subterranean emotion but here was naked anger. He gestured to the chair into which Hannah had lifted Mason the previous summer and it was taken with an abrupt, speechless movement.

"My dear Mason," said Ashley, "a cordial. Do you keep anything at hand?"

"Brandy — in the lower drawer."

Ashley reached down into the desk and removed a small flask and tumbler. Pouring a measure he passed it across to Mason who drank it with fierce contractions of his throat.

"Your daughter —" he said.

Ashley let the flask knock against the wood; he put it down with care. They never referred to the girl in this way.

"What of her?" he asked.

"You'll have noticed," said Mason, brushing his mouth with his sleeve, "that I've taken an interest in her. As I should — as, naturally, I should to one who is your — even though —" He rapped his knuckles against the arm of the chair and gathered himself. "Many and many a time I've offered to teach her to read. The staff would've tormented her if she hadn't been under my patronage."

My daughter, thought Ashley, in my house. Inside his shirt he felt his skin grow clammy.

"I believed — of course, I know — that she should have better of life." Mason's fists were clenching and reclenching; he held the fingers out straight and separate to keep them still. "This afternoon I met her in the lane. I proposed marriage to her. She refused me."

There was a strange lightness in Ashley's body as if he were floating within his clothes.

"Why did you ask?" he said. "Do you love her?"

Mason looked at him as if he had introduced an unexpected change of subject. He was cooling and regaining control as he spoke. He could not explain his desire to bind himself ever more firmly to his friend and the estate but the insult he had received deepened his determination to be master. Inwardly he raged at the repulsed defiance of this girl who he coveted as a piece of the Claydon properties that could become wholly his. He would have her.

"I — she has been kind," he said. "Remedies and nursing for my bones. I like her to be near."

"My wife tells me she has a weakness for one of the weavers."

"Weakness!" Mason laughed shortly. "Aye — weakness is the word. A barefoot spindle-shank — but she's a woman and a good girl and may be brought to her senses."

Ashley frowned slightly. "You've said nothing of your preference to me before."

You would have seen, thought Mason with contempt, if you had eyes for anything but your guilt.

"I was never one to gossip of my affections," he said. "But if you would use your influence now it would be a true act of friendship."

"Influence?" said Ashley. "What influence is this?"

Heaven help us, Mason thought in exasperation — in what world does he live? In a placating tone he said, "You're her employer and benefactor. She depends on you and is fond of your lady. If you talked to her and explained that you wished her to unite herself with me it would have great effect — especially if it were put to her that the weavers, who are such an affront to you, would suffer if she didn't reconsider. And there are obvious advantages in being my wife — I would treat her well and be as thorough in preserving a good marriage as in preserving the estate."

"I think," said Ashley, adjusting the form before him, "there should be no influence from a third party used in such matters." He looked at Mason with sorrow. "My dear friend — dear Robert — if this — if Hannah is the woman of your heart I do most sincerely regret any pain you must bear because of her but the outcome must be decided by you alone."

Mason struck the desk with the flat of his hand. "You don't want me to be related to you," he said, "even if I still conceal the truth."

A shock of recognition arose in Ashley like the sudden dew on a cold glass in a warm room. It was in this man's mind to denounce him and it was appropriate that his scourging and redemption should come from one who had been the close companion of his evil years. He relaxed into the release that was being offered and smiled.

"Even if —" he prompted softly.

The smile enraged Mason. His own character prevented him from understanding what remorse had done to Ashley and he saw only complacency in the expression.

He leant towards Ashley and spoke with the venom of long and deeply-rooted envy. "If you won't speak in my favour," he said, "I will reveal your history to all who will listen. Your reputation will be lost, your good name worthless and your known daughter will marry a pauper at your gates."

Ashley drew in his shallow breath with exaltation. All that he had done these twenty years had been a struggle towards the good and true. Now he could drive a girl he knew to be in fear of him into a marriage she had already refused or he could sacrifice his public face for what would be an act of honour. Here was penitence; here was choice.

He looked on Mason with eyes that were those of a fanatic.

"I will not speak," he said.

Shortly before midnight Sophia tried the door between her

room and Ashley's and, finding that it was — as usual — locked, she took a candle and went out into the corridor. The house was silent and the darkness beyond her small flame seemed a material thing. She knocked on the dressing room door and when she received no answer she lifted the handle and went in.

As she had expected Ashley was there. He had no fire or lamp and was sitting upright and full-dressed in a wing-chair beside the grate. He had drawn back the curtains and the moonlight and candle gave an effect of extreme cold. He did not speak or seem to notice her and as she closed the door at her back she felt an ache of sadness for them both and thought — how did this come about? We were both so willing to love one another.

"Ashley," she said.

At the sound of her voice he looked at her and there was such a strange euphoria in his face that she had an impulse to turn and run. The hand holding the candlestick began to sweat.

"Ashley," she said again. "I have something to tell you. Perhaps you'll call it a confession." She touched her throat. "Hannah came to me this afternoon in great distress. Mason has been paying her unwanted attentions and today he offered marriage. Neither she nor I trust him not to use some threat or force to have his way. I gave her a gold chain I had before I met you and a note saying she is to sell it on my behalf. It will pay for a licence for her to marry her weaver. She's left the house and will not return. I know the chain was yours but I must defy you in this."

When she had finished speaking she realized that she was trembling. She moved the candle to her other hand and a thin trail of smoke floated between them as they watched each other.

"A licence?" Ashley said. The elation was seeping from his face, leaving the rigid emptiness that she feared was his real self.

"Yes. They left for Norwich this evening and will be wed directly. I had no wish to be devious, Ashley, but I know Mason to be your friend."

She waited for him to reply or give some sign of anger but he sat as if he had withdrawn himself from life. The tick of the clock on the mantelshelf grew louder and louder in her ears. Feeling behind her she opened the door; a shaft of light from her own room lay across the corridor. She looked back at the still figure in the greyness and could not leave him like this. Pushing the door ajar, she went back into his room and began to hold her flame to his candles.

Chapter 25

In the summer of 1834 the New Poor Law was passed. It deprived the parishes of their old authority over the relief of the poor and put it in the hands of six hundred newly formed Unions under the dominion of the Central Board of Commissioners. The instructions of this general administration were clear — that any able-bodied person seeking relief must do so in a workhouse and that — in order to discourage indolence and vice — the workhouses should be deliberately kept to a standard of comfort lower even than the deprivations that had driven applicants to its door.

The constitution and principles of the new administration were a rebuttal of all that Ashley had striven to preserve but, as he sat in his darkened library leaving the paper unread, he was no longer in a state to care.

Life at the Hall was falling gently apart like something rotting. Since the day Hannah had left the Hall, Ashley's health had become rapidly worse. The numbness in his hand, the palpitations and sensation of being crushed in the chest and back had become a daily burden and he had been obliged to give up all participation in running the county. Sophia had hoped that no longer having to sit on the Bench would raise his spirits but the apathy which imprisoned him grew no less and kept him like an invalid. She did not believe the physician's diagnosis that Ashley's lack of interest in the world was a result of his illness and thought that there was some root cause concealed from her which she could not guess.

She blamed herself. If she had been the kind of wife he could confide in, her support might have enlivened him. As things were she did what she could. Without a public, social or intimately private life they had little on which they could violently disagree and a kind of companionship emerged in a snail-like way. Ashley persevered in keeping her without money but turned a blind eye to her gifts of food to the weavers and Sophia felt that these visits to Hannah were what kept her sane.

There were fewer weavers in the barn now. As Mason had predicted, time was breaking the cooperative without force from Ashley. That spring Jed Yates and his sons had left to seek their fortune in one of the expanding northern towns. They had promised to send word of their safety but none had come and the Greaves and Hearnes struggled forward in ignorance of their friends' destination and their own future. They could not earn enough to support themselves and — their move to the barn having brought them into the parish where both John Greaves and his son, Luke, were born — they applied for poor relief. Nathan and Hannah, who were of Norwich and unknown birth, could not persuade the overseers that their work in the district entitled them to a settlement but a dole of bread was granted the Greaves on condition that the men laboured for two days in each week breaking stones for the roads. It was not an activity that suited their health after their sedentary lives but the anxiety it caused them was as nothing compared with the fear put in them by the Poor Law.

They had known it was coming but had hoped against hope that a change of heart amongst the members of Parliament would cause the Act to be thrown out. If it was not, their last painful independence would be stripped away; they could not survive without their dole and would be forced into a workhouse and once inside husband would be separated from wife and parents from children.

The Hall was isolated from much of the agitation as it was isolated from most news of the outside world but Sophia heard the rumours when she visited Hannah and pieced them together with what she read in the papers and learnt from her correspondents. Harriet, whose time was now wholly absorbed by her wardrobe and cradle, was of little interest, but Francis and Mrs Dene — to whom she wrote regular bulletins of courageous lies — both sent her accounts of more unrest — of strikes and meetings of labourers protesting over the breaking

233

of matrimonial ties, of rick-burnings, of six men of Tolpuddle transported for administering an oath. These she recounted to Calder when she wrote Hannah's letters — for, though John and Nathan could both write with concentration, Hannah believed that Sophia and her brother would prefer the old arrangement. She described to him the terror of the poor who did not wish to exchange their familiar out-door hunger for what might wait for them behind high walls. She wrote of the myth that pauper bread was poisoned to reduce the numbers to be admitted to the workhouses and of the riots at Bircham Tofts and Christian Malford where a hundred people took possession of the church and refused to let the overseers enter. In the weeks following the announcement that the old charity hospital between Marlingham and Althorpe St Giles was to be reopened as the district workhouse, she had her own tale to tell. "On Sunday last," she wrote, "a still greater number of the poor attended church. The notice was repeated immediately before the sermon was delivered and again every poor man, woman and child to the number of one hundred and fifty, walked out — the men smoking their pipes in the churchyard. Sir Ashley was hissed as the congregation departed — the people believing that he is in authority in this place. My lady doubts that the poor will have their way or that Robert Mason will be refused the office of workhouse agent for which he has applied."

If the organizing of the provision for paupers had been a task that Mason expected to take him much away from his estate he would not have put himself forward but to one of his abilities it seemed a simple thing to fit into his day. Occasionally now he found a field of docks or an unpaid bill which had escaped his vigilance but they were matters easily rectified and did not disturb his confidence or lower his talent to the level of other agents. This particular increase in his work would have the double merit of giving him the interest of a novelty and of spiting Ashley.

Since the opportunity of marrying into the Claydon family had been snatched from him on the very day he had proposed it, he had wavered between exposing Ashley for the pleasure of revenge or remaining silent in the hope that his uncharacteristic outburst would be ignored. With Hannah married it would be convenient for life to continue as before and — after a fashion — it did since the decrease in rational behaviour in both men prevented each from seeing clearly the changes in the other. However, Hannah's elopement, with the connivance of Sophia, had not only injured what tender feelings there were in Mason but had hurt his pride and, on the passing of the New Poor Law, he saw an opportunity to wound them all which he could not resist.

The parish of which he was overseer had not previously included the land where the weavers had their barn but now that the Unions had been formed the neighbouring areas had been amalgamated for purposes of poor relief. When their dole was removed from them, the Hearnes and Greaves would be obliged to turn to the workhouse for help — and the workhouse would be run by him. The envy which had poisoned his relations with his master had taken a new and tormenting form on hearing from a distressed Ashley that Hannah was with child and the thought of having it in his power to separate the entire family was an exquisite delight to him.

Reckless of any consequence to himself, Mason went to the miller — in his capacity as agent — and told him that Sir Ashley was determined to bear the cooperative no longer. If the rogues did not immediately remove — without further annoyance in the form of petitions — the river would be channelled and all livelihood from the mill lost.

Within the day the weavers were homeless.

In the week following the dispersal of the weavers, the threatening letters began. With the new workhouse almost ready to open its doors there was a mood of incensed justice amongst the poor which was finding an outlet for a rage and despair they knew to be ultimately ineffectual in a violent hatred of those above them. Many landowners and magistrates were secretly delivered notes which reminded them of Swing but in the area of Marlingham it was Ashley who received the most.

It seemed obvious to the people likely to become inhabitants of the workhouse that the man who owned the largest property in the region and employed the most cold-hearted agent and overseer, would be the most powerful and have the yea or nay over the change in the local poor relief. It was known that he had a long-standing spite against the weavers and when it was learnt that the cooperative had been closed, with its members fleeing the county by night to escape the workhouse, it was not Mason, but Ashley, who was blamed.

The first letter at Claydon Hall was found nailed to a stable door — which itself had a particular and gruesome relevance for Ashley, unintended by its leaver. "Gentleman," it said, "You have taken Away All Poor men's Pay and you must take care of your Self, Corn, hay and stock this Wenter. You will get it ham-string." The next morning the pheasants in a lonely covert were found slain and left lying in a manner quite unlike normal poaching and, on hearing of the poisoning of a neighbour's dog, Ashley gave orders that Watch was never to be let out of doors without being fastened to a short leash.

It was not, however, to his dog that the next violence was offered. Two days later, on their way to their work, a field-gang of girl labourers came upon a sheep suspended by a rope about its neck from the branch of a tree. When the gang-master cut the animal down it was found to have tied to it a paper addressed to Ashley which said: "Their will be a slaughter made amongst you very soone. I shood well like to hang you the same as I hanged your beastes."

On receiving the letter Ashley collapsed and was put to bed — where he stayed for a fortnight before being allowed up for a few hours at a time. The disappearance of Hannah so soon before she was to be delivered of his grandchild brought forcibly to his mind the death of Hester, and the threat of hanging was so appropriate a vengeance that it conjured an image of Caleb at his bedside. His dreams were plagued by scenes of courtrooms. He was not afraid of having his life ended by an assassin — indeed, would almost have welcomed it — but circumstances made him dwell on the evil eye he appeared to cast upon his descendents until he felt he could endure no more.

To keep him from further worries Sophia asked Mason to prevent any new letters reaching Ashley without first being shown to, and discussed with, her. Mason, regretting the impulsive action which had led to Ashley's illness without securing the Hearnes in his own mercy, agreed. For the only time in their acquaintance, he and Sophia were united in a common aim — for her husband's sake Sophia wanted to encourage Ashley's recovery; for his own sake Mason was anxious to help her. Nor was this the single subject on which their thoughts were similar — for both of them were consumed by a craving to know where Hannah had gone.

Before Nathan and Hannah had been in London a week, Hannah knew that they should have gone north with the Greaves. The suddenness of the weavers' eviction had scattered the wit of minds already indecisive with anxiety. The miller had paid them a little for looms they had nowhere to take but they had no means of providing themselves with a livelihood — and the terror of being torn from their children in the workhouse determined them to gamble on finding a town manufactory willing to use their skills. It was a poor hope but their choice was small.

Despite the lack of news from their old work-fellows the Greaves decided to take the road to Manchester. Hannah — already so far from the country she knew and desperate that her coming child should be born with a decent life within reach — remembered the opulence and plenty she had seen in London and was convinced that a better chance was open to them there than in the new and unknown towns of foreign Lancashire. Nathan was difficult to persuade — believing, as he did, that their numbers would prove a comfort to them — but pity that she should be brought to such a pass while in her condition convinced him it was kindest to humour her. He knew nothing of cities and she was well-travelled; he trusted in her experience.

They left Althorpe St Giles the night after their eviction. There was nothing to keep them in the parish and it was safer not to linger. It was a hard parting from friends they had lived with so long and, as Hannah leant on Nathan's arm and began to walk heavily towards Marlingham, she wept silently in the darkness for all that had happened to them and the effort that was to come. "Oh, ma'am," she had said once to Sophia as she talked fondly of Nathan, "he can't do anything for himself" — and had laughed at his unworldliness as if it were something to delight in. She feared for them now and they hurried past the lighted Hall like thieves. It was tempting to approach Sophia to ask for help but she had already defied her husband to pay for their wedding — if she gave them more what charges of plunder might be brought against them? Like many in the village it seemed logical to Hannah that Ashley, whose agent had had them turned out, should have had the leading voice in the change to the workhouse and she dared not put her child within his grasp. There was less danger in waiting until they were settled before sending Sophia word of where they were.

They walked for five days before they fell on good luck. A carter, driving down to London with a wagon of saplings, was affected by the sight of a respectable young woman tramping so near her time and offered to let them ride with him if Nathan would take his turn at the reins. It was not a skill Nathan had ever had cause to learn but the roads were straight and empty and, as they sat crushed on the box with Hannah smiling tiredly at the driver's amiable tales, he found himself to have a firm hand with horses. It gave him a brief confidence but the strangeness of the country they rode through and the accents he had to strain to understand undermined it. He was cheerful for Hannah's sake and to keep the good will of the carter but as they left behind the world he knew he felt that their spirits were dwindling and that once they had entered the crowds of the city they would dissolve altogether.

"What are you going to do in the town?" asked the carter as they began to leave the fields behind. "Made any plans?"

Nathan was sitting in the middle of the box with his arm supporting his sleeping wife. They looked too young and vulnerable to be parents.

"I'm a weaver," he said. "We thought to find Spitalfields and try our hand at silk."

The carter sucked his teeth and opened his lips with a smack that was curiously expressive of distrust of their success. "You'll have your work cut out, boy," he said. "Weavers are packed in tight as rats in a nest." He hummed thoughtfully for a moment and then said, "Haven't you got nowhere at all to go back to?"

Nathan shook his head. "That's shut to us," he told him.

"Well now. You're country folk — you'll have done a bit of this and some of that. If you're looking for cheap lodgings you'll do best at Bethnal Green. There aren't the market gardens there were but you've got the Lea marshes and the Essex farms close and the people there still keep some of the old trades — fishing, withy-cutting and the like. Poaching. And it's next to Spitalfields so there you are. It's not healthy, mind, but none of the places you could afford are. They've got the Irish fever and cholera's come down from the north. King Cholera. Is young Mrs strong?"

"Yes," said Nathan, holding her tighter. "Yes, she is."

Hannah woke as they drove into the capital and her courage failed at the sights. She had not realized the size of the city. When she had left the Garnams' house for Norfolk she had been in the care of Ashley's servants who were responsible for delivering her and the luggage safely to Claydon Hall — and because they found their familiar route without difficulty she had assumed that there was only one way in and out of the town. She was a farm-girl and had no experience of places too large for a single main street. Now, amidst the bustle and noise, she looked about her in horror.

She recognized nothing and could not even remember the address of the Square where she had stayed. It puzzled her to be in squalor when all her memories were of luxury. She began to shake and the carter passed her his rug to wrap around her. It was almost night as they pushed through the awkward streets and the combination of dark alleys and the bright stalls mobbed by strangers, now shadowed, now over-lit by the smoking candles, frightened her and made her want to cling to the cart. When a rice-water seller tugged her skirts and pointed at his basins she drew her legs away as if he were a snake.

They were heading for Covent Garden market where the saplings and pots of shrubs were to be delivered for the costers to sell or exchange for old clothes. The sharp, pungent scent of the vegetables was reviving after the stink of the streets and the magnificence of the ever-replenished abundance of foods was a revelation to hungry eyes. Piles of gold could not have impressed them more.

The carter tethered the horse to the railings of St Paul's church and he and Nathan carried his wares to the booths under the Piazza where the costers bought. He was to carry back oranges and lemons into the country and they piled a half-load into the cart and slept — like three cigars in a box — in the space that was left. Around them on the pavement the bird-catcher piled his cages and the squares of turf to floor them and the flower-girls sat amongst their baskets dividing their dripping blooms into bunches. So it was that the Hearnes woke on their first morning in the city to the song of larks and the scent of violets and the sight of women with their heads bowed beneath the weight of apples.

The carter bought them coffee and bread in return for Nathan helping him to finish his load and while they ate and blew at the steam he tried to persuade them to go home. Finding they would not, he stationed them on the edge of the stalls and told them to follow the blue barrow with the one-eyed donkey that would lead them to Spitalfields vegetable market. He wished them good luck and meant it — but as he drove away and looked back to see them standing, each with an orange, he was depressed by his thoughts and said to himself: "Lambs to the slaughter."

Chapter 26

At the time that Hannah and Nathan were leaving their home in Norfolk Calder was lying in his shared bunk in the hold of a ship, taking in sail on an easy sea, outside the Thames estuary. He carried with him a packet of letters and articles on the communal life to be published in the *Cooperator*. Neither Sophia nor his sister were aware of his movements and he was, in fact, travelling a little in advance of one of his own writings to them in which he gave no suggestion of a return.

His intention to recross the ocean to persuade Sophia from her husband had almost matured into an action when the illness of a visitor from England, who had been making a tour of the American communities, left a booked berth empty. Since Calder was ready to make the expedition and willing to perform various errands on behalf of the invalid he took over the proposed passage and found himself on the threshold of a meeting that would decide the course of his life.

His plans depended on whether Sophia would reward his love by leaving her home for his. He recognized that it was no small thing he would ask of her; only an extraordinary woman would exchange her lawful husband and familiar country for a poor man from another world. His present way of living meant security and comfort to him but to her it would be all strangeness and poverty. And if she agreed to go with him they would have no choice but to flee back to Pennsylvania. He could not imagine a man like Sir Ashley giving his wife freedom by divorce and if they remained in the jurisdiction of English law she would always be at risk of being legally dragged back to her husband. He hoped with all his heart that she would come with him.

If she would not he was unsure what he would do. He had benefited from his years in his Community and it was tempting simply to turn about and return to his friends but he wondered whether it was his place to be in his native land trying to improve a situation that had killed his brother. Was it his duty or merely a delusion that would put him again on the brink of transportation? Although the language of the religious revival, with its fiery imagery and promise of the Second Coming, irritated him he was in his element in the general swirl of practical idealism that was the undercurrent of the times. He had experience of new forms of working and it was possible that he could be of use as one of the missionaries who were moving amongst those struggling towards self-improvement.

As he walked down the gangplank on a bright and glistening morning, with his mind alert to his chances, even the salt rottenness of the wharf-planks was delicious to his hold-dulled senses. The sky above the city was full of wheeling gulls, squawking and crying, and he watched them and the people of the docks with fresh eyes. He was returning as the same man but with his bonds released. In his wide-brimmed Shaker hat and open knee-length coat he looked foreign but it was not in his clothes or the coins in his pocket that the root difference lay. There was a confidence in his bearing that had not been there before and when he swung his pack up on to his shoulder and began to walk with purpose towards the streets it did not look as if he would fail in his resolve.

The sound of raised voices broke suddenly into the silent house. Sophia, reading a book and eating an apple as she brushed her hair, sat upright like a startled fox and listened. It was past eleven and the Hall had been shut for the night. She had given Ashley his drops and seen him settled; the servants were dismissed; all should have been quiet. The noise persisted — a door banged and she thought she heard some kind of shouted order on the ground floor.

Wrapping herself in her robe, she took a candle and went out on to the landing. There were no movements in Ashley's room but here running feet and excited words were plainer from below. A figure was coming up the stairs. Since her flame would already have been seen she went to the head of the staircase and looked down.

Mason was climbing the steps in limping bounds, hauling himself upwards by the banister. He was dressed for the outdoors and, where his overcoat swung back with his efforts, she saw that he had pistols in his belt. Oh, God, she thought, are we to have all this misery again? She ran down the first flight to meet him, her robe billowing behind her, and he leant against a newel post waiting for her and catching his breath. The candle guttered from the draught of the run and they both put up their hands to shield the flame. The light shook unevenly in the darkness and their faces were made livid and distended by the glare and shadow.

"The mob are tearing down the workhouse," he said. "I came to warn you there's talk of firing the Hall. The Riot Act's been read and the troops sent for but it'll be a time before they get here. I've unlocked the gun cupboard and given weapons to those who can shoot. My man's gone to rouse the keepers. The women are fetching water."

You take much on yourself, thought Sophia, to arm my servants. "Where are the rioters now?" she asked. "I heard nothing through the shutters."

"Most at the workhouse," said Mason. "They carried out the sick who were taken there this morning and are smashing the rooms. They say they will have blood for supper. I saw torches by the lake as I came in but no one near the house. I've ordered two horses to be made ready. If the rabble surrounds you a carriage would be overturned but riders may escape."

"Ashley would never ride away from his household," said Sophia. "Even if he were fit enough to do it. Nor would I want to."

Mason glanced downwards as a door banged in the kitchens. He was tense and angry but Sophia could see a pleasure in his eyes that reminded her of Francis. If the night did not destroy them it would feed his arrogance and power.

"I'll have Ashley dressed and taken down to the breakfast room," she said. "If it comes to fire we shall at least not be trapped upstairs and the window's large enough to climb out of. A warning may be given us if the Hall is to be burnt. Swing never hurt people. If the threats against us were real we must

prepare to stand the worst. Ashley will stay with his servants."
She began to turn but a thought stopped her. "If any man or
maid," she said, "wishes to leave now — let them go and lock
the house behind them. I'll keep no one unwillingly in danger.
And you — you have an illness. Go if you choose it."

"No," said Mason. "I — No. I'll stay."

"Then if you would take charge of the servants?"

They parted and Sophia ran back up the stairs and on to the
landing. Remembering the window, she put her candle down
where it would not be seen from outside and unlatched the
shutter. There were lights moving in the distance but none
seemed to be approaching the house. She could not see who
carried them but from their erratic wanderings towards the
village she supposed them to be — not the soldiers Mason
hoped for — but rioters on their way to the workhouse. Or
spectators, she thought — please God this is sound and fury
signifying nothing. Let the threats to my Ashley be idle. Let no
one on either side be harmed. It was just such a night that led
Caleb Young to the gallows.

Pushing the shutter closed, she lifted her candle and hurried
to Ashley's room. As she entered she saw that he was awake. He
lay against his pillows, still and silent, with eyes as wide and
dark as a seal. She went softly to his side and lit the candle on
the table by his bed.

"My love," she said. "Mason is here. We must go downstairs."

He took the edge of the sheet in hands that were all bone. "Is
the house burning?" he asked.

Sophia slid the covers from under his bitten fingers and put
her arm about him to help him sit up.

"No," she said "but there're men mobbing the workhouse
and we must be on our guard lest they come here. Let me dress
you."

There were clothes placed ready for his few hours out of bed
the next day and she began to draw off his night-shirt and fasten
him into his linen. His shallow breathing was all that she could
hear and the strain of not knowing whether they were being
encircled made her hands shake.

"Are they here?" Ashley asked. "Have they come to hang me? They said they would."

"There're intruders in the gardens, love, but they're passing down to Marlingham. Mason has armed the men and the troops and keepers are summoned. It will come to nothing."

She tied his cravat loosely and knelt to fit the loops of his trousers beneath his feet. It was quiet downstairs now and she wondered why. Ashley stroked her loose hair.

"Take the grooms and ride away from here," he said. "I want you to be safe."

"No," she said.

"I could order you," he told her — and his voice was rasping and uneven from the exertion of being dressed. "I could have you forced to go."

"Put your feet into your shoes."

"Why should you suffer?" he asked. "I should be hanged. I deserve it. No one more so. I'd welcome it."

She laid her head against his leg. "Oh, Ashley," she said. "Ashley, please be ordinary."

He patted her gently. "My own Sophie. Give me my waistcoat. I'm well today."

Rising from the floor, she held out his waistcoat and jacket; he stood up shakily and put his arms into the sleeves. She buttoned him into his clothes while he balanced himself by gripping her waist. How domestic and respectable we are in the face of disaster, she thought. Caleb Young wore a clean suit to be hanged. She reached up and, pulling Ashley's thin face towards her, kissed him — then, setting her shoulder under his arm, she took his weight and together they began to walk to the stairs.

In the hall the door to the kitchen-quarters lay open and the light that came from it, and the lamp on the table, showed a regular and orderly file of maids carrying water through to the rooms. A young girl, with her night-cap dangling about her back, took fright at her master's sickly appearance and knocked her pail against a chest as she went by. Hearing the sound, Mason came from the library and met Ashley as Sophia supported him down the last steps. He had discarded his overcoat, but not the pistols, and was holding a lantern; he smelt cold as if he had just entered from outside.

"Well, old friend," said Ashley, faintly. "We've come to a pass."

Mason gave a brief, severe smile. "Aye," he said, "we'll see sport tonight but we'll live a day yet."

They looked at each other with a shared, unstated grimness and Sophia, clutching at the banister with her free hand, felt the barrier of their years together excluding her from her position in her home.

"We must make a choice," said Mason. "The mob is destroying the summer-house and the gardens around but has come no nearer. Shall I take the men and at them or will we wait to defend the house?"

Ashley moved his arm on Sophia's shoulder and pressed his hand against her sleeve. His face was a dead-white with exhaustion and his skin was wet. Sophia watched him anxiously and Mason held himself ready to break a fall. Ashley drew a breath between his teeth.

"Wait," he said. "They may content themselves with that damage — and, God help us, I want no more deaths. Let there be no shooting unless we're attacked — then," he looked down on Sophia's upturned face, "we must protect what is valuable."

A stable lad came out of the kitchens and stood uncertainly in the path of the maids. Mason beckoned him and he stepped forward towards them. The shadows flowing with the passage of the girls drew themselves across him like the surging of the sea.

"Sir," he said, "the gamekeepers are here."

"Ah," Mason stirred and grew alert. "I must go," he said. "Can you walk as you are? Shall I send —"

"We can manage," said Ashley. "Sophie — another try."

The breakfast room was in darkness when they opened its door but Ashley, letting Sophia lower him into the chair in the bay-window, told her not to bring light. He pointed instead at the shutter and, fumbling for the catch, she unfastened it and swung it back. In the quiet room, away from the servants and with the wood no longer muffling the noise, they could hear the sound of breaking glass. Sophia stood close to the window and looked out.

There was only a quarter-moon and the night was almost black. A scatter of flames — such as she had seen from upstairs — were moving in the distance but seemed to come no closer. From her knowledge of the gardens she judged that Mason was right in saying that the summer-house was being destroyed. The avenue and flower-garden lay between them and violence. It seemed very still in the room.

"How strange," she said, "that we can hear no cries."

Ashley leant back in the chair; his energy overspent by their walk. His hands hung loosely over the padded arms.

"My dear," he said. "I'd like you to put on a gown — we may have visitors."

She glanced at her robe as if she had forgotten what she was wearing. Hesitating whether to leave him, she kissed him again lightly and went quickly from the room. He heard the sounds of the household as she opened and closed the door but then all was again silence but for the occasional, far-away shatter of glass. He rested his head against the back of the chair and tried to take charge of his body. His left hand was numb and the familiar pressure in his chest and back had worsened and spread round his neck and down into his arm. He thought, as he strove to fix some rhythm in his breathing, that the pain gripped him as he had gripped Sophia. A film of weakness drifted about his mind and eyes; it would be so easy to lose his consciousness and be away from all this but he had sent Sophia away for a reason and to carry out his intention he must be strong and calm.

It was fitting that this night had come. The workhouse was the symbol of his failure in all the paths of his life. He had forsaken his family, caused the death of his son and — through his hatred of the weavers — the disappearance of his daughter who he now felt certain had died. The sins of the fathers shall be visited upon the children. The man he had believed to be a loyal friend was warped by self-seeking; the wife, whose admiration he longed for, was lonely in his company and there was no new generation. What had he lived for? All was sorrow and despair.

He levered himself to his feet and took hold of the window. The action made him giddy and he leant, open-mouthed, against the glass while his heart-beats juddered and the pain grew tighter. It was his duty to face the mob and he had so little time. Using all of his strength he raised the sash-window. His left hand was useless but he forced his elbow into the corner of the frame and lifted. Odd, he thought as he half-fell on to the flags outside, that he who had loved all old ways should be freed at last by this modern addition.

The movement of falling forward from the sill carried him staggering down the wide steps to the garden. He had no physical sensation except his pain and a sudden nausea. Without feeling in his legs, he reeled over the gravel and on to the grass. A pillar of clipped yew-hedge stood in the corner of the central lawn and he found himself supported by it, with his good hand amongst the leaves. It was as if his body were dead; his muscles had no power they could call on and he had no benefit from his breath.

Even at a few yards from the house he seemed to be isolated from it completely. The night was cool and the dew on the flowers was fresh and sweet. The scent of a rose entwined amongst the yew choked him. Here in the sunken garden he could not see along the avenue to the lights and he wanted to lie down in this safe place and be removed from life. Voices drifted to him but there was no more breaking glass. Perhaps the destruction of the summer-house was over; now the crowd would approach the Hall and he must meet them.

By an effort of will he crossed the garden. His pain was like a grief made manifest to crush his bones; his heart seemed to contract within him until his blood could not flow. Stumbling up the stone steps he lurched into the longer grass in the avenue. He could not tell whether it was his vision or the night but the torches he had seen from the house appeared to be fewer and moving — not nearer — but further from the Hall towards the village. Was this then only a wanton diversion by those on their way to the workhouse? He had a sacrifice to make and there would be none to take it. He tried to cry out but no sound came and he floundered forward to the edge of the gathering.

A young man was standing amongst the shattered glass before the summer-house. He carried a banner that trailed at his feet and his eyes, lit by the brands of his followers, were burning with the fervour of his words. His head was thrown back and Ashley, swaying forward and clutching at the bushes, heard him ranting amidst the "Amens".

"Go to now, ye rich men," the speaker chanted, "weep and howl for your miseries that shall come upon you. Your riches are corrupted and your garments —"

A convulsion of pain stopped Ashley and dragged him to his knees.

"Behold the hire of the labourers who have reaped down your fields, which is of you kept back by fraud, crieth: and the cries of —"

Ashley covered his right ear with his hand but his left arm would not move and the spasm in his chest curled him down into the wet grass.

"— a day of slaughter. Ye have condemned and killed the just; and he doth not resist you."

Yes, thought Ashley, yes — it is right. His nails dug into the earth and his legs jerked. In his agony he moaned aloud — and the listeners turned to see him.

Under the trees, Calder watched — attentive but cautious. He despised useless behaviour and religious pretences with equal ferocity but he had done much travelling that day to see things that made him weary and a time spent observing would both rest him and give a warning of any danger to Sophia and Hannah.

He had passed a week in London, attending to the business of the man whose berth he had taken and sleeping amongst the lathes in the home of a shoemaker, before setting out on his journey to Norfolk. He rode part of the way with carriers, once on the roof of a coach and walked the remainder. Such expeditions were not new to him and the anticipations, desires and uncertainties that stirred within him made all that he saw vivid and alive.

That morning he had been fifteen miles from Marlingham,

enjoying the summer day, when he had stopped to take a can of tea with a pedlar. The pedlar, who was coming away from the town, had offered Calder the hospitality of his camp because he looked foreign and the pedlar, himself, loved to hear tales of wanderers. In return for Calder's gossip he gave him the news of the region and as Calder sat on the verge in the early sun, drinking unsweetened tea and toasting old bread over a weak fire, he had heard the rumours of the destruction of the workhouse and the threats to Ashley Claydon. Preferring to keep his own counsel on his involvement with the Hall, Calder had not expressed worries born of information so kindly given but after buying two ribbons had returned to the road intending to reach his destination that night.

He had no luck with passing carters, who were more suspicious of strangers than the pedlar had been. There was distrust in the air and by dusk, when he entered the town, he found himself walking amidst knots of young labouring men — some rowdy, some drunk, some bitter and some with their neckerchiefs tied to hide their faces. He had turned aside for a glass of ale to refresh himself and to avoid being caught up in any trouble. His sympathies were for those who had no say in what would be done with them if they were destitute — but he was sure that any protest they made would be fruitless and harshly suppressed and he did not trust his innocence to protect him from that suppression. One hanging in a family was enough.

Taking the directions of the barmaid he had skirted Althorpe St Giles by footpaths. From what he supposed was the workhouse there was the clamour of an excited crowd and the sound of bricks being thrown down from a height but it had grown dark and he could see nothing across the flat fields. Losing the narrow track in the last half-mile he had come to what must be the wall of the Claydon park and, throwing his pack ahead of him, he had climbed it. His way was unexpectedly lit on the other side.

He was in a copse of beech and oak but, in glimpses between the shrubs beneath them, he saw the flicker of burning brands. With care he moved closer and stood behind a laurel whose branches gave him a view of the activity, while hiding him from anyone who did not expect him to be there. The twigs in the undergrowth cracked as he walked but a smashing of glass covered all other sounds and for a while as he watched, uneasily conscious of the darkness around him and the stir before, the air was full of shattering and calling and ungoverned, inarticulate rage. There was a wide, grass avenue in front of the trees which met a white pavilion where the figures with their torches ran and hurled their stones. The other end of the ride, which he assumed led to the house, faded into the night and it was from this blackness that a movement, different from the others, attracted his eye. The windows of the summer-house were in ruins and most of the vandals were drifting away towards the village, taking their light with them, but in the dim moon and the glow from the flames of the few who had stayed to listen to a ranter, he saw a man approaching.

He was coming forward in uneven staggers and seemed less like a human than some stricken creature limping to shelter. As he passed Calder his clothes showed him to be wealthy and Calder, staring in fascination, realized from the description he had had from his sister that this must be Ashley Claydon. Involuntarily, he shuddered and his face touched the leaves on the bush, smearing him with their cold dew. He put up his hand to brush his cheek and the roughness left from his last shave leapt into his mind as a disadvantage and a reminder that he was still a shepherd and come to set himself as rival to a gentleman. A spurt of anger against this soft, elegant, creeping thing made him crush the green twigs nearest to his hand but he mastered it and watched with a forced resignation.

The scene was not without interest. Here was a man, who had earned his hatred, putting himself freely and alone into the mercy of men incensed by a grievance against him. Why? To what end? It was an extraordinary action and appeared to be being done in the grip of extreme pain. As Ashley sank to his knees under the harangue of the ranter, Calder almost stepped forward — and found himself puzzling over the contradictions of life in which so much that seems fair is foul and courage is discovered in cowards. Could he stand by if Claydon were attacked? Well, he thought with an inward smile, I shall find out within the minute.

The listening men, interrupted by a moan, turned to find Ashley in convulsions on the ground behind them. Gathering about him, they gazed at the landlord they had never seen so near before. Ashley writhed on the grass and one youth pushed him with the toe of a heavy boot and had his arm taken in a restraining gesture by another. In the shadows Calder silently put down his pack. I've come so far to do harm to this man, he thought — am I jealous of others who try? There was a murmured conversation amongst the watchers, with glances down the dark avenue towards the house, and then, in a furtive, half-bashful fashion, they began to filter away, as their fellows had done, in the direction of the village. Two passed Calder under the trees but, seeing that he was neither a keeper nor a gentleman, they merely looked at him with startled expressions and moved on into the darkness. They had won too great a prize, Calder thought, and decided it not worth a rope. And I am relieved in several ways.

Ashley lay hunched on the wet ground, breathing with a shallow, wheezing grunt as if he were wrenching life from the air. Calder walked over to him and crouched at his side. Now that the flaming torches had been taken away there was no light but the moon. To Calder there was a sameness between this moment and his previous life; he had so often knelt in the night beside a suffering creature that it was automatic to him to lay his hand gently on Ashley to calm the shuddering body. There was little in the sweating face that was not animal pain and, as Calder looked on it for the first time, he could find no clue to the man that Ashley was. What did Caleb see, he thought, as he heard his years being taken from him?

On the grass, Ashley struggled up through his agony to see who touched him. He could not understand the familiar features being worn by a man. "Hannah?" he said. "Hannah?" but his voice was so low that Calder could not make out the words. He put an arm under Ashley's shoulder and raised him slightly from the ground. The coat was cold and damp where it had lain and there were leaves clinging to the cloth. Ashley let his head drop back against Calder's sleeve; without thinking he began to know who held him. He took as deep a breath as he could drag into his lungs and thrust words out into the air.

"I have condemned and killed the just," he whispered and his eyes as he looked into Calder's were bright and deep with tears.

Calder cradled him. He felt a desperate tiredness of all the small deceits and wilful blindness that lead men into cruelties. Here in such solitude he could put his hand over this wounded face and push it back until the neck broke as Caleb's had done — and he saw that Ashley knew it and was waiting.

He shut his eyes and sighed. "For everything," he said bitterly, "there is a season," and, bracing his feet firmly on the ground, he slid his other arm under Ashley and lifted him from the grass. He stood a moment to get his balance and then, wearily, began to walk towards the house.

Chapter 27

Had Sophia kept a journal she would have been unable to express in it adequately the sensations that afflicted her from the time she returned to the breakfast room. Even the simplest of a rich woman's clothes were not easy to put on alone in the dark, with fingers that fumbled with ties and catches, and, being called aside by Mason as she hurried down the stairs, an excursion into the kitchens detained her further so that it was twenty minutes or more since she left Ashley that she again entered the room.

She was surprised to find it still in darkness. Relying on the maids to have seen to Ashley's well-being, she had not brought a candle with her and, at first, could see nothing.

"Ashley," she said. "My dear, did you want no light?"

He did not answer and, blaming herself for not having given specific orders to attend to him, she walked carefully forward. Her eyes were adjusting and as she reached the table she realized that not only was Ashley gone from the chair but that the window had been opened enough for someone to climb through. Had an intruder forced his way in Ashley could, surely, have raised the alarm — if only by knocking an ornament to the floor. She stared about her but the room seemed empty. Crossing gingerly to the window she examined the frame as best she could in the moonlight. It had not been forced. She folded her arms along it and laid her head against them. Ashley, with his waning strength, had raised this window and gone out into the face of the rioters. The cold night air drifting in from the garden made her shiver and it occurred to her, as she decided what to do, that there was a selfishness in his action.

She was gazing out through the glass as she gathered herself and was on the point of leaving to muster a search when it seemed that part of the blackness was growing denser. Bending a little, she looked out from under the window to make her view more clear.

There were no longer any torches burning and the garden was so dimly lit by the moon that it was not until the illusion had climbed the steps on to the terrace that she could see that it was real. A shock — that she knew she had expected — burst in her. A man, exhausted by the weight he carried, was holding Ashley in his arms. He staggered as he walked and Ashley's heels dragged roughly on the flagstones. Sophia bunched her skirts and began to climb out but the stranger said, in a voice almost inaudible with fatigue, "No — help me in." Stepping back, she reached out to take Ashley's shoulders as the man edged him in through the window. There was a moment of confusion as they struggled to lower him into the armchair without doing him any harm and as they manoeuvred Sophia glanced up and saw Calder's face.

She gave a low cry. Calder, wearied beyond the ability to stand, rocked back against the corner of the window and slid down the wall to sit on the floor. Pushed by the shutter, his hat fell slowly from his head and lay beside him. Sophia, aghast at the deterioration that she saw in Ashley, looked from his unconscious body to Calder. In an instant, recognition and unbelief rushed through her mind and were replaced by an irrational comfort and an undefined guilt. Did she remember his face or Hannah's? What could she say of his sister?

"Did you call, ma'am?"

Sophia turned to the door as if she had been caught in some shameful act. A footman with a lantern was standing in the entrance. With the light so near him he could not make out the composition of the group at the window but the night air told him that something was wrong.

"Fetch Mason," said Sophia. "Tell him your master is much worse and a physician must be brought — though God knows," she went on as he left, "how he will come or whether he'll find us a-fire."

Calder reached out to take hold of the shutter to pull himself up. Strength was returning to him but the effort of standing made him giddy and he leant against the wing of Ashley's chair. Sophia held out her hand to steady him and he took it and held it in his own. His skin was harder than on hands she had known and she could feel that his palm was calloused. It was a hand that was outside her experience. This is no time, she thought, no time for — She stared at him as if he were an apparition, then slowly withdrew her hand and looked down on Ashley who lay so still and quiet in his seat. She had not put up her hair and it fell down around her white face. She smells, thought Calder, as I remember her; I have a ribbon for her in my pack.

"Don't fear for your household," he said. "What rioters there were have gone. And your — husband is easier than when I found him. He was alone on the ground but it was from illness not attack."

There were sounds of people approaching but his voice, with its slight foreign tang, was as soft and drawing to her as it had been on another night when all else had faded when he spoke. The touch of his hand was as strange and potent as it had been on the Bredy road so long ago. Oh, God, she thought, this is not the time. Ashley, Ashley, you tear at me as you lie there and now I have this.

Again the door was pushed open. Mason and two servingmen came in abruptly and suddenly the room was full of the lights they had brought. A moth wavered in from the darkness and flew mutely towards a flame. Mason limped hurriedly past the table and confronted the figures at the window. Sophia beckoned him as he came.

"Ashley," she said, "is grievously ill and see — see who has come to his aid."

In a small, bare room to the rear of the kitchens Calder lay on his back on a low, trestle-bed with one arm behind his head and the other around his old dog. Watch sat on the floor, resting his chin on his master's chest, and now and again Calder ran his finger from the dog's nose to his ears in the way they both liked. He was touched by the affection that had survived the years and grateful for the care that had obviously been shown to the animal.

"So," he said to the dog, stroking its polished collar, "my lady can love a mongrel."

It was three in the morning and though the house was quietening it was not yet fully a-bed and there were those in it who did not think of sleep. The information that Calder had given about the progress of the riot and the relatively harmless nature of the intruders had encouraged Sophia and Mason to send out a party of armed and mounted men to fetch a physician. A journey to Marlingham for Ashley's usual attendant would have been to invite trouble but a Dr Kerr was known to be staying with cousins in their country house two miles beyond the old weavers' barn and, since there had been no reports of danger from that direction, a note was sent begging him to show the utmost urgency in doing Sir Ashley a kindness.

Neither Calder nor Mason — nor, in her heart, Sophia — believed that medical help would be of much assistance and when the stout, scholarly doctor arrived and examined his patient he was unable to give an optimistic forecast. He was a serious man who did not believe that giving false hopes was a mercy and he put the gravity of the case plainly. It was of some relief that news was brought that the troops had re-established order and the household need no longer be on the alert for attack but one anxiety was merely replaced by another and the house was put on the footing of an infirmary.

During Dr Kerr's private inspection of Ashley, who had emerged from unconsciousness only as far as delirium, Sophia appointed watchmen to guard against a resurgence of rebellion and sent the rest of the servants to bed. She was highly distressed by the events of the night but was preserving a rather taut calm. Calder's presence was a particular agitation for her in several ways — not least because rumours of the number of arrests at the workhouse filled her mind with Caleb — and it did not ease her situation to offer him her hospitality and discover that he had intended to join Hannah and Nathan in their barn.

As Calder lay on the hastily-made bed, trying to rouse himself to undress, he thought on Sophia's expression as she had told him of his sister's departure. No guilt attached to her but it was obvious that she felt that it did — and that her concern was real. He was himself deeply worried by his sister's absence; it did not seem to him that Nathan would be able to fend for her and, even before she was with child, Hannah was too gentle and loving to protect herself in the world. Hester rose before him.

He covered his eyes with his hands and sighed. He must rest and tomorrow life would begin again. Sitting up slowly, he stretched his aching shoulders. His pack had been rescued from the trees and he was leaning over to pull it closer when a light knock disturbed him.

"Yes," he said.

The door opened outwards with a sudden rush and the draught from its movement sucked his candle-flame towards the visitor. Sophia was standing uncertainly in the doorway. From far behind her, beyond the short corridor and across the great kitchen, there was a faint, red glow from the range but that and the flickering flames of Calder's candle and the one she held herself only seemed to emphasize the darkness she stood in.

Calder rose from the bed and Watch, seeing his mistress, beat his tail twice and slumped to the floor.

"Will you come in?" Calder asked.

She walked tentatively into the room and he saw that in her free arm she was clutching a pair of fine leather boots to her breast. Her hair was still down and this, with the unornamented gown and the fatigue in her face, made her seem more of a girl and less far from him. Since entering this house, and walking for the first time on carpets, he had been again struck by his audacity in thinking of her but having her before him in this way made her human and reachable. It was as if his love were a prepared canvas and he was now beginning to paint detail upon it. He drank in the wariness in her eyes, the shadows thrown on her white neck, the creases in her skirts and he learnt what he loved as he looked on her.

She glanced down at the boots and almost spoke but, at the last, no sound came. There was an embarrassment and trepidation about her that he did not like to see.

"Yes?" he asked, softly.

She burst out: "It isn't charity."

258

She was gazing at him with wide, pleading eyes and it was not in him to prolong her distress.

"You've brought the boots for me?" he suggested.

"Yes," she gestured with them, not quite giving them to him, and put them down beside the stool on which his candle lay. She clasped her hands together.

"Ashley will not rest," she said, "he's distraught. He insisted again and again that you are to step in his shoes. I was obliged to come to soothe him. Forgive me. I don't understand. Forgive me if I — Were you barefoot?"

"No," he was puzzled by Ashley's direction and uncomfortable in receiving such a gift in this way. Sophia noticed the hesitation on his face and interpreted it as offence.

"Have I insulted you?" she asked. "It was my last intention."

"No," he said. "No, you have never done that." They stared at each other in the pool of yellow light. It was as if, at the same moment, they were alone and yet watched by all who lived and had lived in that house. Ghosts of duty and honour flitted between them waiting to see whether they were understood.

Calder said: "Is he dying?"

"Yes," said Sophia, her voice breaking. "I believe he is." Her face twisted and she turned her head away. "He wants to die," she exclaimed, "he's calling and calling on his judgement."

Tears began to run freely and silently down her cheeks. She was shaking with the effort to reassert her self-control; she put up her hand to her face but the tears spilled through her fingers.

"Oh, God," she said, "this night is so long."

Calder moved forward and took her into his arms. She stiffened, then softened into him and laid her head against his shoulder. Her fingers hurt as she gripped him but he did not show it. He held her as his sister had held her on another night.

"Hush now," he said. "The day is coming."

By morning Ashley was obviously failing to maintain what weak grasp he had on life and the presence of a doctor in the house was merely a matter of appearance. At intervals Ashley's damaged heart convulsed him with pain and left him less able to withstand the next assault but between attacks he grew more lucid.

259

It was a morning of muffled, but brisk, activity. Directly the sun rose the Claydon solicitor was sent for on Ashley's orders and arrived promptly, bringing with him tales of the night's destruction and the number of arrests made. In his capacity as workhouse agent Mason was obliged to go to view the damage and meet the Guardians but returned to the Hall before noon. While the solicitor was closeted with Ashley, five men — including the two who had stared at him under the trees — were brought for Calder to identify and he said — no, these were not the men and he had seen no faces clearly in the darkness. At the suggestion that Sir Ashley should inspect the prisoners Dr Kerr intervened to prevent him being subjected to any such excitement and Sophia backed his words strongly and pointed out that her husband's delirium would have caused him to have no reliable information to give. As the constables — reluctantly admitting that they had nothing on which to charge the men — and the young men themselves, terrified and regretful of their acts, were filing out, the solicitor came slowly down the stairs and, looking strangely and pityingly at her, told Sophia that Sir Ashley wished to see her alone.

Sophia walked to his room with exhaustion dragging at her limbs. Her head ached and she was at that point of waiting when a watcher would almost rather their invalid died if only it would end the tension. Yet she knew Ashley's death was not what she wanted and, when she had exchanged nods with the dependable, middle-aged maid — who sat with her mending outside the sick-room door — and entered his old chamber, it grieved her to the heart to see him so near his end.

The chair the solicitor had used was still next to the bed and she went forward and sat on its edge. The rustle of her skirts was loud in the room. She had bathed and eaten a little for the sake of strength but had not slept and as she first looked at Ashley's ashen face she thought tiredness was giving her fancies. Always thin and white, he now looked as though the pulp of life had been sucked from him leaving only an empty, misshapen rind. He was breathing in the shallow, gasping fashion that was so painfully familiar to her and she placed her hand lightly over his to comfort him. His fingers moved within hers and the image of a smile was briefly on his graven face as if he lay contented on a crusader's tomb.

"My love," she whispered. "You asked for me."

He tried to speak but his mouth was dry and she took the water glass from beside the bed and held it to his lips. When he had swallowed, she put back the glass and sat attentive.

"Sophia." His voice was hardly more than a sigh and she leant closer to him, holding herself awkwardly so that she put no weight on the bed. "Sophie, I told Norton. I thought it best my legal man should know. I — There's something in my past I never told you and must set it right now. Set everything right. All that I can. I must meet my Maker soon, Sophie, and I can't go without —" He paused to strain for a breath.

"Ashley, dearest, don't —" Sophia began but he stopped her with his eyes.

He could not turn his head but he stared up at the ceiling, where the plasterwork drooped its endless garlands, and began to speak as if he had learnt by rote.

"When I was young I could not make the Grand Tour. I went, instead, to Scotland. Mason was my companion. There I loved a girl not of my station and married her." He felt Sophia's hand tremble but went on. "No one in my world knew of this. Mason and I contrived a secret. I had three children from her. Twin boys and a girl. But she was not suitable to be the lady of this house. I put her away for my family name and the children I — the children I gave to Mason to abandon in a far land. My wife died some fifteen years ago. Two of the children live." He gasped for breath again. "Their names are Hannah and Calder Young."

The muslin curtains at the open window stirred and a soft breeze brought in the scent of summer. Outside Sophia could hear the chatter of boys spreading straw on the gravel and a man's voice quieting them. She felt as though she sat in some high place that was separate from all else.

"Oh, love," she said at last, "you've had a fever. When you're well —"

He made an agonized croaking deep in his throat. The back of his head pressed deeper into the pillow and shook in short, wild jerks. Sophia half-stood to call for the doctor but Ashley found strength enough to grasp her arm. In a moment he was still again but for the shudder of his breathing.

"I wanted," he said, faintly, "wanted people not to believe it if they heard — as you don't — but Fate has searched me out. Surrounds me, draws me into my past. The packet on the —" once more the fight for air, "beside the jug. Documents to prove my marriage — the monies paid to my wife. Her burial. Mason brought them this morning before he left. Mason — always been invaluable to me. Norton read them. Can't prove who the children are. Kept too secret — but you know how the Youngs came to Dorset. Go to your room — read them."

At the writing table in her room Sophia undid the fastening of the parcel and took out the papers. She was humouring him but had no belief in his account. When she had examined the certificates and letters in their old, fading ink she closed her eyes. She thought — if I sit here and do not move or speak, hear or see, there will be no world out there. No deception, no intrigue, no demands, no suffering. I will sit here and be. She sat for an interval in a false calm and then opened her eyes. The room was swaying and the letters blurred. She sprang up, knocking over the delicate chair that was unsuited to tragedy, and backed away from the documents until she rested against a bed-post. Here was horror. Beyond the window the sun was as bright, the day as fresh. A hundred oddities in Ashley's words and actions came scattering through her mind and fell into what were now their correct positions. Oh, God! Oh, God! What he had done to Caleb. She turned her head violently aside as if she were being offered poisoned meat. The ruined lives; the anguish of them all. She understood so much of Ashley's behaviour since their marriage but not — *not* — the perversion of mind that had begun the misery. There was the sound of movement and voices in Ashley's room. Was he worse? Had he cried out? She had not heard him. He disgusted her — yet she had been witness to the breaking of his spirit. He had not taken his guilt lightly — and he was the man she had sworn to love and honour. Death was coming to him and she had not the luxury of time for anger and reconciliation.

Tearing herself from the post as if she were breaking chains, she strode from her room into Ashley's. Mason and the maid were standing watching the doctor as he bent over his patient. They glanced at her as she entered but did not speak. Ashley was convulsed on the bed but when he saw her he shrank back, then put out his hands. She went forward and took them. He summoned his frail breath and tried to speak but tears of relief and shame prevented him. At last a whisper slipped from his rigid lips.

"Sophie," he said. "Sophie, I wanted you to love me."

She pressed his cold fingers and tried to find something to say to help him but could not. It was bitter to her that he had not spared her this knowledge and let her share herself freely with him in his last hours. A confession through Norton would have been enough. He thought this way was right — and what damage he had always done by doing what he thought to be right.

Now she must do what she believed her duty. She took her chair again and, through that long and sunlit afternoon, she learnt that a hard dying is not a pretty thing. Death smells of sweat; it tastes of saliva running from the corner of the mouth; it crushes the mind of its victim so that he does not know who is by him. She kept her hold and it was as if she held the hands of two people — her husband and a stranger. She knew him for what he was and if she could not love she could pity — and so she sat beside him, until his breathing stopped and the room grew quiet.

Chapter 28

Ten days after Ashley's death, Sophia was walking in the garden. She was not wearing mourning. It was a fresh, bright day with grey-white clouds being driven further east, yet despite the warmth there was a feel of autumn in the air and the first scatter of crimson and orange leaves was lying on the grass. If Hannah had been there she would have talked of the sea.

The funeral had taken place the week before, with all the formality appropriate to a Claydon, and Ashley's remains had been followed to their vault by a line of carriages containing the somber dignitaries of the county. The service was made remarkable by the sight of Robert Mason weeping and by the rumours that had begun to circulate concerning a young man from America.

It was expected that the widow would not attend the funeral and that the family solicitor should be frequently back and forth to the house but the determination Sophia showed in being "not at home" to all callers and the continuing presence of the stranger were beginning to incite a vigorous interest in the household affairs. It was known through the servants — and through his own inquiries after the whereabouts of the weavers — that the man's name was Calder Young, that he was the brother of the maid Lady Claydon had brought from the west and the owner of Sir Ashley's dog, that he had discovered Ashley in mysterious circumstances during the workhouse riot and had effected a rescue that had done no good. Some said that he had been a shepherd; others that his speech and manners were not those of a working-man — though also not those of a gentleman. He had turned down a room in the main house and kept to the servants' quarters — when not closeted with the solicitor or Mason. There were odd tales of a hanging that connected him with Ashley and of having been reared on

Ashley's Dorsetshire estate. Questions of inheritance began to be asked and laughed at. It was said that Sophia was shy and eager when with him in a way completely unsuited to her sad condition.

On this particular afternoon, the recusant was strolling aimlessly on the terrace that ran along the side of the flower-garden. She was protected from the breeze by the old brick wall that bordered the path and had brought out neither shawl nor head-covering, trusting to the warmth of the sun. If she had found no shelter she would not have cared — being entirely absorbed by the thoughts that tormented her. At intervals she stopped to bury her face in the soft, fat roses that were clustered on the wall — perfect rich, pink blooms that hung heads heavy with that morning's dew — but it was less for their beauty than to avoid what she most wanted to watch. She touched her mouth to a rose and her lips were left cold and scented. Turning round, she stared out over the garden and park to where Calder stood by the distant lake.

Thrusting her hands into her loose sleeves, she gripped her arms and began again to pace the terrace. She was ashamed of the terrible, physical craving she felt for this man who was so disgracefully related to her. A longing to press herself to him, and absorb the comfort she had gained from his nearness on the night of the riot, made her evade opportunities to be with him. Life had soiled her. This was the man it was natural she should be united with — yet barriers of class and wealth had masked her understanding of her feelings until it was too late. And now a most repulsive disclosure was to sunder them before a word of love had passed. What had Ashley's guilt to do with either of them? What cause would they be serving by parting now?

She turned on the gravel with a sharp movement of her heel that sent stones rattling down into the lower garden. She was angry with all the rules of the world — the appearances and performances that had driven Ashley to begin his long deception and herself to give her life into his hands. Her memories of her grandfather and Mrs Dene — and of the unorthodox relations she had encountered when she first began to read radical tracts — were present in her mind and many times in the last days she had been ripe for any persuasion that offered her love. Convention had brought neither happiness for her nor good to others. Was she now free to live outside man-made canons or did a deed done in ignorance condemn her to loneliness for the rest of her years? Oh, Ashley, Ashley, she thought, how could you have done this to me? To any of us? She could not think of him or the horror of his actions with any reason. At times she was numb and passive; at others rage slashed and raked at her until her eyes blinded and her stomach retched. She barely ate and slept only a few hours before dawn; she kept her solitude as much as she was able and thought of Calder and Ashley until she believed her mind was turning.

If she had seen Ashley to be a cruel man it would have been easier for her to despise him but she had known him to be of kind intention and had witnessed his decline. Once, walking on the heath above Chesil Bank, she had come upon a nest of adders, entwined and writhing, and her feelings for Ashley were as confused and knotted as they. She was revolted that he could once have been so vile but it was also a sorrow to her that the house and estate were running as smoothly without him. The only one to be truly mourning him was Mason, who had found his love of his work to have been riddled with an emotional need for the man he had helped to warp in his youth and tried to harm in his last years. Sophia had seen him, bereaved and desperate to keep the management of the estate, attempting, without success, to ingratiate himself with Calder.

And now, thought Sophia, it is necessary for me to talk to the new heir — for that is what he is even if he will not acknowledge it. She had discussed their position with Norton and, though the legal searches he had put into operation were not yet completed, they had decided that Calder should know his change of fortune before it could reach him by gossip. Sophia was determined to do what was just and to avoid any suggestion that she had dragged her feet over what would disinherit her. She had been an heiress and was now a wealthy dowager but all her life had been lived in another kind of poverty and it was of no importance to her whether she retained the whole of Ashley's property or only her widow's jointure; it was, however, vital to her injured spirit that Calder was aware that her actions concerning him were open and true.

She stopped again on the gravel and looked across the park. Calder had left the lake and was crossing the grass towards her. She did not know whether he could see her in her green gown against the leaves on the wall; she told herself he could not — yet she felt that he was looking directly into her face. He walked with his usual long, easy pace, occasionally turning his head to the old dog that lumbered at his side, but there was a purposefulness about him that made her step back as if she were afraid.

He had received the revelation of his birth calmly and declined to accept an inheritance that he said belonged to her; when informed by Norton that the rights and duties of the heir were not his to refuse, but were a condition of his blood, he had merely told the solicitor that it would be a difficult thing to prove conclusively that the children discarded by Sir Ashley and the children supposedly discovered by Mason were one and the same. He had not approached Sophia since the interview had taken place — instead, occupying himself in journeying to Norwich to ask at the weaving manufactories for news of Hannah — and she had convinced herself that she must speak to him personally to encourage him to accept his position. She knew clearly that this was not the course a conversation would take.

Making a few quick strides towards the house, she almost fell against a stone urn that stood in her way. There were weeds amongst the marigolds and she pulled them out of the damp earth and laid them neatly on the rim. Then, glancing at the figure in the park, she turned indecisively and wandered back along the wall. She had no doubt that if she talked freely with this man — who had courted her so delightfully and obviously through his letters — she would join her future to his and, as the moment came, she grew frightened of rejecting so much of her upbringing. They could not marry and there would be no life for them without scandal. They would be pariahs; untouchable. She put her hands to her head and shut her eyes. Let her run to the church and sit in Ashley's pew, beneath the hatchment that announced his death, and be a proper widow.

She looked over her shoulder and saw Calder still approaching. She could not yet distinguish his face beneath the wide, Shaker hat but she loved his walk. If she rejected him because the law said "No" would she have fallen into the trap of upholding a false honour? And would Ashley have made her as hollow as himself? There was love to give and work to be done. Her barren life had damned a torrent of loving in her and was it to dry to nothing for the sake of a book of rules? She stared with hunger at the roses by her side; they were full of thorns and soon to die — but they were beautiful and their smell was sweet.

Calder, walking across the smooth turf from the lake, raised his face to the sun. The breeze, that carried with it the cool taste of the water, bent the few tall grasses left by the scythe but did not spoil the thin warmth of the day. He was in his shirtsleeves with a dark-blue neckcloth and was holding his long, foreign coat hooked over his shoulder so that it swung against the backs of his drill trousers as he walked. With the exception of the boots Sophia had brought him, his clothes were plain and serviceable but not those likely to be worn by the heir of this estate. He had no wish to make any effort to wear gentlemen's suits but wore the boots because he had been poor too long to be prevented by sentiment from using what had belonged to others. As he progressed towards the garden, where he could see Sophia strolling on the terrace, he wondered whether she was as unburdened by maudlin sensibilities as he.

It was true that he was suffering from shock and revulsion that Ashley should have both been his sire and have sent the mild Caleb to the gallows, but he was far less innocent of the ways of the world than Sophia and could accept the common tale of a rich man abandoning the results of his pleasure. It was what had prompted a Claydon to marry a serving girl that puzzled him. He looked at this great house and was bitter for the plenty and influence that could have saved Caleb and Hester and had Hannah in her rightful place in the Hall. While he had pitied Ashley his physical suffering, he could not mourn the man who had killed his brother and had lived out a guilt in ease and comfort.

268

It angered him that a new dimension should have been added to the jealousy he felt of Sophia's husband and that a new complication had replaced the fact that she was married. He was, himself, without carnal experience, having always refused himself the luxury of leaving unwanted children behind him. It was loathsome to him to think that Ashley's lack of the same self-control had led to so much misery — and to imagine Sophia in Ashley's bed. His own celibacy had not been easy to maintain and it was natural that he should desire the woman he had loved and wooed so long — but would she flout convention for him now?

His dog, pushing its head against his hand, distracted him and he first stroked Watch and then looked back to the terrace. Sophia was no longer in the garden and, for a moment, he thought he would have to seek her out in the house — but then he saw her. She was walking towards him across the turf and her face was welcoming.

When she met his eyes she became more shy and began holding her skirts away from the grass, so that when he came up to her she was absorbed in gathering her gown into her hands. He took off his hat and stood before her. She let her skirts drop back to brush the grass and looked at him. There was a subtle, unspoken, delectable tension between them. It was plain to Sophia now what mysterious recognition she had found in Ashley and as she faced Calder on this sunlit afternoon she was again in mist and fire on a western hill and a shepherd was bidding her to come forward into the light.

With her before him Calder was confident but aware of their strangeness to each other. The differences between them were like birds of prey who flew beside them but did not attack.

He said: "Shall we walk to the water?"

They turned and walked forward together with the dog scouting before them. The surface of the lake was being ruffled into small, rippling waves and in the centre, where a group of mallards were riding with folded wings, a drake reared up and beat the air.

"Soon the birds will be leaving for winter."

"Yes," said Sophia.

They strolled to the water's edge in silence. There is one more distance to cross, thought Calder — but how to get from here to there? They gazed out across the lake, watching the reeds swaying in the breeze.

"He should have told me," said Sophia, suddenly. "Oh, God, he should have told me. I can understand almost anything people do if only I see its beginning. I could — perhaps, I could have forgiven him."

"Could you?" said Calder. "My sister is lost and my brother sent to his death."

"He thought it would be transportation."

"Then to worse than death."

"He believed he was doing right." She looked at him in a way that was pleading for compassion for Ashley and yet hoping that he would reinforce her own distress.

"Ah," he said wryly.

She turned abruptly back to stare at the water. It was grey and green but blue where the wind caught it.

"Hannah will know she can write if she's in need," she told him. "I did all that I could for her."

She shivered and he threw his hat on the bank and holding open his coat laid it over her shoulders. Startled, she put up her hands to it and he touched them with his own. While he was behind her, she said, "During the years —" she paused and began again quickly, "apart from the few weeks at the start of our marriage Sir Ashley and I never lived as husband and wife."

Calder slid his arms around her waist. His coat made her bulky but he did not notice it.

"You know," he said, gently, "that if we were free I would ask you to wed me. I love you and will love you always. I would that I am with you all the length of my days."

She gave a stifled cry and leant into his arms; he held her as if she were a precious vase he had caught an instant before it shattered.

"My honey," he said, "my rose of Sharon."

Such fond and undisguised emotion was new and delicious to her. She put her hands on his and, as the breeze rustled the reeds beyond them and the old dog slumped at their feet, it was as if their young lives had not held the sadness that they had and they were any man and woman learning of each other.

As they relaxed, Calder's coat slipped from her shoulders and he kissed her softly on the pale skin of her neck.

"I have the Prayer Book that you gave me still," he whispered, his mouth brushing her ear and hair.

"And I your thrush's egg," she said, "a little broken."

"There now. There now," he rocked her slightly, "how true of us all."

She laughed painfully and he, thinking her crushed by his arms, released his hold. The coat slid again and she pulled it about her as she turned round. She felt a stirring of youth in her tired mind and possibilties running in her veins; she was willing to dare the leaving of her home and country if she could be sure of one thing.

"Let me be understood," she said. "I can bear no more deception and I will not be ordered and my opinions ignored as always in the past. If we are to pledge ourselves to each other it must be as equal partners. I will have nothing less."

Calder smiled. "I didn't cross the Atlantic," he said, "to return with a milksop. I came for the woman who stood against the magistrates for me — who offered me all that she had. I took an equal share then and I'll take it now. She was a woman fit to be an emigrant."

He leant forward and reached into his own pocket to draw out the ribbon he had bought her. It fluttered in the wind, with the sun glinting on its satin surface. It was blue and gaudy and he looked at her as he had done on that May night when he had let the egg fall into her bowl. She laughed again, but more easily, and he took her hand and pulled it out into the air. She held it before her while he bound the ribbon three times about her wrist and tied it, with a tender concentration, into a bow. When he had finished she turned her wrist this way and that for them both to admire.

"A token of my word," he said. "Come with me to Philadelphia and rest until we're free of this hurt. We each have something for the other. You will teach me to be gentle in my ways and I will teach you that I am safe to trust. There is a future as well as our past and we will take into it only what is good."

Some two weeks later a well-dressed woman and a man, whose arm she held, descended from a carriage in the crowded streets of Spitalfields and entered the workhouse. They brought with them a letter written on behalf of Nathan and Hannah Hearne and permission from the Guardians to take them — and the son born to them in the hospital ward — away from that place. The man, who had a foreign way about him, took the baby when it was brought and held it as if he were its mother, asking whether he would like lands in Pennsylvania. The young parents — described by the Master as "indigent weavers, unable to prove their place of birth" — showed a sad lack of gratitude to the authorities and a strong relief that their plea for help had been answered. Reunited after their weeks apart, they embraced each other and the man, told him several times that their child was named "Caleb" and bowed and curtseyed to the woman. Caleb, showing a determination to thrive in all conditions, slept placidly throughout the encounter and the woman, raising her veil above her sad eyes, smiled and said, "We will take what is good."

As they left, the matron remarked on the pleasure their meeting had put in the faces of all — but later, when she came to write her report, she was unable to describe their relation.